Copyri₁

CW00493351

ISBN: 9798364475060

Cover design by: Erelis Design
Library of Congress Control Number: 2018675309
Printed in the United States of America

For Sean, Rian, and Liadh.

FROM HERODOTUS, ANCIENT
GREEK HISTORIAN;

"Bloodthirsty Cyrus... give me back my son and depart unpunished from this country... if you will not do this, then I swear by the sun, the lord of the Massagetae, that for all you are so insatiate of blood, I will give you your fill thereof."

WORDS ATTRIBUTED TO TOMYRIS, QUEEN
OF THE MASSAGETAE PEOPLE OF CENTRAL
ASIA IN 530BC.

The Curse of Naram-Sin
Book One in the Time Warrior Series
By Peter Gibbons

ONE

530 BC.

A snarling, scorched-faced horseman chased him, and Xantho ran for his life. His heart thundered in his chest like a war drum, and he swerved hard to the right towards a rocky escarpment as the screaming and crying of his fellow slaves rang around his skull. The tribesman howled with vicious fury, brandishing a wickedly curved blade as he closed in for the kill. Xantho whimpered as he scurried across the steppe, his head hunched deep between his shoulders. He could hear the panting, rhythmical breath of the horse over his shoulder and the jangling of its traces as the beast and its rider came within striking distance. Xantho threw himself into the short dry steppe grass, landing heavily with a grunt and rolling to his left, away from the scything blade and its pitiless master. The horseman shouted in his guttural, clipped language, savaging the reins, yanking the horse around in a flurry of hooves and steel.

Xantho's jump gave him a few vital extra

seconds, and he used the time well, leaping to haul himself up onto a jutting spit of rock. He climbed over its lip and then sprang to an adjacent boulder and onto the rise of the escarpment, scrambling up its face on his hands and knees like a lizard. Xantho risked a glance over his shoulder, and his heart lifted to see his attacker wheel away in search of new prey on the flat grasslands. If there was one thing Xantho was good at, it was running. He had been running and hiding his whole life.

The Massagetae horsemen had appeared from the steppe like ghosts, whooping and snarling and slashing with their long-curved blades, peppering the Persian slaves with vicious whistling arrows from their recurved horn bows. Now, from his safe position atop the rocks, Xantho watched them, swirling like devils as the last of his fellow slaves met a grizzly end beneath their flashing blades. He alone survived. Being a coward had its advantages, he supposed. A score of slaves, including Xantho, had made the trek around the steep hills to the river from the vast army encampment of Cyrus the Great, Emperor of Persia, and King of Kings. The slaves had hauled their masters' clothes and war gear to wash in the cool, fresh river water to prepare their Persian lords for the battle with the tribesmen, which must come soon. The Massagetae roamed the sea of grassland to the north of the Persian Empire and remained a thorn in the Great King's side. They were yet to be conquered, and Cyrus had brought his vast and terrible army into their lands to bring the wild tribesmen to heel. Guards had escorted the slaves as they brought the clothes and gear to the river, and those brave soldiers had stood their ground in the face of the swift attack. In reward for their bravery, they now lay still and dead, looking like cacti, feathered shafts sprouting from their chests.

Xantho's stomach turned at the sight of so many dead. Their corpses seeped lifeblood into the slow-flowing river, staining it crimson. It wasn't their deaths that made him sick; he had stood close to death many times before. The appalling truth of their deaths was that the slaughtered slaves would never see their homelands again, the places they held in their hearts, clinging on to dreams of freedom and a better life. Like all slaves with the army, they had marched here to the inhospitable and unexplored far north alongside their Persian masters, led by their King, Cyrus the Great. So many slaves, men and women from distant lands across the vast Persian Empire, were dead now, murdered by heathen plainsman. Xantho clenched his fist and slammed it down onto the cold stone where he lay, chest heaving with the exertion of the mad dash to safety.

He turned away from the bloody scene, climbed up and over the ridgeline, and slid down the opposite rock face scattered with scree. Tiny stones were skittering beneath his sandals and hands as he gathered pace, a plume of dust billowing behind him. Xantho looked at the sprawling camp on the plain below. More tents, horses, and men than any man could count, thousands upon thousands of souls to wage war on the tribes of the Massagetae. Xantho spat a clump of dust from his mouth and nearly lost his balance as he reached the foot of the rock face. He knew he must notify the Persians, his father, and the other lords; he must tell them of the surprise attack and slaughter at the river. Xantho swallowed hard, knowing he must now bear his father's wrath. That anger would come not because of the deaths of so many slaves at the hands of the Massagetae but from Xantho losing his father's fine clothes, silk tunics and underclothes, and his shining war gear during the attack. Those items were worth more to his father and master than the lives of easily replaceable slaves. A Persian warrior frowned in his direction, oiled beard gleaming in the sun. Xantho hated these Persians, hated their glossy beards and the superior look in their eyes. Perhaps because his father reinforced his lowly status at every opportunity, making sure that Xantho didn't forget, not even for one second, that he was more Thracian than Persian. Xantho's mother was a Thracian slave, but she was long dead now. She had raised Xantho amongst other Thracian slaves, and although his father was indeed a Persian, Xantho thought of himself as a Thracian and a slave.

Xantho ignored the haughty Persian's gaze and scampered through the camp, jumping over tent ropes and skidding around busy warriors and animals as he went. Then, out of the corner of his eye, he saw a flash of azure, and it stopped him in his tracks. Xantho turned, hoping to see someone smiling and glad to see him—someone he knew could not possibly be there, no matter how much his heart desired it, his wife, Lithra.

But it wasn't her. It was another slave girl, her blue scarf fluttering in the light wind as she hustled along to perform some task for her Persian master. It couldn't have been Lithra. She, too, had died years ago. Sadness forced Xantho's eyes closed. Beautiful Lithra. He snapped himself out of the painful memory and pushed on toward his father's tents.

"Where have you been?" demanded a familiarly gruff voice as Xantho reached his father's camp.

Jawed was the owner of that voice, his father's man at arms, short and swarthy, standing with his arms crossed and a look of pure disdain on his face. Xantho slumped, hands on his knees and his chest heaving.

"The tribes…they attacked us," Xantho said between gasps.

"What madness are you talking, boy?"

Boy. Xantho wasn't sure how old he was, but he had seen twenty summers at least. Two since Lithra had passed.

"Horseman…all dead…surprised us."

Jawed took three spry steps forward and grabbed Xantho by the tunic, hauling him upright. Once at his full height, Xantho was taller than Jawed. Rather than look down his nose at his father's man in the eye and risk a beating, Xantho did the age-old slave trick of picking a point in the distance just to the left of Jawed and focused his gaze on that.

"When, where?" asked Jawed, his dark-ringed

eyes boring into Xantho's.

"Behind the escarpment, all dead. Clothes gone, the guards dead."

"How many of the enemy?"

"Maybe twoscore, I'm not sure."

"Where are the others?"

"All dead. I was the only one to escape."

The corners of Jawed's mouth turned down, sneering as he let go of Xantho's tunic. The man at arms span on his heel, yelling at everyone around him, raising the alarm. Jawed had a second thought and turned back to Xantho.

"You. Stay there. Don't move."

Xantho hadn't planned on going anywhere. He only hoped his father inflicted his wrath on the Massagetae and not on him. Losing his father's gear would certainly mean another thrashing, even though he could not possibly have saved any of it, even by giving his own life up to the Massagetae's blades.

He wiped the dust from his face with the back of his hand and shook his head, a cloud of dirt tumbling from his shaggy brown hair. Xantho dusted down his shabby clothes, hanging loose as they did from his lean frame. He was toneless and colourless against the bright pageantry of the Persian army. Tents of blue, red, and green spread as far as the eye could see across the flat steppe. All around him, warriors milled about with tunics of yellow and white, men with skin tones from east to west of the known world. Cyrus' empire was vast, running from

Lydia close to his mother's home in far Western Thrace, south to Pasargadae and the Great King's summer palace, and further east to the mystical land of elephants. A vast empire built on conquest and blood, and the broken backs of slaves.

Xantho closed a nostril with his finger and blew dirt from the other. A string of muddied snot trailed from his nose, and he leaned forward to avoid splattering his clothes. But, given how dirty they were, it was pointless. He opened his eyes to see his father standing before him, a grimace stretching across his stern face. Xantho commended himself on his impeccable timing.

"You were the only survivor," his father sneered. His eyes poured with accusation, delighted to have a new opportunity to degrade his half-breed son.

"Yes, Fath…Yes, my lord," he said. Almost uttering the unforgivable.

Xantho's father was Tiribazos, satrap of a swathe of land south and west of Pasargadae. Tiribazos had brought over four thousand warriors and horses—and the supplies to feed them all—to Cyrus' banner. Under no circumstances was Xantho to address his father as such. His back bore scars that served as a painful and unforgettable reminder of that.

"How is it, brave Thracian, that you alone survived?"

"I ran, lord."

His father reared up to Xantho's chest. He was not as tall as his son, and Tiribazos' belly barged

Xantho backwards.

"You ran. That's the Thracian in you—your first instinct is to flee, to save yourself. No thought to the other slaves or the valuable clothing in your care. The craven nature of you and your barbarian people never ceases to amaze me. I go now to avenge the glory of Persia on these filthy desert dogs. You stay here and clean my tent. Keep out of my sight."

Xantho again found a spot behind and to the left of his father and stared at it. How could his mother ever have lain with a man like Tiribazos? Maybe she'd had no choice. Such was the lot of a female slave. Thinking of her lifted his spirits a little. A feeling of warmth enveloped Xantho's heart as the smell of her hair, and the glow of her kiss found their way into his mind. His mother had always been a slave. They had captured her as a child during Cyrus' conquest of Lydia. Her father, Aristaeus, had been a mercenary, fighting for the Lydian king across the sea from his home in nearby Thrace. As his mother told it, Aristaeus was a great and noble warrior who fought to the end and was the epitome of honour and strength. Cyrus had crushed Lydia, Xantho's grandfather was killed, and his mother was sold into slavery. Tiribazos had bought her and subjected her to this half-life of servitude and drudgery that it was to be a slave. All in the name of Cyrus, the greatest warlord in all history. King of Persia, Media, Great King, King of the World, and of Sumer and Akkad.

Tiribazos spun on the heel of his supple leather boots and waddled off. His men hustled around him, weapons jangling in scabbards, shouting erupting from across the camp as the brave warriors rode out to be avenged on the Massagetae for their stinging attack on Persian property.

Xantho sighed, wondering if his life could be any worse. He didn't think so. He made for his father's tent, easy to find as it was standing bright yellow and tall amongst the smaller tents of the army's grunts. As he walked, he felt eyes upon him, burning and judging him for his cowardice. But he was alive. Would it have been better if he had stood his ground? Honourably washing clothes in the river to the bitter end whilst rabid steppe horseman shot him with arrows or hacked him to bits? On reflection, Xantho thought maybe it would. After all, would the world miss a mixed-blood slave? He didn't have a family. Yet most of the other men he knew from the slave pens had wives and children, which gave them something to live and work for.

He reached his father's tent, and the two guards at its entrance completely ignored him as he entered. Shoulders hunched and exhausted from the slaughter by the river. He shuffled past those guards in their shining soft blue, and yellow tunics and conical helmets polished to a gleam. Their tall, wicker shields rested against their legs, and sleek, poled spears pointed straight up to the sky, sharp and deadly. Xantho carried on, avoiding a red-dyed tent rope as thick around as one of his wrists. Spiky, dry grass ended and gave way to a luxurious carpet under his sandals like a warm cloud. He ducked under the tent flap and into the tent proper, his senses assaulted by the perfumed burners smoking nearby. Aromas of sweet and spiced meats attacked his nose, making moisture appear in his mouth where there had been only dust and dirt before. Xantho swallowed his saliva and saw the trays of meats on a trestle table placed at the centre of a gathering of intricately woven carpets. Short, deep goblets of watered wine and other delicious drinks dotted the remnants of one of his father's war councils.

Xantho craned his neck and peered through the tent opening. All quiet, the guards still standing silent and alert, Tiribazos' horse warriors off chasing shadows on the open steppe. Xantho licked his lips and swallowed hard. He lowered himself slowly to his knees and took another long look at the tent flap. Still quiet. Xantho crawled across the rugs, low and sleek, like a lion stalking its prey. He reached for a wide plate filled with wonderful meats and fruits. Xantho snatched up a slice of chicken and devoured it, juices running down his chin into his beard. With his other hand, Xantho grabbed grapes and pomegranate seeds and stuffed them into his mouth with the meat. Cheeks bulging, he munched as fast as he could, staring all the while at the tent opening and expecting to see his father or Jawed burst in at any moment to lop his head off for his insolence. He gulped before the food was fully chewed, and the lump of it went down like swallowing a horse whole. He picked up a goblet and swigged a mouthful of sweet wine. It slid down his throat like honey, caressing his insides.

Noise, shouting. Xantho stopped dead, frozen

and staring at the opening. Nothing. He shot to his feet and jumped from the rugs, away from the food. Visions flashed through his mind of floggings and other hideous punishments he would surely endure if caught eating from Tiribazos' table. Nobody entered, though. Xantho wiped his mouth on his sleeve and breathed out, not realising he had been holding his breath. More shouting, some screaming. He moved to the opening of the tent and peeked outside. One guard had gone, and the other had his feet planted wide, shield raised on his left arm, his spear lowered. The guard's head flicked right and left, searching for danger. All around, people ran here and there, aimlessly panicking. Xantho heard a wet thud and his head snapped back to the guard who had fallen to his knees, a black feathered arrow jutting from his eye. *We are under attack.*

Horses exploded from the tent across from his father's, the riders crashing through the tent itself and whirling their mounts in search of targets. A slave ran past them, head tucked into his shoulders and arms raised, waving in terror. A Massagetae warrior laughed and threw a short spear at the slave, which slammed between the man's shoulder blades, flinging him to the ground. Xantho looked at the sun-darkened faces of the attackers, hungry and lean, their small ponies quick and relentless. He looked at their broken teeth and savage snarls and fled back into his father's tent.

Xantho ran four long strides and then halted. *What am I doing? There's no way out of the tent other than the entrance.* It could only be a matter of moments before the Massagetae warriors crashed through the tent, and they would trap him. Succulent meats and fragrant wines would not protect him from the vicious tribesman. He looked about him for something, some way out. Xantho's heart pounded. Noise from the tent flap whipped his head around. They were coming. Resting between a silver tray of fruits and a tasselled pillow was a knife, a short knife with a jewelled hilt used for cutting food. Xantho dived for it, rolling across platters and cushions as he picked it up. The metal felt cold and unfamiliar in his hand. He stood and sprinted to the rear of the tent and slashed at the canvas. Two deep cuts and he could get his arm through. Two more, and he could poke his torso out. Harsh cries erupted behind him. They were upon him. Xantho heaved himself out of the hole he had cut. He sucked in his stomach and twisted, jerking desperately against the canvas walls. Suddenly he surged forward, and he was out, collapsing to the grassy steppe outside, breathing hard.

Xantho ran, dashing between tents, swerving around horseman, spear thrusts and tent ropes. The camp was in disarray. The sheer number of the Massagetae was astonishing. Cyrus' army itself was beyond count, but the enemy was everywhere, swamping the Persians like a tidal wave. The attack at the river had been a ruse, a trap to draw out the Persian warriors. Once those warriors had charged off in pursuit, the tribesmen launched their actual attack on the main camp. Xantho was running aimlessly, just running to stay alive. He needed a plan, and fast. He saw the enormous tent of Cyrus to the west, massive and billowing, rising above the throbbing attack like a great cloud. That would be the focus of the attack. The tribesmen must surely believe that could they kill Cyrus, the Great King, then the war would be over. So Xantho ran in the opposite direction.

Massagetae warriors rushed in and out of Persian tents, blades dripping in gore and arms full of silver, gold, and fine clothing. Xantho headed back towards the escarpment he had crossed earlier to escape the initial attack by the river. He hoped it would save his life again. Reaching the hard yellow stones, he was about to leap up the face when he heard a woman's scream, long and terrible. It stopped him at once. Something at the back of his mind told him he should stop and help, which was odd. He had always dreamt of living up to the ideal image of his grandfather, to be brave, strong, and noble, but that was a fantasy, and Xantho knew it wasn't truly in his nature. Throughout his whole life, right up to this point, his instinct had always been to run, hide, and protect himself. However, an overpowering tingle in his neck now told him it was time to do more. *What would Aristaeus do?* He turned towards the direction of the scream; it seemed to have come from a collection of three enormous boulders to his left. The scream peeled out again, and Xantho urged himself to leap into action and overcome the gut-wrenching fear. He crept towards the boulders, realising he was still holding the jewelled knife from his father's tent. He held it out in front of him as though a ludicrously thin, jewel-encrusted eating knife would help defeat whatever vicious tribal warrior awaited him behind the rocks.

Xantho stood, frozen. Battle and slaughter raged through the camp to his left, and ahead, just around the boulders, suddenly felt like a turning point, a chance to be brave and, for once, to honour the memory of his grandfather. His mind told him to do what he always did: run and find safety. Yet his heart told him he should do what an honourable man would do, not a half-blood slave, but a man like any other. He should spring into action and rescue the screaming woman from her attackers.

TWO

The scream erupted again, so loud it made Xantho jump. *What kind of man jumps in fear instead of rushing to defend a woman under attack?* He heard harsh, guttural voices shouting at the screaming woman. Despite the neck-tingling urge to leap heroically into the rescue, Xantho decided to take the cautious route instead. He clambered up the side of the boulder, using footholds on the adjacent rock face to propel him onto its top. From that vantage point, Xantho hoped for a better view of what was beyond. *Better to be safe than sorry, even if my grandfather would never have uttered such words.*

Below, on the opposite side of the boulder, three tribesmen surrounded a woman. With weapons drawn, they reached for her, trying to grab her arms and clothes. She looked like a Greek slave, wearing a chiton tunic and with braided hair piled atop her head. She was fiercely fending them off with a sword, which she held before her in two hands. The blade shook and wavered as she moved the weapon's point between her attackers. She was halfway between snarling and sobbing, but one thing was for certain, she was putting up a fight. Xantho didn't know what to do. His pounding heart told him to leap down and help her, and his head told him to hide and wait until the attack was over. *What could a mixed-blood, untrained slave do against such fierce warriors, anyway?*

A horseman thundered into view from a bend around the rocky outcrop. He shook his bow above his head and shouted at the tribesmen who attacked the woman. They yelled an incomprehensible curse at her and then ran to follow the rider and join the battle at the Persian camp, leaving their prey, faces twisted in hate and disappointment. She had fought them off, and she had defended herself. *Thank the gods.*

"Hey, you there," Xantho hissed down to her.

Her head shot around to look up at him, face smeared with mud and lined by the tears cascading down her face. She had green almond-shaped eyes, glassy and sparkling with the wet of her tears.

"Who are you?" she said, flipping her sword around, so it pointed at Xantho.

"You did it. That was brave. You saved yourself." He grinned down at her, but she responded with a puzzled frown.

"What…how long have you been there?"

"I'm Xantho; I'm a Thracian. Come on," he

reached down to her, ignoring the question and the barely hidden accusation of inaction. She was petite and willowy, with sallow skin beneath the dirt and grime of the steppe.

She flicked a wide-eyed glance at his outstretched hand and then back to his face before looking off towards the swirling fury of the battle. She took a deep breath and reached out to take his hand. The moment her flesh touched his, Xantho felt a surge of energy pulse up his arm and flood deep into his chest and belly. It felt like a bright light coursing up through his veins, and the sheer unexpected force of that energy crackled in Xantho's brain. At that moment, he felt truly alive for the first time in his life. His vision became brighter, his hearing keener, and his body trembled with a strength he had never felt before. He looked at the young woman. Her cheeks were flushed, and the emerald centre of her eyes quivered. She felt it too, whatever this was. He tightened his grip around her hand and pulled. Expecting her to have to crawl up the boulder whilst he helped to pull her up, it astonished him when she launched into the air. One tremendous leap, and she was up and kneeling next to him. Xantho's breath caught in his chest, unsure how he could suddenly have found the strength to haul her up like that. It should not have been possible. The surging feeling in his body was exhilarating, but its strangeness made Xantho edge back from the woman.

The noise of the battle beyond ebbed and flowed. Xantho saw the torrent of Persian cavalry returning from the ruse at the river amidst a churning cloud of dust and those cavalrymen descending on the Massagetae with all their vengeance and fury. Xantho wheeled around to stare at the mysterious woman, wondering what she had done to impart such power to him with a single touch. They looked at each other, the strange force crackling between them like a cluster of lightning held in place and alive with force and danger.

"How did you...?" the young woman said.

Xantho didn't know how. She'd felt as light as a feather in his hand as he had hauled her up. Xantho thought he could have launched her over the whole rock escarpment, or at least close to it. He had never felt such strength. He shrugged and stared at his hand.

"I don't know. Who are you?"

"I am Penelope, property of Ariamnes of Cappadocia."

"You are Greek?"

She nodded. Penelope rubbed each of her slender bare arms, causing a smile to flicker at the corners of her mouth.

"You feel it too?" Xantho asked.

She nodded again.

Penelope had rested the sword against her leg as she held herself tight and fixed him with her large green eyes. She had a soft, round face and had to look up to meet Xantho's gaze. They held that look between them for what felt like an age. Something had happened when they touched, some spark or link that neither could explain, yet it had imbued him with unnatural strength, enough to lift her to the top of the boulder as though she weighed nothing at all. Powerful, but also frightening.

"Where did you get that?" Xantho asked, nodding to the sword resting at her hip.

"I took it from a fallen guard when I ran. What's happening?" She looked across at the battle still raging amongst the countless tents of Cyrus' army. Great clouds of dust rose, swirling in the steppe breeze, as the warriors of Cyrus found order in their ranks. Xantho could just make out a tide of organised spearmen advancing through the camp against the whirling horsemen.

"I was across these rocks washing my fath… my master's clothes at the river when the tribesmen attacked us. I ran to tell my lord of the attack, and he rode out with the main bulk of the cavalry. But it was a trap."

"Are these the enemy we are here to fight?"

Xantho nodded. "Yes, the Massagetae."

"Look, there," Penelope said, pointing to a group of warriors emerging from the tumult, heading in their direction.

Xantho saw horsemen thundering across the plain. There were two out in front, being pursued hard by a band of eight warriors. The two looked to be Persians by their bright clothing and larger horses. The pursuers rode small but hardy steppe ponies and fanned out in a wide line. One of those being chased unslung a bow from his back, using only his knees to control his horse. He turned in the saddle and shot backwards across his body at the assailants on his tail, expertly executing the famed horse bowmanship usually reserved for the tribesmen who attacked him.

"They're coming this way," observed Xantho.

The fleeing riders veered right to ride around the escarpment and toward the river where the tribesmen had attacked Xantho earlier that day, but something changed their minds, and they continued in a flat gallop straight toward Xantho and Penelope. There was no time to think. In a few heartbeats, they were below them, reining in their mounts in a swirl of dust. Now that the pair were close, Xantho saw it was a warrior and a priestess. The warrior wore the armour of an Immortal, the ten-thousand-strong elite army unit of Cyrus the Great. His breastplate was hard leather, faced with golden fish scale metal plates, and he wore a conical helmet with a full, snarling bronze faceplate, which gave him a fearsome appearance, faceless, and pitiless.

Xantho reached down and took Penelope's sword, without knowing why but feeling the urge to protect her. He didn't even know how to use the weapon properly. As a slave, his only knowledge of weapons had been how to clean and sharpen them. Nevertheless, Xantho stood in front of Penelope, shielding her from whatever danger was about to unfold below them. Yet she snatched the sword back from him and shoved him out of her way, shooting him a mocking look. Not expecting that reaction at all, he took a step back. But she was right. She had just fended off two vicious tribesmen and was far more likely to put up a fight than he.

The Immortal vaulted from his horse and shot three rapid shafts from his recurved bow. Xantho saw one attacker fall and another leap from a hit pony. The shots had been fired at such speed that they were almost a blur. The woman knelt beside the Immortal. Garbed in the long black robes of the Zoroastrian religious priestesses, she tore her face-covering headdress away to reveal long, shining black hair flowing freely in the melee. The attackers reined in and raised their bows to fire upon their cornered prey. But then something astonishing happened.

"What should we do?" Penelope said. Her sword raised as she bounced from one foot to the other.

No sooner had the words left her lips than the priestess below kneeled and thrust her hands out, palms outstretched. An ethereal glow came from her left palm, and a pulse shot outwards from where she kneeled. Xantho stood open-mouthed as the flow of energy shot out in an arc. It was invisible other than a shimmer over the land as it passed. In an instant, the grass of the steppe bent away from her, and the dust flung outwards in a projectile cloud. The attackers had launched arrows from their tribal bows, short, powerful recurved weapons not unlike the Immortal's bow. The priestess' surge flung the arrows back mid-flight and threw the assailants from their knees.

Xantho looked at Penelope, who stood with her mouth agape. She looked back at him for an explanation of the extraordinary act, but all he could do was shrug. Below them, the priestess spoke to the Immortal and then pointed up in Xantho's direction. He felt his stomach tighten and his bowels squirm. *Why are they looking at me?*

"You there," said the Immortal in a sonorous voice while dropping his bow and drawing his war axe—a short-hafted thing with a wicked-looking blade.

"You there," the Immortal called again, this time more forcefully.

Xantho swallowed hard and nodded.

"Get down here. Now."

Xantho nodded again and knelt on his bottom to slide down the face of the boulder. He couldn't deny the Immortal. He couldn't just run away now that Penelope was there. She would think him a coward.

"Both of you, quickly." The Immortal pointed at Penelope, and she, too, moved down the boulder.

The Immortal's voice was deep, and he had a strange accent. The aloofness of the warrior's gaze and the clipped tone of his voice were the signs of nobility that Xantho had been taught to recognise his whole life—to know when to bow and scrape, to be obedient. Clearly, the warrior was a lord, and though Xantho didn't recognise the accent, it was a voice to be obeyed. Their assailants rose and gathered themselves for an attack, drawing their curved blades and advancing on the Immortal and the priestess. The priestess poised herself again, kneeling with palms open, and another surge pulsed out from her across the plain. The attackers had braced themselves this time, yet it was in vain as they were thrust back with immense force, and only three of them stayed on their feet. The priestess placed a hand on the grass and bowed her head, sagging and gasping for breath.

Whatever magic she was using must take a toll

on her, Xantho thought.

"Siduri, look," the Immortal said, holding his left palm out to the priestess. Embedded in the skin inside of his hand was a shallow orb, which glowed a deep gold colour. The priestess turned to him and raised her own palm, where a matching orb also glowed gold.

What magic is this? Who are these people? Xantho wondered, conscious again that he was still clutching the ornate knife from his father's tent. It must have looked incongruous to the Immortal, given that Xantho was a man, yet Penelope held a sword. Xantho glanced at her, and she was staring at the strange hands of the two newcomers.

"They must be the ones," the Immortal said.

Xantho felt heat rising from his belly and into his chest. *I am not the one for anything, washing and running errands, maybe, but nothing more.*

The three attackers who had stayed on their feet charged at the Immortal, shouting and brandishing their blades. He ran to face them before they reached the priestess, who remained on her knees. Then, in a flurry of blades, the Immortal met them, parrying their attacks and slashing with his axe, moving between them like a dancer, lethal and impossibly light on his feet. One attacker fell, and another reeled away with a bloody cut across his face. The remaining attackers rushed to join their comrade, and the Immortal faced six enemies alone. Surely impossible odds.

"You must help him," the priestess implored, looking directly at Xantho.

"What?" was all he could reply.

The priestess rose and strode towards him, stumbling a little, but onward she came. Xantho took a step backwards from her stern, angular face.

"I will explain later," she said, and ahead of them, the Immortal became pressed by his attackers, weapons clashing, locked in a fight for his life. "She strengthens you. Use your power. Help Naram-Sin."

Xantho looked at Penelope. She nodded at Xantho, her face stern and teeth gritted.

"Come on, Thracian," she said before charging ahead.

What is she doing? Where is she going?

"Go, help Naram-Sin," the priestess urged again.

Xantho cursed to himself and charged, thinking of Aristaeus and his legendary bravery. He had to suppress his instinct to run, and he forced it down. He had felt power when he hauled Penelope up to the boulder. What if she had transferred some sort of power to him and somehow made him stronger?

He reached the enemy, and all thought left

him. Penelope was hacking at a foe with her blade, and Xantho just charged. He thundered into one adversary, amazed when that man flew backwards ten paces. A blade arced towards him, wielded by a thick, bearded, tall man. Xantho moved quicker than he thought possible and positioned himself inside the swing, grabbing the attacker's arm and flinging him backwards.

The Immortal had dispatched two more foes and moved to help Penelope with her adversary. The tribesman Xantho had felled and reeled away, shouting curses and running for his pony. Xantho rested his hands on his knees and gasped for breath. He had done it; he had fought and fought well. Xantho had mastered his instinct to run away and had helped the Immortal. A strange new feeling swamped his senses, the feeling that he had done well. Pride filled his heart. He had finally done something his grandfather would have been proud of; he'd acted as a warrior. Xantho had moved so fast and felt so strong. He did not know how such a thing was possible, but the priestess was right. It was undoubtedly Penelope who had made it so.

"Well done," the Immortal said, nodding beneath his gold face mask. He strode over to the priestess, took her arm, and whispered to her. But Xantho could not hear what they said.

"Did you feel it?" he heard Penelope say. She was standing across from him, grinning, looking at the blood standing out brightly at the tip of her sword. Her voice was gravelly and cracked slightly when she spoke.

"How did you do it?"

"What?"

"How did you give us that strength, that power?"

She frowned at him and shrugged.

"I did nothing. It just happened."

Xantho couldn't understand. He was a slave, rebuked and spurned by his father and others for being cowardly. All of his life, he had fled or shrank from confrontation, as was his place as a slave. But today, he had run towards danger. Finally, he'd confronted his fear. Not only that, but something had imbued him with new strength and speed. It must be magic or sorcery of some sort. It had to be. Xantho wondered who they were, this strange Immortal and the priestess, and what of the glowing things stuck into the palms of their hands? More fantastic was the surge the priestess had omitted from her hands, actual magic performed right before Xantho's eyes.

The Immortal and the priestess now walked towards Xantho and Penelope. He took off his golden helmet and ran his hand through his close-cropped, sweat-soaked hair. He was tall and lean, with dark circles surrounding his pale grey eyes. The priestess was also tall, almost as tall as Xantho. She was all angles and sharp features, with an ethereal sort of beauty. She had the same grey eyes as the Immortal, and she moved almost rhythmically, seemingly recovered from her draining otherworldly exertions.

"I am Naram-Sin," said the Immortal in his strange accent, and he dipped his head slightly in greeting.

"I am Siduri," added the priestess, nodding in recognition. "It seems you are the ones we have been searching for."

THREE

The vicious Massagetae attack broke off as soon as Cyrus the Great marshalled his forces and organised his commanders to strike back at the raiders. The Massagetae assault on Xantho and his fellow slaves at the river had worked and drawn most of Cyrus' cavalry off in pursuit of that small force, allowing the full Massagetae horde to descend on the Persian camp. Tiribazos had led the Persian light cavalry pursuit of the raiders, and along with most of the heavy cavalry, they had charged off hunting for retribution, leaving the camp open to attack from the fierce enemy steppe horsemen.

From their vantage point at the rocks, Xantho and Penelope watched the tribesmen race away, back into the endless grass sea of their homeland, leaving a vast cloud of dust and dirt in their wake. They had infiltrated Cyrus' camp and left a swathe of death and destruction, which was certainly a defeat for the Persian King of Kings.

Naram-Sin retrieved his horse and that of the priestess Siduri and strode towards Xantho. Xantho had kept quiet since Siduri had spoken. He was unsure and troubled at what in the gods' names she'd meant by him and Penelope being the ones they had been looking for. Those words had made the hairs stand up on the back of his neck. A brief hope fired within him.

What if it isn't my destiny to be a slave my entire life? Maybe I can be brave and useful. What if some of my grandfather's blood really does flow through me?

Such dreams, however, were fleeting. His well-developed self-preservation instinct kicked in, and Xantho did not allow himself to dwell on such infantile thoughts. He was born a slave and would always be a slave. He glanced at Penelope; she stood straight-backed, her chin raised, ready for the approaching Naram-Sin.

The Immortal was light on his feet, taking long strides with the grace and athleticism reserved for the nobility and elite fighting classes of the Persian Empire. Only those without the debilitating experience of hunger or servitude walked with such confidence. Xantho stared at the ground, feeling his shoulders hunching.

"So, tell me who you are?" said Naram-Sin, his iron-grey eyes flitting between Xantho and

Penelope.

Xantho looked at Penelope. She looked at him sideways, slanting her green eyes without turning her head away from the Immortal. Xantho didn't want to speak, so he returned his eyes to the ground. Penelope, however, spoke loud and clear.

"I am Penelope. I am the property of Ariamnes of Cappadocia."

Naram-Sin tilted his head and placed his hands on his hips.

"A slave?" he said. Penelope nodded, and Naram-Sin shook his head. He turned to Xantho. "And you?"

Xantho felt those grey eyes upon him, but he couldn't lift his own to meet them. His belly was in knots, still frightened by the magic and bloodshed he had witnessed.

"A slave. Xantho. Thracian." Xantho could have introduced himself as the grandson of Aristaeus, warrior and hero, but that seemed a lofty and remote claim. He risked a peek under his eyelids, and his heart sank as Naram-Sin threw his hands into the air and blew out his cheeks.

"Slaves. We lose warriors and mages in every battle. Is this the best Enlil can do? Every day Gula'an grows stronger, and Enlil sends us slaves."

Naram-Sin stormed off towards his mount and ripped open a saddlebag, searching its depths with deep thrusts of his arms, muttering to himself. Xantho didn't know where to look. Penelope still had her eyes fixed on the Immortal. She placed her sword tip down into the grass, leaning on it with both hands, shaking her head to one side to toss away a loose strand of her dark hair. Xantho didn't have the faintest idea who Enlil or Gula'an were. He often overheard conversations in his father's tent, where Jawed and other warlords would discuss tactics. He knew Cyrus had brought his army to the steppe to conquer the Massagetae and extend his dominion over yet more lands. Cyrus had already conquered the Medes, the Lydians, and mighty Babylon. However, a fearsome warrior, Empress Tomyris, led the Massagetae, and her son Spargapises was her general. Despite what he knew, Xantho had heard no one, Persian or slave, speak of Enlil or Gula'an.

The priestess retrieved her headdress and came to stand with Xantho and Penelope. She shook her head in Naram-Sin's direction.

"Ignore him. He speaks rashly. You did well today, both of you," she said, in a soft voice, not much more than a whisper. "He isn't exactly the greatest at dealing with people. Chopping off heads and charging into battle, yes. But, talking and explaining...well..." She waved her arm in Naram-Sin's direction and shrugged. Siduri smiled at them, a wide smile that stretched the skin tight across the hard angles of her face. "We all start somewhere. You were slaves this morning. What you'll become is a different matter," she said, and her pale grey eyes glinted.

There it is again, Xantho thought, *the promise of something more than a life of drudgery and servitude.* Penelope was smiling back at Siduri. *She is buying into everything the priestess is saying. What do they want from us?*

"Why were you looking for us?" asked Penelope.

"We search for those with the power, those who Enlil has entrusted with an elemental and ancient magic to join our ranks," replied Siduri.

"Who is Enlil?"

"He is an old and powerful god. Lord of wind, air, earth and storms. We are his warriors," said Siduri.

"Where does the power come from? I saw what you did to those men. Is it magic?"

These two strangers and their peculiar tales of magic and gods did not cow Penelope. Xantho couldn't string two words together through the shock of it all, but she was firing out questions like arrows from a bow. Xantho's mother had always taught him to stay quiet around lords and ladies and to only speak when spoken to, which likely added to his restraint. Siduri held her left hand in a fist and opened it to show the golden orb Xantho had seen earlier. Now that it was closer, his eyes became drawn to it. It nestled in her palm, and its golden glow was a swirling mass of smoke deep within. It glowed like the heart of a fire on a cold dark night, exuding warmth and brightness but also danger and threat.

"The power is within us, but the Palmstone is its indicator. It tells Naram-Sin and me how much we have used and, therefore, how much we can use before we become exhausted. I am a mage, blessed with magic and power by mighty Enlil. But only when I am close to Naram-Sin. We are a warrior-mage pair. Each makes the other stronger. We must be together for the power to work."

Penelope looked at Xantho, and he was sure she was thinking the same thing as he. It was clear some kind of power had passed between them on the boulder. He had felt supremely strong when pulling Penelope up to the top of the boulder and again in the fight with the raiders. Stronger and faster than ever before. Xantho couldn't deny it, but he didn't want to believe it. It signalled danger and threat, and opportunity. He just wanted to go back to Jawed and his father. As much as they cursed and kicked him, that was his home. He knew it, and it was safe. What Siduri was talking about was beyond understanding, and Xantho's head swam with questions. How could it be? How had he never sensed it before? Why him? Could there be some part of his warrior grandfather echoing down to him, in some way imbuing Xantho with this opportunity to rise above slavery and into a life of honour?

"You must decide now," Siduri pressed. "Will you become Warriors of the Light and join Naram-Sin and I, or go back to being...well... slaves?"

"Come, let us find the others. Leave these slaves to their fate," said Naram-Sin. He had mounted his chestnut mare and wheeled her around.

"Decide. We will find you," Siduri uttered as she, too, mounted her horse, and the two galloped away in a thunder of hoofbeats.

Xantho coughed and rubbed dirt from his eyes. The horses had thrown up a fog, and it rasped in his parched throat. They left him and Penelope standing there in front of a hill of rock. Xantho watched Naram-Sin and Siduri disappear into the distance as quickly as they had arrived. He scratched his beard, not knowing what to say to Penelope. So much had happened in the short time since they had met. He had felt the power from the moment they had touched; there was no mistaking that. He had also fought, actually charged into combat, and fought bravely. Recalling the skirmish made Xantho stand with his shoulders straighter—a coward no more. Perhaps. But all that talk of Palmstones, magic, and strange names he had never heard of…that was all too much to believe. The Palmstones had looked real, and Siduri had emitted some sort of magic to fend off her attackers. Yet Xantho thought it best not to think about it. It was too dangerous. Any slave getting ideas above his station would be severely punished. He should simply put it down to experience and return to his father and his duties. Being with Penelope and talking to Naram-Sin and Siduri would get him into trouble. There would be lots to do after the battle. Injured men would require treatment, and there would be the dead to tend to. For a second, he wondered if his father or Jawed were dead. What would happen to him?

Best not to think about that either.

Plus, if he were dead, who would care? Would anyone shed a tear that Xantho had died? He doubted it.

"So, what now?" asked Penelope. She tucked a loose strand of her hair back into the voluminous pile of it atop her head.

"We'd better get back. Looks like the fighting's over. There'll be work to do."

Penelope raised an eyebrow.

"What?" he said. She looked him up and

down.

"How can we go back to being slaves now, after…"

He held up a hand to stop her. "We are slaves. Nothing more. You can't just walk away from that; you would be hunted and killed. Don't listen to the crazy words of a crazy priestess. I don't know about you, but I'll be flogged if I'm not back soon."

"Haven't you ever dreamed of something more? Of freedom or a different life?"

"No, certainly not," he lied. But, of course, he had. Every slave dreamed of freedom, especially he of all people, being the grandson of Aristaeus, the hero. But Xantho had thought of it a lot less since his wife Lithra had died. They had shared dreams of escape, freedom, and a peaceful life together, that distant and impossible dream of all slaves. The dream had lost its lustre since she had gone.

"Well, I have. And I know you felt what I felt too. It's not crazy; you saw what happened. Siduri did magic, real magic."

Xantho kicked at a stone in the grass. He had seen it and felt it, and maybe it was real.

"She is a priestess of Zoroaster. Maybe they can all do magic. How should I know? I only know of my mother's gods, the gods of Thrace."

Penelope stuck her chin out. "We share some

of the same gods... What of it? You can't just go back, Xantho, back to them." She pointed her finger towards the Persian camp and then made a fist, slamming it into her thigh.

"I have to get back. I'm...sorry," was all Xantho could say. And then, with a heavy heart, he began the trek back to the camp.

"You're afraid, Xantho. You're a coward!" she called.

That word made him wince, but he didn't stop walking. *Maybe she's right. What if this is the one chance for a different life? But it's not; it can't be.* He carried on.

"You're going to mess it up for me, too, Xantho. Don't take this chance away from me."

Her shouts rang in his head. *Best to forget about Penelope, Naram-Sin, and Siduri.* He thought he should forget about the stories his mother and the other Thracian slaves told about his grandfather, too. There would be work to do, slave work.

The army of Cyrus the Great was packing up. The Massagetae surprise attack had torn through it like a knife through a ripe fig. Slaves had been butchered, tents had been ransacked, and supplies and equipment had been stolen. Xantho learned from his fellow slaves that Cyrus had given the order to march out, pack up and go back the way they had come. The Great King had decided to leave the filthy tribesmen to their empty steppe. When Xantho had returned, his father's tents were all abuzz, with injured soldiers lain out for treatment and horses being cleaned and watered. He had spotted Jawed waving his arms and shouting orders to everyone who passed him by. Jawed noticed Xantho and pointed at him.

"You! Where have you been? Hiding? There's work to be done. Start collecting weapons. They need to be cleaned and stored for the march."

Xantho nodded and scampered towards the other slaves, who were busy making piles of arms and armour in the space between his father's tent and the smaller tents of his commanders.

"Wait," barked Jawed in his harsh voice.

Xantho froze on the spot. He heard Jawed's heavy steps behind him and felt a tug at the back of his trews where Jawed pulled something free. Xantho spun around. The knife. He had forgotten about the knife he had taken from his father's tent during the raid. Jawed brandished it before him in all its bejewelled glory.

"So, we are under attack, brave men are dying, and you, dog, steal from your lord's tent?"

Before Xantho could reply, Jawed cuffed him around the head and thrust a knee hard into his belly.

"Take this animal away, tie him up," Jawed

snapped at his men, and he grabbed a tuft of Xantho's hair, twisting it savagely. "I will deal with you later."

Jawed's men were rough and unforgiving. They tied Xantho's hands to a post above his head and left him hanging there overnight. The steppe after dark was a cold and soulless place. Xantho barely slept, shuffling and shifting himself in his awkwardly bound position, looking for a sliver of comfort. He squinted to look up at his hands, the glare of the bright sun in a cloudless pale blue sky creasing his eyes. He couldn't flex his fingers. A dull tingle had replaced the feeling there, but at least they hadn't turned blue. Xantho squirmed his arse on the grass beneath him to shift his position. The morning dew had soaked through his trews, leaving him damp. Xantho coughed and winced. *My throat is dryer than a snake's belly.* He squirmed again to change position, hoping it would help shift the hunger hole in his belly.

He watched his father's warriors coming and going as they hurried to pack up camp. The army would leave today and begin the long march south back to Persia. Since he had awoken earlier that morning, Xantho had watched tents collapse across the camp's skyline, like a great city falling to ruins before his eyes. The enormous canvas tent belonging to his father billowed and sank to the ground, and slaves rushed to begin the effort of rolling the thing into a tight bundle for transportation.

He had not seen Jawed since the discovery of the knife. Xantho had tried to explain to the warriors who'd tied him up that he had not stolen the knife and that he had actually used it to escape the attack. But, of course, they didn't listen; they didn't even respond. The warriors ignored him and went about their knots, just as they would if they were securing a donkey or cow. Such was the life of a slave, to be less than a man. Xantho had slept little that night, which wasn't surprising given that he was tied up and left in the open, likely facing a lashing the following day. However, his mind was left to focus on the events of the battle as he sat there restlessly in the dark. He kept coming back to the worry that he had been a fool to walk away from Penelope and potentially a life of freedom, a life with honour. Sitting there, wet-arsed and bound, it felt like a mistake. But one did not simply walk away from slavery. If he had gone with her, they would be runaway slaves, and men would hunt them. If it were so easy for a slave to walk away, everybody would do it. Yet all knew the penalty for runaway slaves was death.

Then there was the magic. Xantho had tried to convince himself that his mind had played tricks on him and that he hadn't seen Siduri create that surge powerful enough to throw eight men from their feet. But he had seen it; she had done it.

He had felt power flow through his body when he and Penelope touched. Naram-Sin, whoever he was, had turned his back on them upon discovering their status as slaves, and Xantho had given no indication that he was, in fact, the son of a Persian satrap and the grandson of a Thracian warrior.

Typical haughty bloody nobleman.

However, Naram-Sin couldn't be that noble, or he wouldn't be an Immortal. All of Xantho's father's sons were lords and commanders— all the true-blooded recognised sons, at least. The Great King's generals handpicked Immortals for their bravery and prowess, and there were always ten thousand of them. If one died, another man replaced him. Hence the name, an immortal ten thousand. So, no doubt Naram-Sin could fight, but he was no better than Xantho, no better blood. Just better circumstances.

"Here, lad. Take a drink," came a croaky dry voice, a voice Xantho had known his whole life. It was Bristonis, his mother's friend and fellow Thracian. She had helped raise Xantho, and she, too, had been captured at the fall of Lydia. Her husband had been a warrior in Aristaeus' mercenary band, and she was one of the few people in Xantho's life who remembered being a freewoman. She had also known his grandfather.

"Watch they don't catch you. Jawed will…"

"Don't worry about Jawed. Drink." Bristonis

raised a wooden ladle of cool water to Xantho's lips, and he slurped it down, the liquid washing the dust from his throat. Her arm shook, an old woman's limb of skin and bone dotted here and there with discoloured spots.

"Thank you," he sighed, finishing the last of the water.

"You must learn to do as Jawed says, Xantho, or one day he will kill you," she said, frowning. Strands of her white hair fluttered in the light steppe breeze.

"I know, but the tribesmen ambushed me. I fought yesterday, Bristonis. I fought well."

She smiled at him, stroking his hair with her hand, fingers curled with age. "We are but slaves, Xantho, but never forget, I knew your grandfather. He was the greatest of warriors, the bravest of men."

"Tell me again…the story of how he died."

"I've told you a thousand times, lad. He fell fighting the Persians; the Immortals cut him down. But he took ten of those devils with him. He fought with honour and fame all across Greece and Asia. His blood flows in your veins; never forget it."

"He would never have allowed himself to be a slave, not a man like that."

"Well, it's not as simple as that, Xantho. I have to go. Jawed will be around soon. Take your punishment, and don't give him any cheek. I love you, lad. You are always good to me, and you've always looked after me. I don't want to see you hurt." She bent, kissed his head, and then hurried back to her duties.

Xantho closed his eyes tight to squeeze out some of the tiredness. When he opened them, he saw two pairs of supple leather boots facing him, surmounted by finely woven trews and then elaborate leather and steel-scaled breastplates. His eyes continued skyward to meet the scowling faces of Jawed and his father. Tiribazos was sweating beneath his armour. Trickles of sweat crawled their way down his oiled beard, across the contours of his jowls, and below to disappear beneath the baked leather.

"What to do with you?" Tiribazos sighed.

"I discovered the knife myself, my lord. We lost good men yesterday. It's not just theft; it is betrayal." Jawed was trying his best to steer Tiribazos down a certain route, a path Tiribazos seemed reluctant to take. At this stage, Xantho hoped that meant him dishing out a flogging and nothing worse.

"I don't have time for this. Just flog the dog and have done with it," said Tiribazos. So easy to say, so flippant. They had flogged Xantho before. He bore the scars to prove it. There couldn't be many other punishments so painful, so degrading. Not just the physical pain as the lashes scoured the skin from his back, but the scar tissue to remind him of it forever.

"With all due respect, my lord, it's just one too many crimes and mistakes now. This animal is not fit to serve you, not fit to serve the Great King."

"What would you have me do? Kill him?" Tiribazos stared at Xantho. He licked his lips and pawed at the sweat rolling down his face. "Your mother was dear to me," he mumbled. "She was a kind and diligent woman. So beautiful. I wonder, should I have done more…"

"Ho there!"

A clear voice rang out from behind Tiribazos, interrupting him. Xantho cursed to himself. *What was it his father had been about to say? He seemed to have softened. Was there a chance he could show kindness?*

"I say there, Lord Tiribazos, is it?" the voice called again.

Jawed spun around, snarling.

"Who dares address the satrap… oh…forgive me."

Jawed bowed his head and fell to his knees. Xantho had never seen his father's warlord so humbled. He craned his neck to see who was causing such a reaction. A man with a silver headdress wound atop his head, mounted on a magnificent white horse, nodded to Jawed.

The man's long beard and elaborately curled moustache were as black as the deepest night. He wore the same armour as that of Naram-Sin, but with a bright red sash tied from shoulder to waist. Four Immortals accompanied him, one of whom carried a standard showing the symbol of Zoroaster, fluttering limply in the light breeze.

"Nothing to forgive, rise." He waved an arm at Jawed, who duly rose and glanced at Tiribazos, now stood, hands on hips.

"Who are you, sir, to address me so? I see you are of the—" Tiribazos began.

"It is my turn to ask forgiveness for my rudeness. I am Chitraganda, Commander of the Zoroastrian Immortals, Prince of the Kambojas."

"Very well, Prince Chitraganda. What can I do for you?" said Tiribazos, shuffling from one foot to the other and sucking in his stomach. Xantho imagined the word 'Prince' would make any man nervous.

Chitraganda was as fine a looking gentleman as Xantho had ever seen. He was tall and broad-shouldered, mounted on his pure white horse. Across his saddle was a long-handled mace, topped with a strange sparkling rock which drew one's eye; such was its majesty and beauty.

"I like your style, Lord Tiribazos, straight to the point. Just so. I am here for him, the slave." Chitraganda beckoned to one of his Immortal warriors, who stepped forward and handed a fat purse to Jawed. Xantho could hear the coin inside jingling as he handed it over. "That should more than cover the cost. Do we have a bargain?"

Tiribazos spluttered for a moment, looking from Xantho to Chitraganda.

"How do you know the slave? He is…well…" said Tiribazos.

"He performed an act of great bravery yesterday. I would repay that act now by purchasing him from you. I trust the sum is to your liking? Twice the value of the slave, I should say."

"Well, yes. That is to say, well…" replied Tiribazos, spluttering.

"Good show, my lord. Good show. You drive a hard bargain. I like it. Let's double the price then." Chitraganda motioned to his man again, who duly handed Jawed another equally bulging purse. Jawed looked from the purse to Xantho, his mouth open and slack. "Seems we have a bargain. Come, bring the slave," said Chitraganda and sent his man to untie Xantho.

Tiribazos just stared, as stunned as Jawed. The Immortal led Xantho over to Chitraganda, and the magnificent looking Indian winked and grinned at him, his bright white teeth flashing beneath his black beard. Xantho allowed himself to be led away. The Indian's wink took him aback. A lord would never be so informal with a slave. Xantho looked from Jawed to his father.

They both seemed too shocked to react. Xantho wasn't sure what to think. One moment he was waiting to discover his punishment, and now he had been bought and sold to a new master. The Indian Immortal had mentioned that Xantho had fought well, so this must be something to do with Naram-Sin and Siduri.

"Always good to do business with fine noblemen such as yourselves. Good day, sirs," Chitraganda said.

He clicked his tongue, and his white horse stepped forward, forelegs rising high in an elaborate prancing show. The party moved off, and Xantho looked once more at his father, who stood again, hands on hips. His mouth moved, but no words were spoken. Xantho wondered what his father had been about to say before the Immortal had arrived. He had seemed on the cusp of some sort of change of heart. It appeared unlikely that Xantho would ever learn Tiribazos' true feelings about him. Not knowing where these men were leading him, Xantho shivered, unsure and afraid of what would happen next.

FOUR

Xantho shuffled along between the Immortals, who marched perfectly in time, step to step, with their quivers rattling as they moved.

"Now, that was a grimy bit of business. Untie his hands there," said Chitraganda over his shoulder.

The Indian's magnificent horse hopped from foot to foot. At each step, it raised a foreleg high and pranced forward as though it danced as it moved. Chitraganda rode the beast with poise—rider and mount, moving in perfect unison. The Immortal next to Xantho drew a knife from the rear of his belt and reached over to cut Xantho's bonds. The blade passed through the bindings like a knife through butter, and the Immortal whipped the blade back into its sheath.

Xantho rubbed at his burning wrists and blew

out his cheeks as the blood flowed back into his hands. He opened and closed his fists, trying to get the feeling back into his fingers. "Thank you," Xantho said, unable to take his eyes off Chitraganda's dazzling horse. His thanks were both for the Immortal who had cut his bonds and Chitraganda for paying his release from his father.

Xantho's head was bursting with questions. An Indian prince had bought him from his father, purchased and taken him away from the only life he had ever known. He thought of kind Bristonis and his other slave friends, wondering if he would ever see them again. Xantho assumed this had something to do with Naram-Sin and the events of the day before, but worried that all of this meant that he now belonged to Naram-Sin. Was it his fate to be a slave now to an Immortal warrior rather than a satrap? Xantho gulped, suddenly realising that they might expect him to fight and wield a sword. The strange turn of events had heightened his senses. He carefully observed the Immortals as they marched, a queasy feeling rumbling in the pit of his belly.

Xantho marched with the Immortals, the Faravahar symbol of the god Zoroaster flapping and snapping on its long pole. That symbol of a bearded man with one hand reaching forward above a pair of outstretched wings was poignant.

It spoke of the magical and the otherworldly. Xantho had seen such symbols countless times and had never paid them any attention—them being symbols of a religion he did not follow. But having witnessed the strange power Siduri had used in the battle and the power he had felt flowing through his own body, the flag now made Xantho uneasy.

The Immortals cut an impressive figure in their full-faced helmets and the sun glinting from their golden fish scale armour. Xantho couldn't help but think he had jumped from the cooking pan into the fire. But hopefully, whatever Chitraganda had in store for him was better than a lashing from Jawed. Anything had to be better than Jawed's whip. *Almost anything*. Xantho thought about his father's last words. The satrap had spoken kindly of Xantho's mother. For the first time in his life, Tiribazos had softened, and for a heartbeat, Xantho thought his father would forgive him, would exempt his half-blood son from Jawed and his whip. But he had never done so before, so why would he change the habit of a lifetime?

The group marched on through the cacophony of shouting, the clanking of weapons, the noise of tools being collected, and the crumpling and rolling up of the many thousands of army tents. They passed cavalry horses wrangled into long lines and infantry soldiers coming to muster, presumably to form the advance guard of Cyrus' long retreating column. Then, finally, Xantho and the Immortals came into an open space beyond the infantrymen and were headed towards a grouping of canvas tents, where the flag of Zoroaster flew high from their central tent poles. The Immortal beside him removed his helmet and let out a satisfied groan, running a gloved hand through long, sweat-soaked golden hair. The warrior looked across at Xantho and grinned.

"Good to be free?" the Immortal asked brightly.

Xantho's jaw dropped as he realised the Immortal was a woman. As far as he knew, there were no women warriors in the army of Cyrus the Great. But this woman was broad in the shoulder and bore heavy scarring across her face, her nose pushed to one side out of shape, broken in some fight long ago.

"Am I free?" replied Xantho.

"You are not a slave anymore, which surely is good?"

Xantho supposed it was, depending on where they were taking him. He didn't feel free. They had bought him for two bags of gold, which he was sure meant he was still a slave or that someone owned him unless, of course, these strange warriors planned to make him a freedman. He thought of asking again if he was truly free, with the liberty to come or go as he pleased, but thought better of it.

"I am Xantho."

"I know," she said, grinning again. "I am Agi."

"Where are you taking me?"

"To Naram-Sin."

Xantho clenched his teeth. He had thought, or hoped, never to see the haughty warrior again after his reaction to discovering his and Penelope's slave statuses. Xantho and Agi ducked under the entrance of the tent. The sounds of clashing weapons and the earthy smell of sweat-soaked leather hit Xantho like a wall. He hesitated, but Agi laughed and clapped him on the back.

"No need to be afraid, warrior; our friends are practising their craft."

She drew out the word "warrior" as though aware of the irony of addressing Xantho with that title. If there was one thing he was not, it was a warrior. Despite his lineage and the proud stories of his grandfather, he saw himself as more of a cautious, efficient worker. Or, more accurately, a slave, born to serve, not fight. At that moment, a voice boomed from behind.

"Ho, we return. Behold our new warrior," Chitraganda announced as he entered the tent. Xantho looked over his shoulder, and the Indian was grinning broadly, gesturing to Xantho.

The people inside the tent stopped what they were doing, and each looked at Xantho. He scanned the place and counted two groups of four warriors, clutching weapons and breathing hard. Then another two groups of four sat in small circles cross-legged. He felt his cheeks redden, and a burning sensation crept up his neck.

The nearest group of four nodded to Xantho. He nodded back. Those four all wore the uniform of Immortals but were each very different in appearance. Two looked like Medes or Persians. The third had strange eyes and was short in stature, whilst the fourth had black skin, darker even than an Egyptian. Chitraganda went across to the closest seated group, all garbed as priests or priestesses of Zoroaster, and they greeted Chitraganda warmly.

"What is this place?" Xantho asked.

"This is our camp for now. We march with the army once your mage is here," Agi answered.

"My mage?"

"Yes, we are all pairs. That's how it works, a warrior and mage pair."

"A warrior?" Xantho recalled Siduri mentioning something about that on the steppe, about her and Naram-Sin's power only working when they were together.

"Yes, that's you," said Agi, laughing, and she

raised her eyebrows and shook her head, looking at his filthy slave tunic and trews. Xantho's clothes looked faded and worn at the best of times, but the night before, he had slept out in the open, tied to a post. Not to mention he'd fought in a battle. He looked down at himself, his face flushed.

I look like a beggar.

Xantho was all too aware that he didn't look like a warrior, but that was simply because he wasn't one. He had never trained with weapons, nor had the inclination to use them, despite his Thracian warrior roots. He had cleaned and sharpened them many times in his daily chores, but had certainly never wielded a weapon in anger or battle. Xantho took some comfort in that the people in the tent were not laughing at him. They didn't seem to judge him by his appearance, or at least not that he could tell, anyway.

His thoughts moved to Agi's comments about his mage. To Xantho, a mage was someone who practised magic, but it was a thing from bedtime stories for children, not real life. Xantho felt a pang of hope—Penelope. *Who else could be my mage?* He had been flooded with power when they met and even fought in a skirmish, showing bravery. It was she who had brought on that change in him. Xantho hoped it was Penelope. He thought of her green eyes and their warmth.

He told himself to stop thinking like that and concentrate on the now instead.

"Who are these people?" he asked.

Agi stopped and looked him straight in the eye. "Well, it's complicated. We are the protectors of the light, the soldiers of the god Enlil, and we fight now for Cyrus the Great as part of his force of Immortals. But there is also another war, a hidden war, fought across the ages and in the shadows. So while we are part of Cyrus' army, we also fight for Enlil in his battle against the dark god Nergal."

Agi held up her palm to reveal a stone similar to that of Naram-Sin and Siduri, but where theirs was a rich, golden colour, Agi's was deep blue. It was the same deep unearthly blue of the lapis lazuli stones Xantho had seen in his father's jewellery.

"What does that mean?"

"As I said, it's complicated. I'll let Naram-Sin explain it to you. He was the first. Ah, your mage is here," said Agi, nodding to the tent entrance. Xantho sighed, wondering if he would ever get an explanation of his new circumstances that he could actually understand. Penelope stood there, looking slight and willowy, with her hands clasped in front of her, scanning the inside of the tent. Finally, her gaze fell on Xantho, and she scowled, which was not encouraging.

Two Immortals flanked Penelope, tall and

elegant in their uniforms. These two Immortals held their helmets under their arms, allowing Xantho to see their sophisticated features—long noses and sculpted eyebrows in faces slightly darker than his own. A man and woman. Xantho could see the pattern now, always a man and woman, always a mage and warrior. The man could take either role, as could the woman. If he had to take either role, Xantho thought he would make a better mage than a warrior. He knew less about magic than he did about weapons, but at the battle, Penelope had shown more courage than he, and she had fended off two attackers with her sword.

"Welcome, warrior," came a soft, whispery voice over his shoulder. Xantho turned to see Siduri. She was tall, and their eyes met at equal height.

"I think there might have been a misunderstanding," said Xantho.

Siduri cocked her head to one side and raised a slender hand, tapping a long finger on her chin. "Really, what kind of misunderstanding?" she asked.

"You keep calling me a warrior. And, well...I'm not one. I'm sorry."

Siduri smiled at him, cheekbones standing out atop her wide mouth. "You will see, Xantho. Enlil does not make mistakes. You are the warrior we have been waiting for, and here is your mage."

The two Immortals escorted Penelope to where Xantho stood with Siduri. They nodded a greeting and strode off in Naram-Sin's direction, and Xantho's gaze followed them. Naram-Sin was moving through some exercises with a short sword. He thrust and cut in slow, measured movements, effortlessly darting from one position to the next, always on the balls of his feet.

"Welcome, mage," Siduri said. She held a hand out to Penelope, who took it and smiled warmly, small creases appearing at the corners of her green eyes. Xantho noticed the creases, the eyes, and the smile.

"Thank you for paying my master," said Penelope.

"You are most welcome, little one. The army marches soon, and we must make ready. You will practise for a short time first. Let us see what comes naturally to you both." Siduri smiled again and walked away. She called to a few of her comrades, and they talked in hushed voices.

"Hello again," said Xantho. Penelope crossed her arms and frowned at him.

"I thought I would never see you again...after you ran away."

"I didn't run away."

"What would you call it, then?"

"I walked back to my duties. Hardly running away."

"You ran. You ran from what could have been—from freedom. But, lucky for you, these people have given it to us anyway."

"How do you know?"

"How do I know what?"

"That they have given us our freedom?"

"They paid my master."

"Does that mean you are free or now have a new master?"

Penelope huffed and shook her head at him. Xantho winced. He knew he should have just agreed with her. Now she was even more annoyed with him. Luckily, Naram-Sin approached before the conversation could continue. He strode lightly, almost floating, walking with the athletic menace of a cat from Tiribazos' palace.

"You are here, and we have little time. Everyone…" Naram-Sin announced in his deep nobleman's voice. All present came to listen to what he was about to say. "…we march out today, but it is not a retreat. Cyrus has learned from prisoners taken in the raid yesterday that these tribesmen have never tasted wine. It does not exist on the lands of the steppe. So, he leaves plenty of it behind for the Massagetae to enjoy. He intends then to double back and attack them in their cups."

"Surely this plan is too simplistic? We cannot expect that the whole of Tomyris' army will become inebriated; Gula'an will not permit it?" said Chitraganda.

"I do not know, but this is the Great King's plan. We must be vigilant. As you say, such a simple trick will not fool Gula'an. Likely he has something up his sleeve. So be on your guard. Now, let's see what our newest recruits can do."

Before Xantho could ask those around him who Gula'an was, the group fanned out into a circle, leaving Xantho and Penelope at the centre. Xantho's head was spinning with information, a hidden war, Enlil and dark gods, Gula'an. He needed some time to make sense of it all. But they thrust a spear into his hand, and Agi stood opposite him. She also had a spear and smiled, crumpling her twisted nose. Xantho's spear was longer than he was tall, its shaft was smooth, and its blade shaped like a leaf. He could smell the rich pine oil used on the shaft to preserve it.

Siduri stood next to Penelope and whispered into her ear so softly that Xantho could not hear what she said. Siduri braced herself in a wide-footed stance, and Penelope followed her example. Xantho wondered who would show him what to do as Siduri helped Penelope, but nobody came forward. Instead, Agi flashed her spear at him, and the shaft clattered onto his knuckles at the point where he grasped his own weapon. Xantho let out an involuntary yelp and dropped his spear to the ground. A few sniggers rippled through those gathered, and Xantho sighed from the pit of his stomach.

"Pick it up. Hold on to it; fight back," came Naram-Sin's voice from Xantho's left.

Xantho picked up his spear. He watched how Agi held hers, and he tried to match it. He stood side-on, two hands on the spear, one high and one low. As he made ready, Penelope touched him on the arm, and his head whipped around— the feeling again. A wave surged through his body, pulsing rhythmically around his limbs in sync with the beating of his heart. Xantho looked at Penelope, and she nodded. Encouraged by that and by the strength coursing through him, Xantho charged.

He thrust his spear at Agi, and she blocked it with her own. He kept moving forward and swung the butt end of the weapon around in an arc, aiming for her head, but Agi ducked under it, rising quickly and tapping him on the arse with her own spear. He spun around, and a hot feeling caught fire in his belly, which rose up his torso. Anger and rage welled within him, and he let out a shout as he charged at her again, stabbing out with the spear and letting a kick fly out. Agi again dodged his attack with ease. She hooked her foot around his standing leg, and

Xantho toppled to the ground. More sniggers. Xantho's lips peeled back in a snarl. He had never felt so angry, and now he had the power rushing through his body.

Xantho braced himself to shoot for Agi's legs when he caught sight of Penelope. She was moving her arms in a wide circle, copying Siduri, who moved next to her. Penelope had her eyes closed, her mouth set in grim concentration.

"Now!" Siduri urged, and Penelope thrust her arms forward, palms outstretched.

Xantho felt a hot wind whoosh over him, pushing him back to the ground. His hair blew back from his face, and he had to close his eyes at the force and heat of the burst. When he opened them again, Agi was on the floor five paces from where she had stood a moment earlier. Agi sat up, grinning at Penelope, and nodded in her direction. Xantho heard clapping; it was Naram-Sin.

"Fine work. You have a natural ability. Let's pack up now and join the march. Battle is coming, and we will need to play our part," Naram-Sin said, completely ignoring Xantho.

He had fought poorly, and he knew it. Nevertheless, the power had been there. Yet now, Xantho felt it fleeing from him, like throwing off a heavy cloak. He had no skill, but Xantho had felt ferocity and strength. He knew he had embarrassed himself in front of them all.

Some warrior.

He climbed to his feet, dusted himself down, and went to Penelope. She was breathing hard and leaning on Siduri, who was laughing and congratulating her. Xantho ground his teeth.

How was she so proficient at her new skill? She had done actual magic. Penelope had conjured the same power Siduri had used on the steppe a day earlier.

"Well done, Xantho," Siduri said, almost as an afterthought.

"For what? I made a fool of myself."

"You tried, and the skill will come. You have a powerful mage."

"Who is Gula'an?" asked Xantho, wanting to steer the subject away from his failure.

Siduri's face turned serious. "The enemy, the great enemy. He is of Nergal as we are of Enlil. This is the real war we fight. Yes, we fight for Cyrus against the Massagetae, but our real battle is against Gula'an, who fights alongside the Massagetae. He has power, just like we do, granted to him by Nergal as Enlil has empowered us. There will be a battle soon, Xantho. You must prepare yourself. We will speak of this again soon," she said and then moved off, helping the others gather equipment for the march. That explained nothing. It made Xantho slightly more terrified than he was already at his rapid change in circumstances, but he still didn't understand who the enemy was or who Enlil was, for that matter.

"That was amazing," breathed Penelope. Her green eyes were ablaze, and her cheeks flushed. She turned her hands over and back in front of her face.

"You did well," Xantho nodded, prising the words from himself.

"You didn't," she replied. But then she laughed. Her smile was infectious, and Xantho smiled with her. "You did, really. I am teasing you. Agi is skilled; you will learn quickly, I'm sure."

"I'm sorry," Xantho said, which he was. It had been cowardly to leave her after the fight. On the steppe, he had chosen his life as a slave over whatever new opportunity or chance of freedom might have been possible with Penelope. "I shouldn't have walked away yesterday. But we are here now…with these…people."

"Well, no, you shouldn't have. But yes, we are here now. And it looks like we will see a lot more of each other, warrior." She smiled again.

"Thank you, mage."

"You need to find your courage, Xantho. If this is going to work, we have to do it together. We must learn to work as a pair as the others do."

"Do you really believe all this talk of magic

and gods? That the gods have warriors with magical powers fighting a secret war amongst the armies of the Massagetae and Persia?"

She leant her head to one side, frowning. "We don't need to believe. We are in it. This is our life now. You can see it right before you; there is magic within these people and within us." Penelope brushed at a loose strand of hair and fixed him with a flat stare. "I won't let you mess this up for me. This is my chance, and yours, for a different life. So we have to make it work."

Xantho stared back, not knowing what to say. She was right, though. They weren't slaves anymore. But exactly what they were and what kind of danger they were in remained to be seen. "Both Naram-Sin and Siduri said there would be a battle soon. Do you think they will expect us to fight with the army? Like soldiers?"

"Yes, Xantho, I do. We are soldiers now; our old lives are behind us," she said, her face grave and her eyes locked with his.

"I don't think I can do it," he whispered, voicing his fears. They all seemed so sure, Naram-Sin, Siduri and Penelope. But Xantho could not see himself standing in line with the warriors, with the army, fighting a battle. "I am just not a warrior. They have the wrong man for this."

"They do not have the wrong man. You just need to believe in yourself. Do not shirk from this. You have already apologised for turning down this chance once on the steppe, do not do it again. This is our chance to be someone other than a slave. And more than that, we have been given power and opportunity. You must find your strength, Xantho." Penelope put her hand on his shoulder and looked deep into his eyes. She shook her head as though concerned at what she saw there. Then, Penelope left him to prepare herself for the march.

Agi walked past, clapped Xantho on the shoulder, and tossed a rolled-up rug into his arms. Xantho made for the tent entrance with the others to join the march. He was no longer a slave, but he didn't understand what or who he was supposed to be now. Penelope had shown she had magical skills, and he had certainly felt the warrior power flowing through him again, along with the unfamiliar feeling of rage and a desire to attack. Xantho knew he must try; he must do better. He must learn to fight and be a warrior like his grandfather if he was going to play his part in the fight against Gula'an, even if he didn't know quite yet what that battle would entail.

FIVE

Xantho stood in the battle line wearing full Immortal armour, Penelope to his left and Agi to his right. Naram-Sin and his warriors formed up with the rest of the ten thousand Immortals behind the front ranks and in front of Cyrus the Great and his elite bodyguard. Xantho had not seen Cyrus, which was not surprising given the many tens of thousands of men in the Persian army, but Agi had assured him that Cyrus would be there in the rear, mounted on his magnificent war chariot.

It had been two days since the army had packed up and retreated from the lands of the Massagetae tribes. Or feigned a retreat, at least. Naram-Sin's information was correct, and Cyrus had left barrels and barrels of wine for the Massagetae to find when they searched the abandoned camp. Sure enough, a large detachment of enemy horsemen, under their general, Spargapises, had routed Cyrus' rear guard and captured the barrels. Spargapises and his men had stopped to enjoy the nectar, an unfamiliar experience for them, and became stupefied, having never tasted wine before. Cyrus sprang the trap and thundered in to attack Spargapises and his warriors, who made up an entire third of the Massagetae army, butchering them in their entirety.

The leader of those drunken, and now dead warriors, General Spargapises, was the son of the Massagetae empress, Tomyris. The bereaved and enraged warrior empress now faced Cyrus with her massed horde of horse warriors, swirling across the plain from where Xantho stood in line.

Xantho swallowed hard, his throat dry and cracked from the dust flying across the steppe and kicked up by the many thousands of cavalry on the wings of the army. The armour was heavy, too heavy. His breastplate was hard, baked leather, and faced with the same bronze fish scale plates as Naram-Sin and the other Immortals wore. It ended in a kilt of leather pieces which protected his groin. He hadn't asked where the armour and clothing had come from, but he silently hoped it hadn't come from a dead warrior. Xantho had a quiver and bow strapped to his back, which he did not know how to use. He had a short sword in a fleece-lined scabbard at his waist and gripped a spear. It was smooth-shafted, with a blade longer than Xantho's forearm and a silver butt spike to counterbalance the heavy blade. He looked magnificent, but he felt like a fool, like an imposter dressed up in someone else's clothes.

His full-face bronze helmet nestled under his arm, and Xantho had let his shield rest against his leg. It was wicker made and covered in hard leather. Xantho itched at the shoulders of his breastplate and shuffled his feet to relieve the rub of his new boots. To his own amazement, he had managed not to run away from his new life. He had wanted to flee—at night when the others were asleep. Xantho had stayed awake until the rest of the Warriors of the Light snored and slept, and he lay there trying to pluck up the courage to slip away. It would be so simple, just sneak off in the darkness and never return. He had not, though. Xantho was in this situation now, and Penelope was right. For her sake, he had to change. He couldn't be a coward his entire life. In the last few days, Xantho had developed a trick of pushing away thoughts of running and hiding by replacing them with a vision of his grandfather. He would picture Aristaeus standing before him, resplendent in a Greek warrior's panoply of muscled cuirass and full-faced horsehair bristled helmet. There could be no running in the face of Aristaeus. If he had to fight, then Xantho would stand firm and try to live up to his grandfather's memory and reputation.

"Stop it. Stop scratching," said Penelope. She, too, wore the armour of an Immortal, as did all of Naram-Sin's company, including the mages. Only Naram-Sin himself was different. His spear had a golden butt spike, and he wore a golden tiara to mark him out as a commanding officer. Where Xantho felt like a court jester and a slave dressed in fine war clothes, Penelope stood still and straight-backed. To anyone else, she would be just another Immortal warrior, albeit a rather small one.

"I can't help it, it's so itchy, and I'm sweating."

"Stand still. You are going to get us into trouble."

"Won't be much longer," Agi interjected from Xantho's right. "Tomyris is spitting mad with grief that her son is dead. They'll charge soon."

That didn't make Xantho feel much better. Two days ago, he was a slave washing clothes in a river. Now, he stood ready for battle, armed to the teeth and entirely unprepared for what lay ahead.

"Gula'an will be there with his warriors," said Agi.

"I still don't know who this Gula'an is," muttered Xantho. Naram-Sin's soldiers talked incessantly about their enemy and the danger he presented. But none had fully explained it to him yet.

"If you see Gula'an, you just tell me. I'll take care of him," Agi responded, winking at him.

"How will I know if I see him when I don't even know who he is?"

Before his question could be answered, an order rang out with urgency.

"Silence there."

The voice booming down the line was that of Naram-Sin, who shot Xantho a steely frown. Penelope kicked Xantho in the leg, and she, too, frowned at him. *Best to stay quiet then and try not to get killed.* He tried to stand straighter and hold his spear steadier.

Shouts came from the front of the lines, and the conical helmets in Xantho's field of vision snapped left, a wave of one following another. Then, a great cloud thundered from the left of the lines and raced in front of the army in a diagonal path aiming straight for the massed Massagetae.

"Cavalry," said Agi.

Xantho couldn't see any horses, just the cloud. He could, however, feel the rumbling beneath his feet as twenty thousand horsemen charged across the plain, and he could hear the roar of their collective hooves as they pounded across the steppe like a mighty beast from legend. Moments went by in silence. Xantho looked at Agi and Penelope, but there were no answers there. Both craned their necks to see above the lines of soldiers, as did everybody else.

"You are afraid, little mouse," said a deep voice. It was the dark-skinned warrior Xantho had seen back in the tent where he had fought Agi. Of course, he was afraid. He was about to fight in a battle, having never fought before in his life. He ignored the warrior.

"I can smell your fear. It reeks like shit," the warrior spoke again. He loomed over Xantho, his broad frame making Xantho want to step away from him.

"Leave him, Banya," Agi ordered, which seemed to shut him up. He wore his scarf pulled up to cover the lower part of his face, as did Agi. His dark skin would mark him out amongst the men of the Persian army, just as Agi's soft womanly face would. Anyone who stood out would attract attention and questions, which Xantho supposed this odd group wanted to avoid.

Men coughed and shifted position. A warrior two rows ahead of Xantho pissed where he was standing, and nobody reacted. Impossible now to break ranks for a piss. Xantho felt sweat trickling down his sides beneath his tunic and scratched at his underarms. He felt pressure in his bladder and put it down to nerves.

"There, look!" came a shout from down the line.

Xantho could see the cloud still milling ahead, but from that mass of dust, a steady stream of riders, or horses without riders, began careening wildly across the plain. Xantho thought of his father, Tiribazos, and of Jawed and the rest of the people from his home. They would be with the cavalry, out there somewhere, fighting for their lives.

"What's going on?" called another voice three rows ahead.

"Cavalry's blown it. We're in the shit now, boys," came a gruff voice from Xantho's right. He gulped. It sounded bad. But with all the warriors Cyrus had on the field, thousands beyond count, stretching beyond even as far as Xantho could see, how could any enemy attack successfully?

"Silence in the ranks. Hold fast."

That was the sonorous voice of Naram-Sin again. Xantho kept his eyes fixed ahead. More and more horses and riders appeared, charging wildly back the way they had come. A broad brown smear of a line on the horizon emerged through the dust cloud. It glinted here and there where the sun caught metal. It grew larger, coming closer.

"What in the name of the gods is that?" Xantho spluttered.

"Tomyris. Brace yourself," said Agi.

Xantho looked at her, licking his lips and

nearly dropping his spear.

"Shields," came the call from Naram-Sin. All along the line, Immortals fixed their wicker shields to their forearms, the clicking and rustling of the defensive weapons filling the air.

Xantho reached for his own shield. He tried to rest his spear in the crook of his arm, but as he bent, it fell forward, and the shaft hit the warrior in front of him. Xantho cursed to himself.

"Watch it, idiot," the warrior grumbled.

"Sorry," said Xantho, pulling it back. He hefted the shield and got his left arm through the arm loop. He could feel eyes burning into him, and he glanced at Penelope, who just shook her head. She had her shield ready. *How was she so good at this?* Eventually, he snapped back to attention, the shield heavy on his arm as if carrying a bag of wheat.

"Helmets."

Naram-Sin again.

Xantho nearly dropped the helmet, but he caught it and thrust it on his head, twisting it until it was secure. His breath was hot against the bronze face guard, and sweat rolled down his face, already stinging his eyes. Xantho couldn't see left or right now. Instead, he looked ahead and nearly shit where he stood at the sight of what he saw before him.

The enemy was now upon them. A vast

mass of screaming and whirling horse-mounted warriors descended on the army of Cyrus the Great. They whirled in wide circles, monstrous and terrible. Then, when each circle's turn came to face the Persians, they let loose a rain of arrows so that as the circles turned, a relentless torrent of missiles pounded the Persian lines.

Xantho raised his shield and closed his eyes, crouching behind the safety of the thick wicker.

"Get up, Xantho," hissed Penelope.

He peeked around his shield, and everyone was staring at him. Some laughed, and Xantho sighed. He was the only warrior in the surrounding lines who had lifted his shield. So vast was Cyrus's army that the enemy missiles could not reach the depth of the Immortals' lines. But the lines ahead screamed and died in droves.

Xantho was breathing fast, his helmet hot and cloying. He glanced around him, and the lines stood still and unwavering. Xantho wanted to drop his spear and run. If he made a run for it now, he might be away before the enemy cut through the lines ahead of him. Then, he would be free and out of this nightmare. Xantho shook his head. *Too late to run now.* He was in this up to his neck.

Xantho's head rang from an ear-splitting, cracking sound. It sounded like thunder, but at ground level right there before him. He cringed and struggled to see what could have made such a sound. Ahead of him, screaming soldiers flew into the air like so many skittles knocked over by a wooden ball. They landed with sickening crunches, and a wave of hot air swooped through the ranks, driving Xantho back a step. Thirty paces from where Xantho stood, he saw men flying out in all directions as the monstrous, thunder-like sound erupted again. Through the melee, Xantho saw a chariot racing through the Persian ranks. A single man stood in its carriage, one hand on the reins and another wielding a long black staff, which he thrust left and right before him. Warriors were flung away where he waved that staff as though they'd been hurled by a giant. The charioteer wore flowing white robes, and his long white hair cascaded behind him like a horse's mane. At his heels came the vicious steppe horsemen of the Massagetae, pouring into the gap in the Persian ranks. At their head and just behind the chariot rode a snarling woman brandishing two curved blades, one in each hand. She controlled her steppe pony with only her thighs and charged, screaming through the Persian ranks. Tomyris, the battle empress here to avenge the death of her son Spargapises.

"Gula'an!" came a roar, and Xantho saw Naram-Sin take a step forward and launch his golden spear. The weapon arced through the air and seemed destined to strike the charioteer, but at the last moment, he flicked a hand, and the weapon flew by harmlessly. The charioteer, who Xantho now assumed was Gula'an, looked in his direction and smiled, dark eyes shining.

Naram-Sin charged, and the rest of his companions followed. Penelope moved off with them, and Xantho followed her. He was at the rear, but at least he had charged. Hundreds of enemy horsemen had already cleaved through Cyrus' army, pouring into the gap created by Gula'an and his magic. Xantho saw Siduri standing with Chitraganda, waving their arms in unison. They clapped their hands together, and the earth around Xantho shook. He stumbled and watched in awe as the ground ahead was wrenched apart. A long deep crevasse appeared on the steppe, and the attacking horsemen plunged into it, the screaming of the falling horses terrible above the din of battle.

Xantho couldn't see what was happening around him. He heard weapons clashing and men dying, but all was a blur. The battle was joined in earnest now. Persians and Massagetae hacked and thrust at each other. Hot liquid splashed through the eyeholes in Xantho's helmet, and he retched, realising it was someone else's blood. Xantho tore off his helmet and dropped his shield to wipe it from his face. Ahead of him, Agi was battling a tribesman in a whirl of spears and swords. He couldn't see Penelope. A blade scythed towards his head, and Xantho ducked to avoid its strike, feeling it fly past him. Crying out, he sprang forward and cannoned into his attacker, knocking them both to the ground. Xantho scrambled to regain his feet, but his armour was cumbersome, and he cursed. Suddenly, the power surged in him, pulsing around his body. Penelope must be close. He leapt to his feet, roaring with fury. Agi was still battling her attacker, and before he knew what he was doing, Xantho flung his spear, and it flew straight and true, taking the enemy in the throat. Agi turned and smiled at him. Xantho retched again; he had just killed a man. The spear had twisted under its weight and tore a terrible gash in the enemy's throat, black blood poured down the dying man's chest, and his frantic eyes dimmed as his lifeblood flowed onto the steppe.

"Xantho, come on."

He heard Penelope's gravelly voice from somewhere; he turned, and she was there alongside Siduri. The tall mage thrust her hands out, and her power flung a block of four enemy warriors backwards.

"To Naram-Sin!" Siduri shouted.

They set off at a run, charging through the battle. As he ran, Xantho could see and hear the death and carnage flowing around him. His stomach churned, the image of his spear slicing open the enemy's throat playing over and over in his mind. Ahead, there was terrible and vicious fighting. Banya lay about him with his spear, stabbing and wielding it in wide arcs, cleaving the enemy as they raced past on horseback.

Xantho gasped as he spotted a mammoth, deep crater carved into the steppe, like an upturned soup bowl. Inside that bowl lay scores of dead Immortals. Around its edges, warriors fought furiously. Xantho saw Naram-Sin on the far side of that black bowl, his blade swinging and striking, cutting down any enemies who dared to face him. Beside Naram-Sin fought the tall, elegant warrior who had bought Penelope's freedom. Siduri dashed into the bowl, and others followed her. A line of mages formed, chanting and moving their arms in unison; Penelope ran to join them. Xantho found himself rooted to the spot, unsure where to go or what to do.

From the line of mages, a ripple of light flew up towards the sky, and immediately a peal of lightning flashed from the heavens and smashed into the battle melee. Fire and smoke billowed everywhere. Xantho was on his knees. He couldn't see Penelope anymore, and the bowl was deserted. He looked left and right, and there was empty space around him. Xantho stood. An eerie silence fell across the battlefield. Suddenly a steppe pony rushed past him, its rider keening a terrible cry and holding aloft a severed head, blood flying from its gory neck.

The head had an oiled beard and was crowned

with a golden tiara. The rider was Tomyris, and she had killed Cyrus the Great, King of Kings. A collective moan passed across the battlefield like a wave of sorrow washing over the soldiers. Xantho sprang back as a chariot's wheels almost crushed him. He looked up in horror to see Gula'an laughing as he rode.

"I give you souls, Nergal. Bring the underworld forth! I give you souls!" cried Gula'an. Gula'an ceased his terrible chanting and yanked hard on his reins. The chariot stopped dead. He turned his white-bearded, black-eyed face and looked straight at Xantho. Xantho's bowels squirmed, he wanted to turn away from that fearful gaze, but he could not.

"You are of Naram-Sin," Gula'an called in a booming voice. "Behold and despair," he said, waving his arm across the battlefield. At that moment, he was suddenly interrupted by a warrior who charged past Xantho, screaming a challenge. It was Agi, and she flung herself at Gula'an, her sword swinging.

Gula'an raised his staff and touched the tip against Agi, and to Xantho's horror, she erupted into a ball of flames and fell, twitching and screaming. Gula'an laughed maniacally again and drove his chariot on, following Tomyris to her stunning victory over the greatest empire the world had ever seen.

SIX

Xantho's shoulders were on fire, the aching in his muscles deep and sore. The retreat from the field of defeat had been a rolling journey of blood and pain for the army of Cyrus, the slain King of Kings. The Immortals, including the warriors of the light, had fought on the front line of that retreat, and Xantho could have never believed such suffering was possible. Massagetae horseman had dogged them, circling in and out to pour a never-ending torrent of arrows, while the vicious and nimble riders darted in to pick off any stragglers at close quarters. The Persian army had collapsed once Tomyris had taken Cyrus' head, and the flight from the battlefield had been bloody and exhausting. Xantho had retreated with the rest of Naram-Sin's force. Encouraged by his companions, Xantho had kept his shield raised throughout and had even struck out with spear and sword, but he had not taken a life since the battle. His whole body screamed from the exertion, blood was crusted in his hair and face, and Xantho had no clue whose blood it was. It could have been his own, it could have been from the young tribesman whose throat his spear had torn out, or perhaps it could have belonged to Agi, who now lay in a pile of ashes on the battlefield. The death of Cyrus sent a shockwave through the Persian army. Cyrus was a god, the King of Kings, and to see his head cut off and paraded before them by the savage warrior-queen was crushing, leaving the rank and file of the army distraught and lost.

Xantho sat, slumped and exhausted, on the open steppe. Penelope sat alongside him. She was silent, staring bleakly into the far horizon where the evening sun dipped slowly into its night cradle, casting long shadows over the flat grasslands. It was quiet now, save for the sounds of moaning and sobbing from myriad huddles of survivors who had gathered together for safety. The Massagetae had broken off the pursuit as evening fell, and Xantho had thanked the gods for that mercy. Darkness had saved the survivors of the Persian army—that and the need of the victorious and wrathful tribesmen to rest their mounts. Xantho presumed they went to celebrate their stunning victory over the King of the Four Corners of the World and enjoy the terrible vengeance of their empress. Nevertheless, he did not doubt that the onslaught and pursuit would continue at daybreak.

Xantho scratched at his breastplate, where it chafed his neck, and he pulled off his left boot. He tipped out a pile of dust and muck and poked gingerly at the blisters the boot had wrought on his foot. Some movement to his left caught Xantho's eye. It was Chitraganda, the Indian mage. He was leaning forward and moving his hands in small circles, whispering into his palms. A small flame sprang up from nowhere in his clutches, and Chitraganda coaxed it with his hands. The flame grew. Another warrior snapped off a handful of arrow shafts from where they had stuck into her wicker shield and tossed them into the flame.

Others did the same, and the flame grew all the more. The warmth was welcome, and the companions turned to face its glow, all except for Naram-Sin. The tall warrior stood apart, eyes fixed on the horizon. Xantho had never seen a warrior with such martial prowess. It was frightening to see Naram-Sin fight. During the retreat, Xantho had seen him slay endless foes with a bow, spear, and blade; in fact, Naram-Sin had killed beyond count. More than once, Xantho had seen the warrior smile as he killed, eyes flashing with joy.

What kind of man killed like that?

Once again, the face of the tribesman Xantho

had killed in the battle flashed before his eyes. Shaggy-haired and young, a life yet to live. Maybe he had a wife; perhaps he was as happy as Xantho had been to be married. That life was gone now, snatched away by Xantho's spear thrust. For what? Xantho still didn't know. He had seen Gula'an and his terrible power thrusting warriors aside and rending the earth like a god. He had also seen Siduri and the other mages wreak impossible damage to man and land alike. Xantho stared into the spitting orange flames. He needed answers.

"Are you alright?" Xantho asked, leaning slightly towards Penelope. She looked at him, her green eyes dark now in the half-light of dusk. Her face looked drawn, smeared with mud and blood, and Hera knew what else.

"Penelope?" he said, trying to wake her from her daze. Xantho could only assume she had the same images of the day's horrors running through her mind as he did.

"Yes…well…alright, yes," she said. Penelope rubbed her eyes and shook her head. She gazed into the flame and raised her palms to feel the warmth.

"Agi is gone," Xantho murmured.

"I know. I saw. He turned her to ash," Penelope said, looking back to Xantho. Her bottom lip quivered a little, and she bit it softly.

"So much happened today. Magic, death."

"Who would have thought such things are even possible? Did you see the lightning, the crater?"

He had seen it all. He'd watched Penelope work magic with the other mages; she was clearly born for this. She acted without hesitation and with bravery. Xantho had barely made it through the day alive. His companions had saved his life countless times—Naram-Sin, Siduri, and others of the Warriors of the Light he had come to know that day: Wulfgar, Xia Lao, Khamudi.

"I saw," he said.

"What happens to us now?"

He didn't know. He barely knew why they fought in the first place, never mind what would happen now that Cyrus the Great was dead.

"I don't know. But we need some answers," said Xantho. He pulled on his boot and pushed himself to his feet, suppressing a groan as his limbs ached and burned. He had not spoken to Naram-Sin since the tent, where they had forced Xantho to fight Agi unsuccessfully. The tall warrior might be a fierce, bloodthirsty fighter of peerless skill and aloof and impossible to talk to, but if Xantho had learned one thing about himself these last few days, it was that he didn't have to be afraid anymore. The spirit of his grandfather was with him, strengthening him. Xantho had fought in a battle and had taken another man's life. He had wrestled with the fact and come to accept that not only did magic exist in the world but that he had magic flowing through him. So Xantho would be damned if he would sit there afraid to talk to Naram-Sin.

Xantho strode to where Naram-Sin stood. The warrior heard Xantho's boots on the short steppe grass and turned his head. His short-cropped hair was plastered to his head with sweat, and his face was as filthy as the rest of the warriors. But somehow, Naram-Sin still looked better, more noble, like he was in some way more than the rest. He arched an eyebrow above his iron-grey eyes when he saw Xantho.

Xantho stood and stared at Naram-Sin. He wanted answers, but now that he was facing the warrior, no words came. He felt like a slave facing his master again. The only reaction he could muster in such situations was to maintain deferential silence—a reflex driven into him through a lifetime of servitude. Naram-Sin stared at him. Xantho swallowed and opened his mouth. Still no words.

"You fought today. I saw you," said Naram-Sin.

Xantho almost fell over. Although Naram-Sin had not said that Xantho had fought well, he *had* noticed him. That was something. Perhaps the first compliment Xantho had received in years. *Was it a compliment?*

"Who is Gula'an? Where does our magic come

from?" Xantho asked. The words rushed out, and Xantho clenched his teeth, waiting for a rebuke.

Naram-Sin nodded and scratched at his short, angular, dark beard. "Very well. I should have explained earlier. Let's walk a while," he suggested, and he strolled back towards the gathered survivors. Xantho followed, trying not to look like he was scampering to keep pace with Naram-Sin's long strides.

"Today, you witnessed a great battle, perhaps one of the largest of all time. It was a battle between a great conqueror, Cyrus, and an empress fighting for the freedom of her people, Tomyris. There was also another battle today, a battle in a war without end. The war between good and evil, darkness and light," Naram-Sin spoke in his low clear voice. "We fight for Enlil, god of light, wind, air, earth and storms. Gula'an and his warriors fight for Nergal, the god of the underworld. If Nergal and Gula'an win, they will plunge the world into eternal war and strife. Their dream is to give Nergal dominion over a world afire with perpetual war. We are those who fight to stop that."

Xantho had heard some of this before from Siduri—about Enlil and Nergal. But it still made little sense.

"Where does the magic come from?" Xantho pressed.

"It comes from Enlil. The more we push

Gula'an back and increase the chances of peace for the world, the stronger Enlil becomes. The more death and destruction they can wreak, the more powerful Nergal and Gula'an become. Today, Gula'an reaped many souls for Nergal; his power grows."

"Why me? Why us?"

"The power chooses two, always two. Mage and warrior. Enlil chose you and Penelope. Sometimes we lose fighters; today, we lost Agi. She will rise again, but we need to replenish our numbers. Enlil has chosen you."

"Why me, though?"

Naram-Sin stopped and turned to face Xantho.

"You have it in you to be a great warrior for the light, you and Penelope. But, you must learn—and quickly. The war is real. As I told you before, if we lose, they will plunge the world into eternal darkness, war, and strife. So, we must stop Gula'an."

"Well, he won today," Xantho muttered. "It was he who cloved through our ranks and allowed Tomyris to win."

"We should have stopped him."

Xantho shook his head and looked at the ground. It was so much to take in and try to understand. At that moment, a shadow fell across his line of vision, and he looked up to see the hulking figure of Banya staring down at him.

"You need to learn fast, little mouse. You fight like a puppy. You could get us all killed," he said. His spear was crusted with gore from battle, and his eyes were burning with fervour. Xantho wanted to shrink away from the warrior, to block him out. But, instead, he settled on trying to ignore him, and eventually, Banya strode away. What did Banya have against him? He was always there with a snipe at Xantho. There was no reason for it. Xantho couldn't understand what he could have done to upset the warrior.

A groan nearby disrupted his thoughts, and Xantho peered through the shroud of darkness to see who it was. Five paces from where he stood, huddled a clutch of other survivors. He looked across the plain, and little fires had sprung up everywhere, lighting up the steppe like the stars above. The groaning was coming from the fire closest to him, and surrounding it was a group of men in cavalry uniforms. Their breastplates were painted with the eagle of his father's house. Xantho stepped forward, his heart in his mouth. Since the battle, he hadn't given a thought to his father or any of those he had known before.

He approached the huddle of men, and Xantho recognised some of them. None seemed to recognise him, though. The groan came again, followed by a cough, and Xantho noticed a warrior lying down on his side, bloody spittle in his beard and a terrible wound in his belly. Xantho knelt, taking the man's hand—it was Jawed. The two were no longer master and slave. Despite all the hardship and pain that Xantho had endured at the hand of his father's man, it pained him to see Jawed like this. He would surely die from such a wound. Jawed's eyes widened as he saw Xantho. He took in Xantho's Immortal armour and shook his head.

"Xantho…how?"

Xantho realised his armour, and ergo his new role in life must have seemed impossible to Jawed. Only days earlier, Xantho had been a slave, waiting to feel the whip, which Jawed would have gladly administered himself just as he had before, time and time again.

"Tiribazos?" Xantho said.

Jawed closed his eyes and shook his head. Another cough racked his body, and Jawed groaned from the pain, clutching his wound. A warrior held a lump of cloth to it, trying to stem the bleeding.

"Lost…" Jawed lamented, "…fallen in the first charge. Shot to pieces, an arrow in the eye felled him."

Jawed coughed again, and blood flowed from his pale lips. Xantho stood and walked back to Naram-Sin with an empty cavern in his heart, and he wasn't sure if it was because his father was dead or because he had never really had a father to care for him and teach the ways of manhood. Tiribazos had condemned Xantho into slavery from birth, his own son, and Xantho thought that the cavern he felt was perhaps an echo from the hole in his heart—the space which would be normally be filled by a father's love. He thought of Bristonis and the other slaves, wondering what had become of them during the defeat and retreat across the steppe. His heart ached to think old Bristonis was lost and alone, or worse, lying dead somewhere, cut open by a tribesman's blade. For all the stories of the glory of war, of the heroic Aristaeus stories his mother and Bristonis had filled Xantho's head with as a child, this was the real face of war. It was blood and pain, loss and death.

"Your life with these men is over. You are one of us now. We should get back. I must decide what to do next," said Naram-Sin.

Xantho marched sombrely along in silence. His father was dead, and his mind was awash with thoughts, feelings, and memories. The man had never shown any kindness to Xantho. Even as a child, he had been spurned as a half-blood, not allowed to play with the true-blooded sons and daughters of Tiribazos. His own father had made him a slave. Even on his wedding day, his father had not sent a gift. Xantho felt a catch in his throat, but he forced it down. Tiribazos and his men had never loved him. His mother, Bristonis, and his wife, Lithra, were the only people in Xantho's life who had ever shown him any love or kindness. Naram-Sin was right. Xantho was one of them now, a Warrior of the Light. They needed him. A god had entrusted him with power, and Xantho knew now that he must embrace that and learn how to use it to fight Gula'an.

There wasn't much sleeping that night. Naram-Sin had allocated a watch schedule, and Xantho's turn had fallen in the middle of the night, which meant he lay awake waiting to man his post. Then once it was over, eventless as it was, he lay cold on the steppe waiting for morning, flitting in and out of the half-sleep that comes with restlessness. They had to keep watch in case the enemy came screaming out of the vastness beyond to butcher them as they slept.

As the sun crept from its slumber, a sliver of sickly yellow light spread across the grasslands. Xantho sat up, twisting his torso and rotating his arms to ease the stiffness away. Most of the other Warriors of the Light were awake, and Naram-Sin stood waiting, ready to address the group. Xantho nudged Penelope, who slept peacefully beside him, her mouth slightly open as she breathed. She opened her eyes and pushed his hand away from where he shook her. She tutted and frowned at him, but Xantho was too tired to deal with her anger, so he focused on Naram-Sin.

"The battle is over, for now. Gula'an has won this time. You all saw the death wrought yesterday. We have lost some of our numbers, but we will meet them again. For now, we must press for the army to assemble. I will find the…"

"We are lost," Wulfgar interjected, throwing a stone into the distance. "He is too powerful. We are weakened. You saw his power yesterday. We need more of us, Naram-Sin."

Wulfgar was the mage to Agi's warrior. They were both from the far North West, beyond even the Great King's empire, a cold and harsh country of rock and snow.

"We must have courage, Wulfgar; we must fight on," urged Naram-Sin.

Wulfgar held up his hand to show a Palmstone devoid of colour. It was empty, a dull globe at the centre of his hand. Its light and power had been taken away, along with Agi's life.

"We might as well die now and move on to the next battle," said Wulfgar.

"No," said Naram-Sin. "We can fight a rear-guard withdrawal and then fight another battle. Cyrus is dead. If we do not secure the succession, there will be turmoil, and the empire will crumble just as Nergal wants it. More wars, endless death. We must ensure that Cyrus' son Cambyses takes the throne and secures the empire's stability."

"Wise and brave words, old friend," said Chitraganda. He stood now and addressed the group. "We all know what is at stake here and what we fight for. The irony of our current uniform is not lost on us. But Wulfgar is right; we cannot win here. We need to find a fight we can win."

"We do not concede. We do not give in. I am Naram-Sin and do not give way to Gula'an or any Gutian." Naram-Sin's eyes blazed, and as he took a step towards Chitraganda, Siduri rose just in time and placed a gentle hand on his chest. Naram-Sin turned to stare into the distance.

"We have new recruits to our cause," Siduri said, gesturing to Penelope and Xantho. "Our numbers grow. We can fight again."

Wulfgar laughed and shook his head. "These two cannot help us—a warrior without weapon craft and a girl without knowledge of magic. Both slaves. What can they do?" He kicked at a rock and stared at Siduri.

Xantho felt his face reddening. Wulfgar had insulted him and Penelope. He should say something, do something to defend himself. After all, he was a warrior now. But, before he could muster up the courage to act, Penelope had sprung to her feet, fists clenched.

"We didn't ask for this, for this power. We didn't ask to be part of your merry band of miserable, ungodly soldiers. Yet, we are here, fighting for you, with little explanation of who you are or where you come from. We risked our lives yesterday and fought just as hard as you did. Xantho saved Agi's life...before they killed her." She ran out of steam and crossed her arms, looking from Siduri to Wulfgar.

"Say what you like; he is a liability. His weakness puts us all in danger," sneered Banya, seemingly just to rub Wulfgar's message in. The African levelled a flat stare at Xantho. Whilst his comments hurt, at least they gave Xantho a better understanding of what his problem was. Clearly, Banya worried that if the group had to watch out for Xantho and make up for his lack of skills, it would distract them in battle, which made them weaker and put them in harm's way.

Xantho stood and placed himself next to Penelope. He had no words to add; she was right in everything she had spoken. He just wanted her to know he was with her.

"Enough of this bickering. We need to move; we must rally the army," said Naram-Sin, shooting a venomous look at Wulfgar.

Nobody else complained, and they gathered cloaks and weapons for the march ahead.

"Thanks for that," Xantho said. Penelope sighed.

"You should have said something."

"I was going to, but then you did."

"What are we going to do?"

"We are in this now; we must do what Naram-Sin says. We have to fight."

Penelope raised her eyebrows and unfolded her arms.

"Yes. We must."

"You are brave, Penelope. We can get through this together."

"You must be brave, Xantho. You must be a warrior. So please, learn, and quickly. Or we will both be dead, like poor Agi."

She turned away and gathered in the cloak she had slept on. Xantho wanted to tell her about his father and Jawed, but he decided against it; she still seemed distant and angry with him. Penelope wasn't easy to talk to. Yet, as a mage and warrior pair, they would have to get closer and work together. Penelope was right about him, though. If he was to be a warrior, then he must learn to use his weapons. Much of what the Warriors of the Light spoke of confused him. Xantho had listened as they spoke of dying and moving on to the next battle, which made no sense at all.

Xantho picked up his quiver, still full of arrows, because he did not know how to use his bow. He slung the bow and quiver over his shoulder and secured his Immortals battle axe at its belt loop. He had no spear, but at least he was armed. Xantho looked at his companions, wondering who to ask to teach him, who to ask to show him the basics. He couldn't ask Naram-Sin; he was unapproachable at the best of times. Agi was gone. There was Banya, who, of course, was out of the question. Then, there was the Egyptian, or the small, strange-eyed warrior, Xia Lao. Xantho would have to decide who to ask, but regardless of who happened to help him, Xantho would have to learn fast if they were to face the power and wrath of Gula'an again.

SEVEN

The remnants of Cyrus' army trudged homeward, thousands of lost souls making the long, arduous journey south towards their Persian homeland. The survivors were despondent over the slaying of their emperor and the destruction of the army, which had always seemed so monstrous and invincible, and the retreat felt more like a solemn funeral march than an army on the move. Nevertheless, more and more survivors had banded together, drawn from wherever they had fled to the massive column of wraith-like figures making their way across the steppe. The defeated army now had some protection from the enemy tribesmen, with cavalry protecting the flanks and the rear of the march, units formed from horses who had fled the defeat and had been wrangled in by the survivors.

Xantho marched with Penelope at the rear

of Naram-Sin's corps. He had searched for Bristonis and other survivors of Tiribazos' slave contingent amongst the masses, but he had found none of them. The warriors of Naram-Sin had marched mainly in silence and camped exhausted, with little said between the group. A thin porridge was served as their evening meal, and Xantho had finished it each time, still starving and scooping every last scrap with his finger. They bedded down for another night under the cutting, cold wind of the steppe, but Naram-Sin had assured them that the terrain would improve in a few days and that they would reach a wide river and greater cover. Xantho thought it strange that the Massagetae had not harried the Persians harder—the tribes had a chance to finish off the might of Persia forever and massacre the despondent army, but he didn't raise the question.

Xantho lay on his side, wrapped in his thin cloak and staring into the small flickering fire Chitraganda had sparked to cook their meal upon. Siduri had called Penelope, and they sat together at another fire ten paces away, talking and practising hand movements. Xantho assumed she was learning more of the ways of the mage whilst he lay there alone. Across from him, Wulfgar sat cross-legged, hugging a cup of watered wine. The heavy-set Germanic mage stared through the flame at Xantho. The flickering of the light intermittently shadowed

Wulfgar's pale skin, creating the illusion of a shape-shifting beast. Xantho held his gaze, wondering why Wulfgar had spoken out against him. Wulfgar held out his left hand and opened it to show Xantho his dead Palmstone, devoid of colour and life since Agi had died in the battle. Xantho wasn't sure where to look or what the Germanic mage meant by the gesture, so he decided to ignore him. Closing his eyes, he rolled over, allowing the sound of the chill breeze caressing the steppe grass to lull him to sleep.

The next day went the same way, a long march across the flat grasslands, walking atop the short dry steppe. This day, however, Penelope marched with Siduri, and the two talked incessantly. His fellow former slave was thriving in her new life as part of this strange group. She possessed all the skills Xantho assumed they were looking for. Penelope had her mage power. She was brave, quick to action, could stand up for herself, and was learning quickly. Xantho felt like he was just tagging along for the ride. He had learned nothing, really. Xantho still did not know how to use the weapons he carried, nor did he fully understand the strange new power thrust upon him. He kept to the back of the marching column, lost in his thoughts. Images swirling around his head of Bristonis, old and vulnerable, of Tiribazos and Jawed, and of the man he had killed in battle.

THE CURSE OF NARAM-SIN

Morning turned to afternoon, and as Naram-Sin had promised, a range of mountains appeared in the distance, interrupting the steppe's vast flat, grass sea. It meant they were approaching safety, or the end of Massagetae country at least. Xantho thought again about asking one of the warriors to help him learn weapon craft, but he still didn't know who to ask. Clearly, he couldn't ask one of the mages, especially not Wulfgar. The strange staring match from the night before had left Xantho somewhat shaken. He pitied Wulfgar for losing Agi, but Xantho had done nothing to the man, so his mistrust and enmity were unfounded and disturbing.

The evening brought another bowl of sloppy porridge, which Xantho wolfed down gratefully, his hunger getting the better of his taste buds. He watched Penelope and Siduri hard at it again, and just as he was about to launch deeper into his hole of self-pity, a boot kicked him in the back. He looked up from where he sat to see Khamudi, the Egyptian warrior, staring down at him with a sword resting on his shoulder.

"I suppose I'd better teach you to fight...if you are going to help us defeat Gula'an."

Xantho scrambled to his feet, tangling his foot in his cloak, but he managed to recover before tripping and making himself look even more of a fool. "That would be...good, thank you," he responded. Xantho followed the Egyptian away from the fires and out into the open ground.

"I brought you this," Khamudi said, handing Xantho the long sword he'd been resting on his shoulder up until then. "It's two-handed, easier to use. Easier to learn."

Xantho took the blade. Its hilt was bone, wrapped with leather for grip. It had a bronze circular cross piece to protect the hands, and the blade curved slightly. It was just a little longer than Xantho's arm and felt good in his hands, the leather hilt soft, supple and warm.

"First, learn to use the weapon. Then you must learn to use it when you have your power," said the Egyptian. Khamudi then hefted his own weapon and took Xantho through some basic lessons, focused on what he called the 'Guard of the Jackal'.

Xantho held the sword high, following Khamudi's lead. He clasped the weapon in two hands above his head to chop down and effectively block any attack, driving the assailing blade away from his body. The position also allowed him to lunge and cut from a defensive stance.

"Master the Guard of the Jackal first…" the Egyptian instructed, "…then we will learn other forms."

They practised until the sun went down.

Finally, Xantho thanked the Egyptian and fell onto his cloak, exhausted. That night, he felt as though he had improved, that he was, in a small way, closer to becoming a proper warrior. He had enjoyed the instruction, and Khamudi was a patient teacher.

Xantho slept well, but he awoke from his slumber with a sharp object digging into his ribs. He groaned and rubbed the sleep from his eyes, peering through the morning half-light to see what it was.

"We learn the bow before we march. Mornings are bow work, evenings sword work. Come," said Khamudi.

Xantho shot up from his bed roll, eagerly gathering in his quiver and bow. He had carried the weapons ineffectually since Naram-Sin had handed him the Immortal uniform, armour, and weapons. So, he was happy to finally learn and put them to use rather than carry them across the grasslands as an ornament. Khamudi showed him how to nock an arrow and how to aim and draw the bow. They shot at shields, and the Egyptian was a master archer. Each of his shots hit its target, his draw was powerful and lithe, and the shafts flew singing through the air with deadly force. Not only that, but Khamudi could shoot consecutive arrows rapidly, his arms and fingers moving in a blur whilst his legs and torso remained still and firm. Xantho's first few shots flew high and wide, but he got better. Under Khamudi's patient instruction, he soon began to hit the target with consecutive shots. Xantho could barely contain his delight. He was good at this. He felt he was actually getting to a point where he could bring some value and offer some help to Naram-Sin and the others with his newfound archery skills.

Two more days passed in this way, marching towards the mountains, but each day started with the bow whilst the rest of the army slept, and it ended with the sword as they bedded down. Xantho became exhilarated by the training. On the first day, he could barely pull the recurved bow to his cheek, but now the draw was reaching his ear. He loved the thrum of the bow as it loosed and the swift, graceful flight of the arrow as it carried its deadly warhead to thump into the wicker shield target. He was getting better at his aim and faster at his draw. In the evenings, his swordplay was also improving. Xantho could use the Guard of the Jackal to defend Khamudi's attacks and even launch strikes of his own. The tall, lean Egyptian gave him pointers and instruction at each session.

"It's in the wrists, soft fingers and strong wrist," he would say. Or, "Remember to strike, strike from high, to the side, but keep your weapon up. That's the key to the Jackal."

As they walked back to the campfires on

the evening of the third day, Khamudi clapped Xantho on the shoulder.

"You have improved. You have natural skill," he said. Xantho thought his heart would burst with pride. He could bear the glares of Wulfgar, the snipes of Banya and being completely ignored by the others now that he had this. He had his weapons, and he loved them. Maybe he could become a warrior, like his grandfather, after all.

On the evening of the fourth day, Xantho practised the cuts of the sword. Thrust, parry, lunge. He was working through Khamudi's movements when he heard deep, throaty laughter behind him. He turned to see the stocky figure of Banya, arms folded across his chest and shaking his head.

"You are like a child fumbling about with a sword for the first time. You are not even young; you are a grown man. How are you so weak?"

Xantho stared at the dark warrior. He had never been taught how to fight. A person wasn't born knowing such skills. "I never had to fight before."

Banya drew his own short sword and smiled. "Come, let's practice together whilst we wait for your teacher."

Xantho swallowed hard. He raised his blade into the Guard of the Jackal. Banya swung at him, and Xantho chopped his blade down to block it. Banya came again backhand, and Xantho stepped back to dodge the blow. Suddenly, a foot was behind his knee, and he toppled to the ground. Banya leapt upon him, sitting heavily on Xantho's chest. Xantho squirmed, but he couldn't move. Banya leaned towards his face, snarling.

"I'm warning you, little mouse, you put my Idari in harm's way, and I'll take your head. I should take it anyway and do us all a favour."

"Banya, leave him."

Xantho sighed in relief. It was Khamudi. Banya stood and nodded in greeting to Khamudi. He shot Xantho a murderous glance and stalked off. Xantho still did not know why the warrior hated him so much—unless it was as he suspected: Banya feared that Xantho's ineptitude put his mage Idari and the others in peril. But he wasn't sure what he could do to change that besides learning how to fight, so he did not speak of it with Khamudi. They just got straight into their training.

Xantho had seen little of Penelope during the march; she had been stuck to Siduri, the two talking and practising constantly. Strange things could be seen where they practised: dervishes rising from the plains, shimmers in the air, and even rain falling from the clouds on a bright, sun-drenched day.

On the fifth day, after practice, Xantho

had gathered in his cloak and made ready to march. They were about to leave and make for the mountains again when Naram-Sin arrived, riding a chestnut mare, and leading a line of horses.

"Today, we fight back; we go on the attack," Naram-Sin announced as he rode past.

They gathered together to hear his plan. The tall warrior was as grim-faced as ever, but for the first time since the battle, Xantho thought he saw a glint in Naram-Sin's eye as he addressed the group.

"We must ride back and draw out Gula'an. Enough time has passed for the Massagetae to have celebrated their victory and for their horses to have recovered from the battle. Gula'an will be mustering somewhere for an attack, and he will come for us specifically. With Cyrus dead and the army in retreat, he knows we are weakened. There are plenty of souls here he can reave for Nergal before this war is over. Remember, we are all that stands between Nergal, Gula'an and their desire to plunge the world into perpetual war and death. We must deny him that. That is our purpose; that is why Enlil imbibes us with our power. We can ride out and use Gula'an's hubris against him; we can lure him into a fight where numbers don't matter."

Xantho's heart quickened. At least now, there was a plan instead of this endless retreat, with the fog of defeat hanging over the army like a pox—a country mourning its great king and also fleeing for its lives.

"Attack?" Wulfgar exclaimed, "Just us? This is suicide, Naram-Sin."

It surprised Xantho to see others in the group nodding, even Chitraganda. Naram-Sin levelled his cold, grey eyes on the Germanic mage. "You can stay here if you fear death, Wulfgar. I hasten to it, for if we lose, we go to the next life and all it offers. Either way, we go. Only those who wish to fight should come. We ride and hurt Gula'an, kill him if we can. If we can catch him off guard, too confident of his victory, then we can defeat him. The rest of the army will get to the mountains safely and be fully able to ensure the succession of Cambyses, son of Cyrus. Then, although Gula'an has won a glorious victory, stability will endure throughout the empire, and peace will continue to reign. Should Cambyses fall, then Gula'an throws the empire into turmoil and gets another step closer to his goal of war without end," said Naram-Sin. He promptly spun on his heel and strode to his horse to make ready to leave.

Wulfgar's fair skin flushed red, and Xantho could see his cheek muscles working as his teeth ground together. Glances were exchanged between Wulfgar, Chitraganda and some others, but finally, they made for the horses.

"Can you ride?" Naram-Sin called. Xantho looked over his shoulder, but there was nobody behind him. He pointed to his own breastplate, and Naram-Sin nodded.

"Yes, I can ride."

Riding was at least something Xantho knew. Tiribazos used to be the satrap of a vast swathe of land in Southern Persia, and being a cavalry commander meant there were always horses at the estate. Even a slave like Xantho got to ride, travelling from one part of the estate to another, exercising the horses, cleaning and caring for them.

They rode back the way they had marched, the mountains at their back and the steppe stretching away in front of them as far as the eye could see. Naram-Sin ordered them to break off into three groups, all scouting in different directions to find the enemy who must surely follow. Xantho rode with Penelope, Khamudi and his mage, Khensa. The two Egyptians were quiet but companionable as they kept their eyes fixed on the horizon, looking for any signs of riders. Xantho rode alongside Penelope, which gave them a chance to talk.

"You have been working hard," Xantho said, leaning over his saddle to offer her half a baked oatcake. She took it and nodded eagerly.

"Yes, Siduri is amazing. She has such power and such knowledge."

"I, too, have been learning,"

"I noticed. You are improving," Penelope said warmly, and Xantho sat straighter in the saddle, delighted that she had noticed.

"Better than being a slave?" she asked, and Xantho smiled. Of course, it was. He had decided on the march that he was free—as free as any other man in the army. He couldn't come and go as he pleased, but nor could anyone else, unless they wanted to become a pincushion for the Massagetae bowmen. Training with Khamudi had eased the deep sadness he had felt since his father's death and since he had killed a man in battle. Xantho had a purpose now; he was a warrior fighting for Naram-Sin, fighting for peace and against the forces of darkness and death. For the first time in his life, he believed that if Aristaeus was looking down at him from the heavens, he would see that Xantho was trying to make something of himself, to make a difference in the world.

"What do you think will happen?"

She shrugged. "We keep learning, and when we have to, we fight."

"Is that it?"

"Does it need to be more? Don't look for answers all the time, Xantho. Think of where we were and where we are now. We don't need answers; things are better for us. We are valued, and we're learning new skills. So live for that, and don't worry all the time. Naram-Sin plans to draw Gula'an out so that we can fight him… concentrate on that and hope it works."

She was right; he knew. Before he could continue the conversation, he saw a plume of dust travelling rapidly across the plain, racing towards the mountain range.

"There," said Xantho. The others turned to look where he pointed.

"That's it. It's Naram-Sin. And Gula'an follows," exclaimed Khensa. She wrenched on her horse's reins and kicked the beast into a gallop. Xantho saw the large smudge of browns and blacks chasing the dust plume. Naram-Sin had done it—he had lured Gula'an out to fight. That thought left a hole of fear in Xantho's belly, but he followed the Egyptians and made for the mountains.

They rode hard, and the flanks of Xantho's mare were flecked with lather. The mountains grew closer, seeming to rise from the earth like giants rising from slumber. They changed from shadowy apparitions to craggy brown hills, and then grey stone and shale-strewn mountains dominating the horizon. At the base of the range snaked a wide river, starting on the even surface of the steppe on the near bank and then rising steeply as the mountain started proper. To the survivors of the battle against the Massagetae, the mountains had been their goal, as though the peaks were a defined line between the safety of the Persian Empire and the horrors of the steppe.

There was no sign of the Persian army other than a great smear across the plains, stretching to the mountain range as though some monstrous worm had slithered across the steppe, making for the heights. The riders followed that trail now, and behind them came Gula'an and his warriors. Xantho turned in the saddle every so often to see if he could make them out. Still, all he could see was a mass of cloud and occasional spots of browns and greys and glints of sun on metal—the light reflecting on weapons, spears and arrow points, sharpened and ready to kill.

Naram-Sin thundered his mount across the grassland, leading his troop. The river was in sight now, and Naram-Sin made for a broad but narrow turn in the river. Xantho could see rocks on this side of the river and to one side of the bend, with the ripple of rapids beyond. On the far side, the bank rose steeply, too steep for horses and maybe too steep for a man to climb. Naram-Sin meant to funnel the enemy into that river bend and make a stand. Xantho was all for heroic stories and heroes fighting to the end, but he wasn't a hero; he was a slave with a penchant for running away. He conjured the armoured image of Aristaeus again, bringing confidence back into his thoughts. He was afraid, but he would stand against the dark magic of Gula'an and whatever blood-crazed warriors he brought with him.

Naram-Sin leapt from his mount and landed lightly. He slapped the mare's rump, and she raced away. With a flourish, the tall warrior pulled his arrows from their quiver and planted them in the ground before him. They would stand and fight.

EIGHT

Xantho leapt from his horse, landing in a crouch. His left foot shot out as it lost purchase in the shale ground beneath his boots, and he struggled to stay on his feet. The rush of the river behind was a low rumble in Xantho's ears, which combined with the thunder of hoofbeats to drown out any other sounds. He regained his footing and followed Naram-Sin's lead, grabbing a fistful of arrows from his quiver and thrusting them into the ground in front of him. The ready access to his arrows would allow for faster shots at the oncoming enemy. Xantho felt for his sword, his hand resting on the leather-bound hilt. The soft, warm feeling in his grip calmed him a little, his heart still pounding from the ride. He unslung his bow and tested the pull of the string. It felt good, its resistance reassuring. Xantho swallowed hard, Khamudi had taught him how to use the weapon, and now he must use it against an enemy in a fight for his life. The recurved bow was short but powerful, bone and sinew glued together and bent against itself to create the colossal force that could throw a man from the saddle.

Xantho looked left and right. The Warriors of the Light gathered in a line. To his left was Penelope, looking as calm and ready as always. To his right was Naram-Sin. Xantho almost took a step back. He hadn't realised he had set himself so close to their fearsome leader. The tall warrior looked across and flashed a grim smile at Xantho.

"Are you ready to fight?"

Xantho nodded. No words would come forth. But strangely, he did feel ready. Or at least readier than he had a week ago. Then his first thought would have been to turn tail and run—to save his own skin. Now he was drawn up for battle with the rest of Naram-Sin's fighters. Readiness was one thing, but his effectiveness was another. That thought allowed the hollowness of fear to take root in his belly. Xantho felt that root twist up into his chest and suck the moisture from his throat and mouth. Fear—that coiling, grabbing curse that makes a man's bowels loosen and his bladder empty. Xantho felt that now, an overwhelming desire to piss. He pushed those feelings down. *Too late for that. I must be effective. I must fight and kill…or die.*

"Are you alright?" he said to Penelope, more

to distract himself than out of concern for her. He knew that she was capable. She was tough and focused and ready for whatever came her way. Xantho had recognised her steely capability from the moment they had first met when he had watched her fight off two warriors with a stolen sword.

"We must work together. We can do it together," Penelope replied, ignoring his question. Xantho nodded and looked out to the steppe, where Gula'an approached.

Xantho could see the white-haired enemy in his chariot, the starkness of that hair and his flowing robes incongruous against the earthy colours of his tribal warriors and their stocky ponies. Gula'an stood atop his chariot, racing towards them, brandishing his black staff above his head, wild with hate and fury.

"How did you draw him out?" said Xia Lao further down the line. The short warrior had taken up position on the opposite side of Naram-Sin from where Xantho stood.

"It was simple. All I had to do was show myself to him; his hate could not resist the pursuit. They were coming anyway, a half-day behind us, to pick at the bones of Cyrus' army."

Xantho wanted to ask Naram-Sin who Gula'an was, other than the servant of the hell god Nergal, of course. There was a deep hatred between Gula'an and Naram-Sin. It was something far beyond the petty hatred of ordinary men, far more than jealousy or simple tribal rivalries. It was infinitely more searing and powerful—perhaps the very fabric of good and evil itself.

Xantho could hear the roar of the enemy as the stark horror of the force Gula'an had brought upon them became visible. At least fifty horsemen flanked Gula'an, and as he waved his staff above his head, those warriors fanned out into a wide attacking circle, a churning mass of men, horses, and iron. Then, just as they had at the great battle on the plains days earlier, the Massagetae whirled and turned in their circular formation of death, and as they drew closer to the Warriors of the Light, they let their vicious hail of arrows fly.

Shao Ling, the mage to Xia Lao's warrior, took a step forward. She knelt in the shale and turned her arms in a wide circle. Xantho saw her eyes were closed, and she spoke a sort of chant or incantation, the words lost behind the din of the river and the roar of the oncoming enemy.

The Massagetae's shafts arced through the sky, and Xantho felt his stomach clench. The Warriors of the Light had only a few shields between them, and he had none. Surely, they would all be destroyed by those arrows, killed before the fight had even begun. The circular formation of the enemy meant the shafts did not stop. Each warrior loosed his missile as he came around to face his foes and rotated in the circle until he came to bear again—a never-ending rain of death from above as the Massagetae shafts darkened the sky.

Xantho closed his eyes, squeezing them tight, waiting for the pain to come. He was breathing hard, spittle flying from his lips as he breathed through clenched teeth. Yet no arrow struck him. Xantho cracked his eyes open a fraction; he was indeed still alive. He looked left and right. Not one of them had fallen. Ahead of him and ten paces beyond Shao Ling, in a perfectly straight line, lay a growing pile of enemy shafts. Xantho watched, stunned, as the oncoming missiles seemed to hit an unseen wall in mid-air and drop with harmless clicking sounds to the hard earth. Shao Ling was sweating profusely, her face contorted in concentration. To exude that power over the arrows was taking a toll, and by looking at her, Xantho doubted she could keep it up for much longer.

Xantho saw Gula'an race ahead of his warriors. He could see the face of the enemy, twisted in a rictus of hate, snarling and bellowing orders, and immediately the enemy horsemen fell out of the circle formation and drew into a line.

"Be ready for the charge," said Naram-Sin, and there was a perceptible nod down the line, a tensing of muscles.

Shao Ling toppled over onto her side, breathing hard. Xia Lao dashed out from the line and pulled her back to safety, or the relative safety of their line. Xantho could still not comprehend how the magic worked. How had she been able to stop so many arrows in mid-air? He shook his head, remembering what Penelope had said and stopped asking questions, for which the answer didn't matter right now. He needed that magic if he was going to live.

The enemy charged. The savage tribesmen let out a great roar and spurred their mounts. Swords and spears raised, battle cries reverberating around the riverbank, they came on, Gula'an at the centre of their line. Naram-Sin loosed his arrows, firing at a rapid pace. Xantho raised his own bow. He plucked an arrow from the dirt and nocked it to the string. Khamudi's instructions were echoing in his head. He breathed deep and slow. Xantho raised the bow and hauled back the string to his ear, feeling the muscles in his back stretch with the effort. He picked out a target, a rider grasping a spear and wearing a felt cap. Xantho loosed, and he watched the missile fly across its high arc. It found its mark. The rider clutched at the arrow as it slammed into his chest, and he fell from his mount to become lost among the pounding hoofbeats. Another man dead, Xantho's second kill. But he had no time to dwell on that. Xantho loosed another arrow and another until he had exhausted his supply. Most of his shafts had found their mark. He was playing his part.

The enemy line had thinned a little. Xantho looked at Gula'an. Arrows arced towards him, but they bounced away harmlessly in mid-air, the enemy exerting the same power as Shao Ling to bat the missiles away with an invisible force.

"Fall back, closer to the river," Naram-Sin ordered.

The company followed his order, and Xantho dashed back with them. The enemy was within twenty paces. Xantho could hear their shouts. Naram-Sin and the others formed up close to the riverbank, and inside the tight loop, the water curled around the rocks to Xantho's left. This meant they would funnel the enemy into a charge where they could ride only five or six abreast, nullifying their much larger numbers. The first wave came on, and Xantho heard the river change. The rush of it grew deeper for a moment. He looked right to see a flood of that water race across the bank and plunge into the onrushing enemy. Some fell from their mounts but most kept coming, thundering through the water. Siduri was working her magic. Xantho could see her arms moving in a circle as more water flooded the riverbank. The enemy paused, their horses' shying and bucking. Chitraganda let out a roar and clapped his outstretched hands together. At that moment, hot air billowed against Xantho's face. A pulsing force flew across the plain, throwing the first wave of attackers back, horses and all, in a screaming welter of panic and destruction.

Gula'an roared at his warriors. They dismounted and came on foot, faces drawn in terror at the magic thrown against them, their horses too panicked to charge into the mage's wrath wrought by Siduri and Chitraganda. Gula'an held his staff aloft and slammed it down into the steppe, causing the earth to shudder violently and crack in a visible ripple. The shale ahead of Xantho shook, and the stones jumped from the ground. Xantho cried out as something thumped the air from his lungs. It threw him off his feet, and he landed hard on his back. He shook his head; the shock of the punch he had felt left his skull ringing. He jumped to his feet quickly, just in time to see a snarling enemy charging at him.

Xantho had dropped his bow. He reached for his sword, but the scabbard had tangled behind his leg. He cursed as a tribesman closed in. No time. The man thrust a spear in a vicious lunge, yet Xantho swerved just at the right moment to dodge away from its tip. The attacker didn't stop his charge and barrelled into Xantho, knocking him from his feet again. They fell together, rolling and snarling at each other until they stopped, and the tribesman lay atop Xantho, clasping a hot clammy hand around his throat. Xantho croaked and clutched at the man's arm, bucking to get him off, but he clung on. Xantho's face felt like it would explode, red and desperate for air. He scrabbled a hand into the shale and clutched at a rock, twisting as he drove it into his attacker's skull with a dull thud. The enemy fell away, limp and still. Another warrior charged him, and Xantho gasped, certain the warrior's spear would impale him. But Idari darted in front and blocked the blow. She cut at the attacker, and he fell back. Xantho exhaled and almost collapsed in relief. However, there was no respite; he felt a powerful hand on his shoulder, yanking him backwards, and he turned to see Banya snarling into his face.

"Defend yourself, mouse, and don't put my Idari in danger," Banya growled, snarling again as he launched himself into the fray beside Idari.

"Xantho," he heard a shout from somewhere. Penelope. He knew she was close. She must be; he felt the power building inside him, pulsing in his chest, encouraging the rage to take fire. The power surged in him. It flooded through his arms and legs, and where there had been panic, there now was calm. An enemy barged him, slashing wildly with a spear, which Xantho deflected with his forearm. The warrior pivoted, grasping for

Xantho's throat with his free hand. Xantho could smell his attacker's fetid breath, that warrior trying to throttle the life from him. Xantho easily pulled the man's hand away and threw him off. Now that Penelope was close, Xantho felt stronger than ever. He whipped his sword free whilst the enemy was trying to bring his spear to bear, and in one motion, Xantho drew the blade and swung it in a wide arc, opening his enemy's throat in a clean and bloody strike. The man grabbed at his open neck, eyes wide with terror. Xantho turned from him. Another foe killed. The battle raged all around him, flooding his senses with the clash of weapons, the ferrous smell of blood, and the screaming of the wounded and dying.

Warriors fought, and blades collided. The enemy was being pushed back in the face of the warrior-mage ferocity. Xantho parried a sabre thrust, holding his blade high as Khamudi had taught him, and then used the Guard of the Jackal to chop down into his enemy's shoulder, sending him reeling. Pain flushed Xantho's head, and he raised his arms to his ears in response. Before him, the shale ground split open, the very ground cleaved by a long, deep crack. Men sprang back from the chasm as it tore through the riverbank, and on the edge of it was Gula'an. All went silent. The earth was rent, and its sheer power ended the battle.

"No more of this petty skirmish," said Gula'an, his voice deep and clear, even above the roar of the river and the crumbling and creaking of the land he had torn asunder. "You are lost, Naram-Sin, you who razed the Ekur and brought our curse to be. Give yourself to me, to Nergal, and end this war."

"To do that would mean a forever war, raging on for eternity, Gula'an. Just as you wish it to be, bloodthirsty Gutian that you are," said Naram-Sin, stepping forward to stand on the opposite side of the chasm Gula'an had created.

The fighting had stopped, and all were drawn to the confrontation of those two great foemen.

"It's over for you, Naram-Sin; this is all you have left. A rag-tag band of crusty soldiers and weak mages." Gula'an breathed deeply, and his head snapped to look past Naram-Sin. His eyes sparkled, and a grin spread across his dark face.

"Your own warriors have had enough. I sense it. They grow tired of endless defeat, and of loss, and dying. You there, Northman. I feel your conflict. Come, join me; join Nergal and the side of victory. Naram-Sin tells you that you fight for the side of light and good. The hypocrisy! He and his witch Siduri—the most bloodthirsty warlords of all time. They who subjugated the world and attacked the very gods themselves! Free yourselves from his cunning tyranny."

Xantho did not understand most of what

Gula'an or Naram-Sin spoke of, but he noticed Wulfgar looking intensely from Gula'an to Naram-Sin. The Germanic mage itched at his beard and finally shook his head.

"I have had enough. Enough death, enough loss. It's over for me, Naram-Sin. You all should join me, end this forever war," he said. The others looked between them. And to Xantho's horror, Chitraganda and his warrior Anusuya went to stand with Wulfgar, as did Xia Lao and Shao Ling.

"What is this betrayal?" seethed Naram-Sin, his mouth agape and his face turning pale.

"They see you for what you are, fighting against reality, against the new world order. Your time is finished, Naram-Sin," Gula'an hissed. He levelled his staff and pointed it at Wulfgar. The Germanic mage smiled and looked at his Palmstone. He held it up, and it glowed deep blue once more.

"Take up your weapons now. Fight for me. End this war," Gula'an bellowed.

Wulfgar let out a roar and leapt at Naram-Sin, a blood-curdling sound of release, pent-up frustration and envy emanating from his mouth. Slashing with his sword, Naram-Sin darted backwards, barely avoiding the blade. Siduri thrust out her hands, and her power threw Wulfgar backwards. Chitraganda clapped his hands, and Siduri fell to her knees, crushed by an invisible force.

"No!" shouted Naram-Sin, but it was too late. His people were fighting amongst themselves. Xia Lao sprang at Naram-Sin, and they clashed in a whirring of blades. Penelope knelt with Siduri to fling Chitraganda backwards. All was chaos, the air hot and shimmering. Xantho didn't know what to do or where to help. Gula'an leapt across the chasm and landed with a thud. He lashed out with his staff at Naram-Sin's back, which flung the tall warrior ten paces into the water. Gula'an laughed, and with another wave of his staff, he launched Siduri and Penelope into the icy river water. Xantho kept still, horrified by the strength and power of Gula'an.

Gula'an had turned his back on Xantho, ignoring him. Xantho had experienced that his whole life; he had always been insignificant, easy to ignore. This time it was a mistake. Penelope lay face down in the shallows of the river's edge but still close enough that Xantho felt the power. Xantho tightened his grip on his sword. He dashed forward and let out a roar. Gula'an spun around, but not fast enough. Xantho's blade snaked out, lightning fast, infused with the power of warrior and mage. The sword's tip slashed Gula'an's face, and he reeled away, blood sheeting into his white beard. With Gula'an distracted by his injury, Xantho dashed for Penelope and turned her onto her back. She was barely breathing. Naram-Sin and Siduri were caught against the rocks, crawling up the riverbank exhausted. Too late, Xantho saw Wulfgar sprinting with his sword above his head. Too late, Naram-Sin raised his head. Wulfgar stabbed down, and his blade pierced Naram-Sin's back. The Northman pulled the blade free. Siduri knelt with a hand outstretched to Naram-Sin, but Wulfgar cut her down with a slash to the throat, and her blood splashed red onto the riverbank.

Xantho cradled Penelope, staring at the carnage wrought by betrayal. Khamudi leapt upon Wulfgar putting an end to the traitor. So much death. Xantho looked at Penelope. Her green eyes opened slightly. He smiled at her; she was alive. Xantho suddenly felt a blow on the rear of his breastplate and another on his shoulder. He gazed down at Penelope in her Immortal armour; her mouth was agape in horror. Xantho fell onto his side next to her. He was tired now. There was a pain in his back that burned like fire, but deep inside of him. He reached out a hand for her, and she held it. The warmth made him smile. Then, from nowhere, a spear sank into her chest, and before he could react, something made his world go black. A dull thud against his head sent him into the darkness.

NINE

Xantho gasped and sucked in a huge breath. His lungs expanded, filling with air and then exploded in a chest-rattling cough. He clutched at his neck and face, panting in the darkness. Finally, his eyes opened slowly to bright, piercing light. Xantho clenched them closed again. His breathing became fast and shallow, and his ragged exhalation came as a wheeze. He was whimpering, eyes darting back and forth beneath tightly closed lids. Panic flooded his senses, unsure of who he was or where he was, just a being, breathing and living.

He tentatively opened one eye a crack and winced again at the light, but it was just sunlight in a pale blue sky. Xantho opened the other eye. Traces of creamy clouds meandered across his vision, and he felt a warm breeze tickle his cheek. He heard the high-pitched caw of a seagull, and the bird soared, floating on the wind and across his line of sight. Xantho shot his head up, propping his torso on his elbows. *How could this be? Where am I?*

Around him were small dark-leaved bushes clinging to chalky rocks. Beyond that stretched the shimmering green of the sea. Xantho could smell the salt in the air and hear the gentle crashing of waves. He was at the summit of a cliff or hilltop, perched high above the sea. *Penelope.* His memories came flooding back, the fight at the river, Penelope lying beside him dying, and then…Xantho tried to reach around and feel his back. It felt fine. He touched his head where he had felt a blow in his last moments, and there was no blood or pain. *I was dead. I am sure I was dead.* Xantho looked down. He was wearing a simple white chiton tunic, short on the leg and arms. He looked around him, and there was no sign of his Immortal armour or weapons.

Xantho remembered the treachery of Wulfgar and Chitraganda, seeing Naram-Sin and Siduri cut down. Gula'an had torn the earth and won his victory, turning Naram-Sin's own soldiers against him. *Did that mean Gula'an had won? Was the world plunged into eternal war?* A final terrible thought made his breathing pause—*Am I dead? Is this the afterlife?*

A shout from behind stirred Xantho. He scanned the hilltop, but he couldn't see anything. A surge ran through his body, pulsing around his veins, and he felt a throbbing in his left hand. He opened it up, and there was an orb embedded into the flesh there. It pulsed green— the lush green of grass in summer after rainfall, deep and dark. He clenched his fist. A Palmstone. The power surging in him could only mean one thing, Penelope was close by. Xantho realised then that he couldn't be dead. He was very much alive. *But how?*

"Penelope?"

He called her name and went running down the slope, stretching behind him, but his legs gave way, and he tripped, scratching his elbow on the rock. He cursed and rose, and there she was, standing before him, dressed in the same short tunic as he.

"Xantho?"

He stood and stumbled towards her on unsteady legs.

"How?" Xantho said, holding out his hand. She took it, and they drew each other into an embrace. He held her tight, the warmth of her body comforting him, but it was short-lived. Penelope pushed him away suddenly; her face flushed, and she took a step back. She held up her palm where she, too, had a glowing green Palmstone. Xantho raised his hand, and she smiled a small, nervous smile.

"Where are we? Do you know what happened?"

"I don't know. I just woke up here as though I had been sleeping."

"Did you see what happened to the others?"

"I did. Wulfgar and Chitraganda turned to Gula'an. They betrayed us. Wulfgar...well, he..."

"What? What is it, Xantho?"

"He killed Siduri and Naram-Sin."

Penelope's bottom lip quivered, and she placed a hand over her mouth to cover it.

"What now, then?" she said.

Xantho had no idea. He had no clue where they were, why they weren't dead, or what had happened with Gula'an. Memories of conversations between the Warriors of the Light suddenly began to make sense. Xantho recalled Wulfgar talking about waiting for the next life and Naram-Sin alluding to something similar. *Could it really be so?* Penelope walked past him towards the cliff's edge and peered out at the sea beyond.

"Look," she pointed. Xantho went to join her. Stretching out below them was a mass of ships, ships beyond count in tight formation sailing towards them on white-tipped waves. Xantho looked out across the sea. At the hazy horizon, he thought he could see a distant coast, but he couldn't be sure. The day was cloudless, and a warm breeze kissed the land from the green-blue sea. There were so many ships—boats beyond count, and all were enormous vessels with images of sunbursts or strange eye symbols daubed onto their sails.

"We need to find out what's going on here and where we are," Xantho said, tired of questions. He turned and stopped dead in his tracks. At the descending pathway, close to where he had met Penelope, stood four men dressed in armour that Xantho didn't recognise. Each wore a red tunic beneath their armour; some were faded to a pink colour, and some were bright and new. Their armour was unfamiliar. It seemed to be made of a hard cloth-like material, perhaps linen, Xantho thought. It was a breastplate with thick shoulder straps and then a kilt of thick leather thongs to protect their nether regions. The four men clutched clay bottles, and two carried sacks of what Xantho thought was food.

"Nice day for a picnic, eh pretty ones?" said one grizzled man with a curly brown beard and broad face.

"Come to watch the ships? So have we," piped another. He was a young man who stared at Penelope, grinning.

They spoke a language Xantho did not recognise, but for some reason, he understood their words. He held up a hand towards the men. "It's a beautiful view," he said in their language, again unsure where his knowledge of it had come from. "Please enjoy it. We are just leaving."

"There's no rush. We have wine, bread, and some cheese. So stay, please," said the grizzled man.

"What is this place?" Penelope asked. Xantho shot her an angry look. He didn't get a good feeling from these men. They felt like trouble, and he wanted to get away from them.

"This is Asia," said the third man, waving his arm in a wide circle. "Not sure what part this is though, any of you lot know?" The others shook their heads.

"Where do you come from?" asked Penelope.

Enough questions, Xantho thought to himself.

"We are from far Macedon, here to free the people of Asia from the Great King's tyranny," said the young man, grinning.

Xantho had never heard of Macedon. By the Great King, Xantho assumed they meant Cambyses, Cyrus' son, meaning that Naram-Sin's aim had been fulfilled, and the heir had taken the throne, assuring consistency in the empire. That, at least, was something. It had thwarted Gula'an's quest for perpetual war and assured peace in the empire—Naram-Sin's death had not been in vain.

"Well, enjoy your food and wine and the fine view," said Xantho and sidestepped as though to move around the men. Penelope didn't move, so he shot her a frown and nodded toward the downward pathway. She shook her head.

"We need more answers. We must know where we are and what has happened," she whispered.

"Seems your little girly wants to stay here with us. That's alright, lovely. You can stay. But you, boy, be on your way; your master must be hungry for your love," said the grizzled man. The four looked Xantho up and down and laughed. He glanced down at his fine, short white chiton tunic. Xantho looked somewhat ridiculous compared to them in their armour, worn and faded from use. He assumed their joke was that he was some sort of slave boy used for pleasure by his lord. That stirred a flash of anger within him. He was a slave no more and certainly not the lover of some Persian lord.

"We are leaving. Good day to you," Xantho said, moving off again. The four warriors fanned out, and the young man and a tall, middle-aged warrior sprang between Xantho and Penelope.

"You go, she stays," the grizzled man sneered.

"I decide where I do or do not go," snapped Penelope in her gravelly voice. She had thrust her shoulders back in defiance. The warriors laughed.

"You'll do as you're told, whore," spat the grizzled man. He went to grab her arm, but Penelope pulled it away. She stood back and braced herself, quickly bringing her two hands together in a wide clap. The air around Penelope shimmered, and a thrust of hot air launched the grizzled man over the cliff edge. Xantho heard the man's screams as he tumbled towards his death.

The four warriors stood open-mouthed, looking at one another in disbelief.

"Witch!" the young man exclaimed, and they all whipped their short swords from where they hung in scabbards at their waists.

Xantho found himself rooted to the spot, still trying to understand why Penelope had killed the man without so much as a second thought. She smiled at the second man whilst the two closest to Xantho eyed him warily.

"Thought to have your way with me, didn't you? Thought it would be easy?" she said, breathing hard from the exertion of creating the force which had killed the first warrior. She rotated her hand in slow circles, breathing harder, sweat springing out on her brow. The warrior closest to her clutched at his head and wailed in a quiet, muffled voice. He fell to his knees and then writhed on the ground as though being crushed by a giant boot.

"Stop it, witch," growled the tall warrior, and he leapt at Xantho, stabbing with his short sword. Xantho jumped back just in time to avoid the disembowelling strike.

"Let him go!" the other man shouted at Penelope, but she turned her hands, and the warrior continued to writhe on the rocks, blood dripping in dark blobs from his ears. The tall warrior slashed his blade again at Xantho, and Xantho caught the man's arm to block the blow, but the warrior crashed his knee into Xantho's ribs, knocking the air from him.

Xantho fell to one knee, winded but still clutching the warrior's sword arm. The warrior punched Xantho in the face with his free hand, and he closed his eyes, yelping in pain. Then, before he knew what he was doing, Xantho rose to his feet and twisted his attacker's arm back savagely, hearing a crunch as it broke at the shoulder. The power was flowing through him. He had forgotten it was there, or he'd been too stunned to react to Penelope's action, but the punch in the face had awoken him. He flung his attacker back like a rag doll twisting in the air, then grabbed him by his armour and slammed the tall man into the ground, knocking him unconscious.

Xantho spun to see what was happening around him. Penelope stood with her hands on her hips, completely exhausted from the magic she had conjured. The fourth and last warrior moved gingerly towards the edge of the cliff, trying to get as much distance as possible between himself, Xantho, and Penelope. He waved his sword before him, and it wobbled in his grip, the man's eyes wild with terror.

"What are you?" he gasped, stuttering the words, horrified at Penelope and Xantho's other-worldly power.

"A mage," said Penelope, and she clenched her teeth, taking a step forward to brace herself. She brought her arms around and clapped again. The air before her shimmered as it had earlier, and the warrior disappeared, shrieking over the edge. Penelope fell to the rocky ground, exhausted.

Xantho knelt, feeling the soreness in his ribs where the attacker had kneed him and touched his fingers to his cheek. It was sore, but there was no blood from the punch he had taken. He dashed to check on the man he had fought with and found him breathing shallowly but still unconscious.

"Are you going to finish him?" asked Penelope from where she lay.

Xantho swallowed hard. He didn't want to kill the man. Yes, they had wanted to take Penelope for reasons Xantho didn't wish to imagine. But he couldn't reach down now and kill the man where he lay. His mother had taught him the rules of life as a child, and he assumed most people lived by those rules, not to steal, not to lie, not to kill. Of course, a slave had to follow many rules, but there are basic tenets of humanity, or at least Xantho had always thought so. It simply shouldn't be easy to take a life.

"He is no threat to us now. Maybe he can tell us more about where we are." Which was true, he supposed. Penelope rose and picked up the wine dropped during the fight, along with one of the food sacks. She sat on a rock looking out to sea and drank a swig of the wine, then, opening the sack, she took a crust of bread, tore off a piece and bit into it ravenously.

"Come on, eat. I am starving," she said, holding the crust out to Xantho.

His stomach gurgled at the thought of food. He went to join Penelope, taking the bread and a drink of the wine. It was watered, sweet and refreshing as it washed down his throat.

"You have grown strong," Xantho remarked. He wanted to challenge her, to understand why she had been so quick to kill. But he also didn't want to antagonise her any further.

"Those pigs wanted to rape me, and they would have killed you. But we are not helpless slaves anymore," she said whilst chewing. "You should wake up to your strength; you aren't even using it fully."

He looked at his Palmstone and then at the two fallen warriors. One lying dead, and another beaten to a pulp, whilst he and Penelope ate and drank. He had forgotten he even had the power until it came to him by instinct during the fight.

"Ho there, is there any spare for an old man?" came a shout from the pathway.

Xantho and Penelope sprang to their feet in surprise. A man in faded and worn shepherd's clothes ambled up the pathway, stepping over the fallen warrior without pause.

"Are you friend or foe?" Penelope asked.

"A friend. Just a hungry goatherd. Will you share your meal?"

"Come, sit with us," Xantho said, ignoring Penelope's hostility.

The old man shuffled over, giving the crushed warrior a wide berth. He had salt and pepper hair tied loosely at the nape of his neck and a long beard of the same colour. The shepherd walked as though infirm and had the greying hair of an older man, but his face was smooth and almost ageless. He smiled, and his teeth were all straight and perfectly white.

"You are very kind," said the shepherd, grey eyes twinkling under arched brows.

Xantho gave his bread to the old man and handed him the wine. The shepherd took a bite and washed it down with a drink.

"A fine sight, is it not?" he remarked, gesturing to the ships moving silently across the sea below them.

Xantho nodded. He glanced at Penelope, who sat frowning. Her face looked drawn, and her brow was still dotted with sweat from her exertions. There was something about the old man which irked Xantho. He hadn't commented on the soldier lying injured on the hilltop, and he must surely have heard the commotion of the fight moments earlier.

"It is. Who do the ships belong to?" Xantho asked.

"The army of Macedon. The new young King Alexander brings his army to Asia," replied the shepherd.

"Where is Macedon?" asked Penelope.

"Greece, to the north. Between Athens and Thrace."

"I am Thracian," said Xantho. "What is your name?"

The shepherd smiled and winked at Xantho. "I have had many names, friend. Some call me Nunamnir, some, other things," the shepherd responded, waving the crust and taking another bite.

Penelope raised an eyebrow at Xantho, but he shook his head slightly. He looked towards the path, suddenly worried other warriors would approach and see the fallen men.

"Don't worry. No one else will come. We have this spot to ourselves," said the shepherd. Xantho hadn't known the old man had spotted his look, which was strange because he couldn't possibly have; the old man was facing in the opposite direction.

"What land is this?" Penelope enquired.

"This place is called Lapseki, but it is not important."

"What is important then?" she said, quick as a whip.

The shepherd laughed. "You are a smart one, a wonderful choice," he said, wagging a finger. "What's important is that Alexander comes to make war on the Great King, Darius of the Persians. He comes to put an end to the old empire and usher in a new one."

"Darius?"

"Yes, the Great King."

"What happened to Cambyses, son of Cyrus?" asked Xantho.

"He died a long time ago, generations ago. Darius is the son of Artaxerxes."

"How can that be?" asked Penelope.

"It just is. Time moves on," the shepherd smiled.

"But…Cyrus was the Great King until a few days ago. His son is Cambyses," Xantho insisted.

"Cyrus the Great died two hundred years ago, friends," said the shepherd.

Xantho stood, looking from the old man to Penelope. This could not be possible. Two

PETER GIBBONS

hundred years? That simply couldn't be.

"You must be confused, old one," said Penelope. "Please, take us down the mountain so we may talk to someone and see what's going on." She also stood now.

"Sit, please," urged the shepherd. "There is no confusion. You have been kind to an old man so that I will come clean. I haven't been entirely honest with you," the old man chuckled to himself.

"Look, this isn't funny. We are in a war, old man. We need to know where we are and what has happened to our friends." Penelope spoke in a serious tone now, and for a moment, Xantho thought she would fling the shepherd over the edge, but her fury seemed to be contained. For now.

"You will find Naram-Sin and Siduri are here. The others too...well, the ones who remain on my side."

"What?" said Penelope, "How do you know of Naram-Sin?"

The shepherd stood and brushed breadcrumbs from his robe. "I have known Naram-Sin for over two thousand years, my young friend. He serves me in the fight against my son Nergal. He and Siduri are Warriors of the Light, as are you."

"Wait a moment. Two thousand years?

Nergal? That means you are…a god?"

"Well, yes. You may know me as Enlil." Light pulsed from the god's eyes, and where there had been a shepherd, there now stood a shining lord. Power throbbed from his body, and Xantho and Penelope fell to their knees. "Stand, please," said Enlil. "I come to you now, as this is a most troublesome time for you. You died and have travelled two hundred years into the future, as you reckon it. You must fight alongside the army of Alexander. Gula'an now serves Darius of Persia and does his all to crumble the empire and bring in a new age of war and death. You must stop that. He would defeat Alexander and then rend the Persian Empire asunder, plunging Asia and Greece into perpetual war, which means death and despair for people the world over."

"How? Why?" Penelope blurted. "Gula'an won the last time we fought. How are we here to battle him again?"

"Nergal, my son, is the god of death. I placed him in charge of the underworld back when the world was young. His power has grown and grows stronger still. He aims to reduce the world of men to a state of eternal war. That way, his kingdom becomes swollen with souls, and he becomes the most powerful of all the gods. He will cast the rest of us down and rule over a domain of death and destruction on Earth. Gula'an is Nergal's captain, and he must be stopped. I have chosen you both as Warriors of the Light. Young lady, you are realising your power, but you must control it. If you kill indiscriminately like this, you serve Nergal's cause. Xantho, you are more powerful than you know. You must forget your old life; you still think like a slave. You are a Warrior of the Light now, and you must embrace your strength if we are going to win this war."

"How can two hundred years have passed? How did we get here?" murmured Penelope. She had a hand pressed to her cheek, and the other clutched to her chest.

"Do not worry about such things; it all just is. There are things you can never understand, matters of the gods, time, death, life and eternity. But, for now, be assured that you are here, and you are needed; there can never be a battle more important for the future of mankind. Find Naram-Sin and Siduri, and stop Gula'an, or the world as you know it will be lost forever to a horror of death, war and flame. I must go now. I suggest you don the uniforms of these men if you are to fit into the ranks of Alexander's Macedonian army."

Xantho went to speak, to ask one of a hundred questions on the tip of his tongue, but Enlil smiled and raised a finger. He strode to where the pathway began and then disappeared.

"We just spoke to a god," Penelope marvelled,

her eyes wide and glassy.

Xantho's head was spinning. Two hundred years. How could that be?

TEN

The Macedonian army crossed the Dardanelles in over one hundred triple-decked triremes. Monstrous ships, lying low in the water, heavy with infantry and cavalry, including their horses and crammed with supplies to feed them. Xantho marvelled at the organisation of unloading those ships and moving the vast number of troops into camp. It was a massive undertaking, and the surrounding bay held more people than he had ever seen, even at the battle between Cyrus and Tomyris.

Xantho and Penelope had followed Enlil's advice, stripped the Macedonian armour and accoutrements from their fallen attackers, and now walked amongst the army. At first, they had skirted the edges of the milling mass of soldiers, worried they would stand out and be taken as prisoners. But no one noticed them, so being confident that they blended in with the

Macedonian army, they strolled into the seething belly of the mustering force.

Penelope wore the breastplate of the smaller man, the man she crushed with her magic, but it was still too big for her. The breastplate wasn't the problem. She could get away with wearing a large breastplate; many soldiers wore clothes and armour that did not properly fit them, taking what was given to them by the army's quartermasters without objection or choice. The fact that she was a woman was the problem. In the army of Cyrus, Penelope, Siduri, and the other women of Naram-Sin's company blended in by wearing the clothing of a Zoroastrian priestess or the armour of an Immortal with a full-faced helmet to disguise them. She now wore the stolen armour of a Macedonian soldier, and on her head, she wore a felt helmet liner found upon the fallen foe, which at least covered her long hair.

"How are we going to find Naram-Sin amongst all this?" Xantho sighed, looking out onto the many thousands of soldiers, horses, and camp followers bustling across the bay. Finally, Xantho and Penelope found a small hill at the southeast corner of the shoreline, trying to stay out of the way and remain unnoticed.

"We have other problems, Xantho," Penelope said, itching behind the neck scarf she had pulled up to hide the bottom half of her face. The west Asian sun shone warmly onto the sandy bay. It reflected off the glistening water and combined with the hustle and bustle of the army to produce a sweltering heat which amplified the lack of a sea breeze, creating a stifling atmosphere.

Xantho pulled at the neck of his armour. It was made of many pieces of linen folded tightly together. It wasn't too heavy, but its edges were rough and chafed at him. "I don't even know where to begin," he said.

"We died. That's a good place to start. Not to mention we just spoke to a god, and we have travelled through time."

"I don't feel two hundred years old."

"It's not funny. Everyone we knew is dead, long dead. How is this even possible?"

"Wasn't it you who told me not to ask too many questions? What was it you said? Some things just are. Well, maybe this just is," he said, shrugging. Obviously, it was an unbelievable situation they found themselves in. Xantho had barely had time to think since the day of the Massagetae attack by the river. He had been a slave then, and now he was a warrior paired with a mage, and they'd both died and travelled through time. *How do I even begin to make sense of that?*

"How are we going to eat, live? Where do we sleep? We need a plan, Xantho. It could take days, or forever, to find Naram-Sin."

"It looks like we are wearing the uniform of infantrymen. Look," he pointed to a column of men wearing the same pale grey armour as them and with the red tunics, or chitons, underneath. They marched wearing breastplates, a conical bronze helmet, and a small round shield slung across their backs. What marked them out, though, were the long spears they carried over one shoulder. The spears were enormous, twice as long as any spear Xantho had ever seen. The marching column moved like a great forest, the spears making a strange humming sound with every movement and whenever the light breeze fluttered through the pass of timber shafts. The soldiers chanted a rhythmic marching song as they went.

"So, what do we do, just tag along and join in?"

"I don't know. I only know as much as you."

Penelope sighed. She took off the helmet liner for a moment to itch her sweltering scalp. Her hair was plastered to her head with sweat. She held the liner out at arm's length. "This thing stinks. Hera only knows how long that filthy pig was wearing it," she said.

"That pig you killed."

"He would have killed me without a second thought, and you. He deserved to die." Penelope's green eyes blazed, challenging Xantho.

"I just don't find it as easy as you, that's all."

"Well, you need to learn. This world is all about death, Xantho. Death and cruelty. Don't forget...you and I were both slaves, born into slavery, and nobody pitied us—we would have died as slaves. You need to toughen up."

She was probably right. It just didn't sit well with him. He was a warrior now, though, and death was his trade, so he had better learn to deal with it. If Enlil was right, then he had a job to do. They had to defeat Gula'an. His grandfather's stories all involved fighting, death and honour, and if Xantho wanted to live up to that ideal, now was the time.

"We spoke to a god," he said, grinning at her.

"I know. So many strange things have happened. Naram-Sin will know what to do, or he should know what to do. Two thousand years old, I don't even know what that number means."

"Maybe it's over a hundred lifetimes? Either way, it's a long time. We will not find him standing here, let's get moving," said Xantho, trying to consider how large a number a thousand actually was.

"You there, soldiers," a voice called. Xantho looked around to see a burly infantryman standing with hands on hips, staring at him and Penelope.

"Oh no," she whispered.

"Just don't kill him," Xantho muttered, and she rewarded him with a kick in the shin.

"Yes, sir," Xantho said.

"What are you doing here? Lazing about in the sun? Where is your unit? Who is your lochagos?" the soldier asked. Lochagos meant captain, and Xantho did not know what to say, but he knew if his answer was wrong, then he and Penelope might end up being reported for punishment. And if they got hold of Penelope and realised she was a woman...well, Xantho didn't know whether to fear more for her or them.

"Messengers, sir. Waiting for orders," Xantho answered, which seemed like a plausible response.

"Very well. My lord has a message for General Parmenio. Follow me," the soldier said, and he marched off.

Xantho turned and winked at Penelope. The corner of her mouth turned up a half smile, and she shook her head.

"Lucky," she whispered.

They scampered after the soldier. He marched in long strides with a straight back. The three of them weaved through the disembarked units, who all marched towards the landward side of the bay, where Xantho could see tents stretching away into the distance. He dodged around an archer in a wide-brimmed hat; the man cursed at

Xantho for interrupting his step, and the soldier laughed.

"Bloody Cretans," the soldier mumbled.

They wound their way around a pen jammed full of horses, which stank of shit, and came to a stop by a crude timber desk erected amid the hustle and bustle. The noise was a continuous burr of shouting, horses neighing, marching songs, and the clinking and clanking of weapons and supplies brought ashore.

"Wait here," said the soldier, and he approached the desk. Behind it sat a heavily muscled soldier. He wore a bronze breastplate with a bright sun etched onto its front. He had short black hair and an eye patch covering half his face. Xantho felt eyes staring at him, and he glanced to his left. There, in uneven rows and lolling about in the sand, was a group of the roughest-looking men Xantho had ever seen. They were long-bearded and scruffy-haired, and their clothing was a hotchpotch of bronze and linen strapped on around furs. One of them grinned at Xantho, showing brown teeth beneath his crooked smile. The grinning man spat a glob of mucus which missed Xantho's foot by a handbreadth. His companions laughed. Xantho ignored them.

"Here, carry this to General Parmenio. You will find him at the far end of the camp yonder." The soldier handed Xantho a scroll and pointed across the tents stretching beyond the bay. "If he asks, tell him the Agrianians are here. He is waiting for them, as I understand." The warrior nodded his head at the eye-patched soldier behind the desk. "General Cleitus will hold them here until he receives a response. And hurry, this lot stink like a goat's arse."

Which they did. But they looked formidable. Xantho took the scroll from the soldier and headed for the tents. They made it to the beginning of the camp, where orderly lines of beige, four-man bivouacs spread away further than the eyes could see.

"How are we going to find the general?" said Xantho.

"It was your idea to say we are messengers. If you're so smart, you figure it out."

"What happened to 'we're in this together'?"

"Wait a minute," Penelope said, and she grabbed the arm of a boy who ran past them.

"Hey," the boy shouted, wriggling in her grip, but he quickly calmed down. He wore only loose trousers and was barefoot and bare-chested, his skin burnt to copper by the sun.

"Can you take us to General Parmenio?" Penelope asked.

"Yeah, but it'll cost ya," the boy said in a thick, lyrical accent.

"Cost me what?"

"What you got?"

They had little, just a handful of battered coins looted from their attackers on the clifftop.

"Take us to the general, and we will reward you," Penelope promised.

The boy frowned and scratched a scab on his elbow. "It better be worth it. I'll be late for my boss and probably get a whipping," he said. "Come on." The lad set off, closely followed by Xantho and Penelope.

They worked their way across the camp, which was just as busy as the bay beyond. Once they reached the lip of the beach, Xantho turned to look out at the view behind. Ships crisscrossed the vast sea, incredible vessels of timber and rope painted in bright yellows and reds. They spat out their cargo of soldiers and iron onto the beach and then pushed off to allow the next one in. So many ships, so many men. The war ahead would be terrible. Xantho wondered how that served Enlil's purpose. *More death and more war surely served Nergal?* He turned and followed the lad and Penelope. Enlil had mentioned that Nergal was his son. Father and son locked in conflict across time.

Xantho had always believed in the gods, in his gods. Ares, Dionysos, Artemis and the rest. He had never really thought to question their actual existence. Tales of the gods were told at firesides on cold evenings, stories of love and wars. People said prayers and made offerings to the gods in the hopes of helping with things like a harvest, the birth of a child, or war. Xantho had never asked the gods for anything. His only love had died after just a few years of marriage, leaving him broken and alone. He was a slave; the gods had passed him by, so he gave them thanks for nothing. Now, though, he knew the gods were real. He, a slave, or a former slave at least, had met and spoken to a god. *Do my gods exist? Do they sit alongside Enlil?*

"Where are you lot from them?" chirped the boy, stirring Xantho from his thoughts.

"Thrace," said Xantho.

"Where's that, then?"

"Across the sea, to the north," Penelope answered. Xantho supposed that was right.

"Gonna be a big fight soon," said the lad.

"Looks like it," nodded Xantho.

"I'm gonna be a soldier. Just like you."

"Very good. Can you fight?" asked Penelope. *Trust her to think of violence first.*

"Like a demon," said the boy, grinning as he walked. Penelope let out a small laugh, which surprised Xantho. He could not remember the last time he had heard her laugh. The sound made his own spirits rise.

"Are you from here?" Penelope pressed.

"Yeah, nearby. I got no family. All dead. I come

here to help, for pay."

"You are a slave?" asked Xantho.

"I am not. You gotta pay me, friend," the boy said, and he thumped his chest, which made Xantho and Penelope laugh.

After a time, they reached a large open space where soldiers practised with their weapons. It was a dusty square ground afore a long river that stretched away into the mountainous distance. A group of horsemen reposed at the edge of that open space, watching the soldiers train.

"There's the general." The boy pointed to the group. "He's the grey beard, older than the hills that old lion is. But they say he's wicked clever."

Xantho approached the group and delivered the message to a junior officer, who nodded and ran to his general. The old man sat tall on a bay mare. Straight-backed, with a face cut from granite, all sharp edges and long features. He wore black armour and looked every inch a general. The junior officer dismissed Xantho.

"Well?" said the boy, holding his hand out, smeared with grime, and beckoned for his coin.

Penelope laughed. Again, the sound brought warmth to Xantho, and he smiled. She delved into a purse stowed beneath her armpit and drew a coin. She flipped it to the boy, who promptly bit it to check its value.

"Not bad," he nodded and made to scurry away.

"Boy, wait," Xantho said. The lad turned around.

"What's your name?"

"Tiki," the boy replied.

"Tiki, I need to find someone. Can you help?"

"I can help for the right price," the boy grinned and held up the coin.

"Well, I need to find a man. He will be here in the army somewhere. He is tall and lean and has grey eyes and short hair. Likely an officer," said Xantho.

"Sounds like all officers," Tiki gibed. "How would I know it's him?"

That was a good question. Xantho looked at Penelope, and she shrugged.

"Alright then. Take us to where the officers of the different units are. That might help."

"This I can do," said Tiki.

They followed Tiki as he twisted and turned through the camp. As they wove in between more heavy infantry units with their long sarissa pikes and light infantry in sandals and cloaks, the cavalry units inevitably comprised the Macedonian nobility, and Xantho wondered what would happen if he couldn't find Naram-Sin. What would happen if he just walked away? If he just turned around now, left the Macedonian camp, and left Naram-Sin to his war through time? After all, what difference could he make? He looked at Penelope standing beside him, short and willowy but ferocious and skilled. He had a connection with her. Even though their time together had been brief, they had experienced so much, and he couldn't leave her alone in the midst of this army, even if it was she who was more likely to protect him than the other way around.

Naram-Sin had taken Xantho from slavery. Saved him, maybe. So, he owed Naram-Sin. Also, he still remembered how the tall warrior had initially dismissed him and Penelope when he discovered they were slaves—and the look on his face when Xantho first held a spear and was beaten by Agi. He wanted to prove Naram-Sin wrong; he could be a warrior, and he could help in the fight of light against dark. If a god said he could do it, then who was Xantho to argue?

ELEVEN

Tiki knew the Macedonian camp like the back of his hand. He knew where to go and who to see, and people called his name in greeting wherever he went, but some shouted curses at the lad, and Tiki would scurry away laughing. Nevertheless, Xantho enjoyed Tiki's company. With the importance of his new calling weighing him down, the boy lightened his mood. And Tiki made Penelope laugh, which made Xantho happy too.

"You two hungry?" asked Tiki, as the three of them walked along a wide intersection which cut straight through the Macedonian army camp. It bustled with soldiers, horses, carts and locals, bringing food and other items to sell to the newly landed forces.

"Yes, very," said Penelope, "do you know where we can eat?"

"Does a goat shit up a mountain?" smirked

Tiki. Xantho and Penelope laughed again.

Tiki wove around until they came to the far eastern side of the camp, where the tents ended and gave way to open grassland covered by a monstrous herd of cattle and sheep. The animals were wrangled by what Xantho thought were local shepherds but kept in order by Macedonians. Tiki ducked under a guide rope, and from behind a canvas awning came the mouth-watering smell of roasting meat. Saliva flooded Xantho's mouth, and suddenly his stomach felt like an empty pit. The thick smell of roasting lamb swamped his senses. He looked at Penelope, and she looked back with a cheeky grin. As he watched her there smiling at the sheer adventure of exploring the camp with Tiki, Xantho wondered what she would have been like had they met before all this, before the fight at the rock face. It was hard to imagine her as a simple young woman, going about her duties as a slave, when she now carried power beyond the ken of most people, and she was certainly not to be trifled with by even the greatest of warriors.

"Tiki, you rascal. What are you doing here?" boomed a voice. It was a big-bellied man in a blood-soaked apron. He had a bald head and red cheeks; in one hand, he held a carving knife, and in the other, he turned a roasting spit. On that spit turned a leg of lamb. Xantho's stomach growled, and he put a hand on it. Penelope licked her lips, her eyes fixed on the roasting meat.

"Theo, I need a bit of grub for me and my friends here," said Tiki, resting his elbow on a nearby table, talking with the confidence of a man thrice his age but looking barely in his teens. Theo laughed, tilting his head back whilst his belly wobbled with raucous laughter.

"You little rogue," he said.

Tiki wagged a finger at him. "I got you talking with the washing girl, did I not? Tana with the pretty eyes?"

"You did, you did," nodded Theo, his eyes watery from laughing so hard. "Very well, come, eat."

Theo gave them each a chunk of the roasted lamb wrapped in a thin flatbread. They thanked him and went on their way. Xantho bit into it, and juices flowed down his chin as the succulent meat melted in his mouth. He let out a groan of pleasure.

"You are a valuable friend," he said to Tiki, who grinned between mouthfuls of food.

"How's yours?" Tiki asked Penelope.

"Delicious. What would we do without you?" she smiled, and Tiki skipped along as they continued their search for Naram-Sin.

"Let's try here," Tiki suggested as they approached a set of horse corrals on the edge of camp. In those pens were horses beyond count.

Gangs of boys and young warriors brought more of the animals in as they came from the ships and led them through the camp. There were small light horses and vast numbers of huge warhorses, which Xantho assumed were for the heavy cavalry. Over at one end of the corrals was a set of tents, larger than those of the camp proper, and where clay amphorae were being unloaded from carts.

"Cavalry officers' mess," said Tiki, nodding at the tent.

"How do we look for our friend?" asked Penelope.

Tiki shrugged. "Sit and wait…see who comes by," he said, which seemed as good a plan as any.

They watched the cavalry officers come and go, all wearing bronze breastplates and plumed helmets. Each had a fine sword, and many had junior officers running errands and maintaining their kit.

"These are the big lads," Tiki said as the officers passed by.

"What do you mean?" asked Xantho.

"Alexander's cavalry, the nobles, the ones with the fine horses. And all the silver in the world," Tiki chuckled, rubbing his hands together.

Penelope chuckled along with him. "Were your family from around here?" she asked.

Tiki looked down at his bare feet and kicked

them in the dirt, lost in his thoughts.

"Yes, from a village close by."

"What happened to them?" said Penelope.

Tiki went quiet. Eventually, he sniffed and cuffed at his nose. "They died. Memnon came through with his soldier-sons-of-whores, and burned everyone out, killed all the people."

Xantho put his arm around Tiki's shoulder. The boy flinched at first, but then leant into him.

"Who is Memnon?" asked Penelope. She looked at Xantho and turned her mouth into an upside-down smile as if to say "poor boy" without speaking.

"He's the son of a thousand fathers who the Great King has sent to fight Alexander. He's a Greek, a mercenary."

"Son of a thousand fathers?" said Xantho, and he laughed. He ruffled Tiki's hair, and the lad chuckled, the sadness lifting from him.

"Penelope, Xantho?" came a familiar voice. Penelope spun around and ran to embrace the person who had called their names. It was a tall, thin cavalry officer wearing a Phrygian cap helmet with a scarf drawn high who hugged Penelope in return. It was Siduri.

"I think I found your friends for you," said Tiki, holding his hand out again for coin. Xantho shook his head and tickled the lad's ribs.

"Siduri," Xantho called in greeting. She

removed her scarf. A smile split her long, angular face.

"You are here. It does me good to see you," she said.

"Yes. The last time I saw you, you were dead, and it was two hundred years ago." He didn't mean to kill the joyful reunion, but Xantho thought it better to get the big issue out in the open.

Siduri's smile faded, and she nodded gravely, looking them both in the eye. "We have a lot to talk about," she said, reaching out for Penelope's left hand and turning it over. She saw the Palmstone and caressed it. Suddenly her face was drawn, and her grey eyes distant.

"Here you are, well met," said a tall, lean, grey-eyed warrior in officer's armour and helmet appearing behind Siduri. It was Naram-Sin.

"Come, we must talk," Siduri urged, beckoning them to follow her as she moved her elegant frame into a walk. Xantho followed, hoping for some answers at last or at least an explanation from Naram-Sin.

The tall warrior made to follow Siduri but then turned and frowned at Tiki. "Begone, urchin," Naram-Sin ordered.

Tiki stopped and looked at Xantho and Penelope, suddenly cowed, putting his open palm down.

"He comes too. He's with us," said Xantho, putting his hand on Tiki's shoulder. The boy looked up at Xantho, and a broad smile split his dirt-caked face. Naram-Sin looked about to object, but Siduri shook her head slightly, and he relented. Xantho winked at Tiki, and he followed Siduri's lead.

"When did you awake?" asked Naram-Sin, taking off his helmet and dusting its rim with his hand. They had found a quiet spot behind the corrals and away from the officers' mess. All sat on the edge of an unhitched cart except Naram-Sin, who stood before them.

"Today, at the top of that hill," said Xantho, pointing to the peak of the large rise where they had fought off the four attackers earlier. "We were almost killed, and we spoke to Enlil."

Naram-Sin looked up from his helmet at that comment, his cold grey eyes boring into Xantho's own. "And yet you live," he remarked.

"The last time I saw you both, you were dead, as were Penelope and I. Gula'an had won, we were betrayed, and now we are here, two hundred years later," said Xantho. He could feel more eyes fixed upon him, and he flicked a look at Penelope. She was staring at him, her mouth wide open. He had never spoken to a lord in such a way before, and deep down, his inner self still urged him to behave as a slave. But they were not slaves anymore, and Xantho thought they were due some answers.

Naram-Sin looked at Tiki, who was also staring open-mouthed at Xantho.

"Close that, or the flies will get in," said Xantho. "Take some coin and find us something to drink, Tiki, watered wine if you can." Penelope nodded and handed Tiki a few small coins from her purse.

"But, I…" Tiki began. Xantho stopped him by placing his hands on the boy's shoulders and pushing him gently. Tiki blew out his cheeks but went on his way.

Naram-Sin waited until the boy was beyond earshot. "This is our fate. We are Warriors of the Light. The gods have chosen us to fight this war. It is not a simple matter to understand; I know that. Enlil came to you?"

"Yes, garbed as a shepherd. He said we are now Warriors of the Light and that we must defeat his son, Nergal. He said Gula'an now wishes to defeat the Macedonians to preserve the crumbling Persian Empire. Then, he will crush the empire and further his aim for never-ending war," said Xantho.

"This is the fight. We must defeat Gula'an. He put us to the sword in the war with the Massagetae. That strengthened him, and he is much stronger than we are now. We can't let that happen again."

Xantho held up his Palmstone. The deep green swirled bright and gentle. Naram-Sin nodded.

"You are truly one of us now. You know of our burden, of the task we face. Enlil raises us from the dead at times of great conflict, where we must battle the forces of the lord of the underworld and keep him at bay. It just is, do not look for explanations. I searched for answers for many hundreds of years, but there are none. The gods need us; they give us power, we fight, and we die to rise again. That is all."

Xantho looked hard at Naram-Sin. For the first time, he truly looked at him. They had exchanged few words every other time they had spoken, and Xantho had avoided eye contact. Xantho knew that Naram-Sin also avoided talking to him, perhaps because he still saw Xantho as a slave. He felt the awkwardness there. But then, the tall warrior rarely spoke to anyone; he was always detached, in a state of aloof melancholy. Xantho saw a deep sadness in the pits of those grey eyes. Whilst he had the face of a middle-aged man, a few lines around his eyes, and creases in his forehead, his eyes looked truly old. Xantho wondered if they had once been a different, more vibrant colour and perhaps faded to grey over the millennia. Like an ancient statue once painted in all the colours of the rainbow, washed out by time and weather to grey, cold stone. Xantho had experienced for himself what it felt like to die; he had felt the pain of his wounds and then nothing. No heaven, no glorious afterlife. Just nothing, and then the awakening on the clifftop. *Is there an afterlife, and am I now excluded from it?* So many questions bounced around Xantho's head.

Naram-Sin held up his own Palmstone, bright gold against his dark skin. "Your power lasts as long as there is colour in your stone. This is all that Enlil can give us in the fight against Gula'an. Penelope, when you use your mage power, you will find yourself out of breath and tired, as though you have run a long race. Your Palmstone will also lose its colour as you use your power; once it's gone, you will be exhausted and need rest. Once the colour returns, your power returns. The same goes for the strength with which you imbue Xantho. The longer he uses that strength, the more both your Palmstones will lose their colour. Watch that; it could mean the difference between life and death."

Xantho and Penelope stared at each other and nodded. There was a limit to her power and the power she could give to him. This was new. But before Xantho could challenge Naram-Sin with more questions, four riders approached on light cavalry mounts.

"Xantho, well met," said a deep, friendly voice. Xantho recognised Khamudi instantly. The tall Egyptian swung his leg over the saddle and leapt down to clasp Xantho's hand, smiling. Xantho was taken aback. Even though they had spent many mornings and nights together learning weapon craft, the Egyptian had been a man of few words and even fewer smiles. But, of course, Xantho returned the smile, happy to see his teacher again. Khamudi turned over Xantho's left hand and nodded when he saw the Palmstone. His face became serious. "You are of the light now. We live and die together, brother," he said. Khensa also jumped from her horse and ran to greet Penelope and Siduri.

"Where are the others?" asked Penelope.

"We were betrayed by Wulfgar, Chitraganda, Anusuya, Xia Lao, and Shao Ling. They are with Gula'an or lost. Who knows? They are no longer of the light," said Khensa.

Whilst the greetings and welcomes continued, Banya ignored Xantho completely, tending to his horse. *No change in him, then*.

"What news?" Naram-Sin asked Khamudi. The Egyptian removed his helmet and tucked it under his arm.

"Lord Hephaestion orders us to range out and secure a small town, walled and with a well. Priapus is its name. It's mid-way between here and Zeleia, where Memnon gathers his army. Memnon has called together all the satraps in west Asia under orders from Great King Darius. We must secure the town as a base for a push towards Zeleia."

"Very well. What force rides out?" asked Naram-Sin.

"We go with four squadrons of light cavalry, one squadron of heavy cavalry led by Amyntas. Hephaestion himself will follow with a squad of Agrianians. We are to ride ahead of the light cavalry and scout for trouble."

"Good. Let's prepare. This time we bring the fight to Gula'an. This time we use speed, aggression, and surprise. He is out there somewhere with the forces of Memnon. I feel him," said Naram-Sin. He gave a lingering look to Siduri and then strode away towards the officers' mess.

"Well, let's see what you have remembered," Khamudi chimed, drawing his sword.

Xantho grinned and drew his sword from the scabbard at his belt. The Macedonian weapon was much smaller than the sword he'd learned to use in the fight against the Massagetae. He held it up in the Guard of the Jackal, but Khamudi shook his head.

"This sword is too small for that. Watch."

He beckoned Xantho to try it, so Xantho raised the blade above his head. Khamudi lunged at him, and where Xantho would have blocked the blow easily with a downward motion using the Guard of the Jackal, the Macedonian sword fell well short, and Khamudi tapped his blade on Xantho's ribs.

"I'll try to find you a longer sword. And a bow. We will practise again," said the Egyptian, clapping Xantho on the shoulder.

Xantho smiled his thanks. It felt different this time, being with Naram-Sin and the others. Xantho felt like one of them. They had only been back together for a few brief moments, but Xantho felt they were genuinely happy to see him. They seemed pleased that he and Penelope had arrived there with them and believed he could play a part in the battle to come. Despite the unanswerable questions buzzing around his head, Xantho had a warm glow. For the first time in years, he felt needed, for the first time since Lithra had died.

Khamudi, Khensa, Banya, Idari and Siduri followed Naram-Sin back to their quarters to prepare to leave. Xantho and Penelope sat together and watched them as they left.

"It starts again then," said Penelope. She flicked at a loose strand of hair poking out from the rim of her helmet.

"The fighting?"

"Yes. Are we ready?" She turned over her hand and stared at the Palmstone.

"I don't know. Readier than we were last time, at least."

She looked up at him. Her scarf had rolled down away from her face since they had eaten with Tiki. Her mouth was set in a flat line, and her eyes searched his own.

"We died, Xantho. There was nothing. We died hundreds of years ago and awoke now. The others have died and awoken many, many times. This is our life now. How can it be?"

"You said to me before, don't question these things. Some things just don't have an answer. We spoke to a god today; I can't even begin to fathom that. All I know is that he has picked us for this fight, chosen us to have this power."

Suddenly Tiki came hurtling from behind a tent, panting, his face stretched and eyes wild. He cannoned into Xantho.

"Steady there. What is it?" Xantho asked, bending down to look at Tiki's face. One side was raw and swollen, and he had a bloody lip.

"He's after me," Tiki whimpered. Where his voice had been confident before, even cocky, it was now broken and small.

"Who is?"

Tiki didn't need to answer. At that moment, three men came running from the same direction as the boy had. They wore the breastplates of infantry soldiers but with a brown sash tied around their waists.

"There he is. Come here, you little bastard,"

growled one man, a short, bandy-legged soldier with a clean-shaven face.

"No, he's going to beat me again," cried Tiki.

"Hold on," said Xantho calmly, raising his hands to the soldiers. "What has he done to you?"

"He's a thief and an urchin. He's coming with us; he's a slave."

"I'm no slave!" Tiki shouted.

"You are now," hissed the soldier, and he reached out to grab the boy.

Xantho pushed Tiki behind him and thrust the soldier's arm aside.

"The boy is not a slave. He is with me," said Xantho. The soldiers laughed.

"Like that, is it? Sweet on him, are you?" jeered a lanky soldier, smirking.

"I'm a lochagos of the quartermasters, an officer to you, soldier. Where's your salute? I order you to hand the boy over," demanded bandy-legs, hands on hips.

"Enough of this horseshit," Penelope snapped. Xantho felt a pang of panic in his chest, knowing what must come next.

Penelope squeezed her two fists together, and the lanky one and his friend clutched at their throats, falling to the ground. Xantho felt himself swell with power.

"He's yours, Xantho," she said through gritted

teeth.

Bandy-legs looked at his fallen comrades and then at Penelope and Xantho. "What trickery is this?" he spluttered and swung a punch at Xantho.

Xantho swayed away from the blow. He leant into the soldier and grabbed his breastplate at the neck. Lifting the soldier from his feet, he slammed him into the dirt. Bandy-legs cried, and Xantho heard the air whoosh from him. Winded, the soldier gasped for breath.

"Finish him, Xantho, or they'll raise the alarm," Penelope warned.

"It's done. We don't need to kill them. Let's go," Xantho said, and he stepped away from the soldier. "Leave them," he told Penelope, raising his voice.

She broke off her magic and shook her head at him, puffing from the exertion, her eyes scornful. The soldiers writhed in the dirt, groaning and coughing. Xantho checked his Palmstone, and just as Naram-Sin had said, its colour had faded a little.

"You're coming with us," Xantho said to Tiki. The boy smiled.

TWELVE

The black mare was a good horse. Xantho's head felt clear as he rode with the wind in his hair. The mare responded well to his control, and being in the saddle drove away all the fear and uncertainty of his new life. He just focused on the horse and the land before him. Xantho had joined the Warriors of the Light in a light cavalry unit tasked with ranging out and scouting for the town of Priapus and any enemy in the vicinity. He felt like a warrior now; he looked like a warrior. Xantho wondered whether his grandfather would view him as one if they met in the afterlife. Fifty horsemen in the unit split off into separate squadrons to scout the countryside. Naram-Sin commanded their squadron, which included the Warriors of the Light alongside four other soldiers. They rode on light ponies allocated from the corral, Penelope rode behind Xantho on a roan pony, and she was a competent rider.

The plan, as Xantho understood it, was for the light cavalry to range ahead of the army and make sure there were no impediments to hinder the advance, with the main aim of securing the town of Priapus, which would act as a staging point on the push against Memnon and his army. Ahead of them, Hephaestion, Alexander's friend and trusted commander, had already marched out with a company of Agrianian specialist light infantry and a unit of two hundred Companion cavalry, who were the Macedonian heavy cavalry. This force would assault and secure the town and, more importantly, its well, once the scouts had located and made sure there were no enemy forces around the town in large numbers.

The land they rode through was similar to the estates of Tiribazos, where Xantho had grown up. Valleys and hills marked it, with dry grasses on the higher ground and lush greenery in the low valleys. The sun was warm on his face, and a light breeze cooled the air.

Xantho rode at the front of the company alongside Naram-Sin, who, until this point, had said little in typical fashion. It was an honour for Xantho to ride at the front of the column. He had worried mounting up that morning, worried about the awkwardness of riding alongside Naram-Sin, but so far, the companionable silence had allowed Xantho to enjoy the countryside.

Xantho had started the day by training with Khamudi just before sunrise, picking up where they had left off on the Massagetae steppe. The Egyptian had found a kopis sword for Xantho; it was longer than the xiphos sword he had taken from the soldier on the clifftop and suited him better. The xiphos was a standard issue short sword, whereas the kopis had a longer single-edged curved blade and a comfortably shaped wooden grip. It was not as long as the weapon Xantho had used on the steppe, but it felt better balanced. Khamudi had worked him hard in the early sunlight and noted that Xantho continued to improve. So Xantho had started the day with a spring in his step. Khamudi had also found a bow, for which Xantho was especially grateful. He felt more comfortable with the bow than with the sword or spear, likely because it was a ranged weapon, not an up close and personal one. Khamudi said he had bought it from a Cretan archer—they were exceptional archers from an island in Greece—along with a quiver of white fletched arrows. To complete the morning training, Khamudi introduced Xantho to some Egyptian wrestling holds and throws, which were difficult at first, but once Xantho got used to his balance and using Khamudi's momentum against him, it became easier.

"What do you make of these Macedonians?" Naram-Sin said as they rode past a clutch of rustling pine trees.

Xantho almost fell off his horse. He spluttered to get his words out. "Their forces are vast. A lot of cavalry," he said. Xantho knew nothing of armies and tactics. Until a few days ago, in his reckoning of time, he had been a slave responsible only for washing and cleaning. And having been born a slave, he had never needed to understand war, strategy, or tactics. He didn't know what to say to Naram-Sin, so he hoped his comment was insightful. Or, at least, not foolish.

"Did you see their sarissae?"

"The long spears?"

"Yes, I cannot imagine charging into a mass of those. No horse would do it. This Alexander is young and daring."

Xantho waited to see if Naram-Sin would say more, but the pause dragged on. "What do you know of Alexander?" asked Xantho. Relieved to have thought of a question.

"His father, Philip, completely redesigned their army. The sarissae, the heavy cavalry. From nowhere, they've come to rule all of Greece, and now Alexander attacks the Great King. The king of a Greek backwater launching an invasion against the Lord of all Asia."

"He must be brave."

"It's a fine line between bravery, arrogance and hubris. Unfortunately, I know it too well."

Xantho tried to look at Naram-Sin without

turning his head, forcing his eyes left, but he couldn't see the warrior's face. *Is the aloof commander ready to talk about himself and his history with Gula'an?* "Where do you come from, lord?" he asked.

"I am not a lord. You can call me Naram-Sin. I am from far Mesopotamia, Akkad, the greatest of cities. Or it was, at least, back then."

"And Siduri?"

"She was the daughter of a Gutian chief, but she came to be of Akkad."

"What is a Gutian?" asked Xantho. He had heard mention of the Gutians before but couldn't quite recall where. Perhaps about Gula'an, but he couldn't be sure.

"They are, or were, the enemies of Akkad. Wild hill tribesman, fierce and heathen. Not unlike the Massagetae."

Xantho wanted to ask Naram-Sin many questions—had Siduri gone to Akkad to be with him, how had they met, had they married, and if Siduri was a Gutian, what was that to do with Gula'an? The words almost came out, but at the last minute, Xantho bit his lip, too afraid to incur the warrior's wrath. "Is Gula'an here?"

"Certainly. If I am here, and Enlil has brought us here, then Gula'an is here."

"How does it serve him to defeat Alexander?"

"That is a good question. Nergal must believe

that if the Persian Empire continues and is allowed to crumble, it serves his purpose. Chaos would reign, and regions and satrapies would battle for supremacy and independence, signalling the start of the perpetual war he craves. However, if Alexander defeats Darius and ushers in a new age, a new empire, then peace reigns starving Nergal of souls."

"Why does Nergal want perpetual war?"

Naram-Sin twisted in the saddle to look at Xantho with one eyebrow cocked.

"Full of questions today," Naram-Sin said, and Xantho's cheeks flushed.

"Nergal is the son of Enlil. They are gods older than time. My people in Akkad worshipped Enlil thousands of years ago, and the Sumerians even before that. He created the world, separating Heaven and Earth. He also fathered Nergal on the goddess Ninlil. Nergal is the god of the underworld and hates his father for his power; he hates his father for granting him dominion over the underworld. Nergal seethes with jealousy over his siblings, gods of the moon, sun, and earth who live above ground, whilst he skulks in the darkness with the dead. Nergal wants to be the ruling god; to achieve that, he needs the underworld to swell with souls for his army. Once he is powerful enough, he will attack his father. Gula'an is cursed to serve Nergal for eternity; he is Nergal's warrior of darkness on

Earth."

"How did Gula'an come to be so cursed?" asked Xantho, knowing he was pushing his luck with questions.

"That is a tale for another time. We should make for that rise to the north; it will give us a good view of the lands ahead," said Naram-Sin. He clicked his tongue and urged his horse ahead. Xantho let him go.

Xantho patted his mare's neck and reached into his saddlebag for an oatcake. He leant forward and gave the cake to the horse, who ate it with glee. Talking of the gods and of Darius and Alexander was a new way of thinking for Xantho. In his old life, he had thought only of his duties, what must be done that day, getting his work done and avoiding the watchful eye of Jawed. It had been different for a time with Lithra; Xantho had been truly happy then. They had met as slaves, he tending horses and taking care of his father's estates whilst she worked in Tiribazos' palace as a serving slave. His father had bought her as a young woman, and she came into Tiribazos' service at around the same age as Xantho. Perhaps sixteen or seventeen summers. He could never remember correctly. She had been captured as a child from a Greek coastal city and sold by her previous master to Tiribazos. From the moment they had met, during an evening meal in the slaves' quarters, he had been taken with her. She had deep brown eyes and long, flowing black hair. Her skin had been like milk, and he had loved her. Lithra had been kind to Xantho, aware of his nervousness but appreciative of his jokes and attentiveness. Xantho had asked Jawed if he could marry Lithra, and he had consented. Of course, a master always encouraged marriages amongst the slaves; it kept them happy and also bred new free labour. They had married on a spring day, and Tiribazos allowed them both to take a day off from their duties.

They were happy times. Jawed had permitted Xantho and Lithra to take living quarters together. In the evenings, they could walk together and talk by the fire. A simple life with no gods or emperors, and no death, nor fighting. They were slaves, but they had known no other life, so they were content. Xantho stared at the gently swaying firs and ahead at the hill line rising in the distance. He thought of Lithra, and it was hard to remember her face. Sometimes at night, it would come back to him, yet he could not recall it in the morning. Mere months after they married, she had fallen sick, sick with a pain deep in her chest. It was a gnawing pain wracked her day and night and never ceased. In the end, it was a release for her to die. A release for her, but heart-wrenching emptiness for Xantho. After her death, he was alone with his slavery, without hope for any future or happiness, just his duties and the deep nagging pain of rejection.

The legitimate sons of Tiribazos lived like princes, whilst Xantho walked around shoeless and was treated no better than the rest of the slaves, even though he too was a son of Tiribazos and the grandson of Aristaeus, the noble warrior. After Lithra's death, Xantho became tired all the time and neglected his work—stables left unraked, tools left unclean. Jawed had taken the whip to him, and punishments became increasingly frequent. Xantho winced, recalling the flesh-splitting strikes of Jawed's whip. His back was crisscrossed with those scars, the marks of his slavery.

Since the ambush at the river on the plains of the Massagetae, Xantho had not felt that deep sadness. The rejection, losing Lithra, the resentment of punishment. All had fled from him. Xantho assumed it was because he had not had time to think. He had fled that ambush and ran to the rocks to survive. He had been a slave running for his life, and now he was a cavalry scout, learning weapons and part of something. That something was too huge and frightening to fully comprehend, gods, the underworld, and dying and leaping forward in time. But he was free and had a purpose, which was more than he had ever had before.

A rider came alongside him; Penelope pulled down her face scarf to reveal herself. She, Siduri,

Khensa and Idari tried to keep their faces hidden from the other soldiers. There were no women in the army, and though there was no rule against it, it simply did not happen. In Macedon, women were not warriors. So the three women hid their bodies beneath their armour and tied their hair up inside their helmets. Penelope took a swig from the waterskin secured to her saddle. She handed it to Xantho, who also took a drink.

"What was he saying?" she asked, pointing toward Naram-Sin.

"Nothing really, just talking about the war and all that."

"He barely talks to me, never has."

"You have Siduri."

"But he is our leader, is he not?"

"I assume so, yes. Although no one has ever spoken of it to me."

"Do you think they are together? Or were?" asked Penelope.

"I do, but I am not sure what the nature of their relationship is now. Perhaps they have known each other too long, but at some point, yes, they were together."

She secured her waterskin again and flicked a loose strand of hair hanging in her face. Xantho smiled to himself. *Her hair was always coming loose*.

"You shouldn't have brought him," she said,

nodding over her shoulder towards Tiki.

"What should I have done then? Let them take him and make him a slave?"

Penelope shook her head, her facial muscles working where she clenched her teeth. Xantho looked back over his shoulder, and Tiki bounced along on his mount, looking small and keeping quiet. Before they'd left, Xantho had tried to find the smallest uniform he could for the boy. Unfortunately, most of the equipment in the cavalry tents was gone, and he didn't want to be caught stealing, so in the end, Tiki had to make do with whatever they could scrounge together. The only piece of kit that looked out of place was his helmet. The bronze Phrygian cap with its curled top bobbed around on the boy's head.

"I won't leave him to that life; he's a good kid," said Xantho. The boy looked small, but so did Penelope. Some of the Macedonian junior soldiers were also small and thin, joining the army at fifteen or sixteen, and Xantho hoped the lad just looked like one such boy.

"He could be killed," said Penelope, looking downcast. Of course, Xantho knew she was fond of Tiki. The boy's humour lightened the situation, and Penelope rarely laughed unless Tiki was around. Xantho felt the same way.

"Any of these soldiers here could be killed. Surely that's what it means to be a soldier. But I will look after him."

She laughed at that. "Xantho, the noble warrior, protector of children."

"Penelope, the great mage, killer of men."

Her jaw jutted, and her lips curled in on themselves.

"At least I'm not a coward," she said and took off after Naram-Sin.

Xantho instantly regretted his words. She had irked him when she mocked his attempts at being a warrior. He was trying, learning weapons and consciously suppressing the urge to run and shy away. In his heart, though, he was still afraid. Penelope acted without hesitation whenever they faced danger or an attack, whereas Xantho's initial reaction was fear. He had to force himself to act. She had stung him again by calling him a coward; he had been called that name many times. Growing up, he had refused to fight the other boys when challenged, he had refused to ride the dangerous horses, and he had always run from danger.

They reached the hilltop Naram-Sin had aimed for, and the fields and farms of western Asia spread out before them. Priapus must be to the southeast, Xantho thought, between here and the coast. Mid-way to where Memnon gathered his forces. Amongst them somewhere, Gula'an lay in wait.

"Look, there," Siduri signalled, leaning

forward in her saddle, pointing a slender arm to the north. In the distance, Xantho could see sunlight glinting off steel and riders.

"The enemy," said Naram-Sin.

"Do we attack or watch?" asked Khensa.

Naram-Sin sat up straight in his saddle, but didn't take his eyes off the distant warriors. "Remember. Speed, aggression, and surprise."

THIRTEEN

The valley's bowl curved gently down from three hills, each larger than the other, and the central hill was bald rock coming to a soft point at its apex. The hills on either side were a patchwork of rock and dark green tufts of evergreen trees and bushes.

Three men huddled in the base of that shallow valley, crouched around a fire of dry twigs which they had pulled from surrounding shrubs. The soldiers faced in towards the three hills to keep the wind at their back, and so they did not notice the riders coming upon them until it was almost too late. But that had been the plan all along.

Xantho and the rest of the scout squadron waited behind a dip which traversed the central hill and the third larger peak. The dip hid them from the shallow valley below and anyone approaching from the plains leading out to the east. Naram-Sin lay atop the rocky outcrop which covered the dip and watched his three scouts prepare some tea in a small kettle. He also watched the approaching enemy. Naram-Sin had sent the three soldiers down into the valley after he had spotted enemy riders in the far distance. The three were under orders to prepare their meal and light a fire that would let off some smoke. The soldiers had done well, using green leafy bushes and branches for their flame. A thin line of that smoke drifted into the warm Asian breeze and danced there above them to the wind's tune. It would be irresistible, Naram-Sin had said, for enemy scouts. Three Macedonians out alone with horses hobbled. The Persians could not resist the opportunity to strike a blow against the Greek invaders, and Naram-Sin hoped the Persian scouts could not help themselves but launch into an attack.

So, Naram-Sin's scout squadron lay in wait, hidden, all mounted and waiting for the order to attack. Xantho made sure his kopis blade was loose in its scabbard. All who hid to spring the trap were Warriors of the Light, apart from Tiki. The boy was behind them, eyes wide, flitting from Xantho to Naram-Sin.

"Don't worry," said Xantho, "keep to the back, out of the way. We will get the job done."

Tiki nodded, his helmet sliding over his eyes. Penelope shook her head in Xantho's direction.

"They are close now. Make ready," said Naram-Sin.

Xantho pushed himself to stand in the saddle and could see the three soldiers sipping their tea. They were playing the game to perfection, not peering over their shoulders, waiting as ordered until they could hear the thunder of hoofbeats. Next, Xantho saw the enemy fan out into a wide line. There looked to be ten of them, mounted on light ponies, similar to the mount Xantho rode. Xantho felt eyes on him and looked around to see Banya staring at him. He was sick of the muscled warrior sniping and putting him down.

"What?" said Xantho, returning the stare.

Banya just chuckled to himself and shook his head. Xantho disliked Banya just as much as the warrior disliked him. But the difference for Xantho was that he'd done nothing to incur Banya's contempt, whereas Banya had rebuked and put Xantho down at every opportunity, believing he put the rest of the warriors in jeopardy with his lack of skills. Still, Xantho was trying to get better, to be a better warrior.

Xantho heard a whoop break out in the distance from the line of enemy scouts. It echoed and rattled around the valley. The three Macedonian soldiers looked around as though surprised to hear the sound. Then, upon seeing the enemy, they dashed towards their hobbled ponies, scrabbling to untie them and leap to their backs.

"Wait for my order," said Naram-Sin.

The three Macedonians in the valley scrambled to untie their steeds amidst lots of pointing and shouting at the enemy. They mounted and kicked at their horses' flanks, and all made a beeline towards Xantho and the others. The three had timed their retreat perfectly; the enemy was almost upon them, only thirty paces behind. One of the Persian scouts even tried to throw one of his spears, but it fell short. The valley shook now with the roar of galloping horses and the excited shouting of the attacking enemy.

The Macedonians reached the upward slope to the hill where Naram-Sin waited, and Xantho could see the whites of their eyes.

"Now, attack!" Naram-Sin commanded.

"Go, go!" shouted Khamudi, and they leant forward, pressing their horses into the charge.

Xantho dug his heels in, and the mare sprang off. He fell in beside Khamudi, and they raced past Naram-Sin, who had leapt to mount his horse, having jumped down from his vantage point. The Persians slowed their attack as they saw the riders appear from the hills. Xantho knew their leader faced a choice, continue the attack and fight the enemy with equal numbers, or turn and run and live to fight another day. It took too long to make that choice, and the

Persians decided too late to turn around. A shout went up from their line, and they wrenched on their reins, the horses' heads turning savagely as their hooves slid and turned in the dust.

Xantho could see them clearly now. They were unarmoured, wearing light tunics, and each man held a short spear and had a curved blade at his hip. Khamudi let out an ear-rattling battle cry and flung his own short cavalry spear. It flew in a blur and slammed into the closest enemy, flinging him from the saddle to roll in the dirt. The Egyptian drew his blade and waved it above his head. Xantho drew his kopis and readied himself for the attack, the thrill of the chase quickening his pulse. His pony was fast and powerful, its speed a joy as he raced into the fray.

He heard Siduri shout an order from behind him, and he glanced around to see Penelope and Khensa riding together, but with arms outstretched, preparing to unite their mage powers. Xantho angled back to the enemy, who had lost their momentum in turning, and now the Warriors of the Light were upon them. He closed in on a black-bearded enemy. Xantho extended his kopis but thought he was too far away for an effective strike, so he waited and urged his horse to get closer.

Suddenly the Persian swung his short spear behind him in a vicious arc. Xantho only just raised his blade in time to block the blow as it jarred along his arm, his head flung back in shock, and he had to rebalance himself to avoid falling from the saddle.

He felt a hot wind pulse past him; the air shimmered and shook around his pony. Xantho clutched the pommel before him, almost toppled by the force flooding the battleground. Ahead, the pulse of power lifted the enemy, a tornado-like gust of wind raising their mounts aloft from the ground. They fell in a tumble of men and horseflesh, screaming in terror at the preternatural force.

Xantho felt Penelope's power flow through him, the energy and burgeoning rage welcome and warm. He rode past the fallen enemy and urged his mare to round back towards the Persians. As he turned, he saw Khamudi hacking down on a man's shoulder as he rose from the ground. He saw Naram-Sin leap from his horse to land and roll in the dirt, rising with his xiphos drawn. Xantho kept going and drove his horse into the back of a still-rising Persian, feeling the thud of the impact through the animal's flank. He turned again and watched as Naram-Sin waited for the enemy to rise. He could have cut them down where they lay, tangled in the screaming horses, but he waited, relishing the clash of arms. Two Persians roared and charged at the Akkadian, curved blades held before them, craving blood. Xantho held his mare steady so that he could see the clash, in awe at Naram-Sin and his confidence. The tall warrior swayed away from one thrust and ducked under another. Then he sprang forward, slashing his blade across the back of one attacker and then reversing the blade to sink it into the stomach of the other. Xantho wondered if he would ever be able to fight with such skill, such grace. Naram-Sin moved like a dancer, as though he was as light as a feather and his enemies made of rock.

Xantho felt the power rush out of his body, and he looked to find Penelope. She and Khensa were off their horses and stood on either side of two Persians who knelt with their hands over their ears. The mages had their arms outstretched, stern faces and spread fingers holding the enemy in place. Siduri, still mounted, raised both hands high, then brought them down fast, snarling at the Persians. Those two men flew fifteen feet in the air and then slammed into the ground in a cloud of dust. The screams of those men and the crunching of their bones made Xantho's stomach turn. He looked at his blade, free of blood. He had not tackled down any of the Persians, whereas all the other Warriors of the Light had played their part.

"Xantho!"

It was Khamudi shouting, pointing to one enemy who had avoided the attack and got back onto his horse. The Persian shouted and raced away from the slaughter. Xantho remembered his bow and quickly jumped from his horse, taking the bow from his back in one swift movement. He reached into the quiver tied to his saddle and took an arrow. Xantho's chest pushed against his hard-linen breastplate, and he reminded himself to slow his breathing.

"Don't let him get away! He will alert others," shouted Siduri.

Xantho nocked the arrow and raised the bow. He pulled the string back to his ear, feeling the muscles in his back strain and stretch. He watched the rider moving away fast. Maybe too fast.

"Now, Xantho, he's getting away!" Penelope urged.

He felt heat flush his face. Everyone was looking at him, depending on him. He let the arrow fly. It shot high, arcing towards the clouds. He watched it begin its downward trajectory. *Please be good.* It flew towards the rider, towards his back, but then thudded into the grass, a few paces behind the fleeing Persian. Xantho's heart plummeted, and his stomach went hollow. He thought he heard the collective sighs of each Warrior of the Light. Though he couldn't see him, he felt Banya's eyes burning into the back of his head. Khamudi leapt upon a horse and sped off after the Persian, racing away into the distance.

"It was close," said Tiki. Xantho nodded without looking up from the ground. He couldn't look at any of them. They searched the fallen enemy, looking for water, food, coins, weapons, and anything else of value.

Twenty paces away, Naram-Sin leant over a wounded Persian lying beneath him. The Akkadian asked the injured man a question and worked at him with his knife. The Persian screamed and answered in a torrent of desperate words, too far away for Xantho to hear. Naram-Sin asked more questions, pushed and sliced his wicked blade, and there were more screams. Xantho turned away from the terrible scene but told himself that this was the hard face of war he must get used to. He must steel himself against such things.

The rest of the Warriors of the Light avoided Xantho. The three mages sat together, recuperating from the exertions of their magic. Again, they had worked to devastating effect, felling the enemy and then crushing two of them, working as one. Penelope already seemed to be on par with Khensa, soaking up Siduri's lessons, already an effective mage playing her part in the battle.

Xantho had missed his moment. If he could have made that shot, he would have been the hero, the one who saved the ambush souring from victory into a problem. If the fleeing rider got away, he would alert Memnon's forces that Macedonian scouts were abroad, and it would not take the Greek commander long to figure out that Alexander made for Zeleia, and he would know to reinforce the town of Priapus and deny them water. *How could I have missed the shot?* He had been calm, ready, but they had hurried him, and he had missed.

"Here, have a drink," said Tiki, handing him a waterskin. Xantho took a long drink. He poured some water into his hands and washed the sweat from his face.

"Gula'an is here," Naram-Sin announced as he approached the three mages, wiping his bloody knife on a scrap of cloth. "The Persian spoke of a white-haired wizard with a black staff. He is abroad. The Persian says the wizard came from Darius and is marshalling the army at Zeleia."

"He is close then," said Siduri.

"More than that. The Persian says mercenary forces are in the field, close to here. Skilled warriors commanded by fair-skinned and blonde-haired fighters with great power."

"Could it be Wulfgar?" Khensa suggested. She stood, brushing the dust from her chiton.

"Probably, maybe with Agi. We should assume the other traitors are also with them."

"Agi? Surely not?" said Siduri.

"She is tied to Wulfgar, just as you and I are

tied. Gula'an is persuasive. Wulfgar lost his mage power when Agi died at Gula'an's hands. Gula'an gave his power back for a moment, but if they have both returned, he is a mage again."

"We should double back and warn the infantry. The road to Priapus is not clear," said Khensa.

"What are they saying?" asked Tiki.

"We must warn the Agrianians that there are enemy soldiers between here and the town," replied Xantho.

Tiki opened his mouth as though to ask another question. But Xantho walked away. He put his head next to his mare's nose and patted her neck. Xantho could not believe he had missed the shot. He hadn't killed a single enemy. When they had ridden out from the Macedonian camp, Xantho had felt part of the group; he had felt like a Warrior of the Light. Now he felt like a liability. The worst part was not Penelope's scorn, which he could feel even without looking at her. Nor was it proving Banya right. The worst part was that he had let Naram-Sin down.

"Khamudi," said Khensa from behind Xantho. He turned to see the rider approaching.

Naram-Sin's squadron had all come out of the fight with no casualties. They mounted up, and Khamudi drew close.

"Did you get him?" called Penelope. Khamudi

nodded.

"I got him. I saw the town, Priapus. Southwest, maybe a few days' ride from here. A walled town, small and close to a narrow river."

"Come. Back to Hephaestion," said Naram-Sin.

They headed back across the three hills. None of the others mentioned the missed shot to Xantho, but they all avoided him. So, he rode alone.

They came upon Hephaestion, making camp for the night. His men had set a watch and found some high ground from which they would easily see any approaching enemy. The Companion cavalrymen tended to their horses, rubbing them down with handfuls of brush weed before settling for the evening. The Agrianians were the hard-looking folk Xantho had seen at the Macedonian camp. They were wind-burned, short, lean and wiry warriors. They wore light tunics and cloaks dotted in parts with fur and patchwork pieces of bronze armour. Each had a Phrygian-style helmet and carried three throwing spears strapped to his back. Fifty of these men had accompanied Hephaestion on his mission to secure the town.

Xantho sat with Tiki, and they shared some warm flatbread which Tiki had scrounged up from the Agrianians.

"They're alright," the boy had said, "they might eat you if they were hungry, mind. They are very tough, hard fighters."

"How do you know them?"

"There were many of them back in the bay," Tiki shrugged. "They come to fight with Alexander because they love to fight. They also love wine," he said with a wink.

Naram-Sin stood with Hephaestion, and they talked, looking out at the setting sun. The Macedonian was as tall as Naram-Sin, who was already larger than most men. Xantho himself was above average height, but the Akkadian was a head taller even than he. Hephaestion was broad in the chest. He wore a muscled breastplate and not the folded linen armour of the other cavalrymen. He left his arms bare, rippling with muscle beneath heavy scarring. Despite his size and obvious experience in battle, the Macedonian had a gentle face, soft and round beneath a tangle of curly blonde hair.

"He's Alexander's right-hand man, so they say," whispered Tiki.

"What do you know of him?" asked Xantho.

"Not much. He does these special missions for the king, and he did such things in Greece to secure the kingdom, they say. Working between armies, scouting and fighting and making the advance possible."

Xantho considered the information. *A skilled and respected warrior, then.* The opposite of his own status. "When we ride out tomorrow, you will stay with the Agrianians," said Xantho.

"What? I want to stay with you. Where are you going?"

"I don't know yet, but Naram-Sin will want to hunt. It will be dangerous, so you stay here with the greater numbers. You must, Tiki. I'll come back for you."

The lad nodded, sullen but accepting. Xantho had seen the shock on Tiki's face after the fight with the Persian scouts. It was difficult to see men killed, and witnessing the mages in action was to come face to face with the impossible. Tiki hadn't spoken of the strange events, the magic he must have seen used on the Persian scouts. Xantho knew well enough that it was a lot to take in. Hephaestion clapped Naram-Sin on the shoulder, and the Akkadian approached his Warriors of the Light.

"In the morning, we ride out. We are to find and engage any enemy in the field. Hephaestion will march for Priapus as fast as possible. Therefore, we clear the way," he said.

So, tomorrow there would be more fighting. Xantho lay awake that night, looking up into the clear night sky. He stared long at the stars, looking at the patterns and brightness in the heavens. *Is Enlil up there somewhere looking down, as disappointed in me as Naram-Sin must be? Are the other gods up there?* Only one thing was for sure. More battle was to come. The thought kept him awake. Dark thoughts ran through his head, the worry and fear of the pain which comes from the terrible wound that doesn't kill. The fear of death. *If I die, will I be truly dead, or will I rise again in some future war?* The greatest fear, though, was of his own inability to help his fellow warriors.

FOURTEEN

Xantho woke as the sun's edge cast a pallid red glow over the hills beyond. He knuckled at stinging eyes. It had been a long night with thoughts of his failure and fears whirling in his head until the stars lulled him into a dreamless slumber.

He sat up, both eager and nervous, to see if Khamudi would still want to have morning practice following his missed shot the day before. But sure enough, the Egyptian was already up, stretching and executing the controlled movements he performed every morning. He would lay belly down on the ground and push himself up repeatedly, then flip over onto his back and pull his upper torso up to his knees until sweat sheened his body. Khamudi had a fixed series of these movements, which he said kept him strong. Xantho usually waited until Khamudi had finished his routine before commencing weapons practice, but he knew that if we were going to get better, he had to try harder.

"Can I join in?" he asked. Khamudi smiled.

"I thought you would never ask. Come on."

The Egyptian showed him the movements step by step, and Xantho followed his lead. By the time he had finished, he had stripped to his bare chest and was sweating hard. Next, they practised with the kopis, and Xantho pushed himself, parrying, blocking, thrusting. Then they wrestled, holds and throws and chokes. Finally, archery came just as the rest of the group was waking.

"You must forget yesterday. It was one shot. Practice keeping calm. Control your emotions. Calmness is a warrior's greatest skill, and panic our greatest enemy," Khamudi said.

"How do you stay calm when there is fighting all around, and people are shouting at you?"

"Take a few heartbeats. Breathe from your stomach, not your chest. Focus on the target and the arrow, and continue to breathe deep from the stomach. Be calm."

Xantho nodded. The Egyptian watched him fire a dozen shots, good shots, and then he clapped Xantho on the shoulder. They retrieved the arrows and went to make ready to ride out.

"Khamudi," Xantho began, just before they

reached the others, "thank you for helping me."

"You are welcome, my friend. No one is born knowing these skills. They must be taught and learned. You are getting better."

Xantho thought he was improving. He looked forward to the training drills with Khamudi. He couldn't yet match the Egyptian's skills, but there had been moments when he felt like he was getting close to landing a blow or getting inside his guard. However, Xantho knew from painful experience that it's one thing being good in training but another putting those skills into practice on the battlefield.

Most of Hephaestion's force was still asleep when Naram-Sin's squadron rode out. They headed east, tracking back to where they had fought the previous day. It was as good a place as any to look for the enemy. Siduri rode with Naram-Sin at the front of the column, and Xantho fell in beside Penelope. Tiki had, after much persuasion, stayed with the infantry. Fortunately, the Agrianians had promised to look after the boy. Although reluctant at first, they'd soon warmed to Tiki's humour and easy manner and so were happy to have him march with them in the end.

Later that day, riding across ripe farmland bursting with yellows and greens, they came upon signs of the enemy.

"Large column of riders, maybe fifty," said

Khensa, who had spotted the tracks.

They followed those tracks cautiously until a splinter group broke off from the enemy force, a scouting party whose tracks struck to the northwest. If the group continued in that direction, they would surely come across Hephaestion and his force as they marched towards Priapus. So, under Naram-Sin's orders, they followed the splinter scouting party.

The day drew on into the early evening, and riding across a densely wooded ridge, they saw the enemy. There were five men making camp for the night in a clearing below. Xantho and the rest fell back into the cover of the dense pine forest.

"We wait until darkness falls," said Naram-Sin. "Then we go down there and take them."

"One of them looks familiar," Siduri noted, pointing at a fair-haired warrior with his back to them.

"We can't see his face; it could just be a coincidence," said Naram-Sin.

Day turned to night, and they took turns watching, lying at the edge of the ridge, to observe the scouts as darkness drew in. Xantho sharpened his kopis blade and tried to focus his mind, ready for the fight to come, determined to do better this time. Penelope came to sit close by. She took out her xiphos and tried its edge.

"Do you think I should sharpen it?" she asked.

"I think your skills mean you won't need to use it," Xantho replied. She nodded but kept the blade in her hand, looking at her reflection in the steel.

"Do you think we have changed?"

"Yes, so much has happened."

"Have I changed?"

He hadn't known her before the Massagetae attack, so it was hard to say if she had changed from her old self, her slave self. She had undoubtedly hardened and taken to their new life with aplomb. There was no difference now really between Penelope and the other mages. She had slotted right in as one of them. What shocked Xantho most of all, though, was her cold ferocity. She had taken to killing and battle like a duck to water, with no qualms or concerns for those she had killed. That sent a shiver down his neck.

"Yes, you have. You are stronger, more determined," Xantho answered. He hoped it was a pleasant way of describing the change in her. "Have I?"

She stared at him for a few heartbeats, her green eyes still bright in the early dusk. "Yes, but you seem so disappointed in yourself all the time. You shouldn't be, Xantho."

He was disappointed in himself. He had regularly let himself and the others down. *How could I feel any other way? Especially with Banya constantly putting me down.*

"You missed the bow shot yesterday, but at least you took the shot. The Xantho I first met would not have even tried, or known, how to shoot the bow. Don't pity yourself so much; it makes it harder to talk to you. We are all one now. The others will support you if you let them," she said, giving him a smile where her bottom lip moved up and the corners of her top lip down as if to say she understood and felt for him. He had reckoned she despised him or thought him a fool. Hearing her say those words felt like shrugging off a heavy load, and Xantho sat a little straighter. He had been pitying himself, not just now, but his whole life, which he supposed had been one long, miserable mess. *I'm doing it again. I have to stop.*

"Thank you," he said. "I'll try. Do you miss your old life?"

"No. I hated my old life. Now I am free and feel strong, and these people value us; we have a purpose."

"Do you ever think about those people you have killed?" he asked, reaching over to brush at that loose strand of hair that always fell across her face. Penelope looked up at the treetops wavering gently above them and back to Xantho.

"To be honest, no, I don't. They are killers all. We are at war. They were warriors here to kill or be killed. The men I have slain would gladly have killed me first, but I was stronger. If we lose this war with Gula'an, how many more innocent people will be cast in his world of never-ending war?"

Xantho nodded. He reached behind him for a waterskin and handed it to her. She took a drink and smiled in thanks.

"It's partly my fault you missed your shot," Penelope said. "If I had passed the power to you, the arrow would have flown further. We need to work harder to fight as a pair."

He hadn't thought of it like that. But perhaps she was right.

"Do you fully understand it now, your power?"

"No, not yet. Siduri says there is more I can do. Like when she brought thunder down at the battle against Tomyris. But she also says to be careful, those big powerful actions use up our strength quickly, and once the Palmstone loses its colour, it could take hours to return."

Much later, and under the cover of darkness, they moved off for the attack. The moon was in a waning phase. A sliver of a crescent hung above them, barely casting any light as Xantho and others picked their way down the hillside towards the enemy. Naram-Sin led the way, and the rest fanned out in a straight line. It was hard to see clearly ahead, but the small fire the enemy had made for their evening meal glowed like a beacon, and they could make out the humps of the five men sleeping. Xantho could not tell if they lay with eyes open on watch or if they were all fully asleep.

Xantho did his best to move silently. Fallen pine branches and cones littered the ground underfoot amidst small rocks and bushes, making it hard to keep a firm and confident footing. He thought it would be just his luck to trip and alert the enemy, but then he caught himself. *Was that pitying myself again?* Xantho tried to think differently. He would move like a cat, be as stealthy and quiet as Naram-Sin and strike with equal ferocity.

Sounds of crickets and insects filled the night, their regular croaks and clicks much louder in the darkness than during the daytime. The trees behind blew softly in the breeze, and those sounds combined, allowing the Warriors of the Light to approach unheard.

As they neared closer, Naram-Sin drew his blade, and the others followed suit. Xantho could hear an enemy soldier snoring, blissfully unaware of the impending attack. Then, a loud snap came from Xantho's left. Siduri looked to the ground and then at the enemy as a brittle twig had snapped under her foot. The enemy scouts jolted awake, jerking into seated positions.

"Now!" shouted Naram-Sin, and they leapt to the attack. There was a glint of steel. And the enemy called out in panic, rising to their feet to defend themselves.

Xantho picked his man, still just a shadowy figure ahead, too far away to make out a face. That man did not stand and fight. Instead, he made a dash for his mount, tethered twenty paces away. Xantho heard the clash of steel and the shouts of battle around him as he pursued his target.

The enemy warrior had a head start and almost had a hand on his horse's thongs when Xantho leapt on him, landing on the back of the warrior's legs. The two fell to the cold ground, rolling closer to the horse. The enemy struck at the back of Xantho's head with his fist, but the blow had no strength. Xantho released the man's legs and sliced his drawn kopis across his foe's stomach, but it only scraped against a baked leather breastplate. They clutched each other, breathing hard, and rolled on the ground. Xantho lurched away as the horse pawed the ground, panicked by the noise of the surrounding fight and the smell of blood, its hoof pounding a handbreadth from his face.

Xantho and his enemy sprang to their feet and flashed weapons at each other, each blocking the other's strike in an arm-jarring clang of steel on steel. Then, determinedly, Xantho pulled back for another blow.

"You," his foe said through gritted teeth, and Xantho's stomach plummeted when he recognised the scout.

"Wulfgar, traitor," Xantho seethed, and he launched himself into the attack, slashing and jabbing with his blade. The Northman snarled and cursed, yet he moved back from the onslaught and then stabbed his weapon high at Xantho's face. Xantho dodged it and moved inside Wulfgar's outstretched arm. Instinctively he used the wrestling technique Khamudi had taught him and threw the traitor across his hip. Wulfgar hit the ground hard and paused, stunned. Xantho knocked the weapon from his hand and knelt over him, blade poised for the killing blow. For a fleeting moment, Xantho halted, frozen by a sudden fear—Wulfgar could crush him instantly with his magic, but he hadn't. *Agi must not be here.*

Wulfgar's pallid face stretched tight, his eyes wide and teeth clenched. Xantho hesitated. He wanted to plunge his kopis into Wulfgar's chest, but it was impossible to do it whilst looking into the man's pale blue eyes. Wulfgar's panic turned to fury, and he rolled Xantho, squirming out from under him. He kicked Xantho in the stomach, winding him, then leapt onto his horse, laughing.

"You haven't got the stomach for it, coward.

I was right all along," Wulfgar said as he pulled savagely on the reins and kicked his beast into a lurch forward.

"Wulfgar!" came a shout. It was Naram-Sin. A blade fizzed through the air beside Xantho and flew towards Wulfgar, but it sailed wide. The traitor laughed again and sped off into the night.

"Penelope, Siduri, Khensa, stop him!" Xantho yelled. But he knew Wulfgar was too far away now and beyond sight.

Xantho knelt, chest heaving as he recovered his breath from Wulfgar's kick. He had failed to strike, and to his dismay, he had done it again; he had let the others down.

The other four enemy scouts had died in the attack and expired before they could be questioned. Naram-Sin feared Wulfgar would now return to the larger column and follow their tracks back to Hephaestion's force. It would still be another day before the Agrianians would reach Priapus, and so they would have to double back again to warn Alexander's friend.

The Warriors of the Light rode hard through the morning and heard the infantry engaged in savage, desperate combat before they saw them. The Persians had already found Hephaestion and had launched a cavalry attack. The Companion cavalry was not with the Agrianians and must have pushed ahead to secure the town's position. Fifty enemy horsemen rode around the

Macedonian light infantry, loosing arrows and javelins in a hail of murder.

"We must charge them. If we can disrupt their formation, then the Agrianians can attack," said Naram-Sin. "One of us must break through the enemy and encourage the Agrianians to push out against the cavalry."

There was no time for discussion, and they rode on at full tilt into the attack. The blood rushed into Xantho's head as he felt the power and speed of the mare. The Warriors of the Light thundered across the field towards the enemy cavalry. Xantho pushed aside his regret at hesitating to strike at Wulfgar. It was one thing to kill a man in a battle with the throw of a spear or an arrow into the distance, but it was another to take his life eye to eye, thrusting cold steel into another man's warm flesh.

They came upon the enemy, and the clash between the two mounted forces was an impossible clatter of steel, horseflesh, shouting and dust. Xantho made for a gap between the Persian formation, where two men launched arrows into the Agrianians. He braced himself and closed his eyes, not slowing his mare as he ploughed into them. The shock of the collision almost threw him over the front of his horse's neck, but he kept his balance and struck about him with his kopis. The two enemies fell, and he felt the blade strike, but he couldn't be sure if he had hit armour or flesh. He urged the mare on, but she couldn't move, trapped in the enemy's tumult, who now turned to strike at their attackers. Xantho closed his eyes again. Something smashed against the back of his armour, and another blow glanced from his chest. He felt the familiar mage power build rapidly within him, and a surge of energy pulsed through the air. The surrounding enemy screamed, and some fell. A gap opened up. His horse was still jammed amongst the enemy, so Xantho leapt free. The power had fully taken hold, and his jump from the saddle took him clear over the enemy in front of him.

Xantho landed with a roll and came up fast. He grabbed a Persian horse's bit and wrenched the beast to the ground, his power-fuelled strength dragging the horse down and toppling its rider. Then, Xantho dashed forward and shouldered into another horse, toppling that one as well. He was through them now, and he dashed towards the Agrianians, who hunkered down behind their shields, showing themselves only long enough to launch javelins at their attackers.

"Attack now, attack now. They are broken!" Xantho shouted as he approached. Two of the Agrianians peered above their mass of shields, and the wall opened. Xantho didn't stop moving. He spun on his heel and beckoned them on.

"Now, now! Kill them!" he shouted. He burst forward, feeling the Agrianians at his side. Xantho leapt from the ground, the power launching him high. He landed behind a Persian in the saddle and threw that man aside. He slashed left and right with his blade, and the notoriously vicious Agrianians were among them then, stabbing and killing with their spears amid spine-tingling, undulating war cries. As they surged out from their defensive formation, a body of Persians pushed into the gap and threw a wave of spears into the Agrianians. Xantho heard a great cry go up above the din of battle. He sprang towards that gap, using his power to cross the space in three long leaps. Hephaestion himself was there, wounded with an arrow through his shoulder and enemy warriors upon him, charging with spears outstretched. Hephaestion pressed the enemy back despite being wounded, cutting into them, snarling like a demon. Xantho launched himself before the Persians. He deflected a blow destined for Hephaestion's neck with his kopis before punching the enemy warrior in the chest, flinging him backwards. He cut at another attacker, a short, swarthy man who cried out as Xantho's blade sliced through his nose and took his eye, and the enemy fell back. Xantho felt the strength fall away from him. He checked his Palmstone, and the light had faded from it, leaving him exhausted. Xantho stood with his hands on his knees, gasping to regain his breath, his mind still frantic from the fight. He felt a hand on his shoulder and looked for its owner. Hephaestion nodded to him.

"You saved me there, friend. You fight well," said the Macedonian, face grim and flushed from battle.

"You are injured, lord," Xantho noted, pointing to the arrow jutting from Hephaestion's shoulder. Hephaestion grimaced at the wound.

The fight was over in moments, the enemy peeling away and riding for their lives. Just as the tumult subsided, Xantho caught sight of Wulfgar's blonde hair bouncing as he rode back towards the Agrianians for one more attack. Wulfgar launched a spear overhand. Xantho watched it dart through the first clutch of the light infantrymen. A man ducked, and the shaft thudded into a short warrior, dropping him instantly. Wulfgar thrust his hands forward, disturbing the air, and a clutch of Agrianians flew backwards out of his path. Wulfgar turned his horse and rode away with the other Persian survivors. The traitor had escaped again, and Agi must have been with him this time. Xantho found it hard to believe the friendly warrior, the first of the Warriors of the Light to show him kindness, could have gone over to the forces of Gula'an.

Xantho trudged back through the mess of

fallen bodies, ignoring the cries for help from the wounded.

"Tiki!" he called out, searching through the Agrianians for his young friend. There was no reply. Xantho made it to where the Agrianians had made their shield wall. To his left, he saw a body lying before him, smaller than the rest of the warriors. A short spear had gone straight through the corpse's neck. Dark blood covered the horrific wound. Xantho clasped a hand to his mouth when he rolled the body over. It was Tiki, his small, innocent face pale and drained of blood, glassy eyes open and empty, staring up at Xantho, dead.

FIFTEEN

The Agrianians tended to their wounded, applying salves and bandages from whatever supplies they could muster between them. Xantho carried Tiki's body away from the battle site and laid him down on a clear stretch of soft grass. Those almond eyes seemed to stare at Xantho as though Tiki could see through them still from wherever his spirit now walked. Xantho hoped Enlil would help the boy, take his soul to the heavens, and not allow him to be dragged to the underworld into Nergal's realm. Tiki's eyes were wide open, and his mouth turned down in a permanent look of terror and pain.

Xantho swallowed down the lump in his throat. He closed Tiki's eyes. As he did so, he held his hand there for a moment against the boy's soft face. A boy so full of life and fun, with so many possibilities stretching before him. Xantho shook his head, wiping at his wet eyes. It had surely been Wulfgar's final spear throw that had killed Tiki. Xantho had his chance to kill the traitor, and he let him go. And now Tiki was dead. Not only that, had Xantho left Tiki at the Macedonian beach camp, he would not have been in harm's way, and though the camp soldiers would have made him a slave, at least Tiki would be alive. The thought that he was responsible for Tiki's death burned in Xantho's stomach. He stopped fighting against the tears and gave himself over fully to sorrow. Sobs racked his body, quick breaths jerking his shoulders as salty tears rolled down his face.

"Tiki, please no," Penelope gasped. Xantho hadn't heard her approach, but she knelt next to him. She placed a hand on Tiki's thin arm, holding it tight.

"Wulfgar," Xantho said.

"He did this?"

"I saw him throw the spear."

"Poor Tiki. A great deal of laughter has just left the world," she lamented, and her head sank to her chest.

Eleven of the enemy had died in the fight. The Agrianians and the Warriors of the Light had wounded many more, but most of those men escaped on their fleet ponies. There had been no pursuit. The Agrianians had lost three men, and another eight were badly injured. All the Warriors of the Light had survived the encounter. They would take the day to bury the dead and patch up the wounded before pushing on for Priapus. The Companion cavalry was still out there somewhere, and the hope was that they had reached the town by now and would engage any enemy in the vicinity.

Xantho dug a grave for Tiki at the base of a tall, straight fir tree, which he hoped would serve as a dignified monument for his young friend. It stood alone on a wide expanse of grass high above the landscape, which stretched below to where the Agrianians had made their camp. Xantho dug the grave with his kopis, knife, and bare hands. Penelope sat at the base of the tree in silence. She had offered to help, but he had refused. Xantho wanted to do it himself. He felt responsible for the boy's death. So, he would dig the grave.

Once the pit was deep enough, Xantho lifted Tiki's stiff body and laid it in the ground. He had removed the spear from the boy's neck. It had been a horrific ordeal to pull the thing free. Xantho had gagged with the effort, and he'd cried again at the terrible wound the weapon had left in Tiki's neck. Xantho tore a strip of cloth from Tiki's chiton and soaked it from his waterskin. He then washed away as much of the black-crusted blood as he could and washed Tiki's face clean. He wrapped more torn cloth around Tiki's neck to hide the wound and crossed Tiki's arms over his chest so he looked like he was sleeping. Xantho placed an eating knife, and some dried meat from his pack next to Tiki's body for his journey to the afterlife. He stood then and pushed the dug soil back into the grave to cover the body.

"Wait," exclaimed Penelope. She quickly took a hairband and a comb from her pack and laid them with Xantho's offerings. Penelope knelt and kissed her hand, reaching down and placing it on Tiki's forehead. She stood and wept.

"It's all I have to give him," she sobbed. Xantho walked over to her and drew her into an embrace. He held her tight. She pushed her head into his chest, and he felt her anguish as she shook in his arms. After a time, she looked up at him, green eyes ringed with red. "This is what it looks like," she said.

"What?"

"War. This is what it means. It's not the fighting, the hollow honour, the warrior's pride. It's this. Innocent people dying, people who are loved by someone. A son, a mother, a father, a friend. This awaits the world, stretching across time in a deluge of misery and pain if Gula'an wins."

Xantho had not thought of it like that, but she was right. He had never seen this face of war before. Xantho had known that his father

Tiribazos rode to battle at the head of the cavalry, and he had gleefully heard his mother's stories about his grandfather—of battles and heroes. But it had never been something Xantho had given any real thought to. As a slave, it didn't concern him. He had his duties, and that was it. Since joining with Naram-Sin, he had thought only of playing his part, of fighting well, and not letting the others down. His business now was death. That was his purpose. Enlil had selected him and Penelope for that sole purpose, to stop and kill Gula'an and any of his warriors. Yet the other side of that was the corpses, like Tiki, and what they left behind. The loved ones they left behind.

"This is what we fight for, then, for peace, to stop people doing this to each other," he said.

"Or to reduce it, at least."

Xantho covered Tiki with the rest of the soil until it covered his body, and the grave was level with the surrounding grass. Then he piled rocks on top of it to stop scavenging animals from digging up the remains.

"Should we say a prayer?" asked Penelope.

"We should. But to who? Enlil or the other gods?"

They exchanged a long look, but neither had the answer.

"Well, we have seen and spoken to one

god. And isn't it he who brought us back to life, forward in time to fight his war?" said Penelope. Xantho shrugged, supposing she was right. Penelope cleared her throat. "Lord Enlil, we pray to you now for the soul of our friend Tiki. He helped us, your Warriors of the Light. He brought some laughter and joy to us in this time of war. We ask you to help him find peace in the afterlife," she uttered, but the words trailed away.

"They were fine words," said Xantho, knowing he couldn't have said anything better.

He wanted to tell her he knew he should have left Tiki at the Macedonian camp. Xantho also wanted to tell her that Wulfgar had been under his sword, but he had let him go. Yet he didn't; he couldn't. The words wouldn't come out. Penelope had known it was a bad idea to bring the boy with the warriors; she had said it herself. She was being kind to not raise it now, to not remind Xantho of his mistake.

Khensa and Idari approached and said that Naram-Sin wanted to talk to them all. Xantho paused for a second and looked again at Tiki's grave. There would be no more mistakes, no more hesitation. Wulfgar would die. Xantho would seek him out, and the traitor would pay for his actions. He swore it on Tiki's grave.

The Warriors of the Light gathered with Naram-Sin. They stood in a circle beyond where the Agrianians readied themselves to march.

"You will know by now that Wulfgar rode with the enemy today," said the tall Akkadian. His face was still and calm, grey eyes searching the others for any reaction.

"How can it be?" asked Khamudi.

"It has never happened before, Warriors of the Light joining the forces of the underworld. Maybe Nergal can bring people back the same way as Enlil," said Siduri.

"Treacherous scum," growled Banya. Idari hooked her arm into his. She bit her bottom lip, and Banya drew her into an embrace.

"What about the others, Chitraganda, Xia Lao?" Khamudi questioned.

"Assume they are here also fighting with Gula'an under Memnon," said Naram-Sin.

There was silence for a few heartbeats, each looking at their boots. Xantho had only hate for the traitors, but he assumed the others were conflicted. They had been friends and fought alongside the traitors, for the gods only knew how long. It would not be easy to fight against them now. Xantho had never felt hate, not like the deep, profound hatred which burned within him now. He had disliked Jawed and resented his father, but now, when he thought of Wulfgar and the others, he felt hate in its purest form. Pure in that he wanted to drive his sword into Wulfgar's chest and snatch the life from him.

"We will ride out again. Clearly, the enemy is in the field in large numbers. So we will hunt the company who attacked our infantry today. That will provide a screen for Hephaestion to get to Priapus," said Naram-Sin.

"There could be more enemy bands out there," warned Khensa.

"Yes, there could. The other squadrons will hunt them, and the Companion cavalry is out there."

"When we find them, how do we kill Wulfgar and the rest?" Xantho asked.

The others all turned to stare at him. He realised he had not previously spoken up when the group met to discuss tactics and strategy.

"We should not talk of such things," Idari uttered.

"We kill them the same way we kill any man," said Khamudi.

"I mean, how do we kill them so they can never come back?" Xantho clarified. Everyone looked at him again. He didn't care; he wanted to know. Xantho didn't want to fight the traitors repeatedly across time. He wanted Wulfgar dead, and Gula'an stopped for good.

"Walk with us, Xantho," said Naram-Sin. "Let's ride out as soon as we can be ready."

Naram-Sin beckoned Xantho to follow as

he strolled away from the group with Siduri. Xantho tapped Penelope on the arm. She looked at him, and he gave a nod with his eyes for her to follow.

"You want to know how to kill a Warrior of the Light?" asked Naram-Sin.

"No," said Xantho, "I want to know how to kill Wulfgar."

Naram-Sin smiled, a small smile where his mouth moved, but his grey eyes remained flat and cold.

"We can be killed permanently—if you remove the head from a Warrior of the Light before their heart stops, then they will not rise again. I know this because I have seen it."

So, it was possible. All Xantho had to do was find Wulfgar, defeat him, and cut off the traitor's head. A shiver went down his spine. He couldn't imagine cutting off someone's head, but then the image of Tiki in his grave, throat torn and bloody, flashed into his mind, and he realised he could. Or he hoped he could.

"So, I must take his head," nodded Xantho as confidently as possible. Naram-Sin maintained a stare with his strange eyes, and Xantho did his best to meet that stare.

"You used the power well yesterday," said Siduri, interrupting the silence. Xantho inwardly thanked her for that. It was difficult to hold the tall Akkadian's steely grey-eyed stare. He wondered what Naram-Sin was thinking as those grey eyes searched his own, judging, formulating an opinion. He hoped the Akkadian saw some strength, some determination, at least.

"It makes me faster and stronger. I think I am getting used to using it to fight," Xantho agreed.

"Remember, if you use it, Penelope gets weaker. And if Penelope uses it all herself, you cannot call upon it," Siduri cautioned. "You will get used to it. But don't fall into the trap of needing it at the last moment when it isn't there. Either of you. As Naram-Sin says, we can be killed."

Penelope and Xantho nodded.

"How do I call on the greater power, like thunder?" asked Penelope.

Siduri smiled and looked up at the sky. "We mages are all able to call upon a unique element when we combine our strength. For me, it's thunder; for Khensa, it's water. For you, I don't know yet, but we should test it and see."

"How is it so?" Penelope wondered.

Siduri shrugged and put a hand on Penelope's shoulder. "Like so much of what we do, we simply do not know. But once we find it, use it sparingly, as it will drain you."

Penelope nodded in thanks and looked at her

Palmstone. Xantho wasn't sure what she was thinking, but there was still so much to learn about their new life. So much they didn't yet understand. Naram-Sin looked as though he was about to leave the conversation. But Xantho wanted more information from the leader, more answers.

"Why are we all different? You are Akkadians. We are Greek slaves, Khamudi and Khensa are Egyptians."

"When we permanently lose a mage or warrior, the other dies with them, never to rise again. Then when we awake for our next battle, sometimes we find a fresh pair with the potential to use the power, sometimes not," Siduri explained.

"So, if one of us dies, gets their head cut off, the other dies too?" asked Penelope.

"Not at the same time, but that other cannot rise again if their partner has been beheaded," said Naram-Sin.

"Where are Wulfgar and Agi from?" Xantho pressed. He wanted to know more about the traitor; maybe if he knew more about him, it would help in the battles to come. Xantho was also curious about what qualified one to become a Warrior of the Light, given that he was so spectacularly unqualified when Naram-Sin had found him.

"They are from the far north, beyond your

Thrace. Tribes roam there in vast numbers, and there is a constant war over land and tribal rivalries. The people there are fierce; they must be to survive in the harsh cold of their winters. We fought there once, a savage war. Agi and Wulfgar were the last to join us before you. Wulfgar was the son of a chief, destined to rule someday. But then he met us and became a mage," Siduri answered.

"Lord Hephaestion," said Naram-Sin, and Xantho turned to see the Macedonian commander approaching. Naram-Sin touched his fist to his chest, and the others did the same in salute. Hephaestion was stripped to the waist. He had a makeshift bandage around his wounded shoulder, and the bandage was already spotted with blood.

"Captain," said Hephaestion, "you are ready to leave?"

"Yes, lord, we leave momentarily," Naram-Sin replied.

"Find them, keep them busy. Alexander will be on the march by now. We must take the town quickly. I'll see you at Priapus."

Naram-Sin nodded. Hephaestion took a step towards Xantho. Without thinking, Xantho slipped back into his old slave way of thinking—he found a point behind Hephaestion and stared into it to appear meek and unchallenging but ready to receive a command.

"You saved my life today, scout," said the Macedonian. Xantho felt his cheeks flush, and he nodded. "You fight well, with the same odd strength of your commander here. I won't forget that. Here, take this."

Hephaestion took a ring from his finger and handed it to Xantho. It was gold and bore the Macedonian sunburst.

"Thank you, my lord," Xantho gulped. He slid it onto his finger, and it was a good fit.

"If ever you need my help or need to get a message to Alexander or me, use that. It was a gift from Aristotle, our tutor back home, and will be recognised instantly."

Xantho nodded his thanks again.

"Move swiftly; we have tarried here too long. We must have that town," Hephaestion said to Naram-Sin, and then he marched away shouting orders to the Agrianians.

Naram-Sin gave a slight dip of his head to Xantho. Xantho's heart swelled. He thought that was what it must feel like for a son to be hugged by his father after winning a race or doing well in his lessons. And then he felt foolish and did his best to keep calm and look unruffled.

"Can I see it?" asked Penelope. She was smiling and seemed happy that Xantho had received the recognition. He took off the ring and handed it to Penelope.

"It's so heavy; it's beautiful," she said and handed it back to him.

"It happened when I used the power. I stopped a blow from cutting him down. I could push horses over with my shoulder," Xantho shook his head, the power still hard to believe. "We must work together more."

"We will, Xantho. We can do this... together."

He watched Penelope as she went to her horse and checked its straps and equipment. Her approval meant more even than that of Hephaestion. She had been disappointed in him so many times. Xantho had craved that approval. He allowed himself a smile, the ring was beautiful, and he had saved the Macedonian commander.

The smile faded, and Xantho clenched his teeth. Now they would hunt for a second time, but there would be no mercy or hesitation this time. Wulfgar must die.

SIXTEEN

The Persian cavalry force left a simple trail to follow. Fifty ponies left a tear in the landscape like a great serpent, sliding and churning the land as it wound its way south. Naram-Sin rode the Warriors of the Light hard throughout the day in a relentless pursuit of the retreating Persians. The enemy had lost eleven of their number in the fight with the Agrianians, and a large number were injured, perhaps twice that number again. That would slow them down, and Xantho rode hard, certain they were catching up to Wulfgar and his men.

Khamudi had sighted Priapus in the previous days' scouting and so could keep a good bearing on its location as they rode. The Persians were not retreating in the town's direction but seemed to head further south, likely aiming to join up with Memnon's larger force. Xantho and the Warriors of the Light rode out alone. The rest of the light cavalry squadrons under Hephaestion were now under orders to ride hard for Priapus, join the Companion cavalry and secure the town and its vital well. The infantry could then march quickly and unopposed to the town and begin the assault upon it, and secure water and a strong location for Alexander to begin his attack on Memnon and Darius.

Xantho rode on his own that day. Tiki's death weighed heavily upon him, and he could not get the image of the terrible wound or Tiki lying peacefully in the grave out of his head. He still blamed himself entirely for Tiki's death, first for bringing him from the Macedonian camp and putting him in harm's way, and secondly for his failure to kill Wulfgar when he'd had the chance. Now, Xantho was glad to be on the chase; he was sick of being on the back foot, worried about fights to come and letting people down. All he wanted was another chance at Wulfgar. If the traitor came within reach a second time, then Xantho would take his head, or he would die trying.

As the afternoon drew into the evening and a red-tinged horizon dimmed behind a rising pine forest, they came across the enemy. Khensa had pushed onward to a hilltop to the north to get a view ahead. She came riding back hard once she had sight of the Persians entering the forest, where surely, they would make camp for the night.

"Good. We will attack in the dark and thin them out," said Naram-Sin. Xantho wanted to charge straight in and put them to the sword, but he kept quiet. Deep down, he knew that even with their mage power, forty men could easily overwhelm them just with their sheer numbers. So they stopped where they were, out of sight of the forest, and would wait until nightfall to descend upon their foes. They brushed and fed their horses and then sat to rest before the attack. Xantho sat alone, twisting Hephaestion's ring on his finger, fixed on Wulfgar and revenge for Tiki.

The Warriors of the Light had a small meal of oatcakes and dried strips of beef, and then as darkness fell, Naram-Sin gave the order to march. They would leave their horses and supplies and approach the forest, carrying only their weapons.

"In the night, they will hear our horses for miles. Stealth is our ally," Naram-Sin reminded the group, and they set off on foot.

"We will skirt around the forest to the north and then double back and attack from that side. If they suspect an attack, they will watch from this direction and not behind them. Behind them lies only the forces of Memnon and, so they believe, no threat. That is where we will find our gap."

No one questioned Naram-Sin's orders, despite him never actually asserting his command or asking for any kind of salute or title from the others. Xantho knew little about war and battles, but Naram-Sin's orders always seemed to make sense, and he presumed the others felt the same way. Xantho fell in beside Khamudi as they trekked north in the half-darkness of late evening. The Egyptian wore the same linothorax linen armour as Xantho and the others and also carried a kopis blade. Khamudi and Naram-Sin carried short, light infantry spears with them, which Xantho did not. He had trained little with the spear, and there was no point dragging one across Asia for the sake of it.

"Do you think we can attack forty of the enemy?" he asked Khamudi. Xantho was all for bringing the fight to the enemy now, but eight against forty seemed like extreme odds. The Egyptian smiled at Xantho, the angles of his face shadowy in the fading light.

"It will be dark. They will be asleep. We will surprise them, so I think we can thin them out a little."

"If we each kill two men, that's still only sixteen dead."

Khamudi laughed. "We don't have to kill them all, Xantho; just strike fear into them. Wound some, kill if we can. The mages will take care of more men than we mere warriors can," he said.

"If the others are there, our old friends, their mages will use magic against us?"

"They will, now that they serve Nergal. Gula'an may also be there, so be on your guard, young Xantho."

He hadn't thought of that. Gula'an also now fought with three warrior mage pairs, matching the Warriors of the Light. Suddenly fear nipped at his thirst for vengeance. *What if this is a trap? What if Wulfgar and the others knew Naram-Sin would attack them? If Gula'an or the others take our heads, then it's over. The world is lost to a never-ending spiral of war and death. Only we can stop them.*

"Is Gula'an a warrior or a mage?" Xantho asked.

"Neither and both," said Khamudi. "He carries both skills. He had warriors and mages long ago. But somehow, he absorbed their power, and until now, he had fought alone. His greatest skill is getting close to the army commanders he means to influence. Then he can advise and direct a war to his will, causing as much death and reaping as many souls as possible."

"Does he get stronger the more souls he takes?"

"It's hard to say, but he gets closer to his aim— eternal war and the rule of Nergal."

They marched hard. Picking the way across a

rock-strewn hillside was tricky. More than once, Xantho lost his footing on a loose rock or a thorny bush. They clambered up a hill which began the dark pine forests climb into a range of small mountains stretching away to the east. Xantho's eyes had become used to the darkness, and although the moon was but a sliver, it wasn't pitch black. To their east, Xantho could see enemy fires flickering between the trees. Occasionally he could pick out a cough, a shout, or a warrior moaning at the pain of some injury. Around him and in the darkness, insects croaked and clicked, and the warriors moved silently and unseen.

The fires were behind them when Naram-Sin signalled the turn to the east, and they entered the forest. They were in the night's heart now, and it became harder to see once under the cover of the pine forest canopy. They fanned out in a line, ten paces between them, and doubled back. Xantho searched the forest ahead. Despite the chill in the air, sweat trickled down his sides beneath his chiton. He thought he could see the twinkle of the enemy campfires where the downward slope levelled out. Xantho whistled twice, as quietly as he could, and the others looked in his direction. Xantho pointed to the fire, and Naram-Sin held up a hand for the advance to halt. He waved them in, and they huddled around him.

"Khamudi, you and Xantho move ahead and check the perimeter for scouts. If you see any, take them down. The rest of us will edge closer, but we will wait until we get a signal from you to say it's clear. Xantho, a whistle is as good a sign as any," said Naram-Sin.

"We should attack from two sides, Penelope should come with us, and then we have them in a pincer," Khamudi suggested.

Naram-Sin nodded. "Very well. Siduri, Khensa, and Penelope, we will rely on you to cause as much damage and noise as possible. I want them panicked and in fear. So let's bring the fight to them."

Xantho looked at Penelope. She was staring at Siduri. Her mouth was open, and her eyes wide. Siduri reached out and put a hand on her shoulder.

"You are ready for this, Penelope. Focus and feel for your strength. Remember to flow through Xantho," she said, and Penelope nodded.

Khamudi clapped Xantho on the back, and they set off in a low crouch. Xantho tried to move swiftly but was also careful with his footing. Any slips or the snapping of rotten branches underfoot would alert the enemy, and Xantho was determined that he would not be a liability for once. He would not fail. As he moved, Xantho took his bow from his back and tested the string, then he pulled an arrow from the quiver at his belt and nocked it to the bow. Xantho held it, ready to shoot as they descended the hill. Finally, they came close to the enemy, their multiple fires glowing brightly between the trees ahead. Khamudi raised his hand and gestured right. They set off in that direction, skirting the edge of the enemy fires.

Xantho stepped around a fallen trunk, avoiding tripping on its reaching branches. He looked across at Khamudi, who scanned the way ahead like a wolf, head darting left and right, breath steaming from his mouth in the chill night air. Suddenly a chesty cough rang out only twenty paces ahead of them. Khamudi held up a hand, and they stopped dead. The silhouette of a portly soldier appeared from behind a thick pine tree trunk. Khamudi looked at Xantho and pointed at the bow. Xantho nodded, and then his bowels twisted and turned with nerves.

He set himself, mouth dry, heart pounding. He focused on his training with Khamudi. Xantho breathed deep from his stomach, four long breaths. Ready. He couldn't make a mistake this time. He had to get the shot right. The man would surely cry out if he hit him in a limb or any other non-fatal way. It had to be the chest, neck, or head. Xantho allowed himself another deep breath. He clenched his teeth and raised the bow, pulling the string back to his ear. He looked down the shaft of the arrow and on past its grey iron point. The man was still there in the shadows. He coughed again and raised his hand to his mouth. Xantho exhaled and loosed.

The shot was flat because the target was close; no need for a high trajectory. Xantho leant forward, watching the flight of his missile. *Please be good.* The arrow flew with an almost imperceptible whistle through the trees and struck the enemy in the face, pinning his hand where it was against his mouth. The shadowy figure twisted and fell silently to the earth. Khamudi slapped Xantho on the shoulder and bounded ahead towards the fallen man. *Got him.* Penelope grabbed his arm, and Xantho turned to her. She smiled at him through the darkness, and he nodded thanks. He'd made the shot. Another man killed at his hand, but he wouldn't dwell on that, he told himself. They had shown no remorse for Tiki, so neither would he.

Khamudi reached for the fallen lookout and turned to wave back at Xantho. Xantho raised his own hand in acknowledgement.

"Are you ready?" he whispered to Penelope, and she nodded.

They crept forward ten paces, and Xantho could hear snoring ahead of them.

"Give the signal," Penelope said, her gravelly voice low and determined.

Xantho kept his bow ready and gave two whistles. He saw movement to his left; it was Khamudi dashing at the enemy with his kopis drawn. Xantho and Penelope ran forward. Suddenly, the enemy was there—lumps of shadowy contours of sleeping men lying close to the fires. He nocked an arrow and shot at one lump, nocked another and shot again. Next, he dropped the bow and drew his kopis. Penelope, next to him, had her eyes closed, and her hand moved in slow circles. Xantho grinned as the strength flowed into him; he felt it enraging him, his arms and legs feeling like those of a bull.

A gust of warm wind came from his right, and the campfires went out in a bluster of leaves. Men rose, and then suddenly, the air shook, and all the sleeping warriors in front of him lifted as one, as high as Xantho was tall, and then crashed back to the ground in a sickening thud. Siduri and the mages had done their work. The camp was a chaos of pain and alarm. He looked at Penelope, but she had her eyes closed in concentration.

Xantho attacked. The enemy was groaning and writhing, and he ran amongst them, cutting and slashing at shapes in the night. Screaming and shouting erupted around him. He knew Naram-Sin and Khamudi would also be out there somewhere, attacking the Persian foe. Xantho kicked one kneeling man, flinging him into the air to cannon back into another enemy. Xantho laughed. He felt so strong, so powerful. A blade came at him, and he swerved away from it, crashing his fist into his attacker's face, crushing his skull like an overripe fruit.

"Wulfgar!" Xantho shouted; no care now for stealth. He wanted the traitor. More men fell to his blade, more than he could count. Then he thought of Penelope. She hadn't yet fully brought her mage skills to bear. What if she was under attack? He spun on his heel and charged back the way he came. He could see her now in the distance. She held her arms above her head and knelt down as though carrying a great weight. There was a terrible cracking and crunching sound, and Xantho flinched. From behind Penelope, two tall pines tore from their earth roots and passed slowly over her head. They turned in the air and crashed to the ground. The tree trunks then rolled, thundering across the Persian camp, crushing the warriors and their mounts alike. Xantho leapt in the air to avoid one trunk as it rumbled past. He landed and rolled into a crouch, sighing as the mage power seeped from his limbs, weakening him. Xantho checked his Palmstone, and the light had all but gone. He saw Penelope had fallen to the earth and dashed to her. He raised her head, and her eyes flickered open.

"Go, kill them," she implored before slipping from consciousness. Xantho lowered his head and put his ear to her mouth. He could feel her breath warm and hear her inhale and exhale. So

Xantho lay her down gently and ran back into the screaming carnage, blade aloft and hunting for Wulfgar.

Xantho raged across the desolation of the Persian camp, but there was no sign of Wulfgar, Chitraganda, or any of the turncoat Warriors of the Light. He trudged back up the slope, past crushed bodies, fallen horses and scattered debris. Xantho supposed he shouldn't call the traitors Warriors of the Light anymore, warriors of the dark, maybe, or servants of the underworld. A horse screamed in pain up ahead, and thankfully Khamudi cut its throat to spare its suffering. The Egyptian stood and nodded to Xantho. As Xantho approached him through the night's gloom, he could see Khamudi's face splashed with blood, his beige linen armour discoloured by gore and filth.

"We thinned them out alright," said Khamudi, wiping his blade on a dead man's cloak.

"More than that, there are at least fifteen dead here," Xantho replied.

"Penelope has found her element. What she did there was devastating."

"Her element is what, then?"

"Each mage can control an element. Khensa has power over animals, Siduri fire, Penelope, it seems, has power over trees."

"Is anyone hurt?"

"I saw Naram-Sin in the fight, but ill check on the others," said Khamudi.

Xantho stepped around the fallen horse and returned to where he had left Penelope. She was sitting up now, but even in the darkness, he could tell she was exhausted.

"Is it done?" she asked.

"It's done. We destroyed them—you destroyed them. How did you do that?"

"I just felt it."

"No sign of Wulfgar or the other traitors," he said, squinting into the night. Banya and Idari stalked amongst the wounded, bending and slicing here and there, ending suffering and sending maimed warriors into the afterlife.

He sat beside her, and they looked at the desolation before them. Xantho wished Wulfgar was amongst the fallen, but he was nowhere to be seen. Xantho was unsure how many men he had killed or maimed, but they deserved it. Or so he told himself. They would have done the same to him if they'd had the chance.

"Are the others alright?"

"Yes, I think so. Now let's find the traitors," said Xantho.

He wanted to go immediately. He wanted to find Wulfgar, even if he had to ride or march all night.

SEVENTEEN

The Warriors of the Light searched the destroyed Persian camp for any sign of their old comrades but could find nothing. Injured survivors, mainly those hammered by the rolling trees, limped and hobbled from the site towards the hills in a jagged line. Naram-Sin ordered that they be left to leave unharmed. Those men could play no active part now in the mission to secure Priapus. Xantho had found some freshly roasted meat and bread baked in the campfires, and he broke his fast, looking across at the enormous trees Penelope had uprooted with her mage skill. He had felt the power drain from him like water from a bucket as she channelled her strength into that massive effort. It had been a shocking and devastating way to deal with the Persian light cavalrymen. As he chewed at some still-warm bread, Xantho wondered what he would have thought if he had seen that feat a week ago.

Or rather, a week ago in time as he knew it. He would have thought Penelope was a god here on Earth; surely only they could wield such power.

Xantho couldn't help but come back to Wulfgar. There was no satisfaction in the victory over the Persian enemy here without Wulfgar. For Xantho, it wasn't about the wars between Enlil and Nergal, Naram-Sin and Gula'an, or Alexander and Darius. It was about making Wulfgar pay for what he had done to Tiki. He got up, took a sip from his waterskin and popped the last bite of a strip of warm meat into his mouth. He looked for the others and saw Penelope deep in conversation with Siduri, Khensa, and Idari. Naram-Sin stood with Khamudi looking out to the south beyond the pines, and Banya was collecting up short, throwing spears from the camp detritus, and had a bundle tucked under one arm.

As always, Xantho approached Naram-Sin and Khamudi, giving Banya a wide berth. He was too tired and angry to suffer sly comments or put-downs from Banya.

"Naram-Sin," Xantho said as he came up behind the Akkadian and Egyptian. They turned, and Khamudi smiled at him. Naram-Sin gave him a slow nod in greeting. "Shall I collect our horses, then we can be on our way?" They had left their mounts hobbled beyond the forest and in a defile, unseen from the forest's edge. The way Xantho saw it, the sooner they got the horses, the sooner they could get after Wulfgar.

"Yes," Naram-Sin answered. Xantho nodded and made to leave. "Xantho," Naram-Sin said, and Xantho turned back to him. "Well fought."

Xantho nodded again in thanks and continued. He allowed himself a little smile, and pride swelled in his chest. It wasn't often Naram-Sin gave praise, but hearing it made Xantho walk a little straighter. He supposed he had fought well. First, he'd made the bow shot to kill and silence the sentry, and then he had fought as well as the others in the attack on the camp, he dared say. Banya had certainly not outfought him. Of course, Penelope had made the difference, but for once, Xantho was confident he had played his part. He made his way over to the mages, who dipped their heads to him in greeting.

"Penelope, will you help me retrieve our mounts?" he said. She nodded her assent and smiled a farewell to the other mages.

Xantho and Penelope walked in silence until they had cleared the pine forest. The morning was rising, the sun's bright disk had risen fully beyond the distant horizon, and Xantho felt its warmth on his face. The journey was not as far as the trek they had made in the darkness. In the night, they had marched in a wide arc to come up behind the Persians, assuming correctly that most of their lookouts would watch away from the forest for any pursuing Macedonians. Penelope and Xantho could now walk in a straight line. Once they were clear of the wood, the going became easier underfoot. No risk of tripping on fallen branches or pine cones.

"Have you recovered your strength?" he asked her. She had been completely wiped out following the fight in the forest. She raised her Palmstone, which glowed and swirled in translucent green.

"Yes, I'm fine now," she said. "I couldn't believe how tired I was after... well..."

Xantho checked his own Palmstone, which now also flourished with colour once more. "What you did was unbelievable. Do you think you could do it again?"

She shrugged. "I don't know, but I think so. The others, Siduri and the rest, say I must have power over plants and trees. They each have a special gift, water or fire or whatever."

"Let's hope there are lots of trees everywhere we fight," Xantho said, and she gave a short quiet laugh. "Why trees? Did you have anything to do with plants in your old life?"

"No, I was just a slave. I tended to my masters, washed, cleaned, and served. They had gardeners at my master's estate, but I knew nothing of that job."

"Another question without an answer."

They smiled at each other and walked for a while in silence. The horses came into view as they reached the lip of the defile.

"Things are so different now," she whispered. She had left her helmet at the battle site and let her hair down. He had not noticed before, but its light brown colour also had copper running through it. Walking towards the sun with her hair moving slightly in the breeze and her green eyes bright and clever, Xantho thought she was beautiful. In a different world, maybe, in a world where there was peace, he might have entertained such thoughts. His mouth was dry as he looked at her, and he found himself unable to get words out to reply.

"We are part of this war, of two wars. Before, we were nothing. Now we have to defeat Gula'an and the traitors. Do you feel better as we are now or in your old life?" she said.

"The warriors of the dark," he replied.

"What?"

"That's what we should call them, the traitors. We are the Warriors of the Light; they are the warriors of the dark." She laughed again, brushing her hair behind her ears.

"I feel…well…different now," said Xantho. He felt full of purpose. They had gifted him power from the gods, and he had a war to fight. When he was a slave, he had never thought of his life in terms of happiness or sadness; he just was. He simply did his duties. When he met and married Lithra, he had been happy, he thought. Now he just felt determined. Xantho had to get better with his weapons, and he had to kill Wulfgar. The rest, he would think about that afterwards.

"Different good or different bad?" asked Penelope.

"A bit of both, I think."

They gathered the horses together, roped them into a line, and rode back towards the pine forest. Once there, Naram-Sin brought the group together. The Akkadian had received a cut to his forehead, and his armour was dented and scraped. Nevertheless, he still looked calm, his face as ageless and expressionless as ever.

"It's safe to say we have completed the first part of our task. This band won't be bothering the advancing infantry again. Now we make for Priapus. If we encounter the enemy, we will engage. Once we get within sight of the town, we'll join up with Hephaestion again."

The orders were as clear and straightforward as always, and so the Warriors of the Light mounted and began the ride towards Priapus. Xantho found himself at the column's rear, and Idari held back to ride alongside him. He eyed her cautiously as she fell in beside him. They had never really spoken to one another. Idari was Banya's mage, so Xantho avoided her as he avoided Banya. He assumed she thought, just as Banya did, that Xantho was incompetent and had no place amongst the Warriors of the Light. Her joining him now made Xantho fidget in the saddle. He pulled at the neck of his armour to let some air behind it.

"Penelope is amazing, no?" Idari said, eventually. She was a tall woman, almost as tall as Xantho and the same height as Banya. She was slim and kept her black hair cut tight to her scalp. Her face was open and warm. He hadn't noticed that before. She smiled at him, and Xantho relaxed a little.

"She seems to be powerful. Do you think she is?" Xantho asked.

"Yes, very powerful. Beautiful, too, no?" Xantho felt his cheeks flush, and Idari laughed long and loud.

"It is hard to join with Siduri and Naram-Sin. I remember when it first happened to Banya and me. It's difficult to understand what is happening to you. How can we die and live again? How can we have this magic? How can we understand and speak new languages? Too much for a person to get to grips with."

"It is hard," Xantho replied. "How long have you and Banya been with Naram-Sin?"

"Too long," she said and laughed loudly again, tipping her head back. "Many hundreds of years. But that is but a fragment in the lifetime of he and Siduri."

"Do you always die in battle?" he asked her. As she spoke of the time they had lived and fought with the Warriors of the Light, it occurred to Xantho that they might not always die in battle. What if they won the battle they were waging against Gula'an and survived?

"No. But to be honest, it is better that way. Banya and I have lived many long lifetimes together, growing old. Then we die and wake up for the next battle, young and powerful again," Idari answered. Her face lost some of its warmth, and she looked deep into Xantho's eyes. "Sometimes death is a blessing."

"Are you still, well… together or married, or…" he pried. The brightness came back to Idari, and she grinned.

"Yes, of course. How could my Banya find another woman when he has this?" she said and laughed. Xantho laughed too, and it felt good.

"You could be the same, you and Penelope. No?"

Xantho's face flushed scarlet again. He knew it did, but he couldn't stop it. Penelope was pretty. There was no doubt about that. But she was also extraordinarily powerful and had a cold and vicious side. Besides, how could she be interested in him, a buffoon still trying not to cock things up every time he drew his blade or bow?

"There's no time for that," he said, keeping his eyes away from Idari's in case she got a sense of how he suddenly now felt about Penelope. "Did you suspect the others would turn on Naram-Sin?" he asked, changing the subject.

"Never," she said and spat to the side of the horse. "I do not understand it. They must be here if Wulfgar is. They must serve Nergal with the same power as when they served mighty Enlil. We will see. Banya is driven mad with his desire for vengeance."

"Is he kind to you?"

"Banya? Yes, of course," Idari sighed, smiling softly at Xantho. "He has been hard on you, I see it. Banya worries, for me, for the others. No matter that we die to rise again, to see the one you love die is just as painful every time. He is driven to win this war. He will come around."

Xantho smiled thinly and nodded. He hoped so. He couldn't take much more of the African warrior's barbs. They rode a while longer in silence, and then from behind a distant nest of shallow hills rose a town, yellow and hazy in the far distance. Priapus.

Priapus was not the great town Xantho had imagined it would be. In his mind's eye, he'd pictured it as a high-walled town of shining domes, buzzing with merchants and trade. Looking at it now, however, it was nothing more than a gathering of mud-brick single and double-story buildings, with one larger structure at the centre, visible above the clutch of smaller buildings. Around the town was a starched and crumbling mud-brick wall, which, from his vantage point at the peak of a valley, looked to be only as tall as the height of a man. Xantho knew it was not the size or wealth of the town that Alexander valued but the availability of water. The town contained a large well, used by the townspeople and travellers alike, and Priapus was more of a large trading post and stopover point for caravans and travellers than a town proper. Besides the well, a small brook bubbled and bounced its way around Priapus, winding lazily away into the distance.

The Warriors of the Light had reached the town in the mid-afternoon. It was a clear day, with only a light dusting of cloud across the pale blue sky. Xantho stared hard at the town, almost in a daze. Wulfgar was there; he could feel it. He could feel it just as you can feel someone staring at you in a crowd or if someone is behind you on a dark night. What to do it about it, though? That was the challenge somersaulting inside Xantho's head.

There was no sight of the enemy at Priapus. There were a few sentries on the walls but nothing to suggest any sizeable force in there. Priapus was so small that if there were any over five hundred or a thousand warriors, it would force them to camp outside its walls. Naram-Sin had ordered Xantho and the others to stay where they were, overlooking the town. He, Siduri, Khamudi and Khensa rode off in search of the Macedonian Companion cavalry or the other scouting squadrons.

Being stuck with Banya was not a prospect Xantho relished, so he left the others to brush down the horses and put together some food. He kept watch over the town. Little happened. The sentries walked along the walls, unaware of the forces marshalling against them. Xantho had his bow across his back and a quiver full of arrows hanging from his belt. On his left side was the kopis blade. He had kept the Phrygian cap-style cavalry helmet on, and though it was dirty and sweaty, he had not taken off his linothorax armour.

"Riders!" Penelope shouted from behind him. Xantho glanced to his right and saw a long line of cavalry riding across the crest of hills. He looked back at Priapus. The sentries had stopped their patrol, and he could hear the distant shouts of alarm being raised. The riders came on at a gentle pace. It was a long column of large warhorses flanked by a column of shorter light cavalry ponies, similar to the mare Xantho rode. Banya stood and came to stand beside Xantho and waved at the riders.

"Looks like the rest of the cavalry units," he

said. Xantho waited for the sly look or some dig about his lack of battle skill, but none came. Banya pulled his neck scarf up to cover his dark face, leaving only his eyes visible behind his helmet. The riders wheeled left in front of Xantho and spread out their line before dismounting and tending to their animals. Xantho tried to tally them but lost count at forty. He guessed there were at least two hundred cavalrymen. The sheer volume of horses kicked up a dry cloud of grit and dust, and Xantho coughed, pulling up his own neck scarf to protect his mouth and nose. His ears rang with the din of hoofbeats and jangling of horse tack. Eventually, three riders came towards Xantho and Banya and dismounted. One stepped forward, who was no older than Xantho, maybe twenty summers. He was short with a sun-darkened face.

"Amyntas, commander of Companion cavalry," he said in a brusque, dry voice.

"Xantho, scout," he wasn't sure what rank or name to give himself. Banya stayed silent, but he brought his fist to his chest and bowed his head in a salute, so Xantho followed suit.

"No sign of the enemy then?" Amyntas asked.

"Not here. We engaged a large force half a day's ride from here," said Xantho.

"Yes, I met your captain. He follows and will be here shortly."

"Do you have orders, lord?" asked Banya.

Amyntas eyed the African for a minute, squinting as he regarded Banya's dark skin, which was highly unusual for the Macedonian army.

"Not yet. If we are sure there is no enemy here in force, I will approach the town and ask for their surrender. So, for now, take care of your horses and be ready in case this is some sort of honey trap," Amyntas said.

Another rider came up from the column's rear and reined in ten paces away from Xantho, Banya, and Amyntas. He removed his helmet and ran his fingers through a shaggy mane of chestnut hair.

"Socrates," Amyntas said in greeting.

Socrates saluted Amyntas and took a drink from a waterskin. "No sign of Memnon's soldiers anywhere. No infantry or cavalry. Seems they have all dropped back to Zeleia."

"Do they burn crops and farms as they go?" asked Amyntas.

"No, my scouts report no burning. Just a retreat. Seems Priapus is on its own. No enemy around to spring a trap on us," Socrates replied.

Amyntas nodded and scratched at his clean-shaven chin. "Very well. Rest your horse and meet me here shortly. You are a captain of scouts, and I hold commander rank. We can ask for their surrender."

"And if they refuse?" said Socrates. Amyntas looked at him and shrugged.

"Then we swarm their shitty walls and butcher them. Hephaestion will be here before nightfall."

Naram-Sin returned shortly after, and he, Amyntas, and Socrates agreed to approach the gates together. A force of one hundred cavalrymen would accompany them twenty paces behind, just in case the enemy were unseen and poured out of the gate. Xantho formed part of that force with the rest of the Warriors of the Light. He rode between Penelope and Khamudi. They were under orders to keep silent in the line whilst the senior officers requested surrender from the town.

The three leaders marched to within thirty paces of the town and then halted, which Xantho thought was risky. Any archer on those walls would have them shot down in a heartbeat. But no missiles came. All stayed still and quiet, save the ponies in the line, pawing at the ground, blowing and neighing. Then, after what seemed like an age to Xantho, the twin timber gates of Priapus opened up. They creaked on their hinges, and within the gates, all was shadowed by the walls and buildings behind, so Xantho couldn't see inside. For a moment, his heart raced. *What if the Persians come charging out and overwhelm us?*

A party of ten men in flowing robes

emerged from the town and walked towards the Macedonian captains. On the walls of Priapus, dozens of heads appeared above the parapet. They bobbed and reappeared like flotsam on the ride.

"Good afternoon, my lords. How can we help you?" came a bright and friendly voice from a corpulent man at the centre of the Priapus delegation.

"We are here on the orders of Alexander of Macedon. He approaches with thousands of men. We give you this chance to surrender your town to his rule or face annihilation," Amyntas declared. Xantho was expecting a long and tedious diplomatic discourse before they got to the crux of the matter, but it seemed Amyntas had other ideas. The delegation also seemed taken aback and looked at one another, their feet shuffling.

"I see you speak plainly, my lord," said the portly man. "Can you allow us some time to consider your…proposal?"

"No," Amyntas asserted immediately. "Decide now."

The portly town burgher leant forward and looked down his line of dignitaries. One man, who had remained hooded so far, took half a step forward and pulled down his hood. Xantho's hand shot to his kopis. It was Wulfgar, grinning under his long blonde hair.

"Very well, we will surrender the town," he said in his guttural accent. "But before we do, I want to talk to him. Alone." He pointed at Naram-Sin.

Amyntas and Socrates both looked at Naram-Sin, but he nodded his assent. Amyntas shrugged.

"You have until we retrieve our horses and bring them to the stream here," Amyntas gestured to the thin babbling brook on the opposite side of the town. "Then two hundred of us will enter the town."

The burgher bowed deeply from the waist, and the delegation from Priapus withdrew, as did Amyntas and Socrates. Naram-Sin stayed where he was, facing Wulfgar. Xantho's blood boiled. He clenched his teeth and gripped his kopis so hard his knuckles turned white.

It was impossible to hear their discussion amongst the tumult of retreating Macedonian cavalry. Xantho seethed, his mare becoming skittish, sensing his anger. Wulfgar was within striking distance.

EIGHTEEN

"What are they saying?" Xantho said, craning his neck to hear the exchange between Naram-Sin and Wulfgar.

"Be calm," growled Khamudi next to him.

How can I be calm? Wulfgar was there, and Xantho could be upon him, blade in hand, before Wulfgar even knew what hit him.

"How are they talking so gently to one another after all that's happened?" said Xantho.

"Xantho, calm down," Penelope urged.

"We all want vengeance on Wulfgar and the others," said Khamudi, "but now is not the time. For now, we just need Priapus."

"Not the time? It's a perfect time; he is right there."

"You want him dead because of Tiki," said Penelope, and Xantho stared at her. "It won't bring Tiki back if you kill Wulfgar. It won't make it better."

"It will," Xantho protested. It would make it better, or at least he hoped it would.

"It won't make you feel better for taking Tiki from the camp. Or for…" she said.

So, she did blame him; she had let it slip. But no more than he blamed himself.

"Or for what?" he said. Penelope pushed her shoulders back, and her jaw jutted.

"You shouldn't make me say it. Just stay here and be quiet, Xantho."

"Or for what?" he demanded again. This time, Xantho raised his voice. His teeth were grinding now, and he held the mare's reins tight in his fists.

"Alright then," she said, setting her jaw. "It won't make you feel better or take away the fact that you brought Tiki into danger and that you had a chance to kill Wulfgar, yet you didn't. Instead, you let him go." Penelope's eyes blazed at him, and Xantho's heart sank in his chest. A lump rose in his throat, but he swallowed it down. He dug his heels into the mare, and she sprang forward.

"No!" shouted Khamudi behind him. It was too late. Xantho rode towards where Wulfgar and Naram-Sin spoke. He drew his kopis and reined in beside them, his horse pawing her hooves at the ground.

"What are you doing?" said Naram-Sin, looking aghast that Xantho had dared intervene in the parlay.

"It's the pup. Have you no manners pup? Your betters are talking. Run along, slave, and wash Naram-Sin's underclothes," Wulfgar said, chuckling.

"You are a traitor, a murderous traitor," Xantho snarled through clenched teeth, blade still in hand.

"Oh, we are all murderers. The great and noble Naram-Sin here has killed people beyond count. Now put your blade away before I take offence." Wulfgar said, becoming serious.

"Get back to the others," ordered Naram-Sin, but Xantho had eyes only on Wulfgar.

"You killed the boy with your spear. Fight me now, just you and I," Xantho said.

"How low you have fallen, Naram-Sin, King of the Four Quarters, King of the Universe. God of Akkad. Running with slaves and cowards like a beggar," Wulfgar scowled, dripping spite. Then quick as a whip, he knelt and thrust his arms forward. Naram-Sin flew five paces backwards, and the force of hot air launched Xantho from his horse, clattering him to the hard-packed earth.

Xantho clawed at his chest. The fall had

knocked the wind out of him, and his lungs were an empty cavern desperate for breath. He rolled to his side, gasping. A boot pressed hard on his shoulder, pinning him back, and Wulfgar's face loomed above Xantho, grinning.

"You think you can fight me? I could have been a king amongst my people. You who are nothing but a slave, a dog, the bottom dregs of what Enlil can muster in his last days?" Wulfgar clenched his fist, and Xantho felt his throat squeeze as though strangled by iron hands. Xantho grabbed his neck, writhing; he couldn't breathe, and he felt his face turn red. He was panicking, unsure how to stop the magic. Agi must be somewhere close by, but she was nowhere in sight. Then, suddenly, he heard movement behind him.

"Take one step, Naram-Sin, and I'll burst him open like an overripe melon," Wulfgar hissed.

Xantho felt the darkness creeping across his vision, and his limbs became weak. *I am dying.* He lashed out with his leg, and it connected with nothing. Wulfgar knelt over him.

"As you die, dog, know I will kill all of your friends. I will take your Greek bitch for my bed slave. I killed your little boyfriend and enjoyed it when my spear took his life. He died screaming like a pig," Wulfgar laughed again.

Xantho could hear horses approaching behind him. It must be the Warriors of the Light, but they wouldn't get there in time. Xantho closed his eyes. Give me power, Penelope; give me strength. Maybe she was too far away. The pain in his throat grew less. The dark swamped him. *Maybe it's all over. Death is here for me. Will I wake again?* Suddenly, a surge of energy flashed like a lightning bolt into his heart. It surged around his body, flushing his arms and legs with power. Xantho's eyes shot open, and the strangling ceased, thrown off by his new mage-induced strength.

Xantho twisted at the hip, remembering Khamudi's wrestling lessons; he spun and grabbed Wulfgar's leg. The Northman cried out as he fell to the ground. Xantho twisted the leg viciously into a lock and smiled as the bones crunched. Wulfgar screamed out, pawing at Xantho.

"Naram-Sin! You gave your word!" he cried.

Xantho reached for his kopis but felt a hand on his shoulder.

"Let him go, Xantho," said Naram-Sin.

Xantho ignored him and grasped his blade.

"I said let him go. He has my word he can leave; we have the town. That is the price."

"What?"

"Let him go, now," Naram-Sin commanded.

Xantho released Wulfgar, and he twisted away, crawling back towards Priapus.

Xantho slammed his fist into the ground and glared at Naram-Sin.

"There will come a time to fight him. But, for now, our objective is Priapus," said Naram-Sin, and he stalked off.

Penelope and Khamudi rode to where Xantho sat in the dirt.

"You could have died," Penelope said from the back of her horse.

What would you care if I did? He watched Wulfgar crawling back towards Priapus. Two men dashed from the gates and dragged him inside. Xantho spat into the dirt. At least he had struck a blow against the traitor. Penelope peered down at him, but Xantho couldn't meet her gaze, not after what she had said. She blamed him for Tiki's death, just as he blamed himself.

As promised, the town burghers opened the gates to Priapus, and Amyntas led the long column down the gentle hillside and towards the brook. He then led a company on foot into the town to secure it and scour it for any hidden enemy. The takeover of the town happened without incident. The inhabitants were mainly merchants or locals who ran businesses such as stables, lodgings for travellers, and taverns. Hephaestion arrived with the Agrianians in the late afternoon, and they set about making the town more secure with a ditch and palisade on the side facing towards Zeleia. Hephaestion allowed the scouts the rest of that day for rest, but at sunrise, Socrates was to lead his scouts out into the lands to the south and west to scout for Memnon and report on the ground between Priapus and Zeleia.

Xantho marched into Priapus with the others but kept himself distant. His throat ached from where Wulfgar had throttled him, and he felt a sense of failure that he had met the Northman one-on-one and had failed to defeat his enemy because he had needed to follow orders. They found a table at a tavern on the southwest side of the town just before the place became thronged with the rough and boisterous Agrianian infantrymen. Naram-Sin, Siduri and the others found a shaded table and ate a meal of fresh loaves and roasted lamb. Xantho took his plate outside and sat on the wall alone. He was astonished that Naram-Sin had allowed Wulfgar to walk away after all he had done. There was no sign of the Northman in the town. He had obviously fled somehow as the Macedonians entered the town. Xantho hoped he had broken the bastard's leg and that it pained him horrendously. He overheard the soldiers in the tavern talking about the army's arrival. They were due in the next day or so, and Alexander himself would be here. They boasted of the tremendous battle to come and how they would perform great deeds of heroism and bring the Persian tyrants to heel.

THE CURSE OF NARAM-SIN

Xantho ate his meal and lay the plate beside him on the ground. He sat with his back to the tavern fence in the shade of an awning the owner had erected to shield his patrons from the sun. He jumped in surprise as a body slumped down beside him; it was Penelope.

"Here, it's watered wine. It's good," Penelope said, handing him a battered-looking clay cup. He took it and had a sip, but he didn't look at her. She was right; it was good. Slightly bitter on his tongue but refreshing. Xantho rubbed his eyes and yawned. He just wanted to sleep and rest. So much had happened, and there had been no time to think or understand this new war he found himself in. Magic, dying, jumping hundreds of years and awakening in a strange land. Then Tiki. Part of Xantho wished he was still a slave; more of him wished he was his younger self with Lithra. Life was simple then. He had his duties, as had she. They were together, and it was enough. His life now was complicated and dangerous. They had to win the war with Gula'an, or the world would be plunged into never-ending war and death. *Could the pressure be any greater?*

"Xantho, I'm sorry. For what I said, I..." Penelope began. Xantho groaned and pushed himself to his feet.

"I'm tired," he said and walked away from the tavern. Penelope came running up beside him.

"It wasn't your fault," she said, grabbing his

arm. He spun around to look at her, angry and ready to shout. She should be on his side. They should be a team; they could get Wulfgar together. But when he saw her eyes, green and wide and sorry, the anger left him. He nodded slowly.

"A coin for an old man," came a cracked and shallow voice from across the narrow street. Xantho and Penelope turned to see an aged fellow there. He wore a wide-brimmed hat with his head bowed, and his robes were threadbare. Xantho crossed to him and handed the beggar what remained of his wine.

"Here, grandfather, some wine," he said. Penelope came to stand next to him. The old man took the wine with a shaky hand and drained the cup. He threw it to the ground, where it rolled away into the camber of the hard-packed street. The old man pulled his hat away and looked up, grinning. His teeth were pure white and shone beneath a long beard. That beard was as white as bone bleached by the sun, and his face was ancient yet unlined, ethereal, like Naram-Sin and Siduri. His eyes were grey, and his brows as white as his beard. He was no beggar. He was as tall as Xantho and as lean as a wolf.

"Gula'an," hissed Penelope, and she sprang back, lifting her arms as though to work her mage power upon him. He chuckled and raised a finger, pinning her arms where they were.

"Now, now. I just want to talk to you, that's all. No need for all that. Just a few words," he said, smiling. Penelope relented and nodded. Xantho stared at Gula'an, mouth wide open. *How is he here in broad daylight?* The sheer brazenness of him to be in Priapus, alone and surrounded by Macedonian soldiers.

"So, you are Naram-Sin's latest recruits. I remember you gave me a cut to the face. I saw you both die by the river. How are you finding the eternal war?" he grinned widely. Xantho noticed that the cut he had inflicted on Gula'an's face had strangely left no scar.

"We are Warriors of the Light, you are evil, and…" Penelope said defiantly, but Gula'an threw his head back and belly laughed.

"Warriors of the Light, is it? How quaint. And I am evil? Who told you that? Naram-Sin? Siduri?"

"Yes, Naram-Sin," said Xantho.

"Did he tell you how the war started?"

Xantho shook his head slowly and glanced at Penelope. She was glaring at Gula'an but didn't seem to be in any hurry to attack again or to flee. Xantho sensed the opportunity to get some answers. *Yes, this is the great enemy…he hasn't attacked us, though. What harm could it do to probe him for information even if the information he gives is biased to his cause?*

"No, he hasn't," Xantho admitted.

"Ah," said Gula'an, stroking his beard with long thin fingers. In his other hand, he clutched the tall ebony staff with which he had wrought such devastation on the battlefield against Cyrus. Now, here before him, Xantho thought it quite plain, just a walking stick.

"Naram-Sin is of Akkad, and I am a Gutian. Thousands of years ago, when the world was but young, he was a great king and conqueror—like your Alexander. But Naram-Sin was the most bloodthirsty battle conqueror the world had ever seen and the grandson of Sargon the Great. Naram-Sin stole my daughter, made war upon the gods, and washed the world with blood. Did he tell you any of that?"

"Your daughter?" said Penelope.

"Yes, Siduri. My eldest daughter," Gula'an's eyes twinkled below his white brows, and a strange bitter smile played at the corner of his mouth. "Stolen from me by Naram-Sin. He who smashed the link between the gods and men, he who made this eternal war. You should ask him or her about that."

"Why are you here? Why are you saying these things?" demanded Penelope. She glanced at Xantho, her hands on her hips. He didn't know what to say. *Is Gula'an saying Naram-Sin started this war with the gods? He must be lying, trying to trick us. Siduri could never be his daughter.*

"You must be sure who is good and who is evil," said Gula'an. "Is it ever so black and white? Do the Persians think Alexander is evil? Do the Macedonians believe Darius is evil? Who is right? It all depends on what side you are on."

"We must stop you, or you will plunge the world into a never-ending war," Xantho insisted.

Gula'an laughed again. "Is it not already? How does your Alexander stop that? Is he not a warmonger himself? I am going to give you both a chance, a chance to be on the right side of things." He fixed them with his ancient eyes, boring deep into Xantho's skull. So penetrating was that look that it gave Xantho a headache, making his brain creak and crumple. Xantho winced.

"I give you both one chance to join me, to join your old friends, and help us defeat Alexander, the warmonger. Help me stop Naram-Sin and bury his curse into the earth forever."

"Join you, Wulfgar, and those other traitor scum? Never!" Xantho roared, leaping backwards, hand on his kopis. Penelope shook her head and stood with Xantho.

"Very well." The mirth and affability fled from Gula'an, his face becoming sharp and twisted with hate, his grey eyes flushing and changing to pitiless, deep flints of obsidian. "I curse you both. When you die, when I take your heads, you will go screaming to the underworld. You will burn there for eternity like the slaves that you are. I promise you that I will drag your family's souls there to join you, all the people you loved in your old lives; I will cast them burning and screaming for all time in the domain of Nergal."

He was roaring now, and Xantho realised that he and Penelope had fallen to their knees in the face of his hate and power. A voice came from Xantho's left, but he couldn't make it out. Suddenly the furnace of Gula'an's threat vanished, and Xantho crumpled to the ground. As his eyes closed and he succumbed to the darkness, Xantho promised himself that he must be more ruthless. He must devote himself entirely to this war. The horror he had seen in Gula'an's eyes was like nothing Xantho had ever seen before. Gula'an must be stopped. The thought of his mother, of dear Lithra burning in the underworld, was too much to bear. Just as he fell into darkness, he remembered Gula'an's words. The curse of Naram-Sin, his daughter…

NINETEEN

Xantho awoke with a start. He jerked up onto his elbows and searched around him frantically through bleary eyes. His heart was racing, and his breath came short and quick. Once he realised Gula'an was not there before him, he lowered himself back to lying flat and used the technique Khamudi had taught him to calm himself with slow deep breaths from the stomach. He counted ten breaths and brought himself back to a state of placidity.

He opened his eyes. Above him, darkened timber beams stretched across a low ceiling; he felt crisp, dry straw beneath his hands where they rested at his sides. His senses swarmed with the smell of horse and dung. Xantho was in a stable. He could hear the gentle noises of horses breathing and snuffling somewhere out of his sight. He was still alive. Xantho swallowed, and his stomach twisted as the vision of Gula'an and the black pit of his eyes flashed into Xantho's memory. He had seemed so gentle and honest at first. He had asked Xantho and Penelope to join him, but his true colours had shone through in the end, in all their visceral horror. Xantho shot up onto his elbows again.

"Penelope," he called. Xantho waited, but there was no answer. He rolled onto his side and rose to his feet. He was wearing only his chiton. Xantho saw they had propped his armour against the stable wall along with his weapons. Xantho staggered slightly, but he got himself upright. He wasn't hurt, just groggy from sleep.

"Penelope," he said again. Still nothing. He moved out of the stall he had slept in. Siduri came towards him, smiling. She, too, did not have her armour on. Siduri moved with her usual rhythmic grace, tall and slender, her bare feet crunching on the straw strewn across the stable floor. Xantho took a few steps back from her.

"I see you are recovered, Xantho," she chimed, smiling. The smile creased Siduri's ageless face, softening the hard angles of her jaw and cheekbones. She was Gula'an's daughter. *How could they have kept that from us?* Xantho edged away again, and his back bumped into an upright timber, stopping him dead. "Here, take a drink." Siduri held out a waterskin. Xantho regarded it warily, then looked into her grey eyes. Those same ancient pools as Naram-Sin's and the same grey as Gula'an's eyes had been in the early part of their encounter. Xantho's head was spinning; he wasn't sure what was truth, half-truth, or lie anymore. Gula'an had said that Naram-Sin was the cause of this war, that he had made war upon the gods. Suddenly Xantho wasn't sure if he was fighting on the side of good or evil.

"What is it, Xantho? A drink will help," Siduri said, still smiling.

He took the skin and lifted it to his lips. The water was cooling as it sloshed down his throat. Xantho poured some into his hand and splashed his face.

"Where is Penelope? Is she alright?" he said.

"Yes, she sleeps there, see?" Siduri said and pointed to the stable stall next to where Xantho had slept. Sure enough, Penelope was there, sleeping peacefully. Xantho let out a sigh of relief. "You two had quite the ordeal."

"Yes, we did. Gula'an is fearsome. His eyes... his hate gave off heat. It was unbearable," Xantho murmured.

Siduri's smile faded. "We must leave soon. Hephaestion orders us to scout ahead of the army. Alexander will be here today," she said. "Are you well enough to ride?"

Xantho nodded his head and took another drink. "Gula'an spoke to us...before he showed his malice."

"What did he say?"

Xantho paused, unsure if telling her all that Gula'an had said was a wise thing to do. Yet he resolved to get it out in the open. He needed answers. "He said Naram-Sin was a great and terrible conqueror, that he started the war with the gods. He also said that…well…that you are his daughter." Xantho held his breath.

Siduri sighed and gave Xantho a wan smile. She fumbled with a plait in her long hair. "He was my father all those years ago. Two thousand long years ago. Who would believe such an amount of time is possible? It is so long ago as to be unimaginable. The world was still so young then, Xantho."

"So, it is true. What kind of war are we fighting here? Who are you people?" Xantho said, his voice louder than he had intended.

"We will talk today—you, Penelope, Naram-Sin and I."

He nodded. Penelope stirred, and Xantho went to her, helping her to sit up. She looked as groggy as he had upon waking. He held her hand; it was warm and soft. She shook her head to flick a curly strand of her copper-brown hair from her face.

"What happened? Are we safe?" she asked.

"We are safe. He is gone for now," Xantho

reassured her. She nodded slowly and came up to a seated position. Xantho handed Penelope the waterskin, and she drank deeply, the water glugging and her throat pulsing as the liquid entered her body.

"I am glad to see you well," said Siduri. We will talk. Come outside when you are ready.

Xantho put on his armour, lifting the heavy linen, linothorax breastplate over his head and fastening the bulky shoulder straps. He fixed the leather kilt around his waist, along with the belt. His kopis blade was shining and sharp, held safe within its fleece-lined scabbard, and Xantho attached it to his belt, along with the quiver of arrows. Then, slinging his Cretan bow across his back, he went outside.

Penelope stood there, also now fully dressed, and leaning against the wall were Naram-Sin and Siduri. Penelope took a few small steps towards Xantho, and he moved to stand next to her, the closeness already lifting the unease in his belly. Naram-Sin stood.

"So, Gula'an confronted you. You have seen the face of the enemy," he said in his deep voice. He was a hand taller than Xantho, and his short hair glinted in the sunlight. Naram-Sin had his war axe tucked into his belt, a xiphos blade at his waist, and a pair of cavalryman spears rested against the stable wall beside him.

"He was just right there, in the street," said

Penelope, her gravelly voice higher pitched than usual. After she had spoken, she licked her lips and looked from Siduri to Naram-Sin.

"He fled after you fell unconscious," Siduri told them. "He tried to turn you?"

"He did, and then he threatened us with horrible power. Also, he said things… about you," Penelope uttered.

"I know. So now we will tell you about our lives, before this war, in distant Akkad," said Siduri.

"I think you owe us that," Penelope replied, crossing her arms and jutting her chin.

Naram-Sin nodded slowly. "I was born two thousand years ago. My grandfather was Sargon the Great, the first emperor the world had ever seen. Sargon conquered the Sumerians, who were great kings of the first cities, stretching back into the times when the gods themselves walked the Earth just as we do now. In my time, I was King Akkad, King of Sumer, and King of the Four Corners of the World. My pride and ambition and thirst for conquest knew no bounds. I was King of the Universe. The world was smaller then; we knew nothing of the distant east or any of the countries west beyond your Greece."

"In those distant times, there were few cities," said Siduri. "There was Sumer, Akkad, Babylon. The rest of the world was filled with vicious and primal tribes, war, and darkness. In Sumer, there first came the light of knowledge, handed down to people by Enlil, the father of the gods. Enlil granted knowledge of building, writing, knowledge of the stars, and knowledge of the gods. In those days, gods and men were so close that Enlil built a bridge between heaven and Earth. It sat on a mountaintop in Sumer and was named the Ekur. That bridge to the heavens was a temple where one could commune with the gods themselves. They were such glorious times when the world was bright and new."

Xantho looked at Penelope, and she stood open-mouthed, just as he did, listening to this tale of Naram-Sin.

"Great and vast were my armies," said Naram-Sin, "and our blades were drenched with the blood of our enemies until the whole of the civilised world was under my dominion. I craved power and dominion over all the peoples of the world. Men called me 'God of Akkad', and I allowed it, revelling at that name in my hubris. All fell to my blade but one tribe. The Gutians. The Gutians were a savage and wild mountain tribe of vast numbers, a collection of hundreds of tribes ruled by one chief. That chief had a daughter; she was the most beautiful woman that ever walked the Earth, or ever will."

Xantho's eyes widened as he saw Naram-Sin reach for Siduri's hand, and she took it. They looked into each other's eyes, and Xantho saw love there. A deep love, almost too deep for him to understand. He and Lithra had been in love, he thought, but what passed between Naram-Sin and Siduri at that moment was something more, a bond stronger than time and death. Xantho could almost feel the power of it.

"The Gutians were the last tribe yet to fall to my armies, so I attacked them with all my vast forces. The war raged for two years, a dirty war on high mountainsides, and rock-strewn valleys, filled with ambush and slaughter. Then, one day I caught sight of the Gutian chief's daughter, a beautiful woman who was said to have magical abilities. She saw me too, and we have never been apart from that day to this," said Naram-Sin.

"Wait, so Gula'an was the chief, and you were his daughter?" asked Penelope.

"It was so," Siduri nodded.

"Did you take her from her father?" Xantho asked.

Siduri smiled again. "No. He was the greatest and most noble of men, the King of the World. I saw Lord Naram-Sin and went with him of my own accord. Then he broke off the assault on my people, we went back to Akkad together, and the war was over."

"You left the Gutians alone?" said Xantho.

"Yes, we went to Akkad. To be together. Siduri

was a mage even then," Naram-Sin answered.

"What about the curse?" Penelope pressed. She had her hands by her side now, and a shock fizzed up Xantho's arm as she took his hand in hers.

"The war with the Gutians was over, but my pride and hubris still burned," said Naram-Sin. "The people called me 'God of Akkad'. So, I made war upon the gods, determined to exert my dominance on even the heavens. I plundered the Ekur, Enlil's temple, and his link between gods and men. I sacked and destroyed that sacred place, separating us from the gods for all time. That is my great crime, for which I can never be forgiven. I tried to conquer the heavens and severed our earthly link with the gods forever when I destroyed the Ekur. Then, as my pride knew no bounds, I marched once again on the Gutians, who remained the only tribe I had not yet subjugated. Siduri marched with me against her own people; such was her love for me. And there was a battle such as I hope the world will never see again. We were victorious, but the dead on both sides were beyond count. Blood soaked the land, the laments of the bereaved shook the sky, and souls swelled the realm of the dead," said Naram-Sin. The Akkadian held Xantho's gaze, and all Xantho saw there was sadness, two thousand years of sadness and regret.

"Our crime enraged Enlil," Siduri added. "By

destroying the Ekur, we had unwittingly allowed Nergal, Enlil's son and lord of the underworld, free into the world of men. Empowered by the vast number of souls of the dead Gutians and Akkadians rendered up by our terrible war, swelling his realm, Nergal went to my father, and Gula'an sold his soul to Nergal in bargain for his great wish. My father's one great wish was to destroy Akkad and kill Naram-Sin. Gula'an was consumed by vengeance for the death of so many of his people, for his wife and sons. My own mother and brothers."

"And so it was," said Naram-Sin. "With Nergal's favour and imbued with his strength, Gula'an and the Gutians became powerful beyond measure, and Akkad was destroyed. The magnificent high walls, beautiful lush gardens, and the cool pools within my palace were all torn asunder. Gula'an became a thing of Nergal, and his sons became rulers of the world. Enlil cursed me to live forever, tasked with battling against Nergal and Gula'an for all time to stem the flow of souls into the underworld and stop the dark god from taking over the world. I had unleashed Nergal and destroyed the Ekur, and I must do battle against that dark foe. To my eternal shame, my bride, my love, was cursed along with me." Naram-Sin looked to Siduri, and Xantho thought he saw a tear roll down the Akkadian's cheek.

"And so, it has been, for two thousand long years. We live and die and are brought to life again by mighty Enlil. We are cursed to fight to keep the evil we brought into this world at bay," said Siduri.

Xantho looked and Penelope, and she at him. Their hands still clasped together, hanging between them.

"So, are we, too, cursed?" Penelope asked.

"You are the chosen souls with the potential to wield power. Where it is needed, when our ranks reduce, and the war with Nergal is at risk, Enlil will find such as you to join the fight. Not all have the strength and capacity to be a mage and warrior pair. You do, and we need you if we are to defeat Gula'an," Siduri explained.

"Now, we must ride out. We have orders. We will talk again soon," said Naram-Sin, and he stalked off, picking up his spears as he went.

"It is a lot to take in, I know. But we can talk again. I am sorry," Siduri murmured. She came towards them and placed a gentle hand on each of their shoulders; her face was suddenly drawn, and her eyes wan. "I am sorry for what we did. In far Akkad."

The Warriors of the Light rode out that same day. Priapus was now secure and enabled the marshalling of the Macedonian army before the push towards the great battle that must come with the Persian forces of Darius. The commander of the Persians, Memnon, was still gathering his own forces at his city of Zeleia, where all the satraps of the western Persian Empire were to bring their armies to crush Alexander. Hephaestion ordered the light cavalry scout units, under the command of Socrates, to scour the land between Priapus and Zeleia and report back on enemy movements, formations, and the lay of the land. The Macedonians knew they were outnumbered, especially by cavalry and the dreaded Persian war chariots, and so Hephaestion had ordered the scouts to look for ravines, rivers, and any narrows the army could use to manoeuvre the Persians on to ground favourable to the Macedonian forces.

Naram-Sin had led them out of the town and into the lush green hills and valleys of the western Persian Empire. Xantho rode alongside Penelope, but they had spoken little that day. The story of Naram-Sin and Siduri had shocked him. He could easily see the Akkadian as a king and warlord, but the talk of gods and curses was almost too much to believe. Had Xantho not already become embroiled in this world of warriors and mages and seen and spoken to the god Enlil himself, he would not have believed it. As his mare followed the line ahead, and they wound their way up a set of four hills of differing size, Xantho's thoughts were on that story. He thought of the deep hatred Gula'an must have for Naram-Sin, so intense a hatred that he would sell his eternal soul to the god of the underworld to grant his people victory. He thought of Naram-Sin and his curse. *What a thing to live with, being the man responsible for destroying the link between gods and men.* Xantho also thought of the enduring, powerful love that Siduri and Naram-Sin still held for each other, despite everything, despite all they had done, and all the time that had passed.

Idari's words came back to Xantho, of how she and Banya had lived and grown old together many times between battles with Gula'an. He thought of that, and he thought of Penelope. When they had held hands, he had felt something move in his heart, a feeling he had not experienced since Lithra had died. Penelope must feel something, too. She had reached out for his hand. There was no doubt Penelope was attractive. Her green eyes were dazzling, her hair shining and curled, her skin clear and soft. Xantho had just never allowed himself to notice before. She had been so hard on him since they first met and were thrust into this new life of war and magic. Xantho hoped she felt as he did, sure now that he felt something for her. He watched her riding beside him. She turned and smiled at him, little creases at the corners of her eyes. He smiled back, and he felt warm.

There was no sign of the enemy that first day and they made camp at the summit of a wooded rise and in the cover of a clutch of rocks. Naram-Sin allowed a small fire, and Khamudi had caught a brace of birds to roast. They ate and sat in peace; it was a fine meal. Banya told stories of his homeland and of the strange animals there. Khensa told stories of Egypt and the enormous triangular temples of the gods, which reached the very sky. Xantho ate with Penelope. They listened together and shared glances with one another. Despite the revelations of Gula'an and Naram-Sin, Xantho felt something he had never felt before. He felt part of something; he felt content.

As night fell, and they prepared to lie down and sleep, Naram-Sin stood. The campfire's light flickered on his long face, and his mouth set in a grim, straight line.

"You recall I spoke to Wulfgar at Priapus," Naram-Sin began. "Our old friends will meet us out here, in the field. I let him go to bring that challenge to the others. We must engage and remove them from this war. It's too risky to have them and Gula'an fight in the battle between Alexander and Memnon. Tomorrow, Banya and Xantho will leave early and push hard ahead to the south. Find them. Let us bring their treachery to an end."

The Warriors of the Light exchanged looks

across the firelight. No words were spoken. They must do battle with their old friends. Xantho knew some of them had fought together in battles beyond count across the centuries, yet it must be done. He hoped he would get a chance at Wulfgar. For Tiki. Xantho lay down, using his saddle cloth as a pillow. He lay next to Penelope, and in the clear chill night, beside the warmth of the campfire, he reached for her hand. They lay there, holding each other, fingers caressing gently. Xantho fell asleep, her hand in his, hoping that feeling would never end.

TWENTY

The Warriors of the Light pushed south away from Priapus. The town they left behind was a hive of activity, preparing for the imminent arrival of Alexander and his Macedonian army. As they marched in, the Macedonians already at Priapus threw up defences to protect the vast numbers of infantry and cavalry. Hephaestion already had patrols of Agrianians and Companion cavalry out in the surrounding area, procuring food for the men and horses of the army. Xantho overheard talk that General Parmenio, the wily old battle-hardened general of Alexander's father Philip, was in the field with a sizeable force securing farms and estates to ensure a steady supply of food. With Priapus also secure now to provide water, Alexander had a solid base from which to position for the battle with Memnon, which must come soon.

Naram-Sin led his riders south, trying to

keep to high ground as much as possible to get eyes on the traitors as soon as they could. The countryside turned from open hills and valleys to rich farmland partitioned by small stone walls, dotted here and there with farmhouses or larger villas for wealthier landholders. They rode through one such estate with no sign of its owners or the men and women who worked the land. Xantho found it strange that such rich land lay undefended and ripe for the taking.

"Why does Memnon not protect these lands?" he asked Khamudi, who rode just ahead of him on a white-socked pony.

"He could deploy a scorched earth strategy and burn all before us. Starve Alexander out of Asia. He could be confident of victory and is marshalling his army, not caring what Alexander does with the land on the march. Most likely, however, the Persian satraps and lords do not want their land burned, and Memnon is not the Great King. So, there will be a battle, and we will see," he said.

"Have you fought in many battles?"

Khamudi laughed and leant over his saddle to look back at Xantho. "Many, my friend. I was at Kadesh, the greatest battle of all time. That was a thousand years ago. Since then, we have fought countless times."

"And died how many times?"

"Do not talk of such things, my friend. Too

many times," said Khamudi, and Xantho could sense that the Egyptian would say no more.

They rode to the summit of a rising set of hills dotted here and there by tight pockets of forest. Much of it had been cleared for the farmland covering the lower sections of each rise. As they crested the top of that summit, they noticed a lone rider directly across from them on the adjacent peak. The warrior sat upon a pure white Persian horse, its beautiful coat gleaming in the early afternoon sun. The warrior had the sun behind him and held a long spear, wavering gently in the breeze.

"Xia Lao," said Banya as the riders came to a halt.

Xantho watched the traitor silhouetted against the horizon. He hadn't really gotten to know the far eastern warrior before he had betrayed Naram-Sin, but that treachery was enough to make the man an enemy. Xia Lao moved off from his stationary position, and his horse slowly picked its way down the opposite slope, weaving around the shrubbery.

"I don't like this, Naram-Sin," said Siduri. "They chose this place. If there must be a fight, then I don't like that they have chosen the ground."

Xantho leant forward to peer down the line. Naram-Sin's eyes searched the ground ahead, probing it, deep in thought.

"There's water down there and rock," Idari noted.

Xantho looked ahead. A shallow, slow-moving stream punctuated hither and thither with grey. Slick rock formations traversed the low ground, which wove around the collection of low hills. On the right was a wood, no more than two hundred paces wide but dense and covering the stream in that area. Where the hills tapered away to the right, it opened onto farmland bulging with crops, made fertile and lush by the life-giving stream.

"There are other elements also, enough for us to bring our mage-power to bear," said Naram-Sin. "We end this today. We must remove our old friends from the board so we can concentrate on the battle to come. Also, they strengthen Gula'an. Go with caution. Mages, use your powers sparingly and with care for the flow of battle."

Xia Lao had traversed his slope and now waited on the opposite side of the stream. His white horse dipped its head and drank from the slowly flowing water. Xantho wasn't sure what was going on. He still had very little experience with war. Nevertheless, it seemed that Xia Lao wanted to talk. Xantho half hoped he wanted to make peace and return to the side of light; the other half of him wanted the fight, hungered for it. Wulfgar would be here somewhere and would have to pay for what he'd done to Tiki. No sooner had that thought run through his mind than a band of riders emerged from the woods to Xantho's left. They rode at a canter to take a position on either side of Xia Lao.

Wulfgar was there on the far left of their line, his broad face grinning. Xantho clenched his teeth and gripped his reins tight, trying to keep himself in check. His heart sank to see Agi there, next to Wulfgar. She had been the first of the Warriors of the Light to show kindness to him. Xantho remembered her dying in a ball of flame at the great battle between Cyrus and Tomyris. Gula'an had caused her death that day. *How could she fight for him now?* Naram-Sin called a halt, and they stopped ten paces from the stream. Xantho wasn't sure what would happen next; he felt the familiar knot of fear in his stomach. The stream made a gentle sloshing sound as it poured around a clutch of rocks just ahead. He could see a lone bird soaring high overhead, gliding on the light, warm breeze. In the face of the fight that must surely come, Xantho recalled that in his old life, he would have fled such a confrontation; he would have run and hid for his life. But now he stood firm and ready to fight.

The traitors were all garbed in Persian military attire, not too dissimilar to the clothing they had all worn when part of Cyrus's army. They wore the yellow tunics of the Immortals, covered by bronze-scaled armour and helmets, each armed with a spear and sword. Wulfgar nudged his horse forward a few steps, his face creased by his annoying grin. He looked at Naram-Sin and leant forward against his saddle, looking smug. He opened his mouth and was about to speak when Naram-Sin suddenly shouted and kicked his pony into charge. In the blink of an eye, he was at the water's edge, and Wulfgar's mouth dropped open, and his eyes bulged wide in fear. The Akkadian launched his spear, and it thudded into the muscled chest of Wulfgar's horse. The beast reared, and Naram-Sin charged his own horse into it, knocking Wulfgar from the saddle. All was chaos. Immediately, the Warriors of the Light charged forward to the attack, following their leader and his surprise strike.

Xantho reacted later than his comrades, taken completely aback by the speed and surprise of Naram-Sin's attack. He looked left, and Penelope had leapt from her pony and was dashing behind Xantho to join Siduri and the other mages who gathered together. Xantho nudged his horse forward but saw movement from the corner of his eye. He looked right and pulled back on the reins, heart in his mouth. From the dense forest there, a force of Persian Immortals burst from the treeline, howling battle cries and charging with spears outstretched. These warriors were not dressed in regular Immortal clothing; these Immortals wore their fish scale armour over blood-red tunics.

"Immortals!" Xantho shouted to alert the others. They had already noticed, and Naram-Sin had wheeled around to charge alone at the oncoming force. *Is he mad?* Suddenly Xantho was hurled from his horse by a pulse of energy. He landed on his back, pain bursting across his chest and head. Xantho cursed himself and rolled to his feet. He had taken his eye off the battle, and a mage power burst had caught him. Ahead warriors clashed steel on steel.

"Penelope, the forest!" Xantho yelled, pointing to his right. He pulled his bow free and grasped for an arrow in his quiver. Xantho felt the air shimmer around him, and the forest ahead moved. First, there was an ear-bursting sound of cracking and tearing timber. Leaves and dust swirled ferociously above the high forest eaves and the Blood Immortals, and then the air was filled with the sounds of their screaming. Xantho couldn't see what had happened beyond the tree line, but from the din of rending wood, and the screaming of the enemy, it must have been terrible. Many had already made it clear from the woods, but Xantho knew Penelope had used her power well, and much of their number had fallen in the same slaughter he had witnessed in the Persian camp days earlier.

Xantho checked his Palmstone. There was only a hint of a green swirl deep in the centre.

Penelope had used all her power to bend the trees to her will. It had worked, but she was spent now, which meant Xantho could not avail of her mage strength. He turned to see if Penelope was alright. She had fallen exhausted, and Idari held her close. Xantho nocked an arrow. He swung his aim from the fight beyond the river to where the Blood Immortals charged, unsure where to send his first shaft. Xantho was still dizzy from the fall and was dithering in action. He looked for Wulfgar again but couldn't see him in the clash of horses and warriors across the river.

Xantho turned his aim to his right. Naram-Sin had dismounted and was surrounded by Blood Immortals. The Akkadian moved like a dancer, his blade flashing and twirling as he moved, men spinning away, wounded by his steel. Xantho picked his target and loosed, and a Blood Immortal went down. After that, he sent shaft after shaft at the men around Naram-Sin. Xantho breathed deeply, and his aim was true. He nocked another arrow to his bow and then felt the familiar movement in the air; the magic abounded again. Siduri, Khensa, and Idari were kneeling together and seemed poised to send an energy pulse towards the Immortals. But before they could, a foreboding, sucking sound came from the stream. The water rushed in on itself and formed a pillar as high as five men. That pillar of water then smashed into the ground around Xantho, washing him backwards.

Xantho gasped and coughed. He pulled himself up on all fours, his stomach heaving as he vomited river water. He was soaking wet, half-drowned, and the fight raged on around him. Xantho turned to see Siduri, Penelope, and the other mages also down and trying to recover from the wash of water. Across the river, Wulfgar stood with hands on hips, breathing heavily but smiling his smug grin. It had surely been he who had bent the water to his will. *He must have power over water in the same way Penelope does over the trees.* Naram-Sin was still fighting amongst a circle of Blood Immortals, but a smaller group of those red-garbed warriors had flooded between the traitors and now hacked at Khamudi and Banya. The two Warriors of the Light disengaged from where they fought against Anusuya, Xia Lao and the others and rode hard for Xantho's position.

"I go to Naram-Sin," Khamudi shouted above the din, "you hold here." He veered off and charged towards where the Akkadian fought like a god of war amongst the bronze-armoured Blood Immortals.

Banya leapt from his horse and came to a crouch beside Xantho. He was bleeding from a cut on his neck, and his face was stretched tight across bared teeth. "Now we shall see how you fight, little mouse."

The air shimmered again, and Xantho winced

as hot air swamped him. He forced his eyes open to see the rocks in the stream rise, dripping water from their shiny sides. The Blood Immortals, about to charge across the stream, stopped and fell back in disbelief at the magic.

"No, no," Xantho heard from behind him. It was Idari repeating those words over and over as she strode forwards, hands reaching up to the sky.

Xantho felt heat pulsing from her, and then a clap of thunder roared across the sky. All the warriors, mages, and Immortals on that field of battle crouched in terror at the sound. The rocks fell slightly and then rose again. Xantho peered through his fingers, hands over his face, and crouched, fearing what horror the mages would unleash next. Chitraganda was on the opposite side of the river, holding the rocks high with his power, just as tall and imperious as Xantho remembered.

Idari let out a yell, and light flashed before Xantho's eyes. A lightning bolt flew from the heavens in a crack of jagged white light and thundered into the rocks. The rocks exploded with a shattering crunch, and Xantho's armour rapped as tiny stones pelted the surrounding area. Idari fell, spent, and Banya leapt to help her. Across the stream, Xantho could see Chitraganda on his knees. Xantho picked up his bow, which he had dropped when the thunder shocked him into a fear-induced crouch. He notched an arrow and let it fly low and hard. Chitraganda looked up, and Xantho saw the panic on his face just before the arrow slammed into his eye, flinging him backwards.

Xantho's heart was pounding. He had just killed a traitor, yet Chitraganda was also the man who had freed him from Jawed and his father. A wail erupted, and a warrior charged across the thin line of water where the river was refilling itself after Wulfgar's magic had drained it. It was Anusuya, enraged that her mage partner Chitraganda was dead. Xantho dropped his bow, pulled his kopis free, and ran to meet her.

She swung at him, but Xantho already had his blade up. He swung down and blocked her anger-fuelled attack. Her face was twisted in a snarl, and she beat at his sword whilst tears rolled down her cheeks. Xantho breathed hard and was only keeping her at bay. Anusuya swung wildly, yet by remembering Khamudi's lessons, Xantho took a deep breath and forced himself to keep calm. She swung wild and high, and he ducked under her blade. Coming up inside her reach, Xantho used his sword arm to elbow Anusuya in the face whilst simultaneously getting his foot behind her knee. She fell backwards, and he swung his kopis down hard, point first, slamming the blade through her armour and leaning on the hilt to force the weapon into the heart beyond.

Xantho slumped over her corpse, his chest heaving, trying to suck air into his exhausted body. Two traitors dead by his hand. Suddenly, Banya knocked Xantho aside as he charged past, flinging himself into two attacking Blood Immortals. The African cannoned into the assailants, throwing one man from his feet and cleaving the other Persian's chest open. Siduri had dragged Idari back from the fighting to lay her with Penelope, both mages exhausted. From there, Siduri dashed along parallel to the stream to get closer to Naram-Sin. The Akkadian was still fighting amongst a circle of Blood Immortals. Many had died at his feet, but he was hard-pressed. As Siduri grew closer, Naram-Sin forced his attackers back, his blade carving terrible wounds amongst them as her power surged into him. Siduri had not yet used her mage skills, whereas Penelope and Idari were already wholly spent.

Banya came back and stood shoulder-to-shoulder with Xantho. Across from them, Xia Lao, Shao Ling, and Agi came on and marched through the stream. Wulfgar crouched, still recovering from his mage exertions. Xantho saw Naram-Sin off to the right, cutting through his circle of attackers and breaking into a run. Gorged with Siduri's power, Naram-Sin raced faster than should be possible. He wasn't running in their direction, however. Instead, he was running towards the hill behind the traitors. There, in a shining gold chariot, came Gula'an. With his black staff held aloft, he came hurtling down the hill, and Naram-Sin made for him like a lion hunting prey. Where Naram-Sin had fought the Blood Immortals, the ground was soaked with blood, and enemies had fallen beyond count.

Xantho braced himself to face the three attackers. Wulfgar had spent his power, and Xantho had killed Chitraganda, but Shao Ling had yet to join the fray. No sooner had that thought entered Xantho's mind than Xia Lao charged. Flushed with Shao Ling's power, the blows of his sword were like being struck by an elephant. Xantho raised his blade, and Xia Lao batted it aside with a snarl. The force of that blow felt like it would rip his arm from its socket. Xia Lao kicked Banya, and the African flew backwards ten paces to land, winded, rolling on the ground. Xantho cursed and ducked under a swing of Xia Lao's blade. As he did so, Agi cracked him across the ribs with a spear blade, and he cursed at her.

"How could you turn on us like this?" Xantho said through gritted teeth. She shook her head and thrust her spear point at him. He jerked backwards, and the point hit his armour, punching him in the ribs, and he fell sprawling on the riverbank. Agi and Xia Lao went for Banya, blades cutting and slashing, Xia Lao, still flushed with power, battered Banya to his knees, and Xantho thought the African must die under their attack. Quickly, Xantho leapt forward and shouldered Xia Lao out of the way, bringing his kopis down in a giant swing. The blade chopped into Agi's thigh. It was a savage blow. It jarred up Xantho's arm as the blade jammed into her thigh bone. Agi fell screaming, blood blooming bright on her yellow Immortals tunic. Banya leapt forward from where he knelt and dived on Xia Lao, pinning him.

"Now, little mouse," Banya said. The words came strained as he struggled with the power-flooded warrior. Xantho swallowed hard. So much blood had been spilt already that day, so much death. Xantho remembered little Tiki's body and steeled himself to the task. He took two long strides forward and brought the kopis down hard on Xia Lao's neck. The eastern warrior's head tumbled away in a welter of blood, soaking the riverbank. A scream erupted from across the river, and Shao Ling tore at her hair. Xantho had killed Xia Lao, not just in this life, but forever. The mage charged, splashing across the river. Banya leapt up from Xia Lao's body and met her charge, cutting her down with his blade.

Xantho felt thick, warm moisture on his face as he looked across the battlefield. Xia

Lao and Shao Ling were dead, Agi was out of the fight, and Chitraganda and Anusuya were dead. Naram-Sin had caught up to Gula'an's chariot, but the Gutian had eluded him, and he was heartbeats away from where Xantho stood. Xantho reached a hand to wipe the liquid from his face and retched as he looked at it. It was covered in dark blood—and not his own. *No time to think about that.*

"Banya, move!"

Banya leapt out of the way just in time to avoid the onrushing chariot, and Xantho braced himself. If he could get a swing at one horse, he could bring it down, but as he brought his blade to guard, he was thrown into the air and smashed to the ground by Gula'an's magic. Xantho rolled, coughing and spluttering, pain sparking in his head. He looked up to see Naram-Sin leap onto the back of the chariot and grapple with Gula'an. They fell from the hurtling chariot, but whilst Naram-Sin tumbled into the dirt, Gula'an floated down gracefully, landing on his feet. He swung his black staff around in an arc and thrust it towards where Penelope, Idari, and Khensa lay, still exhausted.

Xantho's heart stopped. Everything moved slowly, the black staff came around, and the air shook, all moving at half pace. Gula'an brought his staff down and hammered it onto the ground. The earth trembled and cracked, like thunder erupting but from beneath its surface. Xantho dropped his blade and covered his ears to block out the ear-splitting sound. The ground ahead of Gula'an opened into a crevice, cracking the earth like ice on a frozen pond. The crack raced across the riverbank, heading for the three mages. Xantho wanted to shout, but no sound came out, paralysed by the silent, desperate, heart-rending fear that Penelope could die. The crack widened, and Xantho saw Idari and Khensa fall into its depths, helpless. Penelope rolled away, and Xantho blew out his held breath through clenched teeth. Gula'an brought his staff around again and drove it into the ground a second time. The monstrous crevice he had created creaked and shook, closing itself, swallowing Khensa and Idari into the earth beneath.

Xantho grasped for his blade, hand still slick with Xia Lao's blood. He pushed himself to his feet. Pain shot through his head from the fall, and he thought he must surely black out. The battlefield reeked with the iron of spilt blood. The cries and moans of the injured filled his ears, and he simply didn't know what to do next. *Dash to Penelope, or attack Gula'an?* He saw Wulfgar standing across the stream, picking up a curved blade from a fallen Blood Immortal. Something deep inside Xantho told him there was another option. He didn't have to stay here and die. He could turn now and run; he could get to a horse and be away, free from the horrific carnage.

Xantho looked at Penelope, lying still and unable to defend herself. His mind told him to go. It was his old self calling to him, and he had to decide: was he Xantho the slave or Xantho the Warrior of the Light, grandson of Aristaeus the Brave?

TWENTY ONE

Naram-Sin rose from where Gula'an had sent him tumbling, and the Akkadian braced himself to attack. Siduri raced across the battlefield to join him, swerving around attackers and leaping over fallen warriors. Banya charged, roaring at Gula'an, but the servant of Nergal spun around and blocked the attack with his staff. Then, with his other hand, he used his power to throw Banya back into the rising flow of the stream.

Xantho swallowed his doubt, pushing his slave self away into the depths of his soul. Gula'an faced Naram-Sin and Siduri, and Penelope seemed safe where she lay. Khamudi was still across the stream, battling the remaining Blood Immortals who had charged from the forest. Xantho grasped his kopis and turned to face Wulfgar. The mage had armed himself with an Immortals sword and came on with a wide grin splitting his broad face.

Xantho thought of Tiki, the terrible wound in his throat, and his little body lying cold in the earth. He thought of it all, and he charged, bellowing at Wulfgar. Wulfgar raised his blade to parry Xantho's attack. There was no sword skill in that attack, just pure hatred and vengeance poured into the long single-edged blade. The Northman fell back from the onslaught but parried Xantho's sword strikes. Xantho hammered at Wulfgar, and his grin had turned into a strained grimace. Wulfgar blocked a heavy downward blow and kicked out, striking Xantho in the belly and forcing him back. The mage then lifted his hand as though to use his magic, but none came. Now it was Xantho's turn to grin, and he sprang forward, kopis singing through the air to chop the hand from Wulfgar's arm. The colourless Palmstone caught the light as Wulfgar's severed hand fell to the ground in a spray of dark blood.

Wulfgar let out a cry of pain and fell to his knees. Xantho swatted away the Northman's sword, and it tumbled towards the water.

"I'll see you in the next life, slave. Get it over with," Wulfgar spat, clutching at his severed hand and ready to accept the death blow, confident that he would rise again on a future battlefield to continue his war.

"You are a traitor and a killer of children. There will be no next life for you," said Xantho.

Then, without hesitation, he swung his blade backhand in a flat arc. The blade flew straight and true. Xantho watched Wulfgar's eyes grow wide with terror as he realised he faced true death. The kopis took his head, and Xantho felt resistance as the blade passed through his neck and spine. The blonde-haired skull tumbled to the ground with a dull thud and rolled away to the water's edge.

Xantho turned to see Naram-Sin and Siduri battling Gula'an. The Gutian was being forced back under their attack. He blocked Naram-Sin's furious blade with his staff whilst Siduri strained to keep the dark magic in place with her own power. Khamudi had dealt with the Blood Immortals and now ran to join the Akkadian, so Xantho himself strode to stand with his fellow Warriors of the Light. Gula'an stepped back from them and smiled, eyes black as coal beneath his long silver hair.

"Daughter, you and your warmonger are here together at the last," he said, his voice silky and calm.

"You cannot win," Naram-Sin uttered, fixing his enemy with a flat stare.

"There is no winning, warmonger. The gods cursed us to fight forever, Nergal and Enlil fighting their war of supremacy through us."

"It can end. Thousands of years of war and pain, it can all end now."

"If I let you take my head, warmonger, my lord Nergal will drag the souls of my beloved family down to the underworld for eternity. Your siblings," Gula'an said, pointing at Siduri. "They rest peacefully, and I cannot allow that to happen."

"You sold your soul to Nergal for victory over Akkad. You made the Gutians supreme, and this was the price," Naram-Sin enounced.

"You had to be stopped, warmonger. Do you not remember how you butchered my people? How you slaughtered women and children by the hundred? How you stole my daughter away? You who broke man's link with the gods for all time when you destroyed the Ekur."

"I know what I was, Gula'an. Such is our curse. Let us finish it now," said Naram-Sin, raising his blade.

"I must get back to Memnon now. He needs my advice on the battle to come. I will let my friends deal with you," Gula'an retorted. He nodded over the head of Naram-Sin, to the peak of the hill behind. Xantho's mouth dropped open. A force of enemy cavalry raced over the crest and roared down the hill in a mass of thundering hooves and a cloud of dust. Gula'an turned and pointed at Xantho.

"You are something different, slave that was. You are a true killer. We will meet again," he said. His chariot came racing towards him, pulled by two white horses. In the blink of an eye, Gula'an leapt into the wagon as it passed and rode away, his long hair streaming behind him.

Xantho watched the servant of Nergal speed away before turning back to the oncoming wave of enemy cavalry. Xantho stood with Naram-Sin, Siduri, Khamudi and Banya. He felt like a tiny insect, looking up at a boot about to crush it with terrible force. The ground beneath Xantho's feet shook, and his legs trembled.

"Get Penelope and go back to Hephaestion," Naram-Sin said to Xantho. "Tell him to head for the Granicus river. I know it of old. It will suit Alexander for his battle with Memnon. Khamudi, go with him."

"No, I stand with you," Xantho insisted. There was no way he was leaving now after so much bloodshed.

"Go, little mouse. You fought like a lion today. Win the war," said Banya, smiling, placing a hand on Xantho's arm. "I will see you in the next life, where we will fight side by side again, with honour."

Xantho felt a lump in his throat as Khamudi raced away toward Penelope.

"Go, now!" shouted Siduri. She raised her Palmstone, and it flushed gold. She smiled at him, and Xantho ran. He ran as fast as he could, and his legs suddenly tingled with power. He looked at his own Palmstone, which glowed faint but green. His legs took off, galloping towards Penelope. Overtaking Khamudi, he scooped her into his arms and sped up the hill they had charged down earlier that day. Reaching the top, Xantho saw their ponies idling ten paces away, so he made for them. The power was draining from his limbs. It had been the last fleeting drop Penelope could muster, but it had been enough. He launched himself into the saddle, the last ounce of strength enough to pull her over in front of him, laying across the pony's neck.

Xantho clicked his tongue and dug his heels into the mare's sides, and she lurched back up the hillside. Khamudi had reached the hill's crest and crouched there, searching for something within his breastplate. Xantho shook his head. *Why hasn't he mounted a horse?* Xantho came closer and saw the Egyptian was striking flints into a ball of tinder he had taken from his belt. The Egyptian blew at the tinder, caressing and nurturing the spark of a flame that flitted there.

"What are you doing? Have you lost your mind? Flee, Khamudi!" Xantho exclaimed, shouting in frustration at his teacher.

"Watch," was all the Egyptian said. Xantho looked down towards the stream. The attacking cavalry hit the three Warriors of the Light like a wall. Xantho saw Banya sliced open by a savage blade, blood spraying high above the fighting. The cavalry flowed around Siduri and

Naram-Sin. Xantho remembered her Palmstone had recovered, and the mage was full of power. The tinder ball in Khamudi's hands sprang into full flame, and he dropped it into the grass. He jumped up and down, waving his arms. Below, between the flurry of enemy horses and blades, Xantho saw Siduri raise her hand.

The flame at Khamudi's feet exploded into a fireball, and Xantho's horse whinnied and shied from the blaze. He fought to keep her in check and watched the fireball leap into the sky. It was a ball of flame as large as a barn, and it hurtled towards Siduri, spitting fire behind it like a wolf's tail. The fireball struck Siduri and Naram-Sin and collapsed to sweep the riverbank in a carpet of fire, the wall of flame engulfing the entire Persian cavalry force. Screaming echoed around the hills, men and horses alike screeching to the heavens in agonising pain, and Xantho shrank back from the horror. Fire was Siduri's element, and she had used it to devastating effect, but she had sacrificed herself and Naram-Sin to destroy the Persian cavalrymen.

Khamudi had found a pony, and the last surviving Warriors of the Light raced away. The blaze behind them lit up the late afternoon sky, dancing and casting shadows upon the clouds above.

Later that day, Xantho rested in a brush-covered defile miles from Siduri's inferno. He looked down upon the glistening surface of the Granicus river as it wound its way into the distance. They had to sight the waterway before reporting Naram-Sin's message to Alexander and Hephaestion. He tore a strip of cloth from the edge of his chiton and soaked it with water from the skin at his saddle. Xantho folded the cloth and used it to wash Penelope's face. He held it to her forehead and then wiped away the dirt from her cheeks and neck. Her eyes fluttered open, and Xantho smiled, his melancholy lightened by the sight of her green eyes. She smiled wanly and then closed her eyes again. She was alive, and that was enough for now. He stretched his aching neck, and the pain in his chest and ribs throbbed. Now that he was resting, Xantho noticed cuts and scrapes littering his body. He thought he had removed most of the dried blood from his face and hair, the blood of the enemies he had killed, the heads he had taken. Thoughts and images of that butchery flashed before his eyes, so he closed them tight, blocking out the horror.

Xantho cradled Penelope across his knees and sat opposite Khamudi. The Egyptian had built a small fire, and he had gathered some herbs from around the fields where they rested and brewed a tea for Penelope. They had, up to that point, sat in silence. Xantho hadn't the energy to speak. All was surely lost. Naram-Sin and Siduri were dead, the others dead. Only he, Penelope, and Khamudi survived. *How can we alone fight against the terrible power of Gula'an?* Now that he was resting and the fury of battle had subsided, Xantho saw flashes of what he had done every time he blinked or closed his eyes. He had killed. He had taken the heads of people who had lived a hundred lifetimes. Xantho remembered the words of Gula'an. He was a killer now; there was no mistaking that. Xantho stared into the flames. What would his mother think of what he had become? He doubted she would recognise him, a blood-soaked butcher cutting off heads, but then surely his grandfather had been just the same. Bedtime stories of heroism and battle skill left out the blood, the screams, and the horror. What would Lithra think? She wouldn't know him. He wasn't that Xantho anymore.

There was no way to carry on. The war was plainly over. Xantho and Penelope were inexperienced, and she was only one mage. If all the power of the Warriors of the Light couldn't stand Gula'an, then what chance did they have now? Better to ride away. Leave Gula'an to defeat Alexander. After all, what did that matter across the span of time? Naram-Sin and Gula'an had fought this battle countless times over the centuries. This was their curse from a time long forgotten, where gods and men walked together. Xantho doubted there would ever be a resolution. Naram-Sin would rise again, with

Banya and the others, at some other distant war in a distant land. Xantho sighed and rolled his aching soldiers. *I am exhausted, bone shudderingly exhausted. Tired of fighting, of riding, of sleeping out in the open. Of being hunted, and of hunting.* It was relentless. If this was to be his future life, then it wasn't a future he welcomed. Xantho wasn't so sure he was any better off now than when he was a slave. He wasn't truly free; he had a duty to Naram-Sin and Enlil. Just as before, he had been his father's servant, Tiribazos.

"So, it's over then," he said, words coming out in a dry croak. Xantho cleared his throat and stared across the fire at Khamudi.

"Nothing is over," the Egyptian replied. "We rest tonight. Then tomorrow, we tell Hephaestion of the Granicus. We'll win this battle."

Xantho let out a mirthless laugh. "We three, against Gula'an? It's impossible. He's won; it's over."

Khamudi took the tea from the fire and passed it across to Xantho. "Let her sip this. It will give her strength," he said.

Penelope opened her eyes again, and Xantho helped her rise to a seated position. He lifted the tea to her lips, and she took a few small sips. It seemed to help, and she nodded thanks. Penelope took the brew from Xantho and sipped at it herself.

"How do you feel?" Xantho asked her. Penelope nodded slowly.

"Better, just tired, is all. What happened?"

Xantho sighed. So much had happened that he didn't know where to start. "They are all dead, but us three," he answered.

"Siduri, Naram-Sin?"

"All gone."

"The others, Gula'an?"

"Xantho took the heads of two who will never rise again. The rest are dead. Khensa is gone. But Gula'an lives," said Khamudi.

"We cannot go on, not the three of us," Xantho muttered. Penelope took another sip of her tea.

"So, what do we do?" she asked.

Xantho shrugged. "We go, leave this place. Live our lives." Xantho said those words but wanted to ask her to go with him. Live with him. They could make a life together. He wanted to make a life with her. Banya and Idari had done it before. When they grew old and died, they would rise again to fight alongside Naram-Sin and his curse, but they could live a whole and happy life together before that.

"We do not leave. We go to Hephaestion, we tell him to bring the army to the banks of the Granicus River, and we fight to help Alexander win, and we fight Gula'an. We honour our fallen comrades; we honour Khensa," said Khamudi. He spoke with a calm certainty. He wasn't speaking as though making a suggestion, more that there was no choice to make at all.

"We march into certain death. Gula'an is too powerful. How can we possibly win?" Xantho maintained.

"We, too, are powerful. You killed warriors and mages today. Penelope again used her power to take down countless foes in the forest. So, we fight, and if we die, then we rise to fight again. We do not have a choice. If we give up, and Gula'an and Nergal win, then how many innocent people will die? War will rage across the world for all time, and people will butcher one another beyond count. How could we value our own lives above the countless thousands who will die if we lose? They will swell the underworld with souls, and Nergal will be the most powerful amongst the gods," said Khamudi.

"Khensa is gone, Banya and Idari are gone. Does that not matter to you?" Xantho demanded. Khamudi's eyes flashed in the firelight, and his face sagged into a sad smile.

"Do not speak to me of Khensa. I have seen her die countless times, my love, my queen. Each time hurts like the first time. The others are like a brother and sister to me. It matters beyond reckoning. For them and for that reason, we do not give up. We don't give up, even if it is down to you or me alone. We fight on for all time."

There was no more talk of what they would or wouldn't do. They lay down to rest, exhausted from the battle. Xantho stared up at the stars twinkling down from the heavens above. He had played his part; he had killed and had even been killed himself in this terrible war. Xantho was tired, and his body ached. He had come within a hairsbreadth of losing Penelope without telling her how he felt about her. It was enough; it was over. In the morning, he would talk to Penelope, and they would leave this pointless war behind and let Alexander fight his battle of conquest. Win or lose. It didn't matter to Xantho. He had killed Wulfgar and taken vengeance for Tiki. The Northman would never rise again, but killing his enemy hadn't made Xantho feel any better about the loss of his young friend. His murderer was dead, but so was Tiki. The killing of Wulfgar would not bring Tiki back. His humour and energy were lost to the world forever, whether Wulfgar was dead or alive. Xantho needed to find peace. He would tell Penelope how he felt, hoping she felt the same. Having gone through so much together in desperate times, it would be good to have some quiet time with her, to talk, to laugh.

Yes, I will talk to Penelope in the morning, and then we will leave this eternal war behind.

TWENTY TWO

The morning sun cast a yellow-orange haze over the far-off hilltops, and birds sang and chirped in the distance. Xantho opened his eyes and yawned, rubbing at heavy eyelids. His muscles tensed as he moved from a curled-up stretch, and pain spasmed across his chest and back to remind him of the battle with Gula'an. He groaned and pushed himself upright. The cavalryman's breastplate rested beside him, the once white Macedonian armour now crusted with blood and smeared with dirt. He slipped an arm out of his chiton and winced as he bent to look at the damage. There was a purple welt of a bruise in the centre of his chest where Agi had hit him with her spear, and his ribs were swollen amidst a lurid mix of purple and green where Gula'an had hammered him into the ground.

"That looks sore," came the soothing tones of Penelope's voice. She poked at the fire, adding twigs to get the small blaze going again. He smiled to see her up and about.

"Are you feeling better, then?" Xantho asked, putting his arm slowly back into the chiton and trying not to cringe at the pain.

She nodded and returned his smile. "Whatever was in that tea, it did the trick. Khamudi is still asleep but left some leaves here so that I will brew some for us."

She did indeed look well. Her skin looked clear in the morning light, and she had tied her brown hair back from her face whilst she worked. Xantho imagined her working like that in a home they might share one day. That thought made him smile again, so he allowed the image to linger.

"So, we must decide," she said. A narrow pillar of smoke wafted from the fire now, so she added more fuel.

Xantho clenched his teeth. Before sleeping, he had been so sure that it was all over. With Naram-Sin, Siduri and the others gone, what chance did they have? But now that Penelope was awake, he wasn't so sure. He had let her down once before when they had first met. That image of her standing alone on the plains of the Massagetae was burned into his mind. He knew now that he had made a terrible choice that day; she had looked to him with hope based on their newfound power and strength, and he had taken the cowardly option and gone back to his father and back to slavery.

Now, looking at her green eyes in the half-light of dawn, Xantho couldn't tell her it was over and that he was leaving. If he was going to say anything to her, he knew he should tell her how he felt and what he hoped they could have together. But he couldn't get the words out as she brushed that ever-present loose strand of hair from her forehead. What use was his new-found bravery if he was afraid to talk to Penelope? Xantho hoped that if he just came out with it and told her how he felt, she would agree, and they could ride away from this mess together. He took deep breaths, breathing from his stomach using Khamudi's technique again. Talking to Penelope about how he felt was an entirely different battle. It was not one with blades or arrows but rather a more painful battle which took place in his own mind. He swallowed and sat up straighter.

"If we left, would you…"

"How could we leave?" Penelope said, cutting him off. He looked at her, the bravado fleeing from him like used-up Palmstone strength. He had plucked up the courage to ask her to be with him, to go away with him, but that fleeting moment had passed as the frown spread across her brow.

"We simply can't win," he said. "It's pointless. We are all banged up and injured; only three of us are left. So what can we do?"

"We can do more than you think. Look how

far we've come."

Xantho shook his head. Since the ambush back on the steppe, it had all happened at full tilt like a horse race on his father's estates. First, they had forced him to become a warrior; second, he had discovered the unbelievable reality of mages and magic, only for that to be trumped upon finding out he could die and be reborn across time. Then, after dying at the hands of his supposed comrades, he had risen again hundreds of years later to become part of the Macedonian army. He hadn't had any time to think or understand what was going on, so he could decide for himself what his part would be in all of it.

"Are we so different? I remember the first time I saw you, fighting off two Massagetae tribesmen. You are still that fierce, brave woman now."

"Have you seen yourself lately? I remember that day too. You were so scared, quivering with fear. You left me there alone, walking back to slavery. The warrior I see before me now is not the slave I met that day." Penelope beckoned to him, and he crawled the short distance to where she tended the fire. She motioned for him to look into the water she'd poured into her helmet to heat the tea. It had not yet boiled and was still.

Xantho leant over and looked at his reflection in the water. A stranger stared back at him. He thought of himself as a young man. In his mind's eye, he was a young Thracian with long dark hair and had always kept his face clean-shaven. The man looking out of that glassy pool was a wind-burned, hard-faced soldier. He scratched at the scruffy beard covering his chin and cheeks and stroked the rough face of the hardened warrior who stared back at him. There were wrinkles at the corners of his eyes and on his brow, and he saw flinty, deep eyes glaring up from the still water. Finally, he sat back, and Penelope nodded.

"You see? You are a warrior, Xantho. A warrior who killed yesterday, who fought with warriors of vast experience, and won. We are part of this now. It is our fight." Penelope held up her hand and showed her Palmstone to him, and he raised his own. He realised that everything she said was right. It was his fight. He hadn't asked for it nor welcomed it, but he was part of it nonetheless.

"We are in this together, you and I," he said to her and reached out for her Palmstone hand. She took it, blushing.

"We are," Penelope agreed, squeezing his hand, "and I'm glad of it, Xantho."

They stared into each other's eyes for a moment. She felt the same as he; he was sure of it now. There was a definite attraction there, a bond between them. Penelope's hand felt warm and soft in his own. It sent its warmth up his arm and enveloped his chest. Xantho felt his cheeks burning red.

"So, we go back to the army and find Hephaestion."

"Yes, and we do our best to help Alexander win, and we bring down Gula'an. For if we do not, and Gula'an wins again, then war and death will flood the world. We are the ones who stand between that terrible future and a future where there can be peace and order."

"Do you think that will ever be? Peace and order?" Xantho said. He still struggled to see how exchanging one Great King for another Macedonian king would bring peace. That change could only happen with war, battles, and death, which surely served only Nergal and not Enlil. In the back of his mind, Xantho still heard the words Gula'an had spoken to him at Priapus. Was he sure he fighting on the side of good, the side of light?

"These questions are beyond us. It's enough that they have selected us for this task, for this war. And it's our duty to see it through," said Penelope.

"What if Alexander only brings more war to the world? Sometimes, I just don't see how that doesn't serve Nergal. That's all I'm saying."

"Don't think so much, Xantho. Here, drink your tea." She lifted the helmet from the small fire and poured him a steaming cup.

He sat and drank the refreshing brew. Xantho looked up at a morning sky now tinged with red. In the distance, a flock of small birds ducked and dived on the breeze, making an intricate pattern as they followed each other, flitting in unison, each part of the greater whole, all working together. Maybe Penelope was right, and she had said it to him before. Sometimes there just aren't answers. Who could say how and why those birds flew together the way they did. *Why don't they fly alone? How do they know how to move together to create such beautiful patterns?* Xantho was part of a bigger pattern: the battle between heaven and the underworld, darkness and light. Just because he couldn't see it didn't mean that Alexander wouldn't set the world on the path to peace. Xantho resolved to forget such questions of how and why. His job was to be a warrior.

Xantho finished his tea, and the brew had indeed refreshed him. The warm freshness seeped through his body and even washed away some of the pain and stiffness in his bruising. He thought again of the reflection he had seen of himself in the water. Deep inside, he still felt like Xantho, the slave, trying to survive in this world of warrior and mage, but the face looking back at him was that of a soldier. Xantho stroked his Palmstone and supposed he was as much a warrior as any of his father's men had been. He had fought in a tremendous battle in the army of Cyrus the Great, and Xantho had fought many times now. He had killed and had been killed himself. Xantho wasn't at the same level as Khamudi or Naram-Sin in terms of weapon skill, and he didn't have the majestic mastery of the blade that those warriors possessed. But he could fight and kill.

Xantho pushed himself to his feet and went to where Khamudi lay peacefully sleeping. The Egyptian's chest rose and fell as he lay on his back, his dark angular face smooth and without wrinkles despite his vast age. Xantho wondered if he thought of Khensa as he lay there. How must it feel to see the woman you love fight and die repeatedly? To grow old together and be reborn young and virile? Khamudi opened his left eye and grimaced as he saw Xantho standing there.

"Why are you staring at me, my friend?"

"I am waiting to practise, friend. Or is today a day off?"

Khamudi stretched his lithe frame and stood with hands on hips. "There are no days off for those who fight for the light," he said and smiled. Penelope brought Khamudi his tea, and he thanked her.

As the Egyptian finished his drink and donned his armour, Xantho followed Penelope back to the fire.

"Before I practice with Khamudi, there is

something I want to ask you, something I have been wanting to say for a while but haven't had the courage," he said. Penelope looked up at him, frowning. She brushed at the perpetual loose curl of her hair hanging over her eyes and shifted her feet.

"This sounds very serious," she replied.

Xantho had to ask her. If he was going to get back into this war, he had to know what was on the other side. "When this is over, if we survive, even if we win…"

"Yes?"

"Well, once it's over, and there is no more fighting…"

"Yes?"

"Well, maybe you and I…well…maybe we could. Well…you know?"

Now it was Penelope's turn to blush. She smiled at him but wouldn't let him off the hook. "Yes?" she said.

"Well, maybe you and I could be together?" There. He had said it. He fumbled at his sword belt and pulled at the neck of his armour, suddenly sweating even though the morning was cool.

"I thought you would never ask," she exclaimed, rewarding him with a crooked grin as she looked into his eyes and then back to the ground.

Xantho's heart beat hard against his chest, as hard as it did amid the fury of battle. A smile broke open on his face, and he stood there grinning at her. She smiled back, her cheeks rosy beneath her bright green eyes. He wanted to kiss her and take her in his arms, but it felt awkward. Khamudi was there, just behind him. Looking at her standing there, Xantho got the feeling she wanted him to kiss her. Knowing Penelope, he was a little surprised she hadn't taken the initiative and made the first move herself.

"Are we practising combat, or do you two lovers need some alone time?" said Khamudi. Xantho turned and grinned at his friend. He smiled again at Penelope and then went to practise.

"Xantho," Penelope blurted as he moved off. He turned back to look at her.

"When we met and were learning, I was harsh on you. I wanted to say I'm sorry for that...I just didn't want to go back to being a slave; I just wanted this to work," she said.

Xantho remembered her harsh words. He thought back to when he couldn't fight Agi and when he had let the others down so many times. Recalling his missed bowshot now gave him a shiver, imagining how the others must have seen him. He remembered how disappointed he had been in himself.

"Don't worry," he said, "I understand. I was

also a slave, don't forget."

Khamudi drew his sword and moved to a position twenty paces away from where Penelope gathered her equipment together. The Egyptian swung his blade above his head and around his body, twisting his torso to loosen his muscles. Xantho did the same and felt the stabbing pain of the bruising around his ribs. *Maybe it would have been better to let the Egyptian sleep.*

"The last time we spoke, I got the sense you wanted to leave us," said Khamudi.

Which was true, Xantho supposed. The night before, he had been truly broken. The death and loss of the Warriors of the Light had brought him to the edge of despair.

"I just don't see how we can fight Gula'an or affect this war. There are only three of us, and Penelope and I are new to this," said Xantho. He lifted his kopis and moved through the slow movements of thrust, parry, and lunge. Khamudi did the same.

"We can make a difference. We three will get the message to Hephaestion that the Granicus is the perfect place to fight the Persians. And we will fight Gula'an."

"So, we will fight. I know we must. I won't leave."

Khamudi levelled his blade at Xantho, the signal to begin sparring. "Because of Penelope?"

"Partly, yes, and for you. For the others who died yesterday."

"Their deaths will not be in vain. My poor Khensa."

Xantho gulped hard, recalling how Gula'an had opened up the ground to swallow Khensa and Idari, trapping them there beneath the earth. "I hope she did not suffer."

"She is courageous. She has always been so."

"Do you think Siduri and Naram-Sin suffered in the flames?"

Khamudi grimaced. "I imagine they suffered pain beyond belief. That is Siduri's element, fire. But the element must be present for the mage to command it. They sacrificed themselves to the pain of that fire. Their deaths must have been excruciating. They died like that to destroy the enemy cavalry, so we could escape and live to fight another day."

"Were you together, you and Khensa, before all this?" asked Xantho. Khamudi lowered his blade.

"I fought for my pharaoh, Ramesses the Great. I was a general in his armies. Khensa was a priestess of Montu, our god of war. She would ride with the army, test the omens, and bless our weapons. She was so beautiful, so bright and clever. I truly loved her beyond all else. The sun rose and set with her. We fought at Kadesh, and that is where we met Naram-Sin and Siduri. That is where we first defeated Gula'an."

"You defeated him?"

"He fought alongside the Hittites. We rode in our shining war chariots, in our war splendour. Siduri and Khensa worked together to trap Gula'an with their magic, and Naram-Sin took his life."

"They trapped him?"

"Yes, they held him, but alas, they could not remove his head."

"Could it be done again, like it was at Kadesh?"

"Yes, I suppose it could. Of course, Penelope would need to be strong. And we would need to get close to him, to strike him down once she had him."

"She is strong."

"And beautiful, no?" said Khamudi, and he smiled. Xantho reddened because he certainly thought she was.

"Are you sad that Khensa is gone?"

"Yes, of course. My heart aches for her. But she died with honour, and it is not an ultimate death. I will see her and hold her again. As long as I can keep my head."

Khamudi raised his weapon again, and they touched the tips of their blades together.

THE CURSE OF NARAM-SIN

Immediately, Khamudi launched at Xantho with a straight lunge aimed at his heart. Xantho dodged to the side to avoid the blade and batted it away with his own. Then, without hesitation, he kept the movement going and used Khamudi's momentum to push the Egyptian off balance, but he saw the move and darted backwards away from the danger.

"Good," Khamudi said.

Xantho didn't raise his blade in the Guard of the Jackal he had used in the past. He felt more comfortable with the blade low; he enjoyed being able to attack rather than counterattack. Xantho took a step forward and cut at Khamudi's face, and as the Egyptian moved to parry the feint, Xantho slashed low at his thighs. Khamudi jumped backwards, and Xantho followed him, cutting and slashing. Khamudi danced from foot to foot, parrying and dodging the onslaught. As their blades came together, Xantho feinted again and struck out with his knee, catching Khamudi's ribs.

The Egyptian groaned and pushed Xantho away. They were both sweating and breathing hard. Xantho felt strong, and he felt fast. That had been the first time he had struck his teacher. Today he actually felt faster than Khamudi. Undoubtedly, the Egyptian was stronger, but Xantho felt he had an edge with his speed.

"You grow more confident," Khamudi smiled,

"soon there will be no more need for lessons, my friend."

"Do you think I have improved?"

"For certain. You are fast, and you like to attack. You fight well."

That was high praise indeed, and Xantho nodded his thanks.

"Enough for today. We should get back to Priapus with all haste," said Khamudi.

They sheathed their swords and gathered together whatever kit they had left after the fight with the traitors.

"Why is the Granicus the right place for the battle?" Xantho asked Khamudi as they saddled the horses. Xantho looked out at the river stretching away into the distance.

"Memnon will have greater numbers of cavalry, elite cavalry and chariots. He is a Greek himself, from the island of Rhodes. So, he will have Greek warriors who fight in this new phalanx way of fighting with long spears. Alexander needs a battlefield where numbers do not matter and where he can use his own heavy cavalry and infantry without the edges of his army being overwhelmed."

"So what difference does the Granicus make?"

"Memnon won't be able to use his chariots because of the terrain and riverbank, and the battlefront will be narrow. Also, the river poses questions and challenges for both armies. And where there are questions, there are opportunities."

"I see," lied Xantho. He might be better at swordplay now, but he still knew little of war and armies.

Khamudi leapt onto his pony, and Penelope sat astride her horse, ready to leave.

"So," she said, "we ride for Priapus and then to the battle at the Granicus."

TWENTY THREE

Priapus was no longer the small town where Xantho had drank sweet wine and lounged in the sun. It was now an organised, sprawling military encampment, and the town of Priapus was in the middle of it, the bustling camp extending around its walls and stretching into the distance. Alexander commanded thirteen thousand infantry comprised of light and heavy units. The light infantry with their javelins and bows were the Agrianians and Cretan archers, as well as the Macedonian Hypaspists with their spears and large aspis shields. The heavy infantry were the pezhetairoi or foot companions with their hugely long sarissae spears. Alexander had also brought five thousand cavalry with him across the Dardanelles, again split between light and heavy units. The light cavalry were units such as Xantho's scouts who rode light ponies and could range ahead of the army and the heavy infantry

THE CURSE OF NARAM-SIN

or hetairoi. The heavy cavalry elite units were drawn from the Macedonian aristocracy on their huge war horses, both horse and rider trained for battle from the time they could walk.

Xantho, Penelope, and Khamudi approached that vast force on their ponies. Xantho had never seen so many people in one place, not even in the army of Cyrus the Great. It stretched beyond the horizon to the east and further north than Xantho could see. As they rode down a hillside shorn of grass consumed by the incredible number of cavalry horses, the noise of the army sounded like a city on market day. There was a constant humming, a burring noise of shouting and whistles, of horses and men about their duties.

Khamudi reined his pony in, and Xantho and Penelope fell alongside him.

"We must find Hephaestion," said Khamudi. His eyes pored over the camp, and the Egyptian sucked at his teeth. "So many people."

"Where do we begin to look for him among all this?" Xantho questioned.

"Isn't it said that Hephaestion is Alexander's friend?" asked Penelope. Khamudi nodded. "So, it shouldn't be hard to find the king. We find the king—we find Hephaestion."

"We have no rank in this army," Khamudi replied, "we are simple scouts and dressed as such. A scout is not simply granted an audience with the King of Greece. We must think."

"He does if he has this," said Xantho, holding up his hand, still sporting the fine gold ring Hephaestion had presented him with for saving his life. "If we can get to the Companions, Hephaestion assured me that showing this ring would get me to him if I ever needed him."

Penelope grinned, and Khamudi nodded.

"Very well. We have a plan. Let us find this Alexander, King of Macedon," said Khamudi.

They rode into the camp unchallenged by the perimeter guards. Scouts came and went across the line, and the three Warriors of the Light blended in. Soldiers wearing the brown sash of the quartermaster's unit directed them towards the camp's far right, near vast stabling pens. The three picked their way through the mass of tents, lean-to's and parade grounds the army had thrown together in the days since arriving at Priapus.

Eventually, Xantho saw the corralled areas appear beyond a fifty-pace square of open ground, currently being used by the pezhetairoi for manoeuvres. Their sarissae were incredibly long, and the infantrymen held them two-handed to keep them steady. A pezhetairoi unit was sixteen men, and they marched and turned under the barked orders of their lochagos, or captain. As Xantho watched the sarissae rise and fall into battle position, they were so long he wondered how an enemy could ever get close to them and strike a blow. It seemed impossible for an opposing infantry unit to charge into that massed forest of sharpened steel.

They skirted that small parade ground and approached a group of quartermasters by the edge of the stables behind which cavalry horses grazed.

"Been out long?" asked a short, grizzled soldier. Xantho dismounted, and the soldier took his reins and patted the mare's neck.

"A few days to the south," Xantho replied.

"See much? Any action?" asked the soldier, flashing a gap-toothed grin

"Some," said Xantho.

"Bloody barbarians, eh? They won't stand for long against us," the soldier quipped and winked. "I'll take care of her, mate, don't you worry." He stroked the mare's leg and pulled something from a pouch at his waist. He offered whatever morsel he held to the mare, and she scoffed it vigorously. The soldier laughed to himself at how much the mare enjoyed the snack.

"I need to get my report to the king's men. Where is he camped?" Xantho said.

"He is in the town, near the little river, or what was the little river. You can deliver your report there, friend," the soldier answered, and he led the mare away.

Penelope had her scarf pulled up to hide the lower part of her face and had her Phrygian helmet on. She had to hide her face and pass for a man amongst the army. A quartermaster soldier had already taken her mount, and she leant against a post.

"The king is behind the town, probably near where Naram-Sin spoke to Wulfgar," reckoned Xantho.

"Let's head that way then," she said.

Xantho left his saddle with the stable soldiers and brought with him the meagre belongings he'd carried from the fight with the traitors and Gula'an. He had his armour on his back and his rolled up chlamys long cloak, which he used as a blanket at night. His kopis blade and a dagger were at his waist, but he had left his bow and quiver on the field of battle. Khamudi and Penelope were similarly dressed and equipped, but Penelope wore her long chlamys cloak to disguise her slim frame. They traversed the north-facing perimeter of the stabling area, and then Xantho got a waft in his nose of cooking meat. He hadn't eaten that day, so they cut to the east to find the source of the smell. Xantho led the trio as they weaved in and out of storage tents and stacks of amphorae and piles of supplies. The scent grew closer. It was the fatty mouth-watering smell of roasting lamb, and Xantho made a beeline for it.

They came upon a fire pit dug deep into the earth and filled with charcoal, where two men sporting the brown sashes tended three long spits, where three lambs roasted slowly over hot coals.

"Hello, friends," Xantho called. The nearest soldier turned to eye Xantho with a cocked eyebrow.

"We are scouts, just in from the field. Can you find us a morsel or two?" Xantho said.

"Piss off. These are for the officers, not the likes of you," the soldier grumbled, shaking his head. "Bloody cavalry. Think they own the place."

"We haven't eaten today. Surely you can spare something?" Xantho asked again. He sensed Penelope bristling beside him, and then she took a step forward. Xantho grabbed her arm to hold her back. He had seen her quick temper before, and it wouldn't serve their purpose if they were placed under arrest.

"Don't mind him; he's surlier than an old whore. Here, sit down," said the second soldier and gestured to a collection of milking stools. Xantho thanked the man, and they sat down.

"What's wrong with you?" Penelope asked Xantho.

"I thought you would choke or crush them, and we'd find ourselves apprehended."

"Me? I was going to talk to them," she said, and

Xantho laughed. The soldier brought each a cut of lamb and a piece of flatbread, which they ate heartily. He then brought them each a small cup of watered wine.

"You are a true gentleman, sir," said Khamudi, bowing deeply to the soldier, who grinned.

"It's alright; there's plenty here, for now. Won't be if we don't push off in a day or two, though. Not with armies full of hungry so and so's," the soldier remarked. "Did you go far? See any barbarians?"

"Some," Khamudi replied. "You will get to see them up close soon enough."

"Do you think there'll be a battle soon, then?"

"Yes, for certain. How many more days will the supplies here last?"

The soldier scratched at his stubbly chin. "Maybe five more days, four or five."

"So, it must be soon. They must keep the army fed," Khamudi said.

They thanked the soldier again and continued the journey towards Priapus itself at the centre of the camp. No sooner had they turned around the corner and beyond the awning where the soldiers roasted lamb than Xantho bumped into a gathering of four men walking in the opposite direction. Xantho apologised to the man he had accidentally barged into and immediately recognised him. He wore the sash of the quartermaster's division and was a squat bandy-legged man. The same man who had chased Tiki through the Macedonian camp at the coast. Two of his fellow soldiers from that day were also there, plus one unfamiliar face.

"Hang on, I know you..." said bandy-legs. Xantho punched him in the throat and raked his instep down his shin, toppling bandy-legs to the ground. He kicked a second man in the belly, winding him, and then went to fight the remaining two soldiers but saw that Penelope and Khamudi had taken care of them. Bandy-legs lay writhing and groaning in the dirt, so Xantho kicked him hard in the face to silence him and used the sleeper hold Khamudi had taught him to send the winded man unconscious.

"What happened to the danger of us getting arrested?" Penelope uttered, out of breath.

"These are different. These were the men who wanted to enslave Tiki. They had it coming. Come on, best get out here." Xantho said, walking away as fast as possible without running. The last time he had run into bandy-legs, he had been a slave, new to the ways of the warrior. Now he had taken lives and seen much fighting, and as he strode through the camp, Xantho allowed himself a slight smile. It felt good to act without hesitation and with determination.

"So, we follow you now?" Penelope intoned as

they moved off.

"What? Well, no...but?" Xantho said. He hadn't realised it, but he supposed he was leading the way and deciding for the three of them, even though Khamudi was clearly the more experienced warrior. He hadn't consciously taken the lead. It had just happened.

"I'm teasing. It suits you, lead the way," Penelope grinned. Xantho blushed and looked at Khamudi, who smiled and winked. Xantho wasn't sure if they were mocking or supporting him, but he pressed on.

They came to the walls of Priapus and a perimeter of pezhetairoi heavy infantry soldiers, standing at five-pace intervals across a wide-ranging line of tents. They followed the line of guards to a more densely patrolled area, where a unit of sixteen infantry checked everyone going in and out of the officer's enclosure. Xantho approached an officer, marked by his muscled bronze breastplate, as opposed to the standard folded linen armour of the common soldiers. Xantho gave him a salute, and he nodded in response.

"We are scouts returned from the field. I must see Lord Hephaestion," Xantho said. The officer was a middle-aged man, clean-shaven, with a bull neck and a dark face. He gave Xantho a flat stare and frowned.

"Very well. Who is your officer?"

"He fell; we are all that's left of our unit."

"Which unit?"

"We are light cavalry under the command of Socrates."

"What's today's password?"

"I don't know. We have been gone for days," Xantho said.

The officer waved a hand and turned away. "I don't care where you've returned from. You're not getting in here without the password."

"It's important; the success of the war depends on the information I have."

"Well, you're very important, aren't you? If you were so important, you'd know the bloody password or which bloody officer to ask for. Now piss off."

The officer moved and looked like a seasoned fighter, all muscle and arrogance. Xantho didn't think it would help to press the issue. He twisted the fine gold ring from his finger, Hephaestion's ring, and held it tight in his fist. It was a risk handing it over to the officer; he could easily keep the treasure for himself. He could easily take the ring from Xantho, slide it over his own finger and send him away with a flea in his ear. If Xantho didn't get the ring to Hephaestion, and Alexander didn't get the message about the Granicus, surely his scouts would have found another suitable location for the battle. Alexander was reputed to be a fine young general, so he likely had his own ideas on where to fight the Persians. On the other hand, what if the battleground selected was not as strong as the Granicus? What if the Persians could bring their much larger numbers of cavalry to bear? Then their war chariots could make the difference. Gula'an would win again. If he won, then Gula'an would likely make good on his promise to drag Xantho's mother and Lithra's souls down into the underworld, where Nergal alone knew what horrors would await them. More than that, Xantho knew that countless lives depended on the war's outcome. Lives beyond measure would be lost in the never-ending wars in the world where Nergal became paramount amongst the gods.

He turned back to the officer, and the sergeant snarled at him.

"Sir, I know you are doing your job here, and I don't have the password," Xantho began.

"Listen, you turd, I warned you already," said the officer, cutting Xantho off mid-sentence.

"I work for Lord Hephaestion," Xantho interjected. "Bring he or his aides this ring, or send a man to do it. But do it; the war depends on it. Do you want to answer to King Alexander when he learns you turned me away?"

The officer stared hard into Xantho's eyes, and he met that stare. Xantho did his best to think of himself as the sunburned, rough-faced warrior who had looked back at him through the water's reflection with Penelope. He hoped that was the man the officer saw.

"Very well. I'll send your ring. You wait here. But if my man returns and you've bullshitted me, I'll rip off your head and piss down your dead neck."

"Fair enough," said Xantho, smiling at the officer. Smiling because the officer had seen the warrior.

The officer called a soldier from behind him. He gave the young man the ring and dashed off into the enclosure. Xantho went to where Penelope and Khamudi rested, sitting in the shade of a pile of sarissae spears.

"Well, how did it go?" Penelope asked.

"I gave him Hephaestion's ring. Let's see if it does the trick."

The day drew on, and soldiers came and went from the enclosure. The camp was a hive of activity. Scouts bearing messages were admitted and came out again with new orders. Carts trundled past with skins of water, hay for horses, and all the endless supplies and needs of the army of Alexander of Macedon. Xantho waited patiently. He shared a waterskin with Khamudi and Penelope. The Egyptian even dozed for a while, much to Penelope's surprise. The war's success depended on the three of them and if they could get the message to Hephaestion. With so much at stake, Xantho found it hard to believe Khamudi could sleep, but sleep he did.

As the sun began its journey into the underworld for the night, Xantho saw the lad sent by the officer with his ring emerge from the enclosure. A tall warrior flanked him with long black hair and a shining black beard. That warrior wore a fine iron breastplate fronted with the snarling face of a lion. This glorious warrior marched to the officer, who gave the crispest salute Xantho had ever seen. He pointed the warrior in Xantho's direction.

"Here we go," Xantho said. He sprang to his feet and kicked Khamudi's boot to wake him.

The warrior approached, and Xantho and Penelope saluted him, lacking the snappy straightness of the officer but offering the best they could muster. The warrior nodded and held up Hephaestion's ring.

"You are the soldier who possessed this ring?" he asked. His voice was serious, as was his long face beneath the jet-black beard.

"Yes, lord. Lord Hephaestion himself gave it to me only a few days ago. He said I should use it if I ever need his help."

"And do you need his help?"

"I have returned from the field, lord, and I have important news for Lord Hephaestion. I wouldn't have used the ring if it wasn't of the utmost importance."

"Very well. My name is Agathon; follow me."

Xantho shot a glance at Penelope. She had her scarf up, but he saw the smile behind her eyes. He winked at her, and they followed Agathon into the king's enclosure. They passed the officer and his men. All sixteen saluted and bowed their heads as Agathon passed by; he returned their salutes with one of his own. As they passed the officer, he followed Xantho with his eyes, so Xantho gave him a wink as well. The officer's face creased in a grimace, and Xantho laughed to himself and followed Agathon into Alexander's headquarters.

TWENTY FOUR

Agathon led them through the walls of Priapus and on into the town itself. They marched past groups of officers and soldiers dressed in similar finery to Agathon. It was a bright day, and a light breeze kept the air fresh within the packed town. There was laughter and singing from unseen buildings and laneways, accompanied by shouting and a distant clash of arms, where warriors no doubt practised their skills. Xantho noted that morale was high. These Macedonians seemed confident and sure of their ability to win the battle ahead. Xantho hoped it wasn't hubris. Macedon was a small country to the north of Greece, not unlike his native Thrace. The Persian Empire was vast, even in the distant past of his father's time. It would take weeks or months to cross it. The empire stretched across an unimaginable land mass, from the shores of Greece to the far east of India, spanning deserts, cities, and jungles. The Great King could muster armies beyond measure. Xantho assumed Alexander knew all this, that he and his officers fully understood the vastness of the Great King's empire, and still they were confident of victory. *They must either be ferocious or foolish.*

"So, you fought alongside Hephaestion?" asked Agathon, looking across at Xantho as they marched. They were of a similar height, but Agathon was younger; Xantho guessed at least two years younger, as he counted time at least.

"Yes, lord. A force of cavalry attacked him, and we came to his aid," Xantho replied.

"He was with the Agrianians then?"

"Yes, lord. They are outstanding fighters. We will need them in the wars to come."

"You are not Macedonians?" Agathon said, casting his eyes over Khamudi with his dark skin and Penelope, who hid her face.

"Thracians, lord. Light cavalry in the service of Commander Seleucus," Xantho said. He hoped that what he said didn't sound too outlandish. As much as possible, Xantho tried to say what he thought Naram-Sin would say. He supposed the trick was to sound confident, even if he was completely unsure if what he said was what Agathon expected to hear.

"You scouts are a strange bunch. I hear all kinds of stories."

"Really, lord?" said Xantho. *He doesn't know the half of it.*

"Here we are. The Companions are at their training. You can wait here in the shade; this Persian also awaits an audience." Agathon led them into the wide square at the centre of Priapus, which Xantho saw had now transformed into a military training square. Bare-chested men covered the square. They wrestled and practised with sword, lance, and javelin.

"Good day to you, scouts. Please wait here," said Agathon, gesturing to where a small, rotund man leant against a building wall dressed in bright yellow and green robes, with his head wrapped in the Persian fashion. Xantho nodded thanks to Agathon and led Penelope and Khamudi over to where the Persian waited.

"Peace be with you," the Persian said, twisting his long moustache in ringed fingers.

"Peace be with you also," Khamudi responded, bowing his head to the Persian. Xantho did the same.

"I see you are Macedonians?" said the Persian.

"Thracians. My friend here is Egyptian," Xantho clarified.

"A more cultured man then, inclined to my own tastes," he said, smiling at Khamudi, who nodded in return. "What to make of these

Macedonians? All they think of is war. Look at them." He flicked his head towards the training square.

"Are these officers?" asked Xantho.

"No, indeed. These are the Royal Companions, ranking higher than officers. Alexander himself is there, somewhere, rolling around and fighting with the others. These are his fellow cavalrymen."

Xantho's jaw dropped. The king himself. He watched them, the aristocracy of Macedonia. They looked like Greeks, much like himself in many respects. Directly in front of him, a group wrestled in pairs. They did not just practice holds, nor did they rein in their strength. Punches were thrown in earnest, and men cried out in pain or submission. To Xantho's right, more pairs fought with kopis blades wrapped with cloth to dull the blade. They fought hard, sweat pouring down their glistening bodies.

Xantho looked across at Penelope, who seemed even more enthralled than he at the display before them.

"Are you enjoying the view?" he asked. Penelope shrugged.

"Where am I supposed to look? They are... impressive," she said.

"Do you think they can win the war against the Great King?" Khamudi asked.

"The empire is soft and fractured. These men are hungry; they are as fierce as wolves. They fight with the viciousness of tribesmen but with the organisation and thought of Athenians. They can win," the Persian nodded.

"Which is why you are here," said Khamudi.

"Which is why I am here," allowed the Persian.

A shout rang out from across the square, and the men moved away to the sides, leaving only two men in the centre. A line of ten mustered to oppose them, each armed with long wooden swords similar in size to a kopis.

"Hephaestion," Xantho said, recognising the taller of the two who stood against ten.

The two Macedonians readied themselves side by side, armed with their blunted kopis blades and their ten foes fanned into a wide line to strike from the front and flanks. The ten stood poised and ready, but whilst they waited for an order, a signal to charge, the shorter of the two men sprang into the attack. He launched forward, cutting and slashing in a blur of speed and power. Hephaestion himself then followed. Where the smaller man was all power and aggression, Hephaestion was speed and skill. Xantho watched in awe as the two men fought back to back in unison. They turned their foes, and the fury and surprise of the smaller man's attack had broken their line. He alone had beaten three into submission in a matter of heartbeats. Hephaestion dealt with two, lunging and parrying, to great effect.

"They fight well," said Khamudi.

"If there was ever a man for an understatement, it would be you, my friend," Xantho quipped, smiling. The two warriors were magnificent, and it was all over by the time Xantho looked back to the action. Most of the attackers had fallen in the dirt, and those who remained conceded the fight. Hephaestion slapped the smaller man on the back as they laughed together. The gathered Macedonian aristocratic warriors applauded and shouted their acclaim at the practice fight.

"You see how they fight? They are like animals, bred and raised to blood and blade. How can we Persians, in all our refinement and culture, stand against such savagery?" said the Persian, his eyes glassy and face ashen. It was a fair assumption; Xantho had never seen noblemen fight like that. Of course, he had seen his father, Tiribazos, and his sons, train for war. But that was mostly to develop their skill at riding, javelin throwing and archery. Not ferocious hand-to-hand combat like this.

Hephaestion handed his practice blade to an aide and strode over to where Xantho and others waited. The smaller man followed. The tall Macedonian smiled warmly and waved, and Xantho held up his hand in greeting. He had barely spoken to Hephaestion and was taken aback by his warmth.

"So, the ring was useful, no?" said Hephaestion as he drew closer. Sweat soaked his curly blonde hair, plastering his locks to the sides of his soft, round face. That handsome face was in complete contrast to the scars which crisscrossed his muscled arms and chest. The arrow wound in his shoulder still angry and red around a tight dressing.

Xantho saluted, and Hephaestion held up a hand as if to show it wasn't required.

"Yes, lord, I would not have been able to get my message to you otherwise."

Hephaestion held up the ring, smiling. He tossed it back to Xantho.

"Keep it. You might need it again. These scouts came to my rescue when I was with the Agrianians. This man here saved my life," Hephaestion said, turning to address the smaller fighter who stood at his shoulder. "They ride with Naram-Sin, the strange easterner I told you about. They fight like demons from Hades."

"Then I, too, owe you my thanks for saving my friend's life," enounced the smaller man. His voice was clear and crisp, but he did not smile his thanks. The man was a head shorter than Xantho and Hephaestion but much broader in the chest. His shoulders were thick with corded muscle, and his neck broad. He had large eyes, and a cleanly shaven face. Xantho bowed his head in acknowledgement.

"My Lord King, I..." began the Persian, but a raised finger from the smaller man stopped him mid-sentence. *'King', the Persian had said.* Xantho swallowed and looked at Penelope sideways. She returned his wide-eyed look of surprise. *Is this short, powerful warrior Alexander?*

"Not now," Alexander bade. "Now we talk amongst warriors. We talk of trade later."

The Persian bowed elaborately, almost prostrating himself on the ground.

"Where is Naram-Sin?" asked Hephaestion.

"He fell, my lord. Persian cavalry and a squadron of Immortals garbed in red attacked and outnumbered us."

"I am sorry for your loss," said Hephaestion, a look of genuine sorrow on his handsome face. "He was a great soldier. He will be missed."

"He took many of the enemies with him into the afterlife, lord," Xantho put forth.

Alexander smiled. "So, you fought against the Immortals?" he said, stepping forward, eyes bright.

"Yes, Lord King,"

"Tell me, how do they fight?"

"They are fearless. Each is highly skilled with lance and bow. They do not, however, have the same quality of arms and armour as your heavy infantry and cavalry," Xantho replied. Alexander nodded, and his head leant to one side as he stared at Xantho, deep in thought. Xantho still felt as though he knew little about battles and tactics, but what he had said was true. The Persians were armed with wicker and wood, whilst the Macedonians wielded steel, and their hard-linen armour would easily turn most blades.

"So, what is your message?" asked Hephaestion. Xantho cleared his throat. He looked at the two Macedonians, at the fierceness behind their gentle youthful faces. He had not considered it until this point, but he was a former slave and bastard son of a Persian satrap who was about to give battle advice to the King of Greece. Xantho suddenly needed to piss, and his mouth had gone as dry as a desert. He licked his lips.

"We know Memnon has his army marshalled at Zeleia and that they have not burned their way into a retreat. The fields remain fat with crops before our advance. So, they want to fight."

Alexander nodded.

"They keep us well supplied," he said, and Hephaestion chuckled.

"I believe, my lords, that we came across a perfect place to fight the enemy."

Hephaestion and Alexander looked at each other and then back to Xantho. The expectation spread across their faces like a child on a birthday morning.

"There is a river, the Granicus, it is called. Swampy marshland protects one side, and on the right, the river splits into its tributaries."

"So, they could not use their numbers against us," said Alexander.

"Correct, Lord King. The ground is not suitable for chariots, either. The river, though, has steep banks, and they will likely be there before us once they discover that we have marched—which they surely will. Our men would need to climb those banks in the face of the Persian infantry."

"True. But I like the sound of this Granicus. Hephaestion, see what further intelligence we can gather on the place. Scouts, I thank you for your service. This information is most welcome. You have done well," said Alexander. Xantho thought his heart would burst from his chest with pride. "Now, Persian, come. Walk with me," Alexander motioned to the merchant, and they set off together.

"Please, stay here for a while. I will have refreshments brought for you all," Hephaestion insisted. "Tell me, are you three all that remains of Naram-Sin's unit?"

"I am afraid so, lord. The rest fell in the fight with the Immortals."

"That's a shame. I am sorry for your fallen comrades. Is there anything I can do for you?"

Penelope was suddenly at Xantho's shoulder, and she inclined her head to Hephaestion. "Yes, lord, we are without a unit now. I would request if you would allow it, that we join one of the heavy cavalry units under your command?" she asked.

Hephaestion raised an eyebrow at her. "You have a strange voice for a soldier. But there are many strange things about the warriors of Naram-Sin. However, by all means, I can attach you to a cavalry unit. I will send a man to you."

Penelope nodded in thanks. Hephaestion waved over a youth from the edges of the training ground and ordered him to bring meats, bread and wine for the three scouts. Hephaestion left, leaving the three Warriors of the Light alone.

"Why did you ask that?" Xantho questioned. Of course, they needed to join a new unit now that only three remained. Xantho had given little thought to that, thinking only of getting the message to Hephaestion.

"I just don't think it's safe for us to be ranging ahead of the army," Penelope said. She was right. The three of them were vulnerable to attack from Gula'an and whatever forces he had under his command, Blood Immortals and cavalry at least.

"It was a good request. We will be at the heart of the battle in the heavy cavalry. Our goal is to help Alexander win," Khamudi remarked. Xantho wasn't sure how he felt at being at the heart of the battle. The other battle he had fought in had been a terrible welter of blood and death. This was likely to be the same.

"Gula'an will be there, somewhere," said Penelope.

"He will," Khamudi agreed, "and it will be up to us to stop him from turning the tide of the battle. Ah, our refreshments arrive."

Four young Macedonians, pages to the Macedonian noblemen, came scurrying across the training square. They carried three stools and a folding table. On the table, the pages lay down platters of sweetmeats, bread, and watered wine. Xantho thanked the young men, who bowed and hurried away. He sat down on the small stool and groaned; it felt good to rest for a while. He hadn't realised how tired he was until he sat. Xantho rubbed at his eyes and yawned. Then, he took a pitcher of wine and poured it into the three cups. He drank deeply, as the wine was sweet and cool.

"Kind of Hephaestion, to look after us so," Penelope chimed as she lowered her scarf to sip at the wine.

"He is very handsome," said Khamudi.

"Yes, very," she agreed.

"Strong, too," the Egyptian added.

"Yes, very," Penelope said again.

Xantho felt himself flush with jealousy. He supposed the Macedonian was handsome, but to hear Penelope say it was a different matter altogether.

"That's enough of that kind of talk," he muttered, but then Penelope and Khamudi laughed together. They had teased him, and he had fallen straight into their trap. Was it so obvious how far he had fallen for Penelope?

"Very funny, well done," he said, and he laughed along with them.

The day lurched into mid-afternoon, and the training square became deserted as the Macedonians returned to their duties. Xantho sat back on his stool, resting his back on a cool stone wall and enjoying the shade. His belly was full of delicious sweetmeats and filling flatbread. The wine was cooling and refreshing, and for the first time in a long time, Xantho felt relaxed. Khamudi had fallen asleep in a similar position, and Penelope sat back with Xantho with her two hands over a full belly.

"We haven't eaten so well since, well…" she said.

"I know. I could sleep for a week," Xantho replied.

"Khamudi has been quiet since we lost Khensa and the others."

"He has. He has lost his love and his friends," said Xantho. Khamudi had lost Khensa, who had been his partner for a thousand years. Xantho could not begin to imagine how that felt. He had powerful feelings for Penelope, but they had only just got to know each other. Khamudi and Khensa had shared countless lifetimes together. Khamudi had also lost his sword brothers and sisters to Gula'an and had seen his former friends slain. Xantho himself had taken two of their heads, and surely now those traitors would be in the underworld realm, where he hoped they would wander in pain with eternity to consider their treachery.

"Do you think they get used to it? Losing one another, over and again?" said Penelope.

"I don't know. At least they know they will be reunited again at the next battle."

"Still, though. I would not like to see you die, Xantho," she said. He looked across at her, her green eyes locked onto his. As usual, there was a curl of her copper-brown hair in her eyes. She had taken her helmet off once the square had become deserted. He reached over and brushed the curl away from her face.

"Nor I you. You are beautiful, Penelope. I think I…" he began, then fumbled over the words he so desperately wanted to get out. He stroked the side of her face, her skin soft beneath his touch. She leant her head into his caress, and he held his hand there, enjoying the feeling. She placed her hand over his own and smiled a warm, wide smile, which lit up her face.

"I know. Me too," Penelope said. Now it was Xantho's turn to smile.

He leant close to her and stopped when his face was a hand's width away from hers. He could feel the gentle warmness of her breath, and their eyes searched one another's. They were bonded by the power of their Palmstones and the mage abilities that she could pass between them. But this feeling they shared, in the shade of the training square at Priapus, amidst the raging war between Alexander and Darius, and Enlil and Nergal, was something else. It was the bond between a man and a woman. He had shared that bond once before with Lithra, but what he felt for Penelope burned in his heart like a fire. Being so close to her now made his heart race. Just as it did in battle, with that same heightened sense of feeling and awareness.

He glanced down at her soft lips, moist from the watered wine. He leant in further and pressed his lips against hers. Her mouth warm and accepting. They shared their first kiss, and Xantho felt the thrill of the Palmstone strength running through his veins, as it must be through hers. He could taste the sweet wine on her lips and never wanted the moment to end. He knew it had to end, however, for they would march on the Granicus in the morning and the battle between Alexander and the might of the Persian Empire.

TWENTY FIVE

Hephaestion was as good as his word, and he found a place for Xantho, Penelope, and Khamudi in the Hetairoi Companion heavy cavalry. An officer had seen to it that they were provided with the heavier breastplates of that unit, a Boeotian helmet, and a xyston which was a cornel wood lance with spear points at either end. The ponies Xantho and the others had ridden on their scouting duties were obviously not sufficient for heavy cavalry duty, and so Xantho, Penelope and Khamudi were now mounted on heavy horses from the hinterland of Macedonia. Hephaestion placed them in a unit of two hundred cavalrymen commanded by Agathon, the same soldier who had led them into the royal enclosure at Priapus.

Khamudi loved the xyston spear. The Egyptian had never fought with a double-ended lance before, and he liked the balance of it. As the army marched towards the Granicus River, Khamudi and Xantho's morning training now consisted solely of sparring with the xyston on horseback. Xantho liked its balance, but at first, he'd found it difficult to master, being so used to the chopping and parrying movements of the sword. Over the course of the two days' march, Xantho became more proficient at the thrust and lunge movements of the lance, and Khamudi himself fought with it as though he had been using the thing his whole life.

Xantho stood in wait with Penelope and Khamudi, along with the rest of their unit, watching the enormous lines of infantrymen march upon the river ahead. The infantry filed past the elevated position where the cavalry waited, their huge sarissae pikes waving above them as they marched like an enormous rolling forest. Xantho could see the river beyond, fringed with short dark green trees extending off into the distance towards a range of hills. Across the river, Xantho could just make out the enemy yonder. They threw a cloud of dust as their cavalrymen patrolled the far riverbank, which looked steep and imposing from where Xantho could see.

Word had filtered through the ranks that the river, though wide, was shallow at this time of the year and should be only knee high. Between Xantho's position and the river water were fields of bright yellow crops. He wasn't sure of their type, but those beautiful bright plants now became crushed and pounded to dirt under the boots of the marching pezhetairoi heavy infantry. Where those fields met the Granicus, steep banks inclined into the river itself, broken here and there by shallow slopes. All led into the river's flow, dotted by patches of bright white gravel, washed to shine by the river's force when it would rise to fill its high banks during winter.

"Are you nervous?" Xantho said, leaning across to Penelope, who sat astride her horse next to him.

"Yes, of course I am. Are you?"

He knew it was a pointless question. Undoubtedly, he was nervous too. He just wanted to check that Penelope was alright. Every man in the thirty thousand infantry and five thousand cavalry of the Macedonian army was nervous. The opposing Persian cavalry outnumbered the cavalry alone three to one. Although he had made a good fist of explaining why Naram-Sin had recommended this location for the battle, Xantho wasn't so sure. The banks of the river were very steep. To march up those banks in the face of Persian arrows and spears would be horrific, and many men would die.

"Khamudi, tell me again why we led Alexander to this place?"

The Egyptian on Xanthos's left smiled and

adjusted himself in the saddle.

"No chariots, and the front, although long, does not enable the Persians to encircle us. Also, if we can get amongst them, their infantry and cavalry are no match for ours."

"That's it; I remember now," Xantho nodded.

"Don't forget to stay close to me, Xantho. We must be close if I am to give you the power," said Penelope.

"I'll remember. I don't plan on leaving you alone in the battle. Save the magic, though, Gula'an is out there somewhere, and you might need it."

"Where will he be, do you think?" she asked. Xantho shrugged and looked at Khamudi.

"He favours the chariot, but the ground does not suit. So Gula'an will probably be with the cavalry. Close to Memnon, I expect," said the Egyptian. "If we see him, we must try to take him. We must stop him before he can bring his power to bear on the battle. Make no mistake, his priority will be to kill Alexander."

The conversation was interrupted as Agathon turned his mount to address his men.

"Alright, men, almost time for us to deploy. Listen up now, and listen carefully," he said. A hush came over the cavalrymen as they leaned forward to listen to their leader. "The pezhetairoi will form up in ranks of eight, half their usual number. The line of battle is long, and they need to cover its span. Parmenio has the left with the light cavalry. We line up on the right behind the Agrianians and the Hypaspists."

The Agrianians, that at least gave Xantho some comfort. Their ferocity would be welcome during the battle. Xantho felt his bowels loosening for the fourth time that day, but he tried his best to ignore the feeling. Even though he had drunk over half of his waterskin, his mouth was dry. He told himself it was just nerves and that every man was the same.

"Questions?" said Agathon.

"Why aren't we behind the centre like usual?" shouted a burly soldier behind Xantho.

"Because we want to draw their horses into the river. The Agrianians will do that. When they do, the plan is that we will charge from the flank."

"How are we supposed to get up those steep banks?" asked another man.

"On your horse," answered Agathon. The rest of the unit laughed.

"It's going to be dark soon, lord. Will we fight today or tomorrow?"

"That's a good question, and I don't know. We'll wait for our orders. When we see the Agrianians in place, then we'll move down. But, for now, have a piss or a shit if you need one.

If you've got food, finish it. There won't be any dismounting when we get down there; you'll be pissing down your horses' backs. And I don't want to be smelling your stinking piss for the rest of the day," said Agathon. The men laughed again, and a handful jumped from their horses and ran behind the lines to do their business.

The Macedonians continued to form up in full view of the Persian army on the further bank, and the Persians took no action to stop or interfere with the dispositions. The whole of the left flank and central infantry positions were fully in place before the Agrianians and the Hypaspists left the column of march and fell into ranks on the right-hand side of the army. Agathon gave the order to advance, and Xantho followed the unit down the hill and along the line of battle to fall in behind the Agrianians. They joined the line with the rest of Alexander's heavy cavalry, and as Xantho brought his mount into position, he scanned the lines for any sign of the Macedonian king, but he was nowhere to be seen. During the complex manoeuvre of moving the army from marching column to battle formation, the din of shouting and marching feet had filled the air, rumbling across the plain. Now that they drew the army up, an eerie silence fell across both sides as anticipation and acute fear took hold. Xantho felt that fear himself, the fear of the terrible pain of the wound that does not kill, the fear of death, the fear of Penelope or Khamudi's death. The fear was real and terrifying for the warriors gathered on either side of the Granicus.

"It grows late," Xantho said, glancing at Khamudi to his right. The day was waning into early evening, and if there wasn't a move from either army soon, then the day would turn to night and surely the battle would be postponed until the morning. Secretly, Xantho hoped that would be the case. Even if it was only a delay, it was undoubtedly better than facing the fury of Persian steel today.

"It does," said the Egyptian, smiling slightly at the corner of his mouth.

"Will we fight today?"

"Didn't we already have this conversation? Try to be calm, we will or we will not. If we do, then be ready."

Xantho supposed he had already asked that question. It was just nerves. He scratched at his neck where his breastplate chafed, trying to think of another question to kill time and avoid the thoughts of pain and blood flooding his mind. A trumpet sounded from the left of the battle line, and a tremendous roar went up amongst the Macedonian lines. In the saddle, Xantho made himself as tall as he could see what caused the commotion, but there was no advance, no movement forward from either army. The roar rippled up the army coming towards Xantho like a wave. His horse became skittish, so he patted her neck to calm her. Xantho turned at the sound of horses behind him.

Just as he did so, Alexander himself cantered past on a huge black beast of a horse with a white patch between its eyes. Alexander held his xyston high for the men to see, and they roared their approval. The man Xantho had seen bare-chested on the training grounds now looked magnificent. He wore a pure white cloak which streamed behind him, his armour shone with the snarling face of a lion at his chest, and his shining helmet crested with a red plume flowed above him. His three-hundred-strong Royal Squadron of heavy cavalry trailed him. All mounted on huge war horses. As Alexander passed Xantho's position, two short trumpet blasts rang out, and ahead of him, the savage Agrianians bellowed as one and advanced on the river.

Xantho's heart sank as he saw them move forward. He looked to Penelope, and she looked back, her mouth set in a straight line and her knuckles white where she held on tight to her horse. The massed ranks of Hypaspists also moved forward now, and together with the Agrianians, they entered the waters of the Granicus. A matching roar now erupted from the opposite side of the river, where the Persian cavalry launched their short javelins and loosed their arrows at the advancing Macedonian light infantry. Xantho marvelled at the sheer determination of the Agrianians to advance under what was a deadly and endless hail of missiles. Those brave light infantrymen held their shields high and kept on pressing forward. Xantho could see they were knee deep in the river now, but they were taking heavy losses. What had been shouts and cheers of advance now became mixed with the screams of the injured and dying. The light infantrymen loosed their own javelins, thousands of the short spears launching up the bank to sink home into the front rank of the enemy lines.

Ahead of Xantho now was open ground. The Agrianians were all committed to the advance and well into the river, almost at its far bank.

"How can they possibly get up the bank? It's madness," shouted Penelope above the roar of the battle.

"Gods help them, but they are falling in their hundreds," Xantho responded.

Agathon rode across their line and waved his spear over his head. "Now, now, on me, on me!" he yelled as he rode past. The unit pushed off to Xantho's right at a hard gallop, away from the light infantry assault.

"We are going the wrong way," Xantho shouted to Khamudi, but the Egyptian couldn't hear him above the thunder of the massed cavalry. Xantho looked behind to see the Agrianians were falling back; they were retreating from the Persian front in good order with their shields raised but retreating nonetheless. Suddenly the Persian cavalry leapt from the far bank like an avalanche, falling on the light infantry divisions without mercy. As the enemy poured across the river and into the light infantry, Xantho thought they must lose the day before it had even begun. But then the river on his right exploded in a torrent of spray as a heavy horse thundered down the stream itself. In his war glory, it was Alexander charging the flank of the attacking Persian cavalry.

Xantho watched the king thunder down the river in a plume of white water, and his heart raced, thumping against his breastplate as he followed Agathon in a wide arc, which led them into the riverbed as they followed Alexander's lead. Amongst the furious clash of arms ahead and the roar of the charge, it was difficult for Xantho to get a sense of what happened in front or to the side of him. He saw flashes of Persian javelins from atop the river's banks to his right, but he did not feel in danger. The charge pitched right, and he followed, his horse climbing the riverbank. Its forelegs slipped on the mud-churned slope, but the mare made it up and drove on to continue. Xantho now charged through the Persian ranks, the power of his war horse driving him forwards. He assumed Alexander had driven his heavy cavalry into the gap the charging Persians had left when they pursued the retreating Agrianians. Suddenly, the charge slowed, and the Persians closed in on them. A bearded face to Xantho's left snarled, and a javelin jabbed his breastplate, shoving him backwards. Xantho clung to his horse and thrust back with his xyston. The longer spear stabbed the Persian in the face, slicing the flesh of his cheek open in a bloom of bright blood, and the Persian tumbled away.

It was chaos now, and the enemy surrounded and pressed them hard. The soldier in front of Xantho tumbled from his mount with an arrow in his eye. A javelin gouged that falling warrior's throat open, and blood splashed back onto Xantho's thighs. Xantho shouted and launched forward with his xyston, feeling the resistance as the point pushed into a horse's flesh and through to the meat beyond. He heard a high-pitched keening beside him, and Penelope was there thrusting with her spear, but the Persians pressed her, and he watched in horror as a javelin scraped her helmet, narrowly missing her face. Penelope winced at the strike, but her face came up snarling. She hooked her xyston in the crook of her arm and thrust her hands forward. The surrounding air shimmered in the now familiar way, and the adjacent Persians flew backwards, screaming with terror at the unseen and impossible force. The Macedonians didn't seem to notice, but the space allowed them to kick their mounts into a fresh charge. Xantho surged forwards, and suddenly, they were through the Persian lines and riding in the open.

Xantho grinned and whooped for joy. Penelope had her teeth clenched and nodded back at him. Khamudi, on his other side, grinned from ear to ear as they rode behind the enemy positions. Suddenly the line arced and wheeled again, and they crashed into the rear formation of the Persian lines. These were not cavalrymen now but Persian infantry with wicker breastplates and light shields. Xantho stabbed with his spear, and his horse smashed through the lightly armoured enemy. The Persians fell to the Macedonian heavy horse cavalry like wheat under the scythe, and in a few heartbeats, Xantho found himself back at the riverbank charging parallel to the advancing Macedonian pezhetairoi and their deadly sarissae. The Macedonian infantry could now climb the banks of the Granicus unopposed and bring the devastating force of their long pikes to bear.

"This battle is over," Khamudi shouted above the roar of battle, "they'll form up again, but Alexander has won."

"So, what do we do?"

"Keep fighting. Gula'an must show his hand

soon," Khamudi yelled.

Xantho followed the charge of cavalry as they swarmed amongst the Persian archers, who fled before them. Xantho used his xyston overhand, striking at the terrified, lightly armed soldiers as they came into range. A trumpet blast sounded again, and Xantho turned just in time to see a line of Persian cavalry charging at his flank. They must have reorganised after the initial shock of Alexander's charge and had come now to wrest the battle back in their favour. It was Xantho's turn now to feel the slam and jolt of a charge as the enemy charge hit home. Khamudi went down in the strike, and Xantho's leg was caught against a Persian horse, its weight driving him backwards. He swung his spear at the attacker, striking the man's face with the cornel wood shaft. The Persian gritted his teeth, then closed his eyes with the pain, and Xantho allowed the spear to swing in a full circle so he could bring the rear-end spear point to bear. He slammed that point into his enemy's chest, rejoicing as it passed through the armour with a crack and sank into the beating heart beyond.

Xantho realised that the Persian javelins were too short. He watched down the line as the enemy wasted their attack outside the range of their cavalry weapons, where the longer Macedonian xyston spear smashed home with devastating effect. An arrow clipped from

Xantho's breastplate, and he brought his spear around again to stab at the faceless mass of enemies on his flank. He couldn't see where the blade struck, but blood splashed across his face, and he stabbed again wildly at the surrounding enemy. That attacking line of Persian horsemen now gave way in the face of a brutal charge from an arriving Macedonian force. Xantho saw the immense bulk of Alexander's black horse driving into the Persians, and the King himself lay about him with his xyston. This charge caused the Macedonian warriors around Xantho to shout and cry out with battle fury, and they pressed forward, attacking the enemy with renewed ferocity.

Alexander and his royal companions drove their way into the Persians but became slowed by the enemy's own elite cavalry. Xantho saw big black-bearded warriors beating back the Macedonians with war axes and swords. Finally, Alexander himself took a blow to the helmet and sagged in the saddle. Xantho's heart leapt into his throat as a huge Persian swung back to aim a blow which would surely take the King's head. But a Macedonian blade snaked forward like a serpent's tongue and cleaved the Persian's arm from his body.

All was chaos now as the Macedonians fought with wild abandon against the enemy, and Xantho found himself caught up in that melee.

The battle lust was upon him. He thrust and parried with his spear, the shaft slick with the blood of his enemies and his own sweat. His xyston became trapped between a falling enemy and his mount, so Xantho pressed the shaft down, bending it until it snapped. He then reversed the shaft and used the butt end spear point to attack again, slamming it into a Persian's eye. Penelope was beside him, her face snarling and awash with Persian blood.

The roar of the Persian lines turned into screams, and suddenly where there had been the shove and thrust of two cavalry lines, there was a break in the fighting as the Persians fell away and retreated, and a great cry went up from the Macedonian lines. Alexander held his kopis blade aloft, and the cavalry swirled around him. The Persian cavalry and infantry were in full retreat now, and Xantho thought that surely the battle was over. However, as the Persians fled, an additional force marched forward on the field. A mass of spear points tramped in perfect order towards Xantho's position, like some multi-spined monster eking its way across the battlefield.

"Greeks!" shouted a soldier behind Xantho. These then were the Greek mercenaries under Memnon's command, coming now in their bristling phalanx to kill Alexander. If the Greeks reached the Macedonian cavalry, their spears would trap him and his companions in a great slaughter. The King shouted an order that Xantho couldn't make out, but the cavalry lurched to ride away from that phalanx when a thunderous crack split the evening air. A warm wind flooded the field, the ground opened up a great crevice, and Macedonian horses fell screaming into the abyss. Where he had been sure they had won the battle, now Xantho felt terror. He clenched his teeth and froze, a hollow feeling tearing at his guts. The ground splitting and destroying the Macedonians' devastating cavalry formations could mean only one thing: Gula'an was at the Granicus.

TWENTY SIX

The Immortals of Gula'an, in their blood-red tunics and fish-scale armour, raced from behind the Greek mercenary phalanx and charged full tilt towards Alexander and his Royal Companions. Their lines bristled with spears. Ever the enemy of the cavalry, infantry spearmen in formation can easily pick off riders with their long weapons, and when spearmen, or better still, a phalanx, are in formation, horses will not charge into that fearsome wall of steel points. These Immortals were the things of Gula'an, the same Blood Immortals who had charged from the forest in the battle against the treacherous warriors of the dark. Gula'an's rending of the battlefield had isolated Alexander from his pezhetairoi heavy infantry, leaving him exposed to the Persian attack.

The Macedonian horseman gaped at each other, their faces contorting as they tried to understand how the ground had been torn asunder.

"It's Zeus; the gods are on the battlefield!" Xantho heard one man shout from somewhere in the melee.

But it was not the gods, it was Gula'an, and Xantho could see the servant of Nergal now behind his Immortals. He rode a pure white Persian stallion, his black staff aloft and urging his warriors on to the attack.

"We have to get them moving!" Xantho shouted to Khamudi. The enemy had knocked the Egyptian from his horse, but he stood now at Xantho's heels, his armour and helmet crusted with blood and gore.

"Get to Hephaestion. The Agrianians are behind us," said Khamudi, and Xantho twisted in the saddle to peer behind him. It was a race against time now. The Blood Immortals were closing fast, and still, Alexander's cavalry remained rooted to the spot in shock at the devastating magic of Gula'an. He could see the Phrygian caps of the Agrianians bobbing above the fray beyond, where they were engaged with the Greek mercenary phalanx. Memnon's mercenaries had half circled behind the Macedonian cavalry in an attempt to encircle them. The Agrianians had acted quickly to meet that manoeuvre, and crucially they were on this side of Gula'an's rend. In the distance, Xantho could see the long sarissae of the Macedonian infantry, but they were beyond the rend and engaged with the Persian infantry.

"Come on, with me," Xantho bellowed, and he dug his heels into the mare's sides, spurring her on towards where Alexander's red crested helmet turned from side to side amongst his companions. Xantho knew that where Alexander fought, Hephaestion must also, and so he made for the king. Penelope and Khamudi followed, the former on horseback and the latter running alongside Xantho's steed. They charged through the press of horses, the Blood Immortals only thirty paces away now, charging and roaring with spears levelled.

"Hephaestion, Lord Hephaestion!" Xantho shouted, his throat scratching with the exertion of raising his voice above the din of battle. Hephaestion turned. His mouth agape, but he recognised Xantho and urged his mount on to meet him.

"What work of Hades is this?" said Hephaestion through clenched teeth. He clasped a xyston thick with blood and had fresh cuts and scrapes on his bare arms to add to the existing crisscross of scar tissue.

"It is indeed the work of Hades, lord. You must trust me. We don't have time to explain, but I will hold the attack. I need to get the Agrianians up here now to support me. You and Alexander focus on the Greeks," Xantho said, fully aware that he, a former slave to a Persian satrap, was giving orders to the second most powerful man in all of Greece and soon to be in all Western Asia if this battle was won. Hephaestion stared at Xantho with wide eyes. He licked his lips and looked at the charging Blood Immortals. Twenty paces.

"Go, I will get the Agrianians," he nodded, and he wrenched his horse around, bellowing orders and shouting to his king.

"We must hold them, Penelope. We need you now. But save some of your power if you can. We will need it for Gula'an," said Xantho. She nodded, face set and as determined as ever.

Xantho dropped his broken xyston and leapt from the saddle. He drew his kopis blade and dashed towards the charging Blood Immortals. He weaved through the press of Macedonian horses and came into open ground, heart pounding but mind clear. Ten paces.

"Throw them back," Xantho said, and Penelope took a step forward. She closed her eyes, brought her arms around in a wide circle, and then thrust them towards the charging Blood Immortals. Their lines were ten across and eight deep, and Xantho saw the familiar shimmer of the air around Penelope. The force she generated howled across the battlefield, and it launched the first three lines of Blood

Immortals into the air, their battle cries turning to screams as the unseen power launched them backwards. Xantho checked his Palmstone. Its green swirling energy had depleted, but he couldn't be sure by how much; he guessed a third.

The Blood Immortals halted their charge, their leading ranks had landed amongst the rear ranks, and the rest had paused, looking to one another for orders. They had been so sure that they would plunge their spears into the flanks of the Macedonian king's elite horseman and were within sight of the king himself, but now their dreams of glorious victory had been torn asunder by Penelope and her magic. Xantho could see Gula'an riding back and forth beyond their ranks, staff aloft, and silver hair flowing behind him.

"Penelope, do something about Gula'an. Khamudi, on me," said Xantho. Penelope's eyebrows raised high, and she shook her head. But Xantho didn't know how she should do it; it just had to be done. He clenched his teeth, nodded to Khamudi, levelled his kopis, and charged. Two men, charging against impossible odds. Xantho ran hard at the Immortals, Khamudi at his side, bellowing an Egyptian war cry. The Immortals levelled spears at their attack, but it was too late, and Xantho batted one aside and was amongst them. He sliced his kopis across a young man's face, cutting him from ear to ear in a bloody gash. Xantho's momentum pushed him deeper, and he cannoned into their ranks with his shoulder, hacking about him, cutting one man across the belly and another across the windpipe. The Immortals fell away from his ferocity, pushing back against the men in ranks behind them to keep away from his flashing blade.

Xantho allowed himself a glance to the left. Khamudi was there, still roaring in defiance at the Blood Immortals, his lithe frame moving amongst them, using all his many years of sword skill to kill and devastate his enemies. Penelope had not imbued Xantho with her force yet. It would be welcome, but he knew she would need it for Gula'an. A spear flashed past his face, and Xantho grabbed its shaft. Yanking the man forward, Xantho headbutted him hard in the face, feeling the gristle of the Persian's nose give way under the blow. Xantho drew a dagger from his belt and continued on with his attack. He felt blows striking his armour at his chest and back, but he ignored them, trusting the Macedonian smith work to deflect the blows. Then, suddenly, a blade cut across his cheek, and he felt a deep dull pain in his shoulder. Xantho roared and took a step back.

He could see the staff of Gula'an waving above the ranks ahead of him, but the Gutian could not deploy his power without decimating his own men. Xantho grinned defiantly, tasting the iron of his own blood on his teeth, where it washed down his face from the wound on his cheek. He ducked under a spear thrust and buried his kopis in that man's guts. He kept the blade there and used the screaming torso of that Immortal as a shield as he turned in a half circle to bring himself back to back with Khamudi. The Egyptian turned, snarling, but then smiled as he recognised Xantho.

"A rare fight," said the Egyptian, grinning.

Xantho kicked the Immortal off his blade and parried another blow with his dagger.

"We will die here if the Agrianians don't come soon," Xantho called over his shoulder. He thought they had maybe five more heartbeats before the spears of the Immortals overwhelmed them. Suddenly the Immortals in front of him fell away shrieking. Xantho couldn't understand, but then he saw ten of them fall, peppered with small sharp wooden darts. He looked back at Penelope. She was on her knees now, breathing hard. Penelope had used most of her strength to pull the small bushes and trees around the battlefield and turn their branches and twigs into lethal missiles. She had thinned out the Immortals' ranks, and Gula'an himself must also have fallen. Xantho could no longer see the servant of Nergal above the heads of the

Immortals. He checked his Palmstone; only a sliver of green remained. Penelope and the mage force were almost exhausted.

Xantho's head snapped up as a wall of bellowing warriors thundered past him. Bearded, wild-eyed warriors armed with short javelins and wicked blades. Hephaestion had done it; the Agrianians had come. Those tribesmen cut at the Immortals with wild abandon, launching themselves into the fray. Xantho ran to join them in the attack, his heart pounding and the joy of battle flooding his senses. He cut at a shining-bearded Blood Immortal, whose face was shot through by Penelope's small twigs in a bloody mess. That man fell screaming to Xantho's kopis. Xantho felt a hand on his shoulder and turned, bringing his blade to bear. He stopped just in time to see Khamudi's face.

"We must finish Gula'an," said the Egyptian.

Xantho looked back for Penelope. She was on her feet again and beyond the line of battle. Ahead of her, the Macedonian heavy cavalry had engaged the Greek mercenary forces flank, and on the opposite side of Xantho, the Blood Immortals were in full retreat now amid the onslaught of the Agrianians. He nodded at Khamudi, and they went to find Gula'an.

Xantho and Khamudi stepped over and around the fallen Blood Immortals. Some were still, and others writhed, moaning and clutching at their wounds. The Agrianians now had Gula'an's force in full flight, and they pursued them across the edges of the battlefield.

"I can't see him anywhere," said Khamudi, halting the grim march amongst the fallen. "He fell close to here, but he is gone."

"Maybe he has fled," Xantho suggested. He sank with his hands on his knees, still clutching his gore-dripping weapons. Xantho's shoulders burned, and it took him a moment to gather his breath. "Come then, back to Penelope."

They turned to make their way back to the mage when Xantho spotted a clutch of five Blood Immortals making a dash for Penelope. She stood, braced for the attack with her weapons at the ready.

"Penelope!" Xantho shouted, and he raced in her direction. As he ran, he glanced at his Palmstone. The last vestiges of light flickered there. Penelope looked from Xantho to her attackers. She could flush him with power, and he would be with her before the Immortals, or she could use the last of her power to throw them off. It was a risk, though, with Gula'an still at large. He ran as fast as he could, sprinting to her aid. He bellowed at her attackers, and three peeled off to face Xantho and Khamudi.

Xantho met them at full pace. He blocked a sword cut with his kopis and leapt into the air, slashing his dagger across the eyes of the next attacker. Xantho landed heavily but kept his feet and charged off again. He didn't look back, trusting that Khamudi could deal with the two Immortals he had left behind him. Penelope was now defending herself, using her sword to fend off her two attackers, just as she had on the first day they had met. Only now, she had the skill to match her ferocity, and she lunged with her blade to cut one man down. Xantho was almost there. He could finish them if she held out for just a few more moments. She wrenched at her blade, but it was trapped in the guts of the Immortal she had stabbed. The other attacker kicked her savagely in the groin, toppling her to the ground. That attacker raised his vicious curved blade for the strike that would surely kill her, but Xantho leapt upon him, his kopis cutting deep into the back of the assailant's neck. The Blood Immortal toppled over, dead before his corpse thudded to the ground.

Xantho ran to Penelope and helped her to her feet.

"I thought I was gone for sure," she panted, slumping against him, breathing hard, beads of sweat on her brow.

"How did you do it?" said Xantho.

"Which part?" she replied.

"Gula'an?"

"I called up the surrounding plants to grasp

his horse's legs, the beast panicked, and he was thrown."

Xantho nodded in recognition of her part in the battle. Had she not toppled Gula'an, the outcome for Alexander could have been much different. He winced at the pain from the cut on his cheek. The fury of battle had masked the pain up to that point, but now he felt warm blood pulsing from the wound washing down his face.

Xantho looked back to make sure Khamudi had fared well against the other two Immortals, and sure enough, he strode towards them, smiling, his long kopis blade resting on his shoulder.

The surrounding battle was over. It had lasted only a few minutes. Alexander's daring attack along the riverbed and up the bank of the Granicus had shocked the Persians. Alexander had penetrated deep into the enemy lines, and their army had disintegrated. Xantho saw that the Greek mercenary phalanx had surrendered; their spears dropped to the blood-sodden ground. Around them, the Macedonian infantry and cavalry whooped and cheered, calling the name of their daring young king.

"Alexander! Alexander! Alexander!"

Xantho turned back to Khamudi, Penelope still resting her head on his shoulder. Out of the remnants of the fallen Immortals suddenly came a rider. That rider held a long jet-black staff out in front of him like a spear, and long silver hair flowed behind him like a lion's mane. Xantho stood straight and pointed, trying to alert Khamudi, but it was too late. Gula'an raised his staff, lifting Khamudi from his feet, holding him there in mid-air, the space around him shimmering like the heat from stones on a hot day. Gula'an raced towards the Egyptian, letting go of his reins and holding a Persian war axe aloft. He swung the blade at the levitating Egyptian, aiming for his neck. Xantho cried out, fearing the servant of Nergal would take his friend's head. At the last moment, Khamudi tilted slightly, and the axe ripped open his throat in a spray of blood. Khamudi fell dead, but his head remained on his shoulders.

Gula'an drove hard towards Xantho and Penelope, Khamudi's blood bright in his beard and hair, teeth showing in the snarl of hate twisting around his ageless face. Xantho's blood rushed to his head, and his mind flooded with horror at the visceral death of his friend and teacher. Gula'an was charging. Xantho could feel the rumble of his horse's hooves beneath his feet.

"Xantho, get down!" Penelope shouted, and he dived out of the way. He rolled over in the mud-churned battlefield and came up to see she had used the last remnant of her power to thrust Gula'an from his horse. The Gutian fell again, tumbling in the dirt. Xantho checked his

Palmstone; it was dull and clear, and the power was spent. Penelope was on her knees, breathing hard. Xantho lunged to his feet and charged at Gula'an, kopis raised to kill the bringer of death whilst he reeled from his fall. He swung his blade within range of Gula'an's neck, but Gula'an recovered himself, and from where he lay, he raised his staff and flung Xantho high into the air. Xantho dropped his kopis. He paused there, the height of two men above the ground, and then fell to crash into the mud. The air whooshed from his lungs, and he doubled over with pain across his sides from the collision as he searched for Gula'an.

For the first time since he had met Penelope, Xantho wished he were dead. He wished he had died in the battle to spare his eyes from what now unfolded before him. Gula'an clambered to his feet and strode towards Penelope.

"You thought to defeat me?" his voice boomed, and it grated inside Xantho's skull. "You, an insignificant nothing, thought to thwart Nergal, god of the underworld, and I, his lord of souls?" He turned his staff to Xantho. "Watch now, puny warrior, see what your warmonger Naram-Sin unleashed upon the world. Death and more death, slaughter never-ending!" he roared.

Gula'an reached Penelope. She knelt there before him. Too exhausted to rise, all her strength exhausted. Gula'an raised his staff and pointed it at her. Xantho closed his eyes tight to avert the horror of what Gula'an would do to the woman he loved. He heard a snarl. Xantho opened his eyes; nothing had happened. Gula'an tried his staff again, but nothing. Xantho gritted his teeth. The Gutian had limited mage power, just like Penelope, and he had exhausted that power on the battlefield. Now he was just a man. Xantho sucked air into his winded lungs and grasped the hilt of his kopis. He stood and dashed towards Gula'an. The Gutian saw him and laughed, throwing his head back in mock glee.

"You come to do battle with me, slave? Come then, come and die with your slave whore," Gula'an spat. Before Xantho could react, Gula'an brought his Persian war axe down onto the top of Penelope's head. The blade thumped into her helmet, crushing it and driving on into the skull beyond. She did not cry out; she simply collapsed to the earth, the life pouring out of her skull in a thick red torrent.

The world stopped for Xantho; everything moved slowly. Penelope was dead, dead just like Lithra. Alexander had won, but Gula'an hoped to defeat Naram-Sin and the Warriors of the Light. Xantho was the last hope to strike a blow for Enlil and change the course of the war with the god of the underworld. Xantho charged forward.

He realised he was screaming incoherently, but he embraced that mad fury. He let it wash over him. The Gutian thought he was a slave, and that made him insignificant. But a slave is a man, the same as a battle lord or a king; the only difference is that the slave is worn down and weakened by his masters. Xantho had stopped being worn down when he had died on a riverbank two hundred years ago. He was a full-blooded warrior now, and as he swung his blade at Gula'an, he let the battle fury and his sword skill take over.

Xantho attacked, and Gula'an parried with his axe and staff. The smile had dropped from his face, and the Gutian moved backwards. His grimace told of his surprise at Xantho's skill and determination. Gula'an held his staff high, and Xantho leapt into the air, bringing the kopis down with full force onto the centre of that black pole. It shattered beneath the blow, and Xantho brought his dagger around in a wide sweep. He exalted as he felt the short blade slice through Gula'an's flowing robes and bite into the flesh beyond. Gula'an yelped and fell to the ground, and Xantho kicked him in the face. The Gutian rose with a snarl and swung his axe at Xantho, but Gula'an still moved slowly, and Xantho was fast. Xantho caught that swing in the crook of his arm and slammed his kopis blade into Gula'an's neck. The Gutian's eyes popped wide with terror as he realised he had lost. Xantho sawed his blade back and forward, and blood sheeted down the front of Gula'an's robes. Then, as the Gutian's corpse fell to the mud, Xantho cried out with anguish at Penelope's death.

Xantho fell to his knees. His body shook and crumpled into an exhausted sob. Xantho covered his face with his hands, and his whole being trembled as he cried. She was gone; they were all gone. Only he remained, but he had won. He had defeated Gula'an and thwarted Nergal, the god of the underworld. But, of course, Gula'an had died before Xantho could sever his head, so he knew the war would go on in some unknown distant future. Yet, for now, the world of men was rescued from the brink of eternal war and never-ending death. Xantho cried for Penelope and their dream of a life together beyond this war of the gods. But he would see her again...in the next life and the next battle.

TWENTY SEVEN

Xantho sat on a dried-out tree stump, its leafy majesty torn down by the power of the wind long ago, leaving a dried husk of petrified timber. He took a drink from his waterskin and looked at the ground below. Peaceful now, but it would soon be transformed into a blood-churned battlefield. Darius, Great King of the Persians and retreating in the face of Alexander's implacable onslaught against his empire, had chosen the field of battle this time. He had made sure his men levelled the field flat, allowing for the deployment of his fabled deadly war chariots, which thus far he had been unable to deploy in defence of his empire against the Macedonian conqueror.

The Great King had fallen back to his city of Arbela in the face of Alexander's relentless pursuit. Arbela was an ancient city deep in the heart of the empire and far from the distant coast where the Macedonians had landed their army at the Dardanelles. Alexander's army was two days' march from the city and had reached a small town named Gaugamela, which lay to the north of Arbela. Xantho was part of an advanced guard of Hetairoi heavy cavalry pursuing a force of one thousand Persian cavalry who had occupied the very heights where Xantho now rested. The Persians had thought to keep this high ground above the battlefield for their king, but Alexander himself, along with Hephaestion, had ridden with the advanced guard, and they had driven the Persians from the heights to secure the advantage for themselves.

It had been two years since Xantho had fought at the battle of the Granicus and lost Penelope. Xantho hadn't known what to do once he had killed Gula'an. For days he had wandered the battlefield, lost and alone in the prison of his own mind, plagued by the vision of Penelope's death and tortured by the loss of Khamudi and the Warriors of the Light. Hephaestion eventually found Xantho, where he trudged amongst the corpses at the Granicus, and the Macedonian had ensured that the Royal physicians cared for and tended to him. When he came around, the doctors told Xantho he had been raving and descended into madness for days on end. Without Penelope and the fight with Gula'an over, Xantho had reconciled himself to the thought that he was better off dead. That way, he would rise again with Penelope, ready for the next fight with the servant of Nergal. He had defeated Gula'an this time, but so it had been for countless centuries, Naram-Sin winning a battle, Gula'an winning a battle. Such was the eternal curse of Naram-Sin, which Xantho had become intertwined within.

Xantho looked down at his left hand. The Palmstone was clear and lifeless, all the bright green strangeness gone. It was hard to remember the actual colour it had been, just as it was hard to remember the details of Penelope's face. More than once, Xantho had panicked, fearing he had lost the memory of her delicate features or the smell of her hair. Then the memory would come flooding back to warm his heart and tear it apart again because she was gone from him.

Hephaestion had thanked Xantho for the part he had played in the battle. Xantho had been awarded a jewelled sword belt in honour of the bravery he had shown charging the Blood Immortals, but the Macedonians spoke little or nothing of the magic Gula'an and Penelope had brought to the battlefield that day. Some things were best left to the gods. Hephaestion brought Xantho under his own command. This meant roving ahead of the army on special missions, riding with the light cavalry, along with a unit of heavy cavalry and the Agrianian light infantry. Xantho, having no lust for life, welcomed these special duties. It meant always being at the forefront of the army and in constant danger, securing bridges, scouting, taking towns, and securing water sources. Xantho threw himself into the fighting with gusto, longing for the sword or spear blow which would send him into death's dark embrace, and he hoped back to Penelope. But it did not come. He fought and killed and fought again.

Xantho looked out across that flat, wide field where Alexander would soon battle the forces of Darius for a third time. The year was waning, and the late summer heat was bearable and cool in the early evening. A light breeze kissed the skin of his neck. In the distance, he gazed at the Gomel river, its clear waters twinkling in the late-day sun. His father's estates were close to here, Xantho thought. The land looked familiar. He couldn't be sure, but they had to be close by. In his old life, Xantho never thought much about where he was in the world. He never considered where the nearest city was or which rivers flowed within marching distance. Xantho had been a slave, an unwanted bastard son of a Persian satrap and a Thracian slave woman. He went where he was told and did what he was told. That had been his life two hundred years ago. He had met Lithra, and she had died. His life back then, he supposed, had been hard. Beatings and endless work. But he had known no different, and when he was a boy, he had enjoyed working with his father's beautiful horses and had dreamed of his grandfather Aristaeus's glory. Xantho now saw the old mercenary for what he was, a brutal warrior, much like Memnon of Rhodes, who he had fought at the Granicus. A man who dealt with death and made his living by the sword and whose choice to fight for the King of Lydia against Cyrus the Great had cost his daughter and his grandson dearly, consigning them to a life of slavery.

He poured some of the water into his hands and washed the grime from his rough, bearded face. This place was dusty. Below him, Xantho could see wisps of sandy cloud whirling across the plain. It was hard to remember what he was like in that life so long ago. It seemed to Xantho that he'd been a very different person compared to the man he was now. Two hundred years ago, Xantho had been a frightened boy, rejected by his father and beaten into accepting the drudgery of his life as a slave, with no hope or knowledge of anything better. His old self would have been afraid if he had come across his current self. That Xantho would probably have fled at his approach. He remembered the horror he had felt when killing his first man in the battle with Tomyris. He had killed so many since; it had become normal to him, like a farmer scything sheaves or a potter at his clay.

Xantho had fought at the Battle of Issus,

another huge clash of warriors beyond count at a river. He had ridden with Hephaestion and Alexander in the Companion cavalry, and they had come within striking distance of Darius himself that day. The Great King had fled the field, leaving most of Asia to Alexander to rule as King. Then, Xantho had marched into Egypt and marvelled at the ancient magnificence of Khamudi's homeland. He missed his old teacher; he missed his smile and calm demeanour. After Egypt, it had been back into Persia itself and on with the war against Darius.

Throughout the two years since the Granicus, Xantho wondered at the futility of the war between Enlil and Nergal. Xantho had seen more death riding with Alexander than he had ever thought possible. Over fifty thousand warriors marched now to fight against twice that number of Persians here on the edges of Gaugamela. *How did that serve the god of light and the enemy of the underworld?* He had concluded, after much deliberation, that the wars fought here on a grand scale ensured peace elsewhere. That back in Greece and Western Asia, there was peace under Alexander's rule, whereas there would otherwise be countless smaller battles raging between warring cities. At least, Xantho hoped that was true. If not, then what was the point of Penelope's death? Or mage and warrior magic? Xantho told himself it didn't matter. What was important was that when he died, he would rise again and see those dazzling green eyes. He would brush the familiar curl from her face and kiss those warm lips. Xantho sighed deeply. *By the gods, I miss Penelope.*

A week ago, the moon had disappeared, stolen from the sky by some work of the gods. The rank and file of the Macedonian army had panicked at the omen. Alexander's seers had taken it as a sign of victory. Xantho hoped it was a sign from Enlil, a sign that this round of the war with Nergal and Gula'an was over. He hoped it was a sign that it would be his turn to die soon, that they needed him at a future battlefield to join his friends and fight anew.

It was almost time to fight again, to ride in the heart-pounding charge of the Macedonian heavy cavalry. Xantho would grip his xyston once more and strike down the Persian foemen. He would do his duty to ensure Alexander won.

Xantho opened his eyes. The sun was bright above him, so he closed them tight again. He gasped, reaching for his chest. There was no wound there. His last memory was thundering across the flat battlefield at Gaugamela, blinded by dust. A fierce struggle between opposing cavalry units had ensued, and Xantho remembered the searing pain of a Persian javelin piercing his armpit as he raised his kopis to strike at the enemy. That white-hot pain had driven deep into his chest and on into his heart. He realised then that he had died and that he lay here breathing, alive again.

He sat up, forcing his eyes open. The sun was too bright, and its glare forced his eyes closed again.

"Xantho, dear Xantho," he heard a familiar voice say. It was a gravelly voice for a woman. He smiled, and a tear rolled down his face as bright green eyes came into focus above him.

"Xantho, come on. We are in danger here. Gula'an is in the field with a large force of infantry."

Peter Gibbons

Peter is an author from Warrington in the United Kingdom, now living in County Kildare, Ireland. Peter is a married father of three children, with a burning passion for history. He won the Kindle Storyteller Literary Award in 2022, and is the author of the Viking Blood and Blade Saga, and the Saxon Warrior Series.

Peter grew up enjoying the novels of Bernard Cornwell and David Gemmell, and then the historical texts of Arrian, Xenophon, and Josephus. Peter was inspired by tales of knights, legends and heroes, and from reading the tales of Sharpe, Uhtred, Druss, Achilles, and Alexander, Peter developed a love for history and its heroes.

For news on upcoming releases visit Peter's website at www.petermgibbons.com

Viking Blood And Blade

865 AD. The fierce Vikings stormed onto Saxon soil hungry for spoils, conquest, and vengeance for the death of Ragnar Lothbrok.

Hundr, a Northman with a dog's name... a crew of battle hardened warriors... and Ivar the Boneless.

Amidst the invasion of Saxon England by the sons of Ragnar Lothbrok, Hundr joins a crew of Viking warriors under the command of Einar the Brawler. Hundr fights to forge a warriors reputation under the glare of Ivar and his equally fearsome brothers, but to do that he must battle the Saxons and treachery from within the Viking army itself...

Hundr must navigate the invasion, survive brutal attacks, and find his place in the vicious world of the Vikings.

The Wrath Of Ivar

866 AD. Saxon England burns under attack

from the Great Heathen Army. Vicious Viking adventurers land on the coast of Frankia hungry for spoils, conquest and glory.

Hundr and the crew of the warship Seaworm are hunted by Ivar the Boneless, a pitiless warrior of incomparable fury and weapon skill.

Amidst the invasion of Brittany and war with the Franks, Hundr allies with the armies of Haesten and Bjorn Ironside, two of the greatest warriors of the Viking Age. Ivar the Boneless hunts Hundr, desperate to avenge the death of his son at Hundr's hand. To survive, Hundr must battle against fearsome Lords of Frankia, navigate treachery within the Viking Army itself, and become a warrior of reputation in his own right.

Axes For Valhalla

873 AD. The Viking Age grips Northern Europe. Seven years have passed since the ferocious sea battle with Ivar the Boneless, and Hundr is now a Viking war leader of reputation and wealth. A voice from the past calls to Hundr for aid, and he must take his loyal crew and their feared warships across the Whale Road to Viking Dublin, in a vicious and brutal fight against Eystein Longaxe.

Amidst the invasion of Brittany and war with the

Franks, Hundr allies with the armies of Haesten and Bjorn Ironside, two of the greatest warriors of the Viking Age. Ivar the Boneless hunts Hundr, desperate to avenge the death of his son at Hundr's hand. To survive, Hundr must battle against fearsome Lords of Frankia, navigate treachery within the Viking Army itself, and become a warrior of reputation in his own right.

King Of War

874 AD, Norway. A brutal place, home of warriors where Odin holds sway. King Harald Fairhair fights to become king of the north.

Hundr, a Northman with a dog's name... a crew of battle hardened warriors... and a legendary war where the will of the gods will determine who is victorious.

After incurring the wrath of Ketil Flatnose, Jarl of the Orkney isles, Hundr and his crew become drawn into King Harald's fight for supremacy over all Norway. Hundr must retrieve the Yngling sword, a blade forged for the gods themselves, and find favor with an old friend, Bjorn Ironside, as he fights a vicious and deadly enemy, Black Gorm the Berserker.

Hundr must navigate the war, survive brutal attacks, and make Harald the King of War in this fast paced adventure with striking characters and bloodthirsty action.

Warrior & Protector

989 AD.Alfred the Great's dream of a united England has been forged by his daughter Aethelfaed and grandson, King Aethelstan.

The Vikings have been expelled from York following the death of Erik Bloodaxe, and for two generations there has been peace between Saxon and Dane.

A new Viking warlord Olaf Tryggvason seeks revenge for Bloodaxe's death and the slaughter that followed, and has set his sights on a fresh assault on England's shores. With Skarde Wartooth they set sail for Saxon lands, hungry for glory, conquest and vengeance.

Beornoth, a brutal and battle-hardened Saxon Thegn, is called to arms to fight and protect the Saxon people from the savage Norse invaders. On a personal crusade, he joins the army of Byrthnoth, Lord of the east Saxons in a desperate fight against the bloodthirsty Vikings.

Beornoth must lay his own demons to bed, survive vicious attacks and find redemption for his tragic past.

Printed in Great Britain
by Amazon

15638625R00243